# POWERS

*Brian Michael Bendis*
*and Neil Kleid*

# POWERS

## The Secret History of
## DEENA PILGRIM

—⁓—

*Characters created by Brian Michael Bendis*
*and Michael Avon Oeming*

THOMAS DUNNE BOOKS
St. Martin's Press
New York

This is a work of fiction. All of the characters, organizations, and events portrayed in this novel are either products of the authors' imaginations or are used fictitiously.

THOMAS DUNNE BOOKS.
An imprint of St. Martin's Press.

www.thomasdunnebooks.com
www.stmartins.com

The Library of Congress Cataloging-in-Publication Data is available upon request.

ISBN 978-1-250-07407-2 (hardcover)
ISBN 978-1-4668-8564-6 (e-book)

Our books may be purchased in bulk for promotional, educational, or business use. Please contact your local bookseller or the Macmillan Corporate and Premium Sales Department at 1-800-221-7945, extension 5442, or by e-mail at MacmillanSpecialMarkets@macmillan.com.

First Edition: March 2016

10  9  8  7  6  5  4  3  2  1

*This one's for Laurie, who could teach Deena a thing or two*

*about being a smart, strong, beautiful, witty woman with the*

*determination to always do what's right.*

*Thanks for partnering with this faded hero,*

*and reminding me what it means to fly.*

Neil

# *Acknowledgments*

⟿

Mike Oeming drew my first-ever convention sketch in 1994. He was working on Judge Dredd, and as a hopeful artist at his first con, it was a genuine thrill to interact with one of the guys "behind the curtain." Mike's austere linework made me a lifelong fan, and I was lucky enough to get a second sketch at my first con as a pro in 2001, shortly after the debut of *Powers*. The sketch? Brian Michael Bendis, *Powers* cocreator, ordering Mike to return to work.

Since that show, I've been lucky enough to work with Mike on an X-Men comic and maintain both a personal and professional relationship. I'd never met Brian, though I'm equally a fan of his work and story: balding Midwest Jew writer made good, a fortune and glory tale I'd hoped to re-create if not best (I'm still coming for you, Bendis). Thankfully, fate and opportunity brought we yidden together and I'm proud to say that I've met and worked with one of the most exciting, endearing writers in my field, a creator who is generous to collaborators and offers a unique (and dialogue-rich!) take on sequential art. With Mike, Brian has created one of the most engaging female protagonists in comics today in Deena Pilgrim. Her voice and presence ride between confident and broken, determined and despairing, loyal and lost, and both boisterous and neurotic. Deena goes the distance, personality-wise, with another famous comic book hero, a web-slinging hero upon whom the Bendis stamp has long been imprinted. But unlike Spidey and some in her immediate circle, Deena wears her enthusiasm, guilt, and turmoil for all to see. She is Bendis and Oeming unfettered by masks, honest and open, offering a grounded point of view in a world where the impossible is just another Monday. Thanks, guys, for allowing me the chance to speed through your world and expand the history of an amazing character I've very much come to know and admire.

Thanks, as well, to Nicole Sohl at Macmillan Books for making the editing process a breeze, and to Brendan Deneen, who was my agent, then my editor, but always my friend. An additional high five to Charlie Olsen, who always has my back. Special acknowledgment to Tony Lee for putting Brendan and me together at a Comic Book Legal Defense Fund gathering, emphatically stating how we had to work together. Well, here you go, Tony. That'll be $25.99 hardcover, please.

And last, but by no means least, extra-special thanks and love to Laurie, Jack, Owen, Olivia, and Connor. It's never fun when Dad suddenly drifts away, staring into space during a family outing because he's plotting new ways to make poor, unsuspecting characters suffer. It's even worse when he disappears each night to orchestrate the horrific results on the printed page until 2:00 A.M. Thank you for being my amazing, supportive partners-in-crime, and for giving me another shot to make good every time I return from the struggle. I love you all. You are MY Powers.

*Neil Kleid*

# POWERS

# Prologue

---

*December. Saturday morning. 3:00 A.M.*

Three drops of blood fell to the floor, one after the other in rapid succession. Strapped to a splintered chair, Joe watched them plummet to the ground. He thrashed against his bonds, elderly body too weak to snap the ropes. The glow of a neon sign bathed the apartment and the old man's fruitless struggle. It flickered through the window, carved into red-white slats by a filthy set of venetian blinds.

Joe's tormentor, hooded and silent, knelt by his side. The man's hands were gloved—the kind of gloves one wears to garden rather than shovel snow. He carried an object on his arm, heavy and distinct. He tested its weight, marveling at the balance before placing it against a toolbox that he'd brought along. A handheld power drainer rested on the toolbox, emitting a faint, green corona. The drainer's signature glow intermingled with the neon from the window, mixing to a muddy yellow and eliminating the last of Joe's fading powers. The hooded man secured Joe's ropes, pulling them tight. The fraying bonds cut into his skin; each time he twisted to free his hands, more blood eked out, hanging in the air before splashing to the floor.

Joe worked his mouth, possibly trying to plead for mercy, but his tongue had been removed along with most of his teeth. The hooded man had taken half the teeth with pliers. Another quarter had been extracted with barbe-cue tongs. The only things left in Joe's ravaged mouth were the remaining molars, flecks of spittle, and additional, fat droplets of blood.

The hooded man massaged Joe's arm, doing his best to soothe the fright-ened prisoner. He reminded Joe why this had to happen; in fact, he detailed the road that had led to this moment. Unfortunately, his captive's recollec-tion proved as hazy as the moonlight. The hooded man completely under-stood. The events leading to the night's proceedings were not as important as the feelings he endeavored to elicit from the deserving prisoner. Pain. Anguish and betrayal. Sorrow and shame.

"That's it," the man said. "Not so bad. We're nearly done." He rustled a hand through the old man's hair, eliciting chills at the back of Joe's neck. Leather rasped against wood as the hooded man used the chair for support, carefully rising to his feet.

"Just two things left," he continued, "then it will all be over."

He gripped the front of Joe's rumpled shirt. Buttons tore away, bounc-ing into the darkness, exposing wrinkled skin to the crisp December air. The remaining nubs of Joe's teeth soundlessly chattered. He'd lost a lot of blood. The scuffle, the beating—both had taken more out of the elderly captive than his tormentor could have dared dream.

*Because he's a fossil,* the hooded man reminded himself. *He let himself get weak. He let himself get* soft. *And goddamned stupid.*

Gloved fingers expertly rolled back one of Joe's shirtsleeves and then the other, folding them away from the old man's biceps. The hooded man arranged elderly, goose-pimply arms so that both of Joe's hands rested palm-up against the armrests. Then he stepped back from his handiwork, walking toward the middle of the room.

"There," he announced. "That's one."

Joe tried to catch a breath, squinting to find his captor. But the hooded man blended expertly into the shadows, a mystery against stacks of rotting newspapers. He'd been surprised to find Joe in such squalid lodgings. The building was a slum and the rental itself a suffocating closet. Dusty posters hung on the walls, tacked into cracking plaster. Discolored clothing was strewn across available surfaces. Molding periodicals, dating back a year or more, completed the hoarder's paradise. And the remains of Joe's dinner—an underwarmed hamburger paired with shoestring fries—dotted the landscape in front of the stove, overturned in their too-brief struggle. He looked around, searching for anything that might speak to the old man's former grandeur. But nothing could be found, because either it lay beneath the refuse or Joe had sold it for bottles of Infinity Light. Nothing at all, apart from the object resting against the toolbox.

"Now," the hooded man began. He spoke with measured tones, indulging himself. "Now," he said again with additional gravitas, "just one more thing."

He rested both hands against Joe's kneecaps. Joe's breath, sour and desperate, wafted against the fabric of the hood. He let the moment stretch out into eternity, relishing the feeling as he listened to Joe's rapid, frantic breathing.

"You know I have to do this. Right?"

Tears sprang to the corners of Joe's shuttered eyelids, oozing out and then coursing down beaten, weathered cheeks. He nodded once, and the hooded man acknowledged the nod, though Joe could hardly appreciate the gesture. After that, the man swallowed beneath the hood and reached down for the object. Adjusting his weight, he hoisted the heavy artifact, swinging it in an arc to gather momentum. It glanced against its target's vulnerable skull, connecting with a sickening crack and driving Joe to the floor. The item bounced away, jarred by the impact, slipping from the hooded man's hands. Vibratory sound rang throughout the apartment, reverberating in his ears. He lifted Joe back to a sitting position, righting the chair, and retrieved the object to strike again. He smashed its edge against Joe's temple and then at the base of his neck. It wasn't until the fourth volley that Joe—gurgling for air through bubbles of blood—recognized what the hooded man had been holding. The old fart forced a smile. The item had been dear to him, like his spilled blood. They made him special in ways others could never understand. No one but a select few, like the man in the hood.

The man rammed the item into Joe's nose. Joe struggled to catch his sputtering breath, but the damn thing proved too fast, and there was too much blood in the way. He choked to death where he sat, wheezing and gasping in the slatted, mud-colored light.

The hooded man looked up, completely drained, letting his head loll back against his neck. He didn't want to look down. Staring at the ceiling provided respite from the blood. The red was gone now. Everything was black.

Black forever.

Joe's corpse settled, and the hooded man got to business. Nosy neighbors might have heard the altercation, and he had moments before somebody decided to call a cop. He knelt again, tugging at the ropes, ensuring the body was secure. Satisfied, he adjusted Joe's collar, pulling it aside to reveal a series of tattoos on the old man's skin. The first depicted a tank—a Pershing, an M26 as used during the Korean War. To its side lay a series of soldiers, bodies twisted beneath the Pershing's heavy tread. He prodded the folds of Joe's skin, trying to best present the details of the tank's lurid slaughter. Grunting, he moved on, turning his attention to the dead man's arm.

Branded into the bicep, an artist had inscribed a pattern of serpents and bullets, culminating in a circle at the top of the forearm. It centered on a fist, five grasping fingers clutched around three bolts, shattering them to pieces in its grip. Three initials were added beneath the fist: T.H.F.

The hooded man rose and started toward the door, snapping off the drainer while gathering his tools. He reached the knob and looked back, taking in the grisly scene one last time. He entertained spending more time with the departing message. He wondered whether or not to leave his calling card of choice. *No,* the man decided, considering the consequences. *Far too premature.*

*Soon enough,* he promised himself. *Let them find the first. Then I can allow myself to take more time.*

*After this, I can take certain liberties.*

There was more to do. More to which he would attend before the week was over.

Outside, flashing through the neon, a man in purple spandex raced around the building. The apartment shuddered from the flying man's passing. Windows shattered inward; glass exploded across the room and rained down over Joe's slumped corpse. The hooded man froze, remaining motionless to avoid attracting attention, but the costumed flier never stopped, moving too fast to register what had happened inside apartment 3A.

It wouldn't have mattered if he had. The ability to fly didn't make one a hero any more than the ability to drive made one a courier. The real heroes would arrive soon, though, armed with badges and drainers and guns.

Smiling beneath the hood, Joe's killer turned the doorknob and let the neon light spill into the hallway. He stepped out, closing the door behind him. The apartment lay silent, the only sounds a faint dripping of blood, the tinkling of glass, and the brisk, cutting wind whistling in through fractured windows.

# 1

~~~

*December. Monday morning. 6:25 A.M.*

"I-I-I won't diiiiie for you . . . it's-a henchman's foll-ee! I-I-I won't liiiiie for
you . . . yes, it's truuuue . . ."

Deena Pilgrim tapped her fingers in time to the music, drumming against
the steering wheel of her SUV. Two teeth bit into her lower lip, boosting
her adrenaline as she pressed down on the gas. Shaking her head, short
hair whipping this way and that, she flashed the passenger to her left a *yes-
yes-yes* as she dug into the song's bridge, number fifteen on a list of the forty
most popular in the nation. The adjacent driver stared and then rolled her
eyes and sped away. *Soccer mom,* Deena ventured. *Soccer Mom can't understand,* she decided with a smirk, rat-tat-tatting her digits on the wheel. *This
here, sunshine? This is the high point of my day.*

The station cut to a commercial, so Deena hit the shuffle to find another.
After several fruitless stabs, she landed on classic rock, shrugged, and
adjusted her rate of percussion to a mellower groove. She steered the
dented SUV through town, heading to a place she didn't want to go, listening
to a song she didn't want to hear.

Despite the suboptimal soundtrack, Deena did her best to enjoy the
moment. Right now, right here; before the day went to hell. Before she got
dragged into another bonkers situation beyond her control. That had been

happening often these last several years. Over time, she'd made the most of the period allotted between receiving a call and arriving on scene. Unfortunately today, she'd completely lost the vibe—the music wasn't cutting it, and her thoughts were already down among the bullshit. Deena stabbed the dial and powered down her radio, fingers still tapping a nervous staccato against the wheel.

She focused on the road, trying to put the pain of the last two years out of her mind. Avenues flew past as she navigated on autopilot through the streets, the happy song that had filled her head fading away as the burden of being Deena bullied itself back to the forefront. She rubbed her eyes, trying to wipe her mind, but she could not block out the horrible memories. That, she knew, would take something special. For that, she would need powers or some shit.

*Been there,* Deena bitterly laughed. *Done that, bought the DVD. Didn't help.*

She'd briefly had powers, sure. Unwantedly gifted to her by a scum fuck thug with loose hands and looser genetics. A Powers virus, spread among the populace, designed to impart killer abilities to its user. That would have been bad enough. Deena being Deena had made it worse. She'd isolated herself, threatening relationships at both work and home—relationships she knew would save her from drowning. Her career trajectory had been flushed down the pipeline, and she'd forced herself into exile, leaving the country before eventually returning to try again.

Oh, and she'd been pregnant, if you could believe that. Until she'd lost it during the fiasco in Los Angeles. The debacle with the motherbitching Federal Powers Bureau.

*Only a little bit pregnant,* she chided herself, laughing at the irony. She had to laugh. If she didn't, she'd probably cry—or worse: make somebody else cry.

Between the disasters that followed the bureau and what came before— the colossal fuckup in Chicago—truth be told, Deena could trace a direct line to this moment back to her apple-cheeked, potty-mouth beginnings on the homicide beat. *Hell, if I'm calling my shot, everything went to shit before I accidentally tore off Johnny Royale's arm. Right before I found out that Walker had powers.*

Walker. As if on cue, her partner appeared in the windshield, big as life and twice the size. He stepped out of a patrol car at 851 Taylor, about to venture inside. Deena pulled up to the curb and rubbed both hands against the vents before exiting the car. She slammed the door and hustled to catch up, blowing into her palms for warmth.

"What," she opened, "no fuckin' coffee?"

Walker ignored her pathetic salvo and pressed into the building, shoving aside the usual gawkers. The early ones were mostly neighborhood passersby, but Deena spied familiar bylines circulating throughout the lot, barely restrained by crowd control. Grimacing, wishing she were huddled in front of the SUV's shitty heater, Deena scrambled up the stoop and followed Walker inside.

Christian Walker and Deena Pilgrim had been partnered years ago, right before the unfortunate (and publicly visible) Retro Girl murder—a case that had defined both their careers. The tragic, personal experience had put them on the map. Since then, Deena had done her best to crack the enigma that was Detective Christian Walker, but was no closer now than she'd been years before. Insular and secretive, the broad-shouldered detective hadn't given Deena much to work with until (after an unauthorized bit of sleuthing) she discovered that Walker had worked the other side of the badge as a masked hero named Diamond. After an illustrious career, Diamond had lost his superpowered abilities. That alone might have engendered crankiness in any human being. But Walker had elevated "bitter and remorseful" into a bravura performance, one that delighted all ages . . . or at least his long-suffering partner, the spunky detective forced to swallow the man's grumpy shit on a 24-7 basis. Thankfully, Deena took on similar tread as the years peeled away, keeping pace with her partner's cycle of nightmares. "Bitter and remorseful" proved kiddie-clown-crap compared to the endless list of shit that had taken its toll on Deena's once bright-eyed, wise-assed demeanor.

*Yet still they expect me to get out of bed. I will admit,* she cracked to herself in return, *it's been interesting. And by "interesting," I mean "exhausting."*

"Which is why," she concluded out loud, "I asked for the goddamn coffee."

Walker glanced back from four stairs up. "What was that?"

"Nothing. Keep climbing; I'm enjoying the view."

"Adding sexual harassment to the list of black marks on your personnel record?"

"One more black mark and I get a free fro-yo."

Walker didn't look back. "Barely worth it. The only flavors at the precinct are 'doughnut' and 'dysentery.' And last I heard, we're out of 'doughnut.'"

Trading quips, they climbed the final flight of stairs, arriving at a barrier of police tape that blocked the third-floor landing. Walker tore it aside and beckoned Deena to follow, leading toward the open door of apartment 3A. She hesitated at the threshold. Truthfully, Deena needed a minute before flipping her day on end. A moment existed for every detective in which a single step led from the blissful paradise of ignorance into the harrowing excruciation of purgatory. A twist of the dial, like shutting off a song, that kicked a ladder out from under a detective's feet, sending him or her down a slippery, dangerous chute. Deena wrestled back her nerves and shook off strangling anxiety.

*Not again,* she begged to any and all of the powers that be, doing her best to assume a brave face. *Please, let this be an easy one. Lob us a softball, okay? Drug addicts. Bangers. Nothing that jams electric death rays up my cooter.*

She finished the prayer and steeled her resolve. Painting a smirk across her face, Deena followed her partner into the apartment.

The air felt metallic and cold. Walker had already circumvented a labyrinth of glass and refuse, reaching the far wall of the claustrophobic rental. Sunlight filtered in through torn venetian blinds. Forensic units clomped around, dropping numbers for reference and placing samples into tiny bags.

Deena tiptoed over a pizza box to arrive at Walker's side. He faced the wall, shoulders blocking the victim from view. His arms were folded and his head slumped; Deena could tell something was wrong. Walker's body language suggested some kind of emotional blow, confirmed by the pass of a hand over his craggy, chiseled features. She ducked his left arm, grabbing her first, eye-opening look at the morning's victim.

The dead man had been strapped to a wooden chair. Bound with thick, bloodstained ropes, the corpse had been situated before a window; shards of glass coated both the body and carpet. Cold wind whistled through the broken panes, circulating through the apartment and ruffling the vic's brittle hair. The deceased wore a shirt and skivvies, the former unbuttoned and flapping in the breeze. Deena's eyes darted to the man's legs, charting trails of bile down to a pool of congealed blood. The medical examiner had his back to the detectives, hunkered down while tapping notes into an off-brand, police-issue tablet. Slight and ratlike, stubble covering a protruding overbite, the examiner wore cheap eyeglasses and latex gloves. The knees of his pants were filthy. Deena looked back to the corpse's face. The victim had been savagely beaten, his features unrecognizable, eyes and mouth a pulpy mess. His teeth littered the floor, yanked and discarded. A technician swept several into a bag with a tiny, sterile broom.

She searched for additional identifiers, hoping to key on any unique items that might stand out. The unit's walls were free of decoration apart from a handful of erratically tacked posters; any personal photos the man possessed had been removed or jarred loose. Aside from the odd framed newspaper or curious knickknack, Deena could see nothing that spoke to whom the vic might be or what had caused his brutal demise.

That's when she saw the shield.

She'd been looking for a murder weapon—a hammer or crowbar, say. But then it had caught her eye, partially hidden beneath the garbage. Deena's jaw sagged, and she tapped Walker. He glanced back, and she noted tears in his eyes. He'd been crying; a bell sounded in Deena's brain, alerting her to the fact that they'd reached that horrible moment. So long, paradise; have a drink, purgatory. Bound to be a long afternoon.

"Got something?" Walker asked, clearly finished with half-assed banter.

She cleared her throat and thrust her chin at the item—barely visible, obscured beneath trash and damage. Despite that, it was instantly recognizable to both detectives. He nodded as if confirming a notion he'd pieced together. Whatever the shield was doing in this dingy locale, it firmly intersected with the emotional turmoil that had given Walker the feels.

"See it?" she whispered, begging the question as if he didn't.

"Course I do."

Deena raised an eyebrow. "And? What are we saying?"

"We're saying it's him."

"Maybe not. People steal shit," she suggested. "Neighborhood fits. The old man could have boosted it."

Walker shook his head. "No, that's Joe. Even with the face, I know it's him. Though I can't for the life of me explain what he's doing here."

*Dammit,* she thought. As they'd been talking, one of the technicians had discovered the shield beneath the glass. He barked excitedly and dragged it out. The other officers expressed skepticism; it had to be a replica, a cheap imitation. But the farther they pulled it into the light, the more impressive it appeared. By the time they set the circular shield on an end table, everyone believed it to be the genuine article. Slightly dented, the pitted disc bore signs of rough use—streaks of blood marred its surface, obscuring the cobalt-and-crimson eagle etched over black steel. Nicks and creases lined the edge; someone had used it as a hammer. Or a murder weapon.

"The victim," the medical examiner droned to Walker, jotting notes in an app as he jabbered away. "His age falls in the eighties, I'm gathering—"

"Hundred and twelve," Walker corrected, eyes glued to the gouged weapon.

The ME looked up. "You sure?"

"Twelve years ago, I attended his hundredth birthday party. I bought him a ducky tie and condoms. So yeah, Frank. I'm pretty sure."

Frank, the medical examiner, shrugged. "Fair enough. Hundred and twelve." He ticked off salient points in a scrolling checklist, tapping his glasses against the tablet for emphasis. "Massive trauma to the skull, knees, and fingers. Multiple fractures at the hyoid, which suggests strangulation. Contusions along temple and heel. Heavy loss of blood due to wounds and chafing—the ropes, of course—and hundreds of abrasions that stem from what appears to be a shower of glass. None of which killed him, though. He's been beaten to hell and back, but the actual cause of death in my humble opinion? Lack of oxygen."

He stepped toward the corpse, pointing out highlights. Deena detected a lilt in his voice, as if Frank enjoyed dragging them on a guided tour of a dead man's wounds. She made a mental note to step on his toes.

"The nose has been irreparably broken," Frank was saying, "and his lungs have been punctured; note stabs to the back. He's been attacked with a blunt instrument, mostly around the face and cranium. A hammer, maybe? Need samples, but I—"

Deena coughed, subtly gesturing toward the bloodstained shield. Frank glanced its way and then dove back into his tablet, tap-tap-swiping away.

"Right. That would do it. So bludgeoned with his shield, but the killer had to swing it with considerable momentum to effect this sort of damage. Really bring it down with enough force."

"So," Deena summarized, "your expert opinion is that somebody drove a living legend's nose through his brain with his own heavy, heavy shield. Yes?" A crowd had gathered, listening to the byplay.

Frank's grin widened. "No, see. You can't kill a man like that. That's a myth. The nose is comprised of cartilage, which doesn't possess tensile—"

"My point," Deena interrupted, "remains that America's greatest hero has been tied to an unflattering chair and murdered to pieces on skid row. Possibly by some psycho seeking revenge. That about right?"

"I deal in facts, not guessing games, Detective Pilgrim. Could be a Power. Could just be a bruiser like Walker. A dude that works out, you know?"

Deena interjected before Walker could reply, "You don't really believe that."

Frank spread his hands. "Come on, Deena. Everyone knows this guy, even with hamburger for a nose. I'm guessing an archnemesis with a grudge—or government payback. Hell, it might just be the landlord looking to collect." Frank turned away, preparing to tidy up. "But like I said, I deal in facts. I'll leave conjecture to you, Detective."

The knot of cops drifted back to their tasks. Walker remained quiet—more so than usual, and Deena gave him space. She took advantage of the moment to grind her heel into Frank's left sneaker. The medical examiner squealed in a way that made her feel vindicated. He gathered his kit and hurried far from Deena Pilgrim's rogue brand of justice, leaving them to the body and their own conclusions.

"You okay?" she asked Walker, concerned. Cases with personal attachments could fuck with a detective's impartial nature. "I can take this," she offered. "Just saying, I can gather leads on who iced the Citizen Soldier."

Walker suppressed a smile, clamping his lips in a way that set Deena on edge. He rested a hand on her arm, the lightest of touches to assure her that everything was copacetic. "I'm fine. And his name was Joe. Joseph Monroe, U.S. Army captain, Fifth Regimental Combat Team."

"A.k.a., the ultimate boy scout. The thrilla in vanilla—"

"Deena . . ."

"Wait, wait—you gotta do these things in threes or you lose the comic theory. The thrilla in vanilla, aaaand . . ." She paused for effect, pushing Walker's patience. "Aaaand . . . ?" She came up blank. "Dammit. I had it. It'll come to me."

"Nice. Dignified."

Deena took a breath. "Okay, so Joe Monroe . . . seriously? 'Joe Monroe'?" A look from Walker suggested it might be best to drop the sass. "Fine. Joe Monroe, otherwise known as the Citizen Soldier. The most visible hero in America, on account that he's won, like, five wars and advises the president. This guy, this magazine-cover celebrity, someone out there got a hard-on for him to die."

"Go on."

Deena gestured toward Joe's mashed face. "Killer uses the shield in a fit of irony, caves in skull, leaves him for dead. We make a list of known enemies. SOP."

Walker set his jaw. "More to it than that."

"Don't overthink it, Walker. Even me, with my new-school, sarcastic sensibilities, even I have mad Citizen Soldier knowledge. Could name five suspects just off the top of my head." She ticked them off with her fingers. "Captain Korea. *Boom!* One. The Tet Offenders. *Zing*—that's two. The Klux Klan Krew, Doctor Diabolical, Ho She Grin . . . those are just from the comics, mind you."

Walker ignored Deena and stepped closer to the chair, placing hands on his hips and looking down at the body. "Call back Forensics. Anyone who's seen this apartment in the last few hours."

She wanted to scream. "Seriously? Dude, we should run names, get ahead of this before it leaks. Someone will, you know—News 12, *Powers That Be*. In two hours, every liberal with an Instagram is gonna fill the Web with sensitively filtered memorial memes, and I want to have a suspect before that happens."

Walker bent his knees and rubbed his chin. He cocked his head and then beckoned for Deena to join him on the floor. Exasperated, she rubbed her eyes. "What—are you kidding me? Look, Walker, come *on*. This guy's the example for what it *means* to have powers. There's half a dozen suspects we can drag downtown based on fucking *history* alone. What are we doing?"

He pointed to a tattoo on Joe's arm. "Look here."

"Yeah, so? Uncle Sam had a thing for ink. Most old soldiers do."

"This ink is why we can't rush this. Why this can't get out."

Deena hunkered down, doing her best to keep from kneeling in human detritus, and angled her head to better see the victim's forearm.

Snakes and bullets. A fist breaking lightning bolts. T.H.F.

She furrowed her brow. "I've seen that before. Where?"

"You've seen a more stylized version. A logo."

Deena nodded, intrigued. "Yeah. With the lightning and . . . but 'THF'? I don't . . . a name? A relative?"

"Nope. Letters go with the fist—and to be honest, the snakes." He lightly slapped his cheek, grimacing and squinting. "Ah, dammit, Joe. Is this a lead, or you telling us something?"

Deena volleyed between the curious tattoo and Walker's distraught expression. "What am I missing? 'THF.' Tight High Fanny? Terribly Hot Fart?"

"Deena."

"Ah-ah-ah. Rule of threes."

He dropped both hands between his knees and looked Deena's way with a tired, expectant stare, waiting for her to finish.

"I got it . . . I got it—yes! Tense Hero Friend! Boom." Deena grinned and faced her partner, softening her eyes when she caught his annoyed expression. "Because you're the friend. This way you're involved. No, no—don't thank me."

"You done?"

"For now. So, THF?"

"The Human Front."

Suddenly, the logo came rushing back to her—as did the reason for Walker's reticence. The Human Front. Citizen Soldier.

Deena stood up and patted dust off her knees. This morning's happy driving song had long been forgotten. This was way past purgatory and out into damnation.

"Shit," she announced to the room at large. "Merry fucking Christmas. There goes my week."

# 2

~~~

**December. Monday morning. 8:13 A.M.**

One hour later, Walker pushed his way through the precinct doors. Deena shadowed him, still grappling with what they'd seen downtown. Forensics had already locked down the apartment and quietly run the body to the morgue. It had been transported via a confusing sequence of routes, designed to lose anyone with unusual interest. Now they were determined to outrace social media and the twenty-four-hour news cycle, but first they had to loop in the captain.

The precinct was busy, packed with the standard assortment of low-level Powers and drug-addled hookers. Sad-looking holiday streamers had been strung through the rafters, a spattering of tinsel taped around the duty roster on the large smart board. In the corner, some snot-nosed banger kid was dry-humping the station's Christmas tree. Walker greeted several ranking officers, pointed out the kid, and then headed toward the large office in the back-left corner. Deena followed, dropping her jacket across her desk as they walked past. Several detectives glanced their way, noting the determination with which the partners crossed the room, and then went back to cases, oblivious to the shit storm about to descend on the overworked, understaffed Powers Homicide Division.

The door to the captain's office stood slightly ajar. Captain Emile Cross looked up from his work—scrolling through budget requests on an ancient mobile tablet—as they walked in. He distractedly waved to a pair of open seats. Deena dropped into one, slapping both palms on the armrests. Waiting for the captain to acknowledge their presence, she took a moment to take in the surroundings. Barely a personal effect in sight; the captain had taken to a minimalist decorative style engendered by more of a practical than an emotional sense of reasoning. Most of the homicide staff had adopted the same policy, unwilling to lose precious trinkets to another riot or attack. Several binders lined a metal file cabinet against the left-hand wall, and a stack of law books had been inserted into a wooden bookshelf behind the captain's chair. A handful of degrees completed the picture, the only nonessential item to be seen an autographed baseball signed by a briefly famous Power with a penchant for sports. The ball rested on the blotter; Cross—a likeable bulldog of a man with a gruff exterior but a good heart—used it as a paperweight, stabilizing the mountains of reports that threatened to overwhelm his desk.

He plugged the tablet into its charger, giving half his attention to the detectives as he dug through his desk. "This had better be important. I don't even know what you want, but today I just don't have time for your usual drama."

Walker folded his arms and leaned against the wall. "That call we took? Murder at Taylor and Kirby? Guy's name was Joseph Monroe."

Cross distractedly registered the name, barely letting it settle in. "Yeah? Got a record? Look, Walker, we need to talk about . . . this . . . wait." He sat back in his chair, finally locking eyes with the partners. "'Monroe'? Like, *Joe* Monroe?"

Walker gave the captain a knowing look. "That's right."

The captain swiveled away from the detectives. Deena and Walker shared a glance, waiting for him to break the awkward silence. Finally, the captain slammed his fist on the desk, sending papers flying and the baseball rolling to the floor.

"Goddammit!" he cried in anguish, capturing the attention of cops within earshot, loitering outside his office. He jabbed an accusatory finger at Walker. "No. You hear me, Walker? Absolutely not. You're off this case."

Walker's face drained of color, and after a moment, he doled out a careful response. "No. Joe was my friend."

"Exactly. You're too close. Pilgrim will run it. I'm partnering you with Detective Kirk. He's new—young, needs some experience, and I think—"

Before Cross could finish his sentence, both detectives voiced their displeasure. "What?" Deena argued, hands wide in disbelief. "No fucking way! I already have a partner." Walker, meanwhile, calmly made his case, explaining the importance of his involvement. "There's a larger issue, Cap. Listen, we have to keep it contained or—"

"Enough!" Cross sliced a hand through the air, indicating that the discussion was at an end. "The *both* of you. I've been dodging bullets all morning—bullets with *your* name on them, Walker."

They paused in their gesticulations and stared at the captain. "Bullets?" Walker asked. "What bullets?"

Cross waved a hand at his door and then pointed up toward the ceiling. "Bullets from above, fired from *god knows* where. City hall, federal—hell, maybe *Washington*. I got special investigators breathing down my neck, poking their nose up my *tuchis* 'cause of that disaster with the Powers Bureau."

"The bureau?" Deena snorted with disdain. "LA was, like, three years ago."

"The speed at which your government works. Regardless, some commission plans to investigate select law enforcement agents. Cops with powers. You read, Walker?"

A sliver of ice slithered down Deena's spine. "Wait, hang on; Walker doesn't have powers. Not anymore."

"Used to, though. His identity as Diamond is more of an open secret than my raging alcoholism." Cross turned to Walker, explaining in measured tones, "You were famous, Christian. That level of fame paints a target here"—Cross stuck a finger into Walker's chest and then out at the bullpen— "and here. Your powers may be gone, but that doesn't make you less of a white whale. And this commission is Captain Ahab."

The captain slumped into his chair, letting the wheels squeak in protest. "And now a dead legend's cooling in my morgue. How do I keep that from Uncle Sam? How can I protect you from the media, Walker, when you have direct ties to an open murder investigation? I'm sorry, but no. You're out."

Deena indignantly folded her arms. "Then so am I."

"No, you're not."

She whirled to face her partner. Walker had turned to stare out into the house, taking in the maelstrom with his back to the desk. He leaned against the window, forehead resting against a fist. "He's right. I'm a liability. It's better for everyone if you handle this alone."

"Don't I get a say?"

Walker pounded on the window. A passing clerk jumped and dropped her files.

"Let it go, Deena."

She fumed with annoyance. "Fine, dammit. I'll handle it. Do I have to babysit this Kirk, though? Partner me with Enki."

"Detective Sunrise is unavailable," Cross replied. "Assigned to another case. Drug stakeout—designer powers near D and Bernardin." That was a shame; despite comparable sets of impressive lady balls, both of which often put them at odds, Deena respected Detective Enki Sunrise. Even though, after Sunrise had partnered with Walker when Deena had gone into exile, she'd later discovered Enki had been investigating them on behalf of Internal Affairs. The two women had buried the hatchet in due course; Sunrise, a cop with a bigger mouth than Deena's, was the only detective in the division she trusted other than Walker.

Deena exhaled. "Goddammit. Fine. I'll take the newborn."

The captain nodded from his seat. "Thank you. What do we got on this?"

She took a breath and launched into it. "We got loud and ugly. Victim beaten with his own shield; the ME likes asphyxiation for cause. No suspects yet, but I'll gather a list of known enemies, possible beefs."

"Work fast. The Soldier's death warrants a week of prime-time debate and touchy-feely, sugary retrospectives on entertainment news."

"Agreed."

Cross cocked an index finger in her direction. "I mean it, Pilgrim. The people can't find out about this until we have a lead. That means keeping secrets in a cop house about to be crawling with feds."

Walker and Pilgrim shared a furtive glance, and the captain flicked his eyes from one to the other. "What? What was that?"

Deena conceded the floor to Walker. "Tell him."

"Tell me what? There's more? What am I saying—of *course* there's more. You're like the bad news Santa Claus, here to impart tidings of shit."

Walker scratched his cheek, hesitating before going on. "We found identifying marks on the vic's body. Tattoos. Some decorative, but one in particular that could get . . . complicated."

Cross arched an eyebrow. "Complicated *how*?"

"It's a tattoo of the Human Front logo. Ho-ho-ho."

The captain fell silent. After a moment, air escaped from his lips, coupled with a whistle. He laced his fingers behind his head. "Fresh? Put there by the killer?"

"Not a chance," Deena replied. "Faded, a few years—if not longer."

Cross placed his hands on the blotter. "You're telling me the most recognizable hero in America—a man who claimed to be the bridge between the Powers and the common man—has a tattoo glorifying the world's most vocal anti-Powers movement?"

The detectives nodded in confirmation.

Cross massaged his temple. "Unless you can prove that someone forcibly tattooed that thing onto his arm, we have twenty-four hours before the world discovers the poster boy for Powers relations might have been a traitor to his own kind. Are you kidding?"

"We look like we're kidding? Gut shot, Cap, same as you."

Cross headed toward the door. "Say nothing, do nothing but work that list. Find me a Human Front bigwig, someone with something to prove by discrediting a living legend."

Deena stepped closer. "Cap?"

"Yeah?"

"What if it's real? What if Monroe put it there himself?"

Walker glared, face reddening. Clearly, he didn't share her concern.

"Beats me," the captain responded. "I imagine there'll be a lot of disappointed kids this Christmas with action figures they'll be too ashamed to keep. For now, locate Corbin Kirk—you'll partner with him and show him the ropes. Keep this closed; say nothing to the press. Meanwhile, I'll try to get ahead of it."

He faced Walker. "And you. A special investigator's on his way. Brush up on whatever shit you have to sling to stay out of trouble. I'll back you up, but I won't do time. Sling like your life depends on it. Because it does."

Cross left the office. The partners followed him back into the hustle and hubbub of the bullpen. He scanned the crowd, ignoring jovial greetings from the detectives and barely subtle threats from nearby perps. Finally, his eyes landed on a baby-faced rookie fresh out of the oven, wearing a stupid-looking suit and an even dumber grin. Nervous eyes; kind of sweaty. Deena knew that she was looking at her temporary partner.

"Kirk," the captain indicated, pointing in the kid's direction. "Partner up, keep it quiet, get it done." He clasped Walker's arm and then rushed away, mingling with the crowd and heading for the commissioner's office.

Deena glared at Cross's retreating form, wishing she had handled him better. The prospect of babysitting in the middle of a high-profile murder case didn't excite her in the least. If Walker hadn't rolled over, she might have fought a little harder, but her docile partner seemed to have checked out. Distracted by the intricacies of the case, Walker would be as useless here as a bag of assholes. This special investigation—slapping the man's lost powers in his face—was just plain mean.

"You're good with this?" she inquired, giving Walker a long, inviting look. "Because I can hand this off."

"Don't do that." He turned her way, widening his eyes to rouse himself. "No, I'm good. It's fine. I have to deal with this bureau thing."

"Apparently."

"That a problem?"

Deena rolled her eyes. "This whole damn thing is a problem. I don't get it. I had powers, too. I was in Chicago and LA. Why aren't the feds tapping my ass?"

Walker smiled. "Feeling left out? I can toss some heat your way."

"Like I don't have enough." She groaned and violently dug her fingers through her hair. "Agggh. If it's not one thing, it's another."

"Got a beef mentoring the new fish?"

"Not just that. I . . . look; I'm not in the mood to end up on TV again, okay? Another high-profile celebrity murder . . . like Z, like Retro Girl. A murder of a guy, by the way, who got his powers through the fucking government, I might add."

Walker grimaced. "That's never been proven—"

"This inconsiderate jamoke who gets the Wonka golden ticket of Powers careers and, what? In his heart of hearts, he might really be a Powers-hater? I'm pissed at the hypocrisy, Walker. The never-ending flood of bullshit. I'm jaded, I'm frustrated, and I'm sick of the three-ring circus that is Powers Homicide, is all."

He let her rant until she finally exhaled, letting out a second groan. Her eyes felt swollen and heavy. "I'm just tired. I can't do this much longer, you know? Things have changed."

"What are you saying?"

"I just . . . I honestly don't know."

Walker frowned and placed a hand on Deena's shoulder. It felt good; supportive. Protective. Warm. She squeezed it with her own, holding it firmly before letting it drop.

"What I do know is, yes," she concluded, "I got a beef mentoring the new fish. I'd work quicker on my own." She moved to her desk, and Walker fell into step at her side. They wormed between the throng of detectives, clerks, and criminals, wending their way toward the waiting rookie. Walker waved at Kirk, indicating that they were coming, which pissed Deena off even more.

He turned back to her and asked, "Where will you start?"

"Human Front, I suppose. They got that big, shiny office building up-town. I can rattle cages, shake loose a name. Who's the top bigot over there?"

Walker smiled. "Crane. The good reverend Malachi Crane. Nasty piece of work."

"Riiiight. Preacher type turned businessman. Ran guns against powers in Atlanta, among others. Now he's politicized and legitimate."

"Careful how you step. The Front used to be thugs with science weapons and hate speech, but these days, they're all lawyers and lobbyists. Malachi Crane can make your life very difficult."

"Just going to ask some questions. Meanwhile, I'll have the baby check to see which of Crane's lynching buddies is still at large. Which are strong enough to have murdered—and maybe framed—your old pal Joe."

Walker took Deena's forearm. Heat radiated through her face, flushing her from neck to scalp. "Thanks, Deena," he said sincerely. "I appreciate this."

"Hey, what else am I gonna do? You play nice with the special investigator."

She grabbed her jacket as Walker eased into his seat. Throwing it over her shoulder, Deena snapped her fingers at the toddler with a badge. "You, six-year-old," she barked. "You're with me.

Let's go bag us a hate crime."

# 3

~~~~

**December. Monday morning. 9:41 A.M.**

Walker had a secret.

Not his powers or his other identity; no, those tidbits had infiltrated the national consciousness long ago. Christian Walker's not-so-secret time as Diamond, a costumed hero with history as deep as public memory, stymied any hopes the detective had for maintaining any kind of private life. Every case that he and Pilgrim examined—no matter the circumstance—managed to let his alter ego cast a shadow on some aspect of the affair. So the powers . . . every intimate detail of his life behind the mask and portions that followed . . . not a single bit had ever been secret.

There were other secrets—Walker's incredible longevity, for one. Though he'd kept the details from many, his confidants knew that he'd worn countless names over the years. "Christian Walker" had been Diamond, sure, but before that he'd been Blue Streak, battling Al Capone's syphilitic crusade against decency, government, and the people of Chicago. Blue Streak had fought other, far bloodier wars overseas, alongside brave soldiers who had lost their lives pushing the line toward Hitler, Tojo, and Mussolini. He'd been Great Walker for a time. And even earlier, in places lost to memory like water through a sieve, he had been Gora. He'd spent an eternity wandering the planet, earning his surname, and gathering thousands of lies and millions of burdens. Yet the knowledge that Walker was centuries old had been granted to a select few. Zora had known, as did Retro Girl and Triphammer. Olympia and Z. Wolfe, may he rot in hell. And, of course, Joseph Monroe. All were dead now, having taken Walker's secrets to the grave. Still, one might have squealed. The information could be out there, circulating among the ether. And Walker had touched so many people in his lifetime that there had to be someone, anyone that still recognized him as Diamond, Blue Streak, or—god forbid—one of his other, tragic identities. So, no. Hardly secret.

The actual secret was this: Detective Christian Walker, Powers Homicide Division, had been Diamond. He'd been Blue Streak and Gora and the rest. He'd lived, loved, killed, and conquered. He'd seen empires rise and fall; villains wax and wane. Friends thrive and wither. Through it all, traversing the world with considerable weight on his broad, slumped shoulders, Christian Walker had endured. He'd persisted.

But so had the guilt.

He'd internalized every death and loss. Each era that flaked to dust at his feet left Walker feeling responsible and ashamed. That he should draw breath; should be allowed to go on while all the others had died. Hadn't he suffered a thousand lifetimes? Would Walker have to withstand watching Deena and Cross and everyone he ever loved . . . no, he couldn't bear thinking it, let alone live it. And so, the guilt—the fear and regret that he could not end the cycle. Instead, he moved forward. He made fewer attachments, regretting those he'd been foolish enough to encourage. And still his friends fell around him. Still he soldiered on while others—deserved or not—laid their lives at his feet. Or in Joe's case, across his desk.

Walker wiped his face, doing his best to ignore the clamor of the precinct. Deena had left twenty minutes ago, dragging the poor, unsuspecting rookie in her wake. He sniffed with remorse. Flashes of conflict filled his head, cities and costumes he hadn't seen or thought about in over ten years.

*Hot enough for you?* Joe had asked.

*The Human Front,* Walker recalled, decades-old arrests flitting through his mind. *Man, that takes me back. I haven't been to Atlanta in a dog's age.*

Walker grabbed a closed manila folder that lay upon his desk. He flipped it around and untied the cord, digging inside for a set of Polaroids. He shuffled through the stack, turning them over, staring at the photographed remains of an old, dead friend.

He stared at a picture of Joe's tattooed arm. The incriminating logo slapped him in the face like an angry, vindictive girlfriend. Walker rubbed his chin, pensively meditating, debating the implications of the image in his hand.

*Talk to me, Joe.*

"Walker?"

He looked up, startled by the unexpected reply. Instead of his dead friend's ghost, Walker faced Melinda, the captain's assistant. She indicated an interview room, turning his attention to a shadow lurking behind the room's pebbled window. "Someone to see you," she said, ending the statement with a questioning lilt.

Walker patted her arm. "Thanks. I'm expecting him."

He navigated the bullpen like a frigate through troubled water. Arriving at the interview room, he held his breath, preparing to open the door to whatever might come. The shadow, having sensed Walker's presence, beckoned for the detective to enter. Putting Joe's case out of his mind for the time being, he turned the knob and stepped inside.

The man was slight and dark, clothed in a charcoal suit and cobalt power tie, both of which seemed expensive. Manicured nails, a silver tie pin, and a better-than-average watch completed the picture of upper-class extravagance—an impression Walker cataloged the moment he recognized the other man's face.

"Hello, Walker. You look like someone put coal in your Jockeys instead of your stocking." He extended a hand as the detective closed the door. Walker stonewalled the investigator, briefly acknowledging the hand and then moving around the table to an available seat. After a moment, the investigator inclined his head in resigned comprehension, sighing as if to say that he understood the slight. He took the seat across from Walker, before which lay several folders, a mobile tablet, and some notebooks.

"I suppose I deserve that," the investigator commented, shrugging and folding his arms across his chest. "This is about Deena, I suppose. I guess she finally filled you in. I thought the water would have moved out from under that particular bridge."

Walker grimaced. "You're wrong, Boucher. And don't be cute." He glanced around, taking in subtly placed surveillance cameras; cracked, green wallpaper; and the intricate system of spiderwebs that had overtaken the far-left corner. There was no one else in the room, nothing to eat or drink.

"What," he demanded, "no fucking coffee?"

Aaron Boucher, special investigator, smiled and settled back. "When's the last time you saw Atlanta, Walker?"

"You drop by to reminisce and jerk my chain?"

"I suppose I asked because I know the topic makes you uncomfortable."

Walker narrowed his eyes. "*You* make me uncomfortable. Atlanta makes me sad . . . and today, it makes me lonely."

Boucher tapped the tablet, bringing it to life. "That's right," he replied. "Just saw that report in the system. Entered by you and Detective Pilgrim?"

Walker flushed at the second mention of Deena's name, and he felt stupid for giving Boucher the satisfaction. He watched the investigator widen his smirk, and he wished he could wipe the smug expression away with a fist. Boucher had dropped her name to rattle Walker.

"Come on," Walker complained. "You and I, we can't do this. There's too much history. You won't be impartial; I won't keep myself from breaking your face."

"I can be impartial."

"Well, I can't promise that I won't break your face."

Boucher dismissively waved a hand. "Look," he said, "this could have been handled differently. See? No drainers."

"I don't have powers, Boucher. Not anymore."

"But you did. Twice, I hear. That alone gives me—"

"We're going nowhere, and I don't have time for this."

"—the right to . . . right, yeah. You have a homicide and a ticking clock. Another friend down," Boucher teased. "Another hero bites the dust."

"Charging me with something, or are we going to play grab ass all afternoon?" Walker sat on his hands, forcing himself to maintain his composure. Secrets and lies swirled about his head, heart thudding against his chest.

Boucher held out both palms in mock surrender. He flashed his teeth and flipped through a notebook until he found an empty page. Lifting a pen, Boucher leaned forward once more, pupils shimmering like the gleam of a shark's dead eyes.

"Let's start with the Soldier. Last time you spoke to one another?"

"Been a while. How about you?"

Aaron ignored that. "So you knew nothing about his death before this morning—or why they found him tied to a chair with his head caved in?"

"Not yet. Will soon."

Boucher glanced at the notebook, flipping back a page. "But you were thick as thieves, right?"

"What does this have to do with your investigation?"

Boucher looked up, wide-eyed and wounded. "Oh, it's a rich tapestry. You, the bureau, the Soldier, the last two years of unchecked damage to the name of law enforcement. Every life you've touched, every mask you've worn . . . I believe it ties together in a guilty, pretty bow."

Boucher stood and began to pace. "See, my mandate is to identify men and women in positions of power—authoritative power, whether in law enforcement or the legal system—with known powers, apparent or otherwise. Now, after the disaster in Chicago and the debacle at the now-defunct bureau, it's become clear that you, along with several key associates, may have been given a longer arm than the law requires."

He spread his arms and jerked both thumbs toward his chest. "Guess who they asked to investigate said arm? This guy."

Walker swiveled away from Boucher, barely able to stomach the man's unwarranted satisfaction. Flashes of memory swam through Walker's head. The incident in Chicago had led him down the road toward disaster; a team of Powers purporting to be gods had been slaughtered by one of their own, including a mama's boy by the name of Damocles. Said mama had decided to forgo the usual *shiva* period and attacked the city, luring Walker and his friends into battle from which many never made it out alive. Over six thousand people had died in Chicago, including Walker's friend Harley Cohen, also known as Triphammer. Walker disappeared for a while after that until they tracked him down and slapped a badge back in his hand, making federal agents out of both him and Deena.

Of course, *that* hadn't ended well, either.

"Look," he opined to Boucher, "we both know this wraps up with you taking my badge because you think I'm dangerous." Walker stood and reached for his pocket. "So let's skip the mind fuck so I can go check the job listings, okay?"

Boucher swept his palm toward the empty chairs. "Whoa. You're getting ahead of yourself. Sure—you don't like me. I hate your guts, because . . . well, you know why."

He tapped the tablet and gestured toward the folders. "But I do things by the book. I rarely let personal feelings get in the way. So we're going to talk, and you're going to get your coffee. And together, we'll decide whether it's in this precinct's best interests that you retain the badge you're so keen to throw in my face."

Walker locked eyes with the special investigator. The noise of the station receded. Boucher was right; there was friction, but at least Walker would be heard and fairly treated. Stomping out like baby Godzilla wouldn't solve a thing. And the longer they stayed in the room, the longer Walker had to figure out how to keep him from seeing Deena. Because if that happened, all bets were off.

Walker sat back down, wordlessly indicating his consent. Boucher retook his seat as well. "Glad we're on the same page. Why don't we get that coffee and start again?"

"The coffee's terrible. Let's get on with it."

"Fine. So again—the last time you saw Joseph Monroe before his murder?"

Walker paged back through the years. "Twelve years ago. Hundredth birthday. Bought him a tie and condoms. Should be in my report."

Boucher offered Walker the ghost of a smile. "Condoms? What size?"

"The autopsy should have any pertinent data you feel necessary for your investigation, Special Investigator Boucher."

"Fair enough. This was back in Atlanta?"

Walker held out a palm as if to pass back the question. "You would know."

"Okay, then. That was the first time you worked alongside the federal bureau, right? You, the Soldier, Zora, several others."

"That's right. Organized by Joe, partnering with police and homicide units to contain the proliferation of evil creeps throughout the city. Powers catching Powers."

"The gang wars."

"Exactly."

"And that wasn't the first time you worked with the Citizen Soldier. First Detroit, Doomtown before that. Then earlier on, in Korea."

"Correct on all counts."

"And during that time, did Monroe show signs of associating with anti-American or anti-Powers organizations, such as the Human Front, the Communist Party, or the Klan?"

Walker screwed up his face with disdain. "No, that's preposterous."

Boucher gathered his folders and removed a set of photographs not unlike the ones on Walker's desk. He tapped the mark tattooed on Monroe's bicep, drawing attention toward the fist-and-lightning lockup. "Are you sure? Because the report states that Monroe's tattoo had faded into his skin—skin that had once contained enhanced blood, which should have kept it bright. Especially if freshly inscribed by the killer."

Boucher steepled his fingers and furrowed his brow in thought. "That implies the Soldier had to have been rocking that logo for longer than a month, even several. Ergo, the killer didn't apply it to frame the man. It was there long before his murder."

"I knew Joe. He had nothing to do with that pack of wolves at the Human Front."

Boucher let the chair squeak as he scooted closer to the table. "I'm sorry, but I gotta say the evidence looks pretty damning."

"Evidence can be faked, especially by those familiar with powers."

"Are you saying a Power did this, looking to frame Joe because of his ties to the Front? Or are you suggesting an anti-Powers agent familiar with Joe's powers tried to position him as a traitor?"

Walker massaged his head, which had begun to throb. "I don't know. We need time to answer those questions."

" 'We'? As I understand it, Detective Walker, you've been pulled from the case."

"The royal 'we.' As in 'we, the precinct.'"

Boucher flipped through his notebook. "Why exactly were you pulled from the case, Detective? Because of a personal connection to the deceased? Is someone afraid that your shared history will reveal certain . . . truths?"

"You're reaching. Joe was my friend; his death affected me on an emotional level. We decided it was best for the investigation if I recuse myself."

" 'We' again. You and the captain? Your partner, Detective—"

"Don't—"

A knock at the door interrupted the heated interrogation. A moment later, Deena pulled it open and stepped inside, Corbin Kirk following close behind. "Hey, Walker? We got a list of possible suspects here, and I know you're off the case, but . . ." They each carried a sheaf of folders, and Kirk balanced a mobile tablet atop his pile. Deena held a printout in her hands, initially waving it to grab Walker's attention, but trailed off when she caught sight of the man sitting across from her partner.

"Oh," she whispered. Her face reddened, and for the first time in his life, Walker experienced what it meant to be in a room with a flustered, tongue-tied Deena Pilgrim. She hastily shoved her document into Kirk's pile, jostling the tablet and forcing him to juggle for his life.

Boucher got to his feet and stepped toward the door. The edges of his mouth curled up with pleasure. Slowly, a smile extended out from his lips, gradually widening the sides of both cheeks. He reached for Deena but thought better of it after a moment and quickly slid his hands into his pockets. He stood there, taking Deena in as she did her best to find her tongue.

Walker gathered his things and edged around Deena toward the door. Confused, Kirk's eyes darted between the partners and with the faint shadow of a frown, Walker beckoned for the rookie to join him outside.

"Come on, Kirk. Let's work your list."

Flustered and confused, Kirk glanced at Pilgrim. "But you're off the case? They told me you were—"

"Move, Kirk."

"But I'd like to work with Detective Pilg—"

"Read the room, rookie." The two cops exited the room, and as they departed, Boucher moved toward Deena and broke the silence. Walker lingered for a moment, hand on the doorknob, gauging the atmosphere before leaving the room.

"Hello, Deena," Boucher said, voice thick with emotion.

"Aaron? Is that . . . what . . . what are you doing here?"

They shuffled closer and, with clumsy movement, took one other in a familiar embrace. Walker frowned again. The guilt returned, slugging him in the gut. As he closed the door, he knew a time was coming where Detective Christian Walker—formerly Diamond, formerly Blue Streak and Gora—would have to dig into secrets to solve this case. Most importantly, though, he'd need to offer full transparency to support his partner—and possibly protect her from the sordid past.

# 4

*—mm—*

*November. Twelve years ago.*
*Thursday afternoon. 4:05 P.M.*

Leaves fell, lining the street with a multicolored blanket of crimson and gold. A chill had come over the last few days, settling across Atlanta like an unwelcome guest. It caressed each window with a layer of frost. North of the city, where elegant homes kissed woodland, a phalanx of automobiles converged on an understated Tudor situated in well-to-do Tuxedo Park. Wheels crackling through leafy carpets, they arranged themselves in a horseshoe around a well-manicured circular drive. Guests emerged in weather wear— smart jackets and coats, leather gloves, and expensive scarves. They greeted one another and angled toward the door, drawn by smells wafting from inside the Pilgrim home.

Ablaze in light and sound, the Pilgrim household had been carefully arranged for a night of football and fun. Salty treats perched on available end tables, and televisions presented the day's games from every conceivable angle. Guests lingered in the kitchen, milling about the granite island on which platters had been laid containing meats and cheeses, paired alongside bottles of reds, whites, and ambers. The man of the house laughed uproariously in the family room, handing out cigars from the comfort of a leather recliner. Detective Waldo Pilgrim wore a Falcons jersey over faded jeans, a counterpoint to the tastefully attired guests dressed in designer sweaters, sport coats, or dress shirts. Deena regretfully skirted the circle of men and the Packers-Lions game—she'd been a card-carrying member of Falcons Nation for years, and any other day, she'd trade dirty jokes and cadge beer from her dad's cronies. Today, however, she had a mission.

Today, Deena Pilgrim was on point.

Breezing past a throng of babbling Atlanta cougars, Deena veered to the right and headed toward the door. Her journey to the foyer had taken her past recognizable faces—several of which had covered national magazines. Her father, whom she idolized, had risen through the ranks of Atlanta's Powers Homicide Division, on a first-name basis with the deputy mayor and several notable masked heroes. Most days, Deena found herself in awe of Waldo. He'd engendered a sphere of influence—most of tonight's guests having arrived in luxury automobiles; other having swooped from above, carried in on brisk, Atlanta winds. She wanted for little, Waldo providing more than his share on a detective's salary. They had clothes, toys, vacations, and a gardener. Her mother barely lifted a finger, relinquishing control of the housework and cooking to a team of dedicated Cubans.

More than that, though, Deena admired what her father did for a living. The toys were nice, but the detective work—being a cop, righting wrongs— that appealed to her on an entirely different level. She asked questions, begged Dad to recount the day's events and tell her his war stories. She soaked it all in, as much as she could, and hoped one day to follow in his footsteps. As much as she'd wanted anything before today, Deena Pilgrim wanted to be a cop.

Why, then, Deena wondered, did Mom act like she hated it? Why did she have to be a *bitch* all the time? *Maybe it's a cop's wife thing. Once I bag Aaron, you won't catch me acting that way. No chance in hell. But then, hopefully, we'll be in the trenches together. Working side-by-side.*

She loitered in the foyer, glancing out at the pebbled driveway. Anxious, she grabbed a jacket and hurried down the porch. She fished a pair of earbuds out of her pocket and cycled through a playlist, listening to music as she waited for Aaron's arrival. She knew he was coming—she'd checked to make sure. But, truthfully, she'd already known; there hadn't been a Pilgrim event for the last six years that the Bouchers did not attend.

Muffled noise caught her attention, echoing from the south. Fighting of some kind, a clash above the clouds. Tinny claps of thunder resounded in the distance. It sounded like a fight; it might have been an explosion. Deena couldn't be sure. Cops and costumes drifted out to the porch, straining their necks to see what might be happening. None of them left, however, choosing to stay rather than check out the source of the thunder. All of them were loath, no doubt, to stray far from the Pilgrims' food or drink.

*Fuck,* Deena thought. *I'd be off like a rocket.* She'd asked Dad to take her for a ride-along, like a "take your daughter to work" thing, but the Homicide Division frowned on detectives dragging family members into active crime scenes. *Soon, though. I'm headed to college, deciding shit for myself. What to think, what to eat, what to* be. *Anything I want. Especially a cop.*

She sat on the curb, watching kids maul her yard—they belonged to Waldo's friends, left to their own devices as their parents drank and smoked. None were Deena's age; only Aaron, slightly older, who had yet to arrive. Deena's brother was away; he lived in California, having moved there for a girl and a job. She folded both arms across her knees. "Come on . . ." She tapped her fingers, keeping time to the rhythm as the clock crept closer to five. *Where are you, Aaron?*

As if on a cue, a sedan rolled down her street and turned into the Pilgrims' drive, coming to rest at the willow near the curb. Her heart surged to see the familiar sight of the Bouchers' car. Deena's stomach burbled; she was nervous. As she battled a sudden infestation of stomach butterflies, a kindly gentleman opened the sedan's driver's-side door. He winked at Deena as he stepped around the car, offering an arm to a tastefully dressed matron exiting the passenger's door along with several pies. They tottered up the driveway, responding to greetings from the porch with beaming, rosy cheeks. The man, in his late fifties, was dressed in a comfortable houndstooth jacket beneath a snug fleece overcoat. A dashing homburg balanced atop his head at a jaunty angle, threatening to topple to the ground. His wife, dressed in an ermine coat, strode past her husband and mounted the steps, whisking off a hat while doling kisses and hugs to those she encountered along the way. Her husband pumped several hands and then continued on to join his wife. Deena's body tensed with expectation, angling back to the sedan to spy the man to whom she hoped to give her heart . . . along with any other parts he desired.

But to Deena's chagrin, Aaron Boucher was nowhere to be found.

They'd met at a family barbecue, before Aaron had entered the police academy. Tall, athletic, bright, and sarcastic, he'd struck up an easy rapport with the opinionated ball of spunk clad in shorts and a belly shirt. Their parents had been longtime friends: Judge Kenneth Boucher tirelessly worked with Waldo Pilgrim to put away the worst criminals that Atlanta had to offer. Their moms belonged to the same charities, and Deena's brother had played against Aaron's cousins in JV basketball. Choosing to abstain from the afternoon's traditional games and sports, Aaron had located a secluded pond where they could splash and horse around in platonic, good-natured fashion. They'd dug into stolen snacks as he briefed her on the history of rock—a passion of Aaron's, as were most types of music. It had been a fun, memorable day.

Only Deena hadn't wanted it to be so platonic. Deena had to admit, she'd developed something of a crush on Aaron Boucher.

Truthfully, this was new territory for Deena. Tomboyish, outspoken, she didn't fit the picture of the lovelorn wallflower. Deena Pilgrim took what she wanted and made her intentions clear to the chosen target. *So why all the anxiety?* she wondered. *What is it about Aaron Boucher that turns me into an idiot?*

Part of it had to do with the way he treated her—as an equal, intellectually and emotionally. They shared passions, discussed goals. He knew what she thought about school and her limited social circle; she knew how he felt about Nine MM's second album and could regurgitate his treatise on the Conspiracy of Similar Chords Throughout the Music Industry. Treatise? More like a thesis. But Deena memorized it because it was important to Aaron. And he was important to her.

Mostly, though, it had to do with their shared desire to become working detectives. Aaron felt that an undercurrent of graft had crippled the police department. He vowed—should he be given the chance—to be as honest a cop as there ever was. Sometimes he intimated that Waldo had dabbled in dirty deeds, tainting the Homicide Division, but Deena chalked that up to a naïveté that came with principles. Everything about Aaron, from his looks to his fervor, made her want to spend time with him. She understood what it meant to covet that badge, just as he did. And he—unlike Waldo and her father's colleagues and cronies—was willing to share that world with her. That's why Aaron, unlike any man before, made Deena feel the way that she did. That's why she dug him, because of their mutual connection and interests. *Also? I want to fuck him all the time have his awesome babies spend our every minute fighting crime and sucking face.*

*I mean, is that too much to ask for?*

*Look,* she explained to the universe, *it isn't just about the sex.* Deena, at eighteen, had notched several dalliances on her bedpost—well, her first had been a notch on a locker room wall (the less said to the universe about that experience, the better). She'd been with guys, but guys in her school were dude-bros, morons, or—worse—weak in a sensitive, nice-guy way. This . . . what she felt for Aaron . . . she mooned over his stupid face when he went on about the Aquachords or Miranda rights. Despite the fact that she was still in school, Aaron already treated Deena like an equal. Like a partner. He'd given her a passport into his world.

*And now,* she yearned, *I want to guide him into mine.* Wind fluttered through her hair, jangling earrings and shivering her skin. The ground trembled; a corona of yellow light appeared in the distance, encouraging her to look away. After a moment, a figure soared through it, dragging clouds in its wake. The front door opened, and Deena's mother stepped out, sucking a drag from an ever-present cigarette.

"Deena," she demanded. "Help me set the napkin rings. Your father will never let me live it down if we don't use your grandmother's silver rings."

"When is Aaron coming?"

Her mother arched an eyebrow. "He didn't come with Ken and Eveline? Who could tell amid the parade of moral turpitude that has descended on my King James living room set?" The last slipped from her tongue with a disapproving cluck. Mom was at the five-drink mark; too soon for insubordination, just at the level of biting sarcasm. "Chop-chop. Dinner in ten, rings or no."

Fifteen minutes later, the horde of dignitaries, police luminaries, and celebrity guests settled around the dining room table. A feast had been laid, comprised of family standards—deep-fried turkey with Vidalia onions and chunky gravy, cranberry-walnut compote, and cheesy grits—along with nods to those of Italian heritage intermingled within the group: pepper-and-beef lasagna, shitake mushroom bruschetta, and a homemade manicotti prepared by the deputy mayor's wife. Deena was seated close to her father—between Judge Boucher and a drunk young man named Harley Cohen, rumored to be inventing anti-Powers technology for the FBI. Cohen absently pawed at Deena's leg, and she cheerfully set his hand aside each time. She kept an eye glued to the door, halfheartedly listening to breakdowns of the day's games (Lions won, Cowboys lost), perking up slightly when Waldo launched into an alcohol-soaked diatribe regarding Atlanta's criminal element.

"Thing about these murders," he mouthed off to the deputy mayor and the judge, "isn't about motive, but—"

"Dear," Deena's mother acidly ventured from across the table, "let's allow our guests to enjoy this delicious meal sans cops and robbers."

Waldo chuckled in reply. "How do *you* know it's delicious? You didn't cook it." He gestured toward the kitchen. "Hey! Get the Cubans out here. They're the ones . . . they . . ." He stifled a belch as his guests ignored the awkwardness. Someone handed him a drink. It might have been the judge; it might have been Deena.

Mom, however, sweetly kept digging. "Yes, but the children—"

"Children? They're outside, riding the dog."

"We don't have a dog."

"Yeah? Maybe it's one of the Cubans, then. Ha!"

"Dear! Not in front of the guests . . . or your daughter."

All eyes turned Deena's way, and her face conspicuously flushed a dull red. "Mom . . ." she deflected, "I like hearing about Dad's job. I want to hear about . . ." She turned to Dad. "What was it again?"

Waldo settled back. "Liberty murders. Coupla costumes over in Druid Hills."

Deputy Mayor Hanover dabbed his lips with a napkin. "Best to table this . . ."

"Kids need to know current events. Keeps them abreast of what's happening in their own front yard. Nothing wrong with the truth."

Mom snorted into her wineglass, and the judge neatly stepped in to cover the tension. "Druid Hills? By the CDC? That's troubling."

Waldo quaffed a swallow of Infinity Gold. "Hardly," he responded after wiping his mouth on a sleeve. "The Soldier's crew has things covered. Ain't that right, crew?" The assembled Powers around the table silently confirmed her father's half-sober conjectures. Even Deena, knee-deep in college applications, had seen the reports in the AJC; Downtown Atlanta had been levied a stringent curfew, and portions of the National Guard were stationed throughout the city, lending a hand to contain the resultant damage. The mayor had granted emergency powers to the both newly established and necessary Federal Powers Bureau along with a team of deputized Powers: names and masks like the Citizen Soldier, Diamond, Zora, Olympia, and Z. They flew around in capes and costumes, beating the tar out of other capes and costumes without ever coming closer to ending the violence. Frankly, she hoped it never ended; maybe she'd see some super shit in action. Maybe Dad or Aaron would put the holy beatdown on some dude with a death ray. For now, the Homicide Division had let the Soldier's goons contain the devastation. But as far as Deena could ascertain, two-thirds of said goons currently sat around her dining room, stuffing their faces with Eveline Boucher's cheese-and-onion pie.

*Amateurs,* Deena sniffed. *Aaron would never stand for affluent supercops eating mushroom puffs while the city burned to the ground. That's why he isn't here, I bet—he's on the job. I get it. I'd be there, too.*

"Fact is," Waldo went on, ignoring the undercurrent of tension, "we can't be sure who's at fault. Maybe it's one of those morons with the lightning tattoos—"

"The Human Front," someone supplied. It might have been the judge. It might have been the deputy mayor's wife, too flushed and engaged to sell an innocent, demure façade.

"That's right," Waldo agreed, satisfied and smiling. "The latest in backward-thinking monkey uncle would-be fascists, too afraid to play with fire, too stupid to know when they're already trapped in a burning building."

"Well, I don't know about that," Judge Boucher stated, putting aside his napkin. "I firmly remain curious about some form of registry or restriction placed on those with powers . . . those without the responsibility to use their gifts for the relative good. Witness this gang war, for example." The Powers at the table quietly seethed into their drinks. Thankfully, before things spiraled out of control, the judge stood up and winked at Deena. "Probably a fine time to extricate myself and stretch m'legs. Join me, dear?"

Out on the porch, settled into a pair of varnished rocking chairs, Deena and the judge ignored the evening chill and looked into the distance. Over the horizon, scattered pinpricks of ongoing battle twinkled in the fading light, like summer fireflies that had lived to see the autumn. Echoes of carnage radiated out from Atlanta, skimming the edge of Tuxedo Park and causing skeletal trees to shiver. Judge Boucher reached into his pocket and removed a fat cigar; once lit, it conjured up a cloud of smoke that rested about their shoulders, obscuring his face in its muddy haze. They rocked in silence, the sounds of debate and boisterous mirth thrumming from back inside the dining room.

The judge allowed himself a lazy, playful smile. "Not exactly the romantic evening you'd hoped for, is it?"

Deena hunched, keenly aware of color rising to her face. She felt hot and stupid; her tongue grew three sizes, unable to form a coherent response.

The judge chuckled. "It's all right. I got eyes."

"Please stop talking."

"It ain't like it's a secret. Both Eveline and I know about your crush on Aaron."

She hid her head in her hands. "Remember when you weren't talking? Those were good times."

"Ah, let an old man have his fun." The cigar blazed in the gathering dusk, casting a ruddy look about his face. "Besides, love—or hell, even lust—is nothing to hide. Don't be embarrassed or keep it secret. Never be afraid to seize love. You'll regret it when it's gone and mourn after it's far too late."

She tucked away an errant lock of hair. "I'm not in love."

The judge rocked and contentedly puffed. "I'm just happy for the company, dear."

"I mean . . ." She searched for the words, feeling them slip away. "I don't know that it's love. But I will say—if it's all right, Judge?"

He indulgently waved a free hand. "Lay on, Macduff."

"I will say I'm excited about his passions—the music and being a cop."

"That boy has strange taste in music, I'll give him that."

Deena grinned. "Strange wonderful. Nine MM. Little Doomsday. Alison Nightbird, Rocket to Planet X. Everything from hip-hop to grunge to—"

"Hmph. Whatever happened to Jimmy Dorian and the Belle City Bass?" The judge tapped his ashes over the porch, scattering them on the gravel below.

"—classic and even country, depending on the artist."

Judge Boucher poked Deena in the arm. "And what do *you* like?"

"Well . . . I like them all."

"But that's what Aaron likes. You must have had your own opinions, some original thoughts before my boy came along?"

She shrugged. "I guess."

"Don't get lost in another person's passions, Deena. Have your own beliefs and principles—desires and dreams independent of the man you love."

"But, his dreams *are* mine. And his beliefs. Like . . . well . . ."

"Yes?"

"Well, like he's a cop. But a *good* cop, right?"

The judge squinted through the smoke. "As opposed to?"

"No one, really. I mean, Aaron thinks—"

"He thinks?" The judge scooted closer, dangling the lit cigar from his fingers.

She felt flush again. "No, it's not like that. I just—"

Thankfully, before she could stick her toes in any deeper, a patrol car banked hard into the driveway. It stopped behind the other cars, and a sharply dressed officer leaped from behind the wheel and started toward the porch. The judge rose to his feet, ashing his cigar, and stepped forward to meet the cop. Deena joined him, heart thumping against her larynx, happy to have been given a reprieve from further humiliation. Happier still to see that Aaron Boucher had finally arrived.

"Son," the judge began, voice tightening with questioning expectation, "your face is the color of cheesecloth."

The younger Boucher mounted the steps. Deena charted every move, mentally cataloging the expressiveness of Aaron's eyes and, to be honest, the way his butt looked in his uniform. She waved hello, but he'd breezed by and ushered his father inside so fast that Deena wasn't sure he'd even registered her presence.

"Time to go, Pop. Get Mom, your coats. You need to get home now."

Judge Boucher liberated his arm. "What is going on, Aaron? Let go of me."

"Dinner's over, okay? You have to get home before—"

"Before what?" The dinner party had filtered out into the foyer, drawn by Aaron's explosive arrival. Waldo Pilgrim stumbled toward the door as Eveline briskly approached her son.

"Aaron, what is it?" Aaron's mother placed a hand against his cheek, and he slid it away, looking past her and into the house. "What's going on?"

"Are you serious?" He gestured out a window. "Have none of you looked outside? Or are you too drunk to care?"

Waldo raised a hand, firmly wrapped around a can of Old Guard. "Hang on. You talking about me?"

Aaron gave him a withering stare. "Go to bed. Sleep it off, okay?"

But Waldo pressed on, shaking off the deputy mayor's wife—his own having melted into the recesses of the house. "What did you mean by that? You, of all people?"

Deena eased herself between the two men. "Dad, how about some coffee?"

Aaron took Eveline's hand. "Let's go, Mom. Say good-bye to your friends."

The judge deftly removed Eveline's hand from his son's grip. "Officer Boucher," he started again, adding authority to his tone, "what exactly happened tonight?"

Aaron rubbed the lower half of his face and sharply inhaled, breathing deeply before continuing. "Aside from World War III blanketing Atlanta while half our Powers drink and fly? Besides cops—good cops, mind, not half the badges in this room—dying on the streets while evading heat vision?" The dinner guests shifted uncomfortably, waiting for Aaron to finish berating them. "You mean what's happening aside from all that?" The judge nodded, subtly holding out a palm to block Deena's father from getting close.

"Well, Pop," Aaron seethed. "Taking all that into account, ignoring the big picture . . . there's been another murder."

Deena scanned the faces of her parents' guests as the statement elicited short intakes of breath. Eveline and the judge exchanged glances, the latter's face hardening with concern. He placed a hand atop his son's right forearm. "You're sure?"

Aaron nodded in reply.

"A note? There was another note?"

This too, Aaron confirmed. Deena waited for an explanation, but it looked as if one wouldn't be forthcoming.

"Take it easy," Waldo said, swaggering forward. "You don't know what it is; who Liberty is. But, listen—"

Aaron whirled, poking a finger into Waldo's chest. "I *know* what it is, and I know what *you* are, Pilgrim. I'll protect my family, and *you* protect *yours*. Course, it's not like anyone here is doing much protecting. Have another beer, why don't you? It isn't as if you're being much help."

Bristling at Aaron's attack, Deena had to admit that she was also rather impressed. Her father was sneering, his face a dull, brick red . . . but he made no move to attack Aaron Boucher. She'd never spoken like that to either parent, much less one of her parents' friends.

Eveline quickly bestowed kisses on the gathering, wishing all a good night. Aaron stared down Waldo as the judge made apologies for the abruptness of their departure. The older couple bustled out into the cold, headed for their sedan. Aaron paused on the threshold and then looked back to address the assembled throng.

"You know," he began, leveling them with a withering gaze. "I love being a cop. Especially in Atlanta. There's something noble about wearing a badge here. Even when we fall, what's our motto? *Resurgens*. 'Rising Again,' it means. Get knocked down? You get up, despite thousands of blows to your pride and spine." The room was silent now, apart from muffled gunfire echoing in the distance.

"Tonight, though, I'm embarrassed to belong. Disgusted to be an Atlanta cop if it means sharing the streets with the likes of you. Police, power, politician—makes no difference. This look-the-other-way policy, the bribes, collusion, and goddamn *apathy* that allow you to party while the town burns down around its motherfucking *ears*? While someone slices bodies in the name of what he or she thinks is liberty? *Liberty*? *That* I will have no part of. *That* is something I can't let '*rise again.*' You're cops. *Cops.* You carry a badge that bestows upon you a mission to create a safer Atlanta—one that ensures the safety of its citizens. One that builds trust, not betrayal. And you"—he pointed to the Powers in their midst—"what would Uncle Sam say if he could witness this? Don't half of you have government grants to end this violence? *Damn.*"

Aaron stepped onto the porch. "You're a goddamn disgrace. *All* of you. I don't know where your collective head is at, but I want no part of it. I'll be damned if I let my parents feast among this den of weak-willed, do-nothing crooks when at any moment all our lives could be in very real danger."

He stalked down the steps and back to the patrol car, the elder Bouchers having already departed. Deena wanted to go with him, but Dad moved to the door and slammed it in Aaron's wake.

*He never said hello,* she thought dejectedly. *He barely even looked my way.*

Waldo had a coppery bloom about his face. Deena gingerly took his arm and led him back into the family room, shooing angry, buzzing guests like cats from a windowsill. One by one, the partygoers ventured out into the night, back to fancy cars or up and away, headed for less conscience-laden environs. The deputy mayor bid his farewell, promising to look into Officer Boucher's claims and smooth the matter with both the mayor's and commissioner's offices. Soon enough, the house was quiet. Father and daughter sat alone in recliners, her mother nowhere to be found for comfort or support.

Deena looked into Waldo's eyes. "You okay, Dad?"

Fuming, he jerked his head, assuring his daughter that all was well. She placed a palm on the back of his hand, and he clapped it with his own, gently caressing her fingers and being careful not to break them in anger. Aaron's speech had stirred something within her father's heart—as it had everyone in the foyer—and she longed to get his read on it. But Deena knew not to press the matter. She never asked questions about her father's relationship with Aaron. Truth be told, she was afraid to know the answers.

Instead, she tugged another thread from the evening's tapestry. "Dad," she asked. "Dad, what murders?"

His face screwed up in thought, eyebrows beetling as he pursed his lips. "What?"

"The murders you were talking about, Dad."

Waldo fixed his bleary gaze on his only daughter. "Hm? Whassat, kiddo? You don' wanna know. Just forget it."

She pressed him. "But there are murders. And a note? Aaron said."

Her father snorted. "Nggh. Aaron . . . what he . . . that kid has some nerve . . . look. This guy, we guess—"

"You *guess*?"

He slowly shrugged and eased back into his chair. "One guy. Maybe two? A woman? Every time we find a victim, it's different from the last. See? And he leaves a note, right? Or they do. Or she."

"Dad," she interjected, keeping him on-topic. "What note?"

He held out his hands, framing it like a marquee. "'*In the Name of Liberty.*' Sometimes in ink. Sometimes blood. Always—*always*—near the body." Waldo passed the back of one hand across his nose. "Coulda been part of the, uh, the gang war. Maybe Powers. Maybe Human Front. Someone who hates everyone. I dunno."

"But you'll catch him? That's what you do." Deena squeezed his knee, trying to keep him awake. Hoping to pump information she could use to get close to Aaron. To make them equals—anything other than what she currently felt: this weird, needy place where he seemed out of her league and in a different world. She needed to know everything she could about the murders, about the madness that had overtaken Atlanta.

Because it was important to Aaron, and it was important to the Atlanta Powers Homicide Division. And so it was important to her.

"You'll catch him," she reiterated. "How about coffee, okay?"

Waldo evaded her statement and dismissively waved his hand. Somewhere in the back, Mom tripped over something and broke a glass or vase. Deena hunched on the recliner, unsure how to jar her parents from their drunken cocoons of self-loathing. She desperately wanted to see Dad in action, to see him save the day. To have him be the man Aaron claimed he wasn't. But there would be no resolution this evening. Tonight, she needed to support her father, to repair his ego and assure him that Aaron hadn't been referring to the Pilgrim patriarch. Waldo was a good cop. The best. How else could he be such a good provider, so connected, so famous and respected?

She would listen to whatever he had to say, soak it in, and use it to arm her mission. Sure, Dad didn't know who or what this murderer was. But he was a great detective; she told him so—words her mother should have been the one to say. Tonight was a stutter-step in the war on crime. Tomorrow, he would wake up fresh and follow leads. He'd question suspects and analyze evidence. No one knew anything? He soon would. Deena believed that in her heart of hearts. She had faith in her father, even if Aaron didn't. She knew that Waldo was a good cop, just like Aaron. And if they would only let her, Deena knew she would be out with them both, cleaning up the streets.

Just as she knew, despite tonight's misstep, that one way or another, she would have a rookie cop's principled, awesome babies.

Just as she knew she had already fallen in love with Aaron Boucher.

# 5

~~~

**December. Monday morning. 3:57 A.M.**

The last of the barflies stumbled out of Der Mann ohne Bier and into the receding dusk. Faint rays of sunlight were visible over row houses and brownstones, painting the slush and streets with flecks of gold. The lights went out inside the beer hall—last call had come and gone—and someone, one of the brothers most probably, flipped the sign in the window from GEÖFFNET to GESCHLOSSEN. The hooded man listened intently from across the way, detecting the faint clinking of glasses and scraping of chairs against a wooden floor. The proprietors were closing down the pub for the night, as the hooded man knew they would be.

He deftly slipped out of the parked van, locked the door, and took confident strides across the filthy sidewalk. Worn Reeboks slapped against the wet concrete, skidding once in the snow as he reached the wreathed door. The man held out a gloved hand, using it to regain balance by pressing against the darkened glass. Someone noticed; a blurry shadow stopped and stared through the beer hall window.

The hooded man sniffed and then stuck both hands in the pockets of his overcoat. He peered out into the cold, wintry night. The barflies had disappeared; he was alone, a mysterious pedestrian loitering on the streets of the German Quarter at 4:00 A.M.

*Truly, though,* he thought, *my presence isn't much of a mystery. They'll know why I'm here. They've been expecting me, or someone like me, for years.*

Securing the objects in his left pocket, the hooded man withdrew the item in the right. He rapped against the glass, continuing to knock on the door with his knuckles until a broad, ugly face appeared in the window. The face sneered; Aryan features twisted into regret as the rest of the body—wiry, muscled, dressed in a simple black T-shirt—subtly gestured toward the GESCHLOSSEN sign. The hooded man glanced down and then looked up and apologetically shrugged and placed the fist against his chest. *I don't understand German,* it suggested.

The ugly Aryan unlocked the door, cracking it just enough through which he could stick his face and rest a fist against the jamb. The hooded man's attention was drawn to a carving on the frame. Graffiti, dug into the wood. It was a symbol . . . a snake circling a fist. Three lightning bolts clutched in its grasp. He nodded at the apologetic proprietor, expressing with his hooded eyes that he recognized the mark for what it was. He might not understand German, the look said, but he understood *that.* The face in the door nodded with approval and then tapped against the glass on the GESCHLOSSEN sign.

"Closed," he grunted, barely an accent discernible in the word. "We're closed."

The man smiled beneath his mask. He reaffirmed his grip on the tool in his right hand. Every tool, he believed, for a specific job. He cocked his head in reply.

"Season's greetings, Dolph," Liberty whispered.

Dolph—that was his name, the densest of three brothers that Liberty knew loitered inside the pub—opened his mouth, fairly dumbfounded. His eyes widened, and the door started to close. *Idiot,* Liberty scolded himself. *He recognized your damn voice.*

Before Dolph could slam the door, Liberty lifted his right hand and held out the item resting securely in his fist. It was a cube—no bigger than a golf ball—black and bristling with electronics. Liberty tapped the back, and an earsplitting shriek emanated from the box, transmitting out to a five-block radius. It was a recorder, equipped with high-decibel playback, and what it currently played was the scream of a dying god. He'd recorded it in Chicago, not so long ago. And now he used it to not only bring Dolph to his knees but also shatter every door and window in and around Der Mann ohne Bier.

Liberty punched Dolph in the face, shattering his teeth. The beefy Aryan fell back and clutched his mouth, blood spraying across the hardwood flooring. Liberty stepped over him, entering the premises, striding toward the long, circular bar. Bottles had shattered, and various types of liquid drenched the floor, so he carefully made his way around the glass and puddles of ale, Jaeger, and brandy. Another man writhed near the bar, rubbing his temple and attempting to dig out his damaged inner ear. Liberty approached just as the man—wearing a suit, slimmer and older—finally pulled himself up and grabbed for a nearby bat.

Liberty lifted the cube, pointing it at the second German. "Tut-tut, Bruno. The first round works you over. The second one kills you."

Bruno lowered the bat. His accent was more pronounced. "You wouldn't dare play it again. Every policeman in the city would be down here to arrest you for property damage, assault, and attempted robbery."

Liberty frowned. "Robbery? Bruno, you know me better than that."

Dolph groaned by the door, and a third man, splayed out on the floor, had yet to show signs of life. *I might have killed that one. That will save some time,* Liberty realized with a smile. He stowed the cube into his pocket and pointed to a nearby barstool. "Sit. I'd like Dolph to join you. We can do this *der einfache Weg* or *die harte Tour,* if you'll pardon the cliché. It's four in the morning, I'm expecting fireworks to kick off at any moment, and I don't particularly have the time to be clever."

Bruno nodded, dumbfounded, and pointed at a particular stool, making sure that it would serve. Liberty gestured toward it. "Please, sit." Bruno grinned. Something moved behind the hooded man.

He ducked left just as Dolph lunged right. Liberty easily sidestepped the big German and clotheslined him with a forearm. Dolph doubled over, the wind knocked out of him, and Liberty snatched the Aryan's white-blond hair with his right hand. His left hand still remained in his pocket, fastened to the other tool he couldn't wait to reveal. He tossed Dolph into a set of tables, breaking several and scattering chairs. Dolph didn't get up. Bruno, meanwhile, had launched himself from the stool. Liberty was forced to swivel and grab him by the throat. Bruno's neck was thick and veiny, but the man in the mask crushed his windpipe with relative ease. Bruno turned red and then blue. Finally, Liberty lifted the German and heaved him over the bar, into broken glass and shattered bottles. Bruno slid down, out of view. The third German—*Johann,* the hooded man reminded himself—stayed where he was, completely unconscious and possibly dead.

Liberty sniffed and stretched. He flexed the fingers on his right hand and caught his breath. Then, finally, he removed the item in his left pocket and pulled it taut with both hands. It glistened and *twanged* in the moonlight filtering in from the smashed window. Morning was only hours away, and he could hear people on the street, stirring as car alarms blared in reaction to his sonic volley.

Liberty shrugged and started toward the closest German.

"I suppose that means we do it *die harte Tour,*" he said to no one at all. "Not to worry, *meine Freunde.* That's what I'd been hoping for."

He hunkered down and got to work.

# 6

~mm~

Traffic snarled as they neared Twenty-Eighth and Gallaher, slowing to a halt ten feet from Deena's destination. Honking the horn, she craned her neck to see the snow-covered terminal ahead, rearing above the holiday shoppers, crowned with frost and graffiti. Crowds weaved around Ellis Station, ten-dollar-an-hour admins hustling past on coffee breaks, careful not to slip on patches of ice. The office drones were interspersed amid cheerful tourists, late commuters, and—more relevant to Deena's concerns—a multitude of police officers. A barricade had been erected across Gallaher, blocking off two of the street's four lanes. Three cruisers stuck ass-backward into traffic, forcing away drivers and cabs in order to cordon off space for approaching, blaring ambulances. Lights splashed red and blue against the station's exterior walls, and the hubbub of the sirens and arriving detectives only served to further add to the urban morass. Deena tugged out her phone and begged it to call Walker for the third time since they'd left the precinct. As it had for the previous attempts, a pleasantly digital voice sent Deena's message straight into Walker's inbox. Cussing, she hurled the phone into the back, doing her best to angle her SUV toward the entrance to Ellis Station.

*Dammit. He's probably underground, the newbie by his side.*

Sitting in the passenger seat, legs braced against the dashboard, Aaron winced as Deena gracelessly pulled her car up onto a curb. She nearly bisected a halal vendor with the two left wheels, and Aaron gaped at the poor man, jerking his hand in an awkward wave, doing his best to impart hasty, sincere apologies.

*Fuck yes,* Deena seethed inwardly while stealing a furtive glance in his direction. *You* should *apologize. This is* your *fault.*

They'd barely spoken since the call had come in. Walker and Kirk had abandoned Deena, having raced to the scene in one of the three already present cherry tops. She would have joined them if not for the fact that she'd been shuttered in a room, awkwardly reconnecting with the former love of her life. The last thing Deena had seen of Aaron Boucher—her first and final big romance—had been his pathetic face, shoulders slumped as she'd stormed out. That was over ten years ago, and so much had happened during the intervening period, far too much to impart in a single encounter. Far too important to impart in a room that faintly smelled of cat piss. They'd traded pleasantries: Aaron caught Deena up on Boucher family matters—Eveline had died three years prior from a case of high-grade lymphoma; the judge, widowed and alone, was now preparing to explore the adventure that was retirement. Aaron, meanwhile, had traveled. First Texas, to which he'd escaped from the madness of Atlanta. Then Chicago for a while, leaving just as Walker and Pilgrim managed to burn it to the ground. Now Aaron lived in Washington, trekking between a two-bedroom off Dupont Circle and his father's guest room on Delsante, here in the city. Still crazy about music, his tastes had evolved from Nine MM and Powers punk to more eclectic fare, jazz legends like Bird and the Count as well as a raft of genres ranging from neue-vogue hip-hop to disintilectronica. He asked what Deena had been listening to lately, but she was too embarrassed to answer; Deena hadn't stacked a playlist in years. The lone CD gracing her glove compartment was a Blonde Ammo single scored during last year's holiday party.

*He never asked about my father,* Deena realized as she inched toward their destination, fishing for an opening in the widening silence. *Mom and the job. But Dad? I doubt it'll come up unless I bring it up.*

Deena hadn't spoken to Waldo in years. Mom got the occasional phone call, along with the odd holiday or birthday exchange. Her mother lived in Wisconsin—Racine or Madison, one of the ones that wasn't Green Bay.

She'd remarried after leaving Waldo eight years earlier, having found sobriety and love with an auto parts dealer named Hoyt. No kids this time, but she spent her days gardening and managing the books for Hoyt, evenings playing cards with the Rotary Club. She seemed happy; Deena couldn't deny that she deserved it, not after Atlanta. But they led separate lives now; both of them had compartmentalized their pasts and futures. As had Deena's shit stain of a father.

So when Aaron had asked Deena about her past, she'd replied that she hated all music, current or otherwise. She hadn't spoken to her parents in a while. And, of course, she was single. Deena had her apartment. She had her partner. And she had her badge. Those were the things that shaped her life; not her past, which she did her best to lose in a bottle or investigation. Deena chose to live in the present. The past was too damn hard.

"So," he'd responded, tracing gouges in the table. "You're single?"

The conversation had gotten easier after that, chiefly because they'd focused on flirting and work. She asked about his commission, and Aaron evaded every question. He, in turn, pried into Walker's life, and she pivoted toward the intriguing shit that they had seen or solved. She caught him up on Retro Girl and Triphammer. The Powers virus and Olympia's death-by-orgasm. Z and Wolfe, and then Chicago and the setback with the bureau (which he, as a Washington insider, knew about). She skirted certain issues and elaborated on others, choosing to conceal her brief stint with powers (and ensuing pregnancy) as well as Walker's more intimate, personal details. Aaron picked up on her fading passion, though—the way she described the events in her past, the manner in which her body language changed from confident to sorrowful made him wonder if she'd become disenchanted with the job. She admitted that the years had taken their toll. Deena balanced on the precipice; she loved law enforcement, never felt more alive than when using honed detection skills to solve a case. But the raft of bullshit that came with that high had begun to outweigh the wins. And truth be told, she had explained to Aaron, Deena wasn't sure how much longer she could endure it.

*I haven't even expressed that to Walker,* Deena thought. *Aaron is the first person I've told about how I've been feeling, That must mean something, right?*

She remained wary, worried he might be leveraging their history and minefield of a relationship to dig up dirt for his commission. But when

Aaron's face softened after that and he'd invited her to dinner, espousing the virtues of a Polynesian stew joint on Dougan and Alimagno, Deena lowered her shields to see where this might be going. She really needed a night out, despite the way her gut recoiled when she thought about how they'd left things. Her last date had ended badly—like "boot in the crotch" badly. So she'd said yes, even though she'd sensed warning lights when Aaron offered to help navigate the red tape of her open investigation: the high-profile corpse in the morgue.

She'd hesitated, and then the call had come in. But they'd gone on reminiscing for another ten minutes, so of course Walker had left her behind.

*And now here we sit,* she mused, *ignoring questions best left unanswered. Meanwhile, I'm forced to cut a swath through snow-covered streets to reach a crime scene in which my superstar partner—who isn't actually on the job—has probably solved the Hoffa disappearance.* She slammed her palm on the wheel, eliciting barks of protest from her straining horn.

"Come on, dammit! Homicide! Out of the way!" Deena sharply turned to the left, driving up and onto the sidewalk, spattering bystanders with slush. Commuters and tourists scrambled to clear a path, flattening themselves against walls as she steered toward Ellis Station. Three policemen warned Deena back, but the squeal of her tires as she launched off the curb sent them hustling for safety, too. She banked right and then left again and brought the SUV in behind the cordon that had been created for the ambulances. Shifting into park, she waved at the shouting cops and then glanced sideways to gauge her passenger's reaction. Hand welded to the dash, left foot wedged against the glove compartment, Aaron was wide-eyed and his breathing was very still. After a moment, his chest unhitched, and he extricated himself from the crash-landing position he'd assumed until Deena inevitably, thankfully, stopped the car.

"Come on, Blitzen," she said, smiling sweetly. Deena exited onto the street, and Aaron joined her after a moment, visibly shaken. Deena started toward the doors, ignoring astonished stares while beckoning for Aaron to follow. They ducked beneath the tape and headed into the evacuated building.

Ellis Station, situated on the city's western harbor, was a sprawling hub into which all sorts of public transportation converged. Seven stories high, comprised of a series of interconnected terminals, Ellis had been named after one of the city's original governors and the building's financier, Tiberius Reginald Ellis. The building's architect, a half-drunken refugee with vast ambitions and scant resources, had taken the assignment in hopes of landing future work from the city leaders. Unfortunately, said leaders deemed his plans too subdued for the forward-thinking metropolis they'd hoped to create, so Ellis paid for three more engineers to come aboard (one of whom may have been the city's first evil genius type). The resultant mess, squalid and odorous due to years of urban decay, squatted upon the west side like a flatulent gargoyle. As successive layers of government continued to mold the city, they built up eateries, pharmacies, coffeehouses, and tchotchke shops around the pulsing, belching arteries through which coursed the life-blood of interconnected multistate transit. Along with the army of stores came a deluge of mouth breathers searching for a way to distract themselves from shitty jobs, shittier vacations, and—during inspired moments—sporadic instances of petty thievery and sexual harassment. Now, striding past a gourmet pastry shop, Deena paid attention to the unusual, welcome silence that had descended on Ellis Station. Boucher nipped at her heels, following onto the escalators.

"So catch me up. Is this case new?" Aaron adjusted his tie and induced color back into his cheeks. "Can you afford the time while dealing with the Soldier fallout?"

She shrugged. "We'll have to find out."

"What did you and Detective Kirk uncover at the precinct?"

"Big list. That's about it."

Aaron raised his hands in mock prayer as they descended. "Praise and hallelujah."

She smiled despite herself. "We compiled a roll call of the Soldier's known enemies with ties to the Front, stretching back to the organization's inception."

"Only the ones who are currently active?"

"Uh-uh," Deena replied. "Can't rule anyone out. Don't know when Monroe got those tats; can't tell how deep it is, if it's deep at all."

"Meaning?"

"Meaning the tats, the Human Front—could be a blind. Someone pointing us away from the culprit." Deena stepped off the escalator and waited for Aaron to join her. They continued down a corridor, heading for a sign indicating stairs leading deeper into the station's bowels. The sign was pockmarked and dented. It read SUBWAY, with an arrow pointing down.

"But you said that the tattoos weren't new. Older, faded . . . Walker all but confirmed that to me."

"True, but even if Joe subscribed to an anti-Powers agenda, that doesn't mean they had anything to do with his death."

He eyed her as they reached the subway stairs. "But you don't believe that. You've got a hunch it's Malachi Crane and his band of goons."

Deena shrugged again. "I follow my nose. It always knows."

She could see commotion on the platform below—lights, stretchers, and more yellow tape. She fidgeted, feeling the moment of paradise-purgatory once again; the same thing Deena had felt before entering Joe's apartment. *Come on. My partner's down there. You're cute and all, but he needs my help.*

Aaron held out a hand, placing it on her shoulder. "You all right?"

Deena tapped her finger against the bridge of her nose and grinned, ignoring the queasiness that had settled in her stomach. "Car ride caught up with my guts."

"Do tell."

"Later. Trying to breathe first." Two cops headed toward them, walking up the stairs. One of them spied Deena, whispered to his partner, and then performed an about-face and hustled back down to the platform. The second kept coming, unconvincingly trying to ignore Deena and her guest as he continued toward the escalator.

"Your case," Aaron continued. "You must have a hunch, something enough to have disturbed Walker back at the precinct. Clue me in; I can run interference with the feds, toss them a lead they can feed the media. Then we can go see what fresh hell Walker's discovered."

"Look," she stammered, unsure if she really wanted to mix her business with whatever she had going on with Aaron. *Why the fuck not? What harm will it do?* "We had a few leads, but only a handful seemed solid enough to pursue. Walker might think otherwise—"

"Walker's off the case."

"Plus there's that, so I'm second-guessing myself a bit. And I'm paraphrasing, of course, because Kirk has the files . . ." Deena trailed off and looked down. As if summoned, Kirk walked past the stairs, his back to the detectives, heading for the far end of the platform. Aaron noticed her distraction and did his best to recapture Deena's attention. "Hey, over here."

"Sorry. Like I said, the key suspect isn't one person, I don't think, but rather a group of THF thugs who had dealings with Monroe and also were suspects during the whole thing we had down South."

"Really." Aaron stepped away and crossed his arms, processing this new information. "I thought we covered all the suspects. There was a *lot* of Human Front activity in Atlanta. Not only because of the gang wars, but also tied into—"

"—the Liberty case, right. Some of these guys were incarcerated in Atlanta at the time of the later murders."

"Guys plural."

"Plural like a motherfucker."

Aaron leaned against the railing, mulling over the data in his head. "Okay, so multiple suspects. Why not bring them in?"

"Kirk and I wanted to run our findings past Walker, but the man had an important meeting this morning."

"Touché."

"Touché like a motherfucker."

"Quit it."

"Detective?"

Deena turned. Corbin Kirk hesitated halfway between the landing and the subway platform, tentatively trying to get her attention. He clutched a tablet and seemed unsure as to whether or not he should approach, eyes darting between his senior partner and the special investigator with whom she was conversing. Aaron waved him closer, and Kirk mounted the last few steps. His collar was rumpled in a way that made Deena want to mother the poor kid; his straw-colored hair, however, was immaculate and glistening with product and sweat. Kirk pointed to the platform where an idling E train sat—the northern line, traveling from the Sprawl to Harrow Falls and Alvindale. The doors were open, and the inside of the car teemed with lights and cops.

"You should see this," he suggested, voice cracking. On closer inspection, Kirk looked green around the edges; as if he'd been sick. *Come on, new fish,* Deena begged. *Keep it together in front of my ex.* Rolling her eyes, she started down the stairs. *Too late.* The impression had been made, and unless Kirk was telepathic, her request wouldn't have helped. Of course, in this town, stranger things had happened.

They reached the platform, skirting the usual array of gawking cops and harried technicians. The medical examiner had yet to arrive, though a handful of paramedics were on-site, consulting with Walker and Forensics. Deena sidled up alongside her partner, arching an eyebrow as she looked into the compartment. Police tape sectioned off a corner of the car, and two men moved about the space, taking pictures and lifting samples. The wall caught her eye; it was red, and Deena thought she saw men on a bench, calmly watching the police at work.

"Whadda we got?" she inquired, craning her neck to see past her partner.

Walker glanced Deena's way, his conversation having been interrupted, finally noticing that she was on scene. "I got this."

"Eff that. What is it? Attack of the Mole People?"

He edged her back from the door toward the middle of the platform. "You have a case, Deena. An important case with a timeline. Go deal with it, and leave this to me."

Kirk lifted two fingers to get their attention. "The thing is, Detectives—"

Deena held out a finger of her own. "Quiet, you. Listen, Walker: I can work both, and by the way? When you whisk my new partner off for an evening of glamour below the city, well—"

"Detective Boucher, escort Deena back to the station, would you?"

Aaron shrugged and peered through the open doors. "Hey, I'm just here for the laughs and wit. Besides, I . . ." Aaron hesitated and then whistled low and long. "*Damn.* Hello, what have we here?"

Curiosity piqued, Deena started for the open doors. Kirk did his best to deflect her, but all that got him was an elbow to the ribs. "Wait," he sputtered, scuttling along in her wake, "I think you should know—"

Deena ducked inside the car, and Kirk followed. The cops turned around, drawn by their presence, and then stepped aside to give the detectives a clearer view. Three men sat next to each other, as Deena had thought, side-by-side on a seat fit for four. A horrible odor wafted off their bodies, filling the car. It smelled as if cheese had been left out in the sun for a week. The men sat demurely, shoulders rubbing up against one another, facing forward as if waiting to reach their destination. At least Deena imagined they had faces; all three had been cleanly decapitated. Their necks were cauterized near the Adam's apple. Blood had spattered against the wall, marring a city map and the adjacent, filthy window. The closest man's arms, emerging from a straining black T-shirt, had been crossed so that both hands rested in his lap. The hands were gone, wrists burned to match his neck. The forearms had been taped to his jeans, and Deena could see they were covered with tattoos: snakes, bullets, and letters . . . a near-match to Joe Monroe's. The other two bodies were dressed more professionally: ties and dress shirts, khakis and argyle. The corpse in the middle had its hands taped to a newspaper; both arms rigged and lifted with wire, making it appear as if he were casually perusing the headlines. His tie was askew, as were his socks, and Deena was horrified to realize the ankles had been stuck into two of the missing heads, mouths agape and teeth shattered. The last dead man protected a bag under his arm; slung over his shoulder, it rested heavily on the fourth seat. The interior had been exposed, and Deena could see the final head peeking out from within the bag, eyes missing and jaw removed. All three corpses had bare forearms; all three inscribed with Human Front tattoos. But Deena barely noticed.

Five words, painted on the wall in blood, had her full attention.

She stepped out of the car, breathing the sour air of the station, doing her best to purge the metallic smell of blood and rotting flesh from her nose. Aaron and Kirk joined her, holding their breath, but Deena sensed the sway in Kirk's step, intuiting the rookie was about to lose his lunch. Perhaps for the second time that morning.

"Let's be honest, Detective Kirk," she suggested, a faint grin reaching her lips. "Santa delivered. This worked out better than we expected."

He slowly nodded. "Happy holidays."

Deena turned to Aaron, gesturing with her chin. "Déjà vu like a freight train."

Aaron steadied himself with a hand against the door. He couldn't look away from the credo written above the dead men's heads. *In the Name of Liberty,* it read. Just as it had twelve years earlier.

Just as it had in Atlanta.

# 7

───〜〜〜───

*December. Monday afternoon. 1:02* P.M.

Corbin Kirk wobbled. Walker caught the queasy look on the rookie's face. He placed a steady hand against Kirk's back. "Easy there," the big man said. "You okay?"

"Sweet baby Jesus, not again," Kirk answered, lurching onto the platform, doubling over and out of view.

Walker stuck a hand in his pocket. "Yeah, I felt that way the first time, too. Ten years back? More?" He looked sideways at Boucher, as if by way of confirmation.

"Twelve," Boucher corrected, the investigator's focus still glued to the wall.

"Exactly. Hits you in the eyes and then sneaks up on the skull and gut. Kicks you over, leaves room in the breadbasket for more to wrench. Hey, Deena?"

"Yeah?" Walker's partner was still wrestling with the scene, mentally cataloging and ascertaining what the triple-homicide meant to her already difficult case. The case that Christian Walker had been warned to leave alone. *Wouldn't be the first,* he mused. *Nor the last.* "Food for thought?"

Kirk retched out on the platform, wetly and loudly. "Sick now," he begged. "Don't talk about food."

Deena moved into the compartment, sidestepping random outliers of gore. She picked her way closer to the decapitated trio, slipping an unsharpened pencil from her coat and—despite squawks of protest from the forensic specialists—gently prodded various body parts to see if they might prod back. The pencil traced intangible lines from corpse to the wall and then down to the bag and up again, coming to a climax at the leftmost forearm. She tapped a thoughtful staccato against the man's tattoos.

"Can't be coincidence, can it?" She peered at Walker, searching for assent.

"Doubtful. Motive seems unclear. Someone simply killing bigots?"

Boucher stepped into the car, cheeks sallow and Adam's apple working. "We don't know for certain that Monroe was—"

Deena touched Boucher's forearm. "Lower," she warned. "Let's not broadcast that. Privileged information between you, me, Walker, and the human sprinkler out there." Kirk showed signs of recovery and moved to join them. "General rule: keep it contained. Understood, new fish?" Kirk weakly nodded, doing his best to remain composed.

"Fine," Boucher agreed. "Even still: different methods, opposite sides of town. Possibly around the same time—bodies have clearly been here for a while. Liberty tag here, but not at Monroe's. Two different killers?"

"Possible," Walker reluctantly ventured. "Bleeding and damage are surgical here. The cuts more deliberate; less carnage. But there's no denying the larger connections."

"Which are?"

Deena flapped a hand at Kirk, and the rookie fumbled with his tablet. He triggered an app, displaying a series of coded departmental photos. He swiped up, flipping them like trading cards, shuffling until he slowed around a series of specific images. Walker recognized the faces—all three were present in the car, though still attached to a set of shoulders in the unflattering photos. Bruisers all, scowls ringed by stitches and the shadows of forgotten wounds. One of the men wore a snake tattoo above an eye; Walker instinctively glanced downward, seeking the flesh-and-blood version, finding it winking at him from within the blood-encrusted bag.

"Aside from matching tattoos," Walker explained, the other detectives paying attention to every whispered word, "these men crossed Joe's path often in the not-so-recent past. Mine, as well."

"Atlanta?"

*"Too hot for you?" Joe asked Walker, nursing their drinks at the long, mirrored bar. "Maybe you're in the wrong goddamn business." They laughed and turned their attention to the girls, naked bodies writhing across a glistening stage, as flashes of hammering gunfire winked outside the only window. The streets burned, riots flared, and people died, but here in the Shaft, the golden gods lived.*

*That was Detroit, nearly forty years ago. Before Atlanta.*

"Walker?" Deena eyed her partner, concern widening her inquisitive expression. He cleared the daydream from his mind.

"Yes, Atlanta. Among other cities."

Boucher furrowed his brow, staring at the motto above the grisly scene. The medical examiner had arrived and rudely elbowed through the crowd that had gathered in—possibly tainting—his crime scene. He shooed them away, and the quartet of detectives huddled against a pylon near the opposite end of the platform. Deena plucked Kirk's tablet from the baby's fingers and scrolled through the police records, sorting and filtering as she searched for connections between the Human Front and Joe Monroe.

Walker leaned in. "The dead gentlemen? Brothers, three of five. The other two died before your time; one in Atlanta. Part of the original Liberty murders."

Boucher turned to Walker, raising an eyebrow. "A copycat, finishing the job?"

"Could be the genuine article. The original murders went unsolved, remember?"

Boucher fumed. "Not for lack of trying. But why here, why now?"

Walker shrugged, understanding how frustrating this was for the special investigator. Boucher made his bones in Atlanta, helping contain the gang wars and trying—though failing—to find the Liberty killer. Or killers.

*Then again,* the ageless detective considered, *hardly coincidence that Boucher resurfaces just as Liberty does.* But the hypothesis and its implications seemed laughable. Boucher had nearly ruined his career trying to catch the killer. And three murders had been committed after he'd left Atlanta.

*C'mon, Christian. The years and circumstances have you looking for conspiracies around every corner. Boucher didn't show up because of these killings; he came to investigate your big, immortal ass. His involvement in the Monroe case is only due to his relationship with Deena. He's here because she's here.*

"The Rampage Brothers!" Deena suddenly hooted, triumphantly flipping through a handful of mug shots. "Three dudes who ran muscle for the pre-corporate Front during the nineties."

"The Brothers were Front-connected well before that."

Deena waved off Walker's contribution. "These jamokes festooned themselves with heavy-duty construction equipment—didja see that alien movie? That power loader thingy? Like that, but with more balls. Also? Monster masks. Like werewolves and gorillas."

Recognition dawned in Boucher's eyes. "Right. Like a merman mask? Creature from the Black Lagoon."

Deena swiped left. "Ernst Rammler. Charbroiled a year after the gang wars ended." She gawked at the mobile device and swiped again. "This app is awesome. Like that 'Powr' dating app, but for douche bags and criminals."

Walker cleared his throat. "Rampage Brothers?"

Deena squinted and got on with it. "Right, so brother Ernst got barbecued. The second-to-last Liberty murder, if you'll recall."

*"Too hot for you?" Joe asked.* Walker squeezed his eyes closed, shelving the memory. This was no time to wallow.

Deena swiped to reveal another image. "Older brother Max had been strafed or sniped in the Detroit Powers Riots."

Boucher glanced Walker's way. "You there for that?"

He nodded in confirmation. "As was the Soldier."

"So that's two connections."

"There's more," Deena confirmed. She launched a notebook app. A short list appeared on the screen, and Walker scanned the list of names.

"What's this?"

"The list our baby compiled this morning. Former associates of Malachi Crane. Associates still at large with connections to Joseph Monroe. Associates with strength enough—powered or not—to pulp the man's skull with his very heavy shield."

"And?"

"And suspects one through three are Johann, Dolph, and Bruno Rammler. The last remaining Rampage Brothers, currently deceased."

They watched the medical team carefully bag their samples, take notes, and prep the bodies for transport. Deena lobbed the tablet to Kirk, who juggled it for a moment before gripping it with both hands.

"All right," Walker began, recapping for the team. "Two murders. One, a legend who'd seen action in Korea and championed Powers rights for as long as I've known him. The second—actually, a chain of three—a group of anti-Powers activists, all of whom have tangled with said legend. All of whom might have *performed* the first murder and share the same collegial markings as, yes, the original victim."

"Let's not forget," Deena reminded them, "that Monroe was present at— or at least in the vicinity of—the murders of the other Rampage Brothers."

"Finally," Walker concluded, "we can't discuss this with anyone outside this circle that isn't Captain Cross because we have to keep the first murder under wraps."

"Because of said collegial markings."

"Which opens up an entirely different can of shit."

Boucher eyed them both. "Do you two always talk this much?"

"Only when we have nothing new to say. The cadence often jars loose an idea."

"How exhausting. Look, there are layers beyond all that. The Liberty tag, for instance. Is it a pretender? The same killer I tried putting away twelve years ago?"

"Can we answer that?" Walker posed. "The Liberty killer never worked the same way twice. The only reason we even knew it was serial had been the tagline."

Boucher paced between pylons. "Of course we can. This has to be a second chance. We might—"

"Boucher," Walker interjected, "the Liberty killer worked *only* in Atlanta. He disappeared ten years ago. This is a scumbag copycat who's getting his jollies by jerking into old newspaper clippings."

"Yeah, but—"

"Let's just figure this out and move on. Leave the past in the past. We have another priority. A bigger, possibly explosive case. The connection between Joe and the Human Front is more important than a decade-old—"

"No!" Boucher rapped his hand against a steel pylon. He turned back, face drawn and haggard, eyes yearning. The medical examiner stuck his head out of the car to determine the cause of the commotion but swiftly returned to work, unwilling to be drawn into whatever drama was playing out across the platform.

"No," Boucher reiterated. "I will not sweep this under the rug and watch it become history. Not again, not because someone may have something to hide."

"Aaron." Deena stepped forward. "Come on, that isn't—"

"Stay out of this. He knows what I'm talking about."

Walker's nostrils flared. He wanted to defend himself against Boucher's erratic pronouncements. But he knew the truth. He knew that Boucher *was fucking right.*

"Fine, Aaron. Reopen the Liberty murders. Connect them to whatever happened to the Soldier. But let Deena take the lead—it's her case. And, besides . . . you're only here to strip me of my badge. Right?"

Boucher frowned. "Which I'll be able to do when armed with the facts surrounding this case and how they tie in to your history of powers."

"No, fuck that." Walker pointed an accusatory finger. "You were ready to burn me before you knew about Joe's death. You have a case? Let's go. Because otherwise, all you got is whatever my partner figured out. And right now? That isn't a hell of a lot."

"Well," a hesitant voice disagreed. "That isn't exactly true."

They swiveled about to behold Corbin Kirk, baby detective, awkwardly shuffling on the periphery of the confrontation. He held something in a clutching fist, and Deena beckoned with grasping fingers like a mother to a troublesome child. "New fish," she said. "I forgot you were even here. What-cha got?"

"I found something," he admitted, warily entering their hostile circle. "While hunkered down to, ah . . ."

"To puke."

"Uh, right." He opened his palm to reveal a handful of metal strips—long and wiry, coated with blood. "These seem important. Definitely more substantial than 'not a hell of a lot.'"

A dull flush rose to Walker's cheeks. He patted the rookie's shoulder. "Good find. Though you should have left them alone. If these are part of the murder weapon, your prints may have covered over the actual killer's."

Now it was Kirk's turn to blush, but the homicide detectives barely noticed as they huddled around the evidence. "Quick, before we hand these off," Deena whispered to the others, "initial conjecture? They look like guitar strings."

Aaron agreed. "That's because they are."

"How do you know?" Walker asked. "Could be piano wire."

Deena bit her lip. "Aaron would know. He's played for years."

"That's right," Boucher confirmed. "I had a set like these. Steel, heavy-gauge for added tension. About a .027. Bought them accidentally for a vintage acoustic, was worried they'd bow the neck. Traded them for a set of nylons. Less stress on the frame."

"Okay, so the Liberty killer decapitated three Human Front associates with a set of guitar strings? Doesn't compute."

"Well, he may have killed them some other way first. Then sliced their heads and moved them here. We could wait for the ME's findings before jumping on this."

Deena shook her head. "No time."

Walker grunted. "Fine. Here's what we do, then—"

Boucher stepped between them. "Ah, ah. You, sir, are doing nothing. You're off this case, remember?"

"The Monroe case."

"While under investigation, Walker, you're off all cases. Especially those with ties to a delicate set of circumstances that could fall into the hands of federal investigators anytime over the course of the next several hours."

Walker fumed. But he knew the pompous asshole was right. He had to sit this out for the sake of his career—and for the sake of both the integrity of the precinct and discovering the truth pertaining to his dead friend.

"Fine," he relented, arms crossing the barrel of his chest. "What's your plan?"

They turned to Deena, who had been mostly silent throughout their argument—which, Walker had to admit, set off warning lights. Deena Pilgrim was rarely silent; Boucher's presence had thrown her off. Walking away from this case, especially during the critical discovery period, was a mistake. But his hands were tied. Walker's place was back at his desk, sweating out Boucher's investigation. Out of the media glare, away from any place he might say too much and embarrass himself, his history, and any late, lamented friendships.

Deena cleared her throat and retrieved Kirk's tablet. She studied the mug shots again and then the photos from the Monroe crime scene.

"Here's how we play this, and we have to work fast. Walker, you and Aaron go back and finish your little drama."

The two men traded hostile looks; Deena ignored them. Forensics was removing all bodies from the train, and she wanted to talk to the ME before he slithered off to a morgue or bottle, whichever came first. "Kirk and I will work our list." She tossed the tablet back to the baby. This time, he caught it, right as it buzzed. A new e-mail, perhaps. Service was spotty below, and they'd been out of contact for far too long . . . especially with the Monroe case hanging over their heads.

"The guitar strings," Aaron suggested. "Track sales to recent buyers. The .027 is rare—only a handful of instruments will take it, due to the bend it induces because of higher tension. Gotta narrow it down within the metropolitan area."

Deena agreed. "Great. Walker, help us by looking into that."

"Sure. After I'm done with the Gestapo here."

"Seriously, dude?" Boucher's hands curled into fists.

Kirk's device buzzed again, and the rookie stared at it in his hand, unsure whether or not to look, whether or not to step in between the simmering detectives.

Deena interceded. "Girls, you're both prom queens. Go back. Find the strings. New fish and I will work the Human Front angle, this time expanding to known enemies. Old rivals of Monroe who might be seeking revenge."

"Someone with musical ties?" Aaron gestured at the strings in her hand. "A Power or hater with an acoustic—or in the market for one."

A lightbulb clicked on in Deena's head, just as Kirk's tablet buzzed for the third time. "Goddammit, fish," she spat. "Check your e-mail."

Kirk dove into the screen, happy to detach from the tension. As the rookie checked his messages, she ventured a guess as to the identity of the next suspect.

"You know, there was a Front member with musical ties. The strength isn't there—I doubt she killed Joe—but I can definitely see her being involved."

Aaron arched his eyebrows. "A woman? You think a woman *twanged* these tractors on legs?"

"Hey, a woman decimated the entire city of Chicago, remember?"

"Fair point. Got a name?"

"Uh . . . guys?" Kirk held up a hand, trying to get their attention.

Deena ignored him. "Actually, you may already know. Wailing Willie Quince. Short for Wilhelmina. Malachi Crane's girlfriend, back in the day."

"Seriously," Kirk raised his voice in intensity. "Guys, you should definitely—"

"She had a way of connecting instruments to a kind of vibratory harness—pounded the decibels. Killer headache; brains-through-your-ears killer. Plus, she was in Atlanta, too. She and my family . . . well, there's history."

Aaron nodded. "Right. She was on the stand that time."

Walker frowned. "Oh, I know who you're talking about. Last I heard, she'd left the cause after the whole Kaotic Chic thing. Retired, far as I know. Singing a different tune now under the name 'Willie Wails.'"

"As far as you know." Deena smirked. "You fucked her, didn't you?"

"Hey, come on."

"You slipped her the mickey. You let her ride the Bologna Express. You—"

"Deena!"

Kirk shoved the tablet in Deena's face. "Detective! You need to see this!"

She slapped Kirk's hand. "Personal space!" Walker removed the device from the rookie's grasp and turned it around to see. He found an open e-mail, linking to an embedded video.

"What's this?" He jabbed the Play button, and all sorts of hell unfolded, streaming as fast as the signal would allow.

A memory stirred again. Detroit, long before Atlanta. *"Too hot for you?"* *Joe had asked. "Then you're in the wrong goddamn business."*

Deena stepped closer, curiously watching her partner's face. "What is it?"

"Aw, hell," Christian Walker moaned in dismay. "Some moron leaked the Soldier's death to *Powers That Be*."

# 8

——✒——

"Commissioner Tate spared little time for reporters, nor did he elaborate on plans for any sort of press conference. But despite outward appearances and claims otherwise, *Powers That Be* has confirmed the lurid details surrounding this morning's grisly discovery. Credible sources—"

"'Credible'?" Deena snorted. "And I saw Hoffa ordering a latte last week."

"Did you?" Boucher asked, lowering the volume on the video as Deena manhandled the steering wheel. "Because we've been looking for him."

Deena scoffed. "Press Play."

"Music instead? Turn the radio to P-Rock, because Alison Nightbird just released a new sing—"

"I said Play!"

He grinned and raised the volume. *Powers That Be,* the incredibly popular opinion newscast, continued streaming on the tablet, Collette McDaniels reporting.

"Joseph Monroe, a name our audience may be unfamiliar with. But for over seventy years, Monroe lived a heroic double life: this patriot battled evil with nothing more than fists and shield. Yes, PTB Nation. Joseph

Monroe—decorated military man, pillar of his community—was the Citizen Soldier. And now he is gone. And with him our hopes and prayers."

"Seriously? What's this 'pillar of his community' crap?" Deena slammed the horn, squawking at traffic as she vented to her passengers. "The guy lived in a roach motel, just him and leftover pizza. The community didn't even know he was there."

"Deena . . ." Walker placed a calming hand on his partner's shoulder, attempting to soothe her nerves from the backseat. Boucher and Kirk appreciated the gesture; they hoped it would ensure they made it back to the precinct in one piece.

Deena threw up her hands in disgust. "Damn! Fine. Whatever."

"Our sources—"

"You mean 'Twitter'!" She seethed and drove. "Keep going."

"—have learned that the Soldier's body, smuggled from an unknown location, has yet to be identified by family members or recognized by government officials. Tate may still be investigating the circumstances behind Monroe's death, but this reporter can't help but grimace at the rotten taste in her mouth—"

"Ha! No . . . too easy."

"—placed there due to unnecessary delay in laying the great man's remains in state. What are police and both federal channels and the Powers community attempting to hide? Have unsavory facts been baked into Monroe's untimely demise? The man, a veteran of countless conflicts, engendered several enemies in his lifetime. *Powers That Be* hoped, however, that Commissioner Tate, Captain Emile Cross, and Homicide Detective Christian Walker would not be counted among their number—"

Deena pounded both hands against the wheel. "Shut it off. Shut it. Oh, that *bitch*."

Walker leaned back and stared out the window, scanning the snow-covered landscape as it quickly sped by. "Nothing we haven't heard before."

"Don't worry, Deena," Boucher coolly replied, handing the tablet back to Kirk. "I'll apply leverage to McDaniels. Hush things up."

"It isn't that. I just can't . . . oh, come on. What fresh hell is *this* now?" Deena peered over the dashboard as she pulled the SUV into the precinct parking lot. A thick, angry crowd had gathered in front of the building, comprised of chanting, picketing civilians and costumed children. The adults, hidden beneath coats and scarves, stomped about in the snow, hoisting placards on which they'd scrawled an equal number of messages both supporting and condemning the Citizen Soldier. The kids gawked and cried, dragged along by the hand and held up to news cameras lining the sidewalk. The usual religious nuts were in attendance, as were local and national news along with a stalwart group of policemen, barricading the steps and doing their best to maintain crowd control. Reporters belted questions at passersby while a handful of men and women, dressed in hats emblazoned with the Soldier's eagle sigil, wept and carried on with abandon. Deena quickly steered the SUV into the garage and was waved through by a warmly dressed, mildly annoyed beat cop who was being peppered with insults by the gathered mob.

They sidestepped Central Booking and entered the hot, crowded precinct. Someone had removed the Christmas tree, possibly into a back room—the bullpen was too crowded, and they needed the space. Walker and Pilgrim beelined for the captain's office while Aaron excused himself to hunt down media relations. Kirk stumbled after the partners, fumbling with the tablet and wiping sweat from his eyes. As he departed, Aaron deftly lifted the mobile device from Kirk's hands, ensuring that the rookie wouldn't get bumped, drop the tablet, and have it shatter into millions of pieces. That easily could have happened; the bullpen was packed—strangled by not only cops and perps but also attorneys and politicians descended from on high to deal with the details surrounding the public relations nightmare. Deena ignored them; they were a distraction, and there was a case to solve.

*Walker's lucky,* she thought. *I should recuse myself, too. Claim emotional distress due to the reappearance of the Liberty killer. Make up a bit of bullshit and hole up somewhere quiet and dark, lined with dusty bottles and inappropriate choices. I should get out now. My heart's not in it. With Aaron here, to be honest, I wouldn't trust my heart even if it were. I should tell the captain I'm walking. I should tell him today.*

Kirk sneezed behind Deena, wide-eyed and gawking at the district attorney, who was quietly arguing with Aaron in a corner, vehemently gesticulating to the crowd outside. The rookie caught Deena staring and, red-faced, scampered to his desk.

*Dammit,* she realized. *If I walk, they'll just give it to the baby. I can't subject him to that.* Deena Pilgrim was in—again—like it or not. But she planned to have a frank discussion with Cross once they wrapped it up. A well-earned vacation. Right after she had a *franker* discussion with the ex-boyfriend who'd shown up from out of the blue. Whatever the case, between the details of the murders, Aaron's reappearance, and the blanket of conversation permeating the cop house, Deena Pilgrim was distracted.

Which, unfortunately, left her vulnerable.

Somebody tugged the back of her collar, hard enough that the zipper of her jacket dug deeply into her throat. She lost her footing, but whoever it was dragged her up and held her close. A guy, by the smell and breathing, possibly two weeks without a shower. He was wiry but strong, sporting a musty jacket and a thick brush of beard. His left arm locked around Deena's neck, crushing it as he raised his right hand before her eyes. She twisted, attempting to free herself, but the filthy man matched her step for step, adjusting his stance to ensure that she couldn't kick or grab a delicate spot.

The room reacted. Several cops drew on Deena's attacker, barking angry warnings as they steadied their aim. The lawyers, stricken with silence, disappeared into offices or plastered themselves against the wall. Hookers and thieves, waiting to be arraigned, hooted and cackled. They cheered for the unnamed man at Deena's back. Walker held out a hand, no doubt locking eyes with whoever it was behind Deena. She couldn't make out Walker's words; the only sound reaching her ears was a rushing wind—adrenaline washing through her body. Then a metered tick—like from a clock—the filthy man's irregular breathing, and Deena's own pounding heartbeat.

Finally, like water through an unstopped drain, the noise rushed back in.

"Get down!" two of the officers shouted. "Put her down and step away!"

"It's all right." That was Walker, using measured tones to calm her assailant. "We're here to listen," he reasoned with the stinky wall of flesh against which Deena was pressed. "Just let her go, okay? It's been a hard day for everyone. Just set her down, lower your hands, and we can talk." Captain

Cross had emerged from his office; she spied him behind Walker, along with a handful of goggle-eyed detectives and secretaries. Kirk watched from his seat. He'd frozen; they all had. No one moved to help her, and sweat began to roll down her cheeks. Why didn't Walker move or do something? If she could breathe, if she could get her hand on the guy's knees or balls this would be over in a minute. But she kept missing her targets, squirming and doing her best to break free. Deena's hands scrabbled for purchase on his arms, throat, his face, but he was smoke—her fingers passed through dry, sticky heat. Deena's heart hammered against her chest. She was losing oxygen, and everyone just *fucking stood there.*

Then the man waved the hand before her eyes, and she understood why. He clenched his fist, and the air . . . swirled. So did his skin, lapping like water as fire and electricity coursed into it, flowing through his veins. He pulled an electric charge out of the air, and it rippled from knuckle to knuckle until the entire hand was bathed in cold, blue flame. He turned his hand on Deena and moved it close to her temple, the open palm directed at her face. She could feel the irregular warmth and a tiny jolt of static strafed her right ear. Deena flinched, and the bearded man reasserted his grip, chest heaving as if about to sob.

"You pigs," the intruder sputtered, his fetid breath no welcome treat. "You swine are responsible; you let him *die.* He's gone, and our enemies . . . they're fuckin' *every*where." Deena locked eyes with Walker, her partner still maintaining a pose of practiced negotiation. Deena knew that if she could see through Walker's eyes, she'd be seeing a crazy person . . . probably dressed in some kind of Citizen Soldier shirt, hat, or jacket. She slackened her frantic attempts to escape and surreptitiously pointed an index finger at her partner. *You got this,* Deena whispered in her mind. *We took down Royale and Wolfe, so this guy's nothing. You got this, all right?*

Walker took a hesitant step forward, and the Power flinched. His body shuddered, and he forced his hand closer to Deena, threatening to speed-tan half her face. "Stay back," he warned her wary partner. The man swiveled to the right, quickly holding out his hand to the assembled policemen, and then he shoved it back at Deena. "I'll broil her, I swear. You just . . . you have to bring him to me, okay? Bring him back."

Walker spread his hands, demonstrating that he presented no threat.

"The Soldier? You know we can't do that. I understand your grief, man; we all knew him. This isn't the way to get him back."

"No!" The Power grew increasingly unhinged. He pointed an unsteady finger at Walker. "No, you *didn't* know him! *I* knew him! The *people* knew him. Hunter fucking *Thompson* knew him. *You* killed him, what with your wars and badge and Facebook satellites bombarding Powers with sterilization rays."

The bearded man sobbed. He cracked his knuckles, and the blue flames popped. "You . . . you were his *partner,* Diamond. You left him to die, and now what do we have? There's no . . . no *citizenry.* Only soldiers and Uncle Tom slave wagers like *you.*"

He brought his beard closer to Deena's cheeks, and she could *taste* the smell permeating the follicles. She couldn't take it. Walker wasn't going to move; Kirk wasn't going to move; no one was going to take a shot. *As always, I have to do it myse—*

Something swung right from the agitated Power's blind spot. It shattered against the man's face and splintered into his eyes and cheeks. Stunned, he loosened his grip on Deena and jerked his right hand around, emitting a blast of fire that consumed a nearby desk. Deena swiftly shoved an elbow into her attacker's gut. He stumbled, mud-covered work boots demolishing shards of glass about his feet. The object that had saved her swung back for a return appearance, shoved into the injured Power's face by Aaron Boucher. Aaron palmed his weapon—Kirk's mobile tablet, hopefully backed up and by now completely useless—and then twisted it left and right, digging jagged shards of glass into her assailant's face. The bearded Power squealed and grabbed his wounded eyes. Deena swept his legs, knocking him to the ground. Walker rushed forward, along with a handful of cops; they swarmed the Power and clapped a set of drainer cuffs over both wrists.

Deena clutched her neck and breathed, instantly regretting it as her throat filled with razor blades. Aaron was at her side, supporting her from falling and protecting her from further harm. Several detectives hustled the Power off to a cell before Deena could get her hands on him. *Smart. I would have hurt him.* Slowly, awkwardly, the precinct released its collective breath, and everyone returned to his or her tasks after a smattering of enthusiastic, much-needed applause.

"You okay?" Aaron asked. "Did he hurt you?"

Deena coughed violently. Sinking to her knees, she rested an arm on one leg while the other massaged her throat. "Only my pride. Need a drink." Aaron nodded and patted her shoulder. He turned and headed to the break room, searching for a glass of water. Walker stepped over, bending down to help Deena to her feet. She shooed him away, preferring to stand on her own, assuring her partner that everything was fine. Walker didn't believe her, judging by his expression. But Deena didn't care. She was fine. *Fine.* All in a day's work, right?

*I'm talking to the captain* today.

"So, thanks." Deena turned to the rookie hovering off to one side. Kirk gawked and stammered. He seemed at a loss for what to say. She clasped him on the arm, squeezing collegially. "I'm kidding. That guy would have roasted you, Baby Kabobs."

Kirk turned beet-red. "You would have tried if it had been me . . . or anyone. I just stood there. I didn't do anything. You would have saved the day."

"Doubt that's true. Don't beat yourself up."

Kirk smiled. "That's your job."

She weakly returned the grin. *God, I'm exhausted.* "Damn right."

"Are you insane? Are you trying to bury me?"

Deena turned around, along with the others, weary and curious to know why Captain Cross was bulling toward the detectives with eyes to kill. "What kind of a stunt . . . I don't know why . . ." He reached the desk and took Deena's face in his palm, turning it this way and that. "Are you okay?"

*I'm fine. I'm* fine. *Tell the captain you're walking. Do it. Tell him now.*

She removed Cross's hand. "Thanks to the special investigator. What's an asshole with barbecue fingers when you've faced down vengeful gods?"

Cross rested his ass on the closest desk. "That never should have happened. *This* shouldn't have happened. This situation is out of hand. I want drainers at every door . . . no one goes in or out without . . . look, I don't know who leaked this, but when I find out—"

"You won't." Boucher came up from behind, carrying paper cups filled with water. Red droplets stained the cups; his hands were bleeding from the broken glass, wrapped in paper towels to stanch the flow. He handed one cup to Deena and the other to Walker. The two men exchanged a curt nod, and Walker drained his cup with a hurried swallow. The district attorney was angling their way, so Boucher talked fast. "Could have been anyone on scene or involved with the transfer. Techs, porters, cops, anyone."

"That's true," Walker said, crumpling the cup in his fist. "Hell, one of the lookie-loos may have caught a glimpse and recognized Joe or figured it out on our way to the station. You'll go nuts trying to figure it out. Let's just solve the cases we have."

Cross jabbed a finger at Walker. "*You* solve nothing. *You* stay put. What the fuck were you even thinking, answering that call?"

"I was thinking that I'd do my job."

"Right now, your job is to stay out of sight." He waved a hand across the bullpen and then pointed out the window to the gathering crowd. "Whoever gabbed to PNN happily identified you as a detective on scene. They're going through your exploits with a fine-tooth comb. Know why they call it a media circus, Walker? Despite the main attraction, they're here to flush out the freaks and throw them to the lions."

"You're mixing metaphors, Cap."

Exasperated, Cross threw both hands into the air. "Do I have to throw you in a cell? *Don't. Fucking. Move.* Got it, Walker?" He pointed to Boucher. "*You*—do what you came to do and then get out. I have too much on my plate to deal with your *mishegas* along with everything else."

"Thought I might dawdle with that investigation, Captain Cross. Stick around. Lend a hand." Aaron glanced at Deena. "Catch up with old friends."

Cross squinted, looking from Boucher to Deena. "Fine. Whatever. Just stay out of the way, and don't talk to the media. Pilgrim, get me a suspect. Anybody. Get one *today*."

Deena saluted in reply as Cross stamped away to deflect the DA in the center aisle. Aaron edged closer to Deena and rubbed her shoulder; she flinched, moving away, unwilling to show further vulnerability. Not here. Not in front of the pimps and clowns. And definitely not in front of Walker or Kirk.

The buzz and drone of the cop house had reasserted itself. She needed to get back to cases, back to tracking down Willie Wails or hoofing down the forensics report from the Rampage Brothers murders. Aaron continued to hover, and she waved him off, sick of his mothering. *Enough, Pilgrim. Stop wallowing, quit second-guessing. This is just another fucked-up Powers situation, and you're the goddamn mother of fucked-up Powers situations. Get up, say something cute yet profane, and bark orders so they quit treating you like the baby.*

"Okay," she began, turning back to Walker. "First thing I need you to do is track down Wails—hey, where are you going?" Walker had risen from the chair, gathering folders and notepads.

"I can't stay."

"Cross said—"

Aaron held out a hand. "Walker, we still have to finish—"

"Cross said to stay quiet. And that's what I'm doing. I'm going home, taking work with me. I'll call if I dig up anything on Wails. Let's pick it up in the morning, Boucher. Deena, take Kirk and talk to Malachi Crane at the Human Front. Find out what he knows about Joe and the Rampage Brothers. Find out what he knows about Liberty."

She placed both palms on Walker's desk. "Are you kidding? You're giving up?"

"I'm just calling it for today, Deena. I'm providing a bigger target for the department. . . . . . and a friend of mine died. I think that earns some time to myself."

He started for the door and then turned around. He looked beaten. "Are *you* all right?" Walker asked. "That guy, I mean. The Power?"

Deena indicated that she was. "Yeah. Just another day in the salt mines, right?"

"Don't."

Heat washed across her face. "Yeah. I'll be all right. Sorry about your friend."

Walker shot her a smile, tight and joyless. "I'm sorry, too." And then he was gone, shouldering through the room, avoiding stares and conspicuous whispers.

Kirk cleared his throat and took a step forward. "So, uh . . . should we. . . . . . ?"

Deena gave him her best fuck-off look. After a second, she felt bad and quietly told him, "Get an address, and find that suspect list. Then ask Dr. Death what he learned from the headless triplets. We'll grab lunch on the way uptown. I want Crane to connect some dots, but I need a few minutes."

Kirk nodded and hustled toward the morgue. She watched him go, angry with herself for taking a shit mood out on the new fish. The baby meant well. It wasn't his fault that her worlds were crashing headlong into one another.

As if on cue, Aaron awkwardly sat on the edge of Walker's desk. He placed both hands on his knees and whistled long and low. "So," he said, scanning the room, watching detectives intimidate criminals. "*Are* you okay? Like, really?"

She shot him a sidelong glance. "*God,* yes. I said I was fine."

Aaron's lips thinned as he sighed. "Yeah. As an ex-boyfriend, I gotta tell you. I've heard '*God,* yes, said I was fine' before. It usually meant, 'Asshole, no, I'm not.'"

Deena laughed. "You throw the term 'ex-boyfriend' around loosely for a guy I haven't seen in years. 'Asshole' fits, though."

Aaron placed a hand on her arm and lowered his voice. "Seriously. You were manhandled by a human bug zapper. Your partner's been ripped from your side. This asshole you used to fuck, a moron who walked out of your life without looking back, just waltzed back in as if he owned the place. And now you're after a suspect whose testimony, along with others', helped ruin your father."

Deena flinched, and her eyes watered. *Don't you fucking cry, Pilgrim,* she admonished herself. *Cry and I'll kick you in the goddamn uterus.*

"Lest we forget," he continued, failing to notice the maelstrom churning behind her eyes, "the reemergence of an unsolved string of murders. Killings, I might add, that took place during an emotional time for the both of us. Back when your dad and I—"

She grabbed his fingers and squeezed. "I *know.* I was there."

Aaron squeezed back. Cross wandered by and raised an eyebrow; he paused for a moment, but Deena waved him on, assuring the captain that everything was fine in Pilgrimtown. *Fine, fine. I'm all* fine.

"All I'm saying, Deen, is that I know you. I know you're not 'fine.' Walker does, too, but he's too much of a . . . fuck, I don't know *what* he is anymore. He's too *Walker* to put himself out there, if that means anything."

"I'm fine."

"And I'm Golgotha, Queen of the Radioactive Monsters."

*Dammit,* Deena thought ruefully. *He always knew how to get me to smile. Okay. I already opened up to him once, and maybe a hundred times when I was in training bras. What's one more humiliating confession going to hurt me?*

*Just get it out before the baby comes back.*

She turned Aaron's way, ducking her head so that the hair hung into her eyes. "You wanna know what's bothering me? How about the fact that three men had their heads sliced off with a guitar string and were artfully posed in a subway car?" She ticked salient points off on her fingers, speaking faster and lower so that Aaron had to strain to hear it. "Or how about the hero who *might* be a traitor to his own kind and *may* have sold out the government, friends, and the country he purported to love?"

"Okay, I get—"

"No, wait. There's also the giant fucking tidal wave that obliterated Chicago and the underworld kingpin I tore apart with a lightning bolt from my dainty little fingers. There's the little girl I helped save who turned out to become a super*fucking*hero and nearly killed my partner in the process. Oh! Yeah!" She was getting louder again, and Aaron urged her to lower her voice. But Deena wouldn't be stopped. Not until it all came out. "And then there's my partner who *used* to have powers and then *didn't,* but all of a sudden he *does,* and he's—*what?*—beating up Satan, and then I don't know? He loses his powers *again*, and gets *new* ones—"

"Wait." Aaron's eyes narrowed, and he held up a hand. "Are you talking about Walker? He had a third power set?"

"And I killed Johnny Royale and the Lance, and of course I was goddamn *pregnant* and then basically died—"

"Wait. What?"

"—but *that* didn't take, and . . . and, *god,* I don't even know." She slumped over, dangling hands between her legs, head between her shoulders. "Old memories. *Bad* memories. The last five years have been a roller coaster, and I used to love this job, but so many people have died on my watch. So many people I let die or maybe even killed. And the weird, fucked-up shit I see on a daily basis? Aaron, you haven't lived until you've seen a man explode from the inside out. I've seen that *twice.*"

Deena lifted her head and stared into his eyes, shutting out the noise buzzing through the precinct. Her eyes were red, rimmed with tears, and her body simmered like a pressure cooker. "I just can't take any more. I loved being a cop. But when you've seen it all, when you've seen kids in danger and spoiled brats offing each other with designer powers because they think it's a game . . . you *lose* that love. You lose the idealism, and all you want is *out*."

She flapped a hand in the direction that Walker had left. "I get it. I totally *get* it, you know. He didn't go home because we told him to stay out of the way. He left because enough is goddamn enough! You get jaded, and the shit becomes the norm, and you forget there was a time you had powers or that you saw some schmuck get raped by those who still do." She dabbed both eyes with her fingers and let out a sigh. "And if that wasn't enough . . . if I didn't have enough haunting me . . . boom. Five words to remind me how much I hate my father. Five words to remind me how much I resent you."

They sat there for a moment in awkward silence. Her throat was raw— sore from where the Power had grabbed it, dry from the sudden tantrum. The intervening years sat between them, marking the great unknown; the time they'd lost. The might-have-been. Secrets, history, countless details they didn't know about the other. Deena didn't think they'd be able to fully understand what happened or the people they'd become. But the memories rushed back, happier moments they'd shared before everything went to hell. The intimate details of a life she fondly remembered. Back before she met Enki Sunrise or Emile Cross or Johnny Royale or even Christian Walker. Before she'd killed anyone. Before Deena Pilgrim had witnessed—and lived—the impossible.

Back when all she'd wanted was to love a man and be a cop.

Now here they sat, in a police station far from Atlanta. Perched on her partner's desk, reliving old wounds and older cases. Shoulder to shoulder, yet very far apart. The silence stretched out, and Deena cleared her throat once more, wishing she had another cup of water.

After a minute, Aaron spoke. "'Everybody got power, ever'body got pain. We take the ride, all side-by-side, and we'd do it again.'"

She looked up. "Did . . . did you just sing me a fucking song?"

"No. I sang you a significant lyric of a fucking Little Doomsday song. Lifted from 'Power Train'—a deep cut off his fifth studio album."

"I never liked Little Doomsday."

"Sure you did. 'Under the Macroverse' was your jam. We totally had sex to it."

She blushed. "I think you're remembering what you want to remember."

"You know why, right? 'Macroverse' subscribed to my BEEBA chord theor—"

Deena laughed and hid her face in her hands. "Oh, shit. I forgot about that damn theory. No, no, no . . . you never stopped talking about it!"

"Look," he said, suddenly shifting away from the lighthearted ribbing, "I get it. I can't say I have answers. And I won't pretend to understand everything you've been through, Deen. It sounds hard. It must have been."

He shifted his weight, sliding closer. He was nearly in her lap now, and she felt the urge to stand. Before she could, he took her right hand in his left.

"But I've lived, too. I have no right to beg you to get what I've endured. I mean, *I* walked away. *I* made that decision. But my life hasn't been easy, either. Mom's death, for instance. Dad's stoic march into twilight . . . he's lonely, Deena. It's been rough."

"But that's normal to me," she said. "That isn't jackal-headed cosmic gods wanting to judge humanity. It isn't a psychopathic criminal choosing to melt your face."

"True," he agreed. "I can't get everything you've been through. And maybe you can't relate to my too-human foibles and frustrations. But . . ."

"But . . . ?"

"*But* I'm willing to listen. And I'm willing to talk. I know you've lost the passion for police work—a passion that I believe I helped inspire." He squeezed her hand, running his thumb over Deena's and offering a smile. "I know I have plenty of apologizing to do. And though you're busy with the case of the century, I hope you'll let me rediscover the wonder, the unmitigated joy I believe to be Deena Pilgrim. A girl I've never stopped thinking about. A girl for whom I feel a great, unconstrained passion."

Now Aaron took her hand in both of his own, caressing it between the two. "And, Deena, if you'll let me . . . I promise to help you rediscover yours."

Her heart was floating. It was an unfamiliar feeling—one she hadn't felt in a long time. Sitting on her partner's desk, relinquishing her right hand to the man she'd once loved, Deena understood that her life was about to become needlessly complicated.

Well . . . more needlessly complicated than usual.

# 9

—⁓⁓—

*July. Eleven and a half years ago.*
*Sunday afternoon. 2:38 P.M.*

Music filled the room, folding Deena and Aaron into its lyrical embrace. She smiled, leaning against his chest as Carbon Copy wailed about a boy who didn't notice because she was one of a million clones. She stole a glance at her boyfriend; his eyes were closed. Deena took advantage and pinched his nipple.

"*Damn*! Cut it out, Deen." He swatted her hand and then took it in his own. She grinned and let him be, happily intertwining their fingers. She looked around the room (*his* room, the room in which he'd grown up), staring at old posters and various high school trophies. His closet was empty, but the wall was lined with CDs, filling a bookcase and several shelves. He'd dug out an old Discman—dusting it off, praying it would work—and they'd settled against his childhood headboard to wait out dinner with a playlist and a bit of light petting.

The bedroom was empty other than Aaron's discography. They'd moved him out weeks ago, into a two-bedroom over in Summerhill. Deena had teased him about it, ribbing how mama's boy had been unable to leave the nest. He, in turn, tickled her until she stopped. They'd fallen into bed that night, too, but Aaron Boucher's music had been the furthest thing from either of their minds.

They'd been seeing each other for roughly six months, ever since she'd returned for winter break. It had been awkward at first, as most relationships tended to be. But after several dates and a thrilling weekend in the Emory dorms, Aaron and Deena had fallen into a naturally romantic groove. He felt guilty at times, worried about dividing attention between a girlfriend and the law. But she reminded Aaron that she would soon join him on the force, and one day they would solve crime side-by-side. He'd worried about that, too—what it meant for both halves of a couple to place themselves in danger. But they were young. Their hearts and . . . other parts made the ultimate decision.

Over a year after the Pilgrim Thanksgiving debacle, Aaron's career had taken off like a rocket. He'd been promoted to junior detective in the same department as Deena's father. The gang war had dwindled to pockets of territorial conflict, and the government had reduced the number of sponsored Powers. Unfortunately, Aaron's meteoric rise had driven a wedge between the Pilgrims and Bouchers; Deena's dad had bristled long after Aaron's diatribe in their foyer, and the two detectives barely got along these days. In fact, her father outwardly condemned Aaron and Deena's flourishing romance, often complaining long and loud to her mother and anyone else willing to listen. More often than not, he bitched to the help.

The Bouchers, meanwhile, had welcomed Deena with open arms. She felt at home in their tastefully decorated Colonial. Teakettles burbled on the range while Eveline puttered in the garden and the judge tackled crosswords on the porch. They lived within their means, few luxuries standing out to a visitor's eye. Most of all, their house was filled with laughter and light— sarcasm, sure, but doled out with a twinkle and a smile, not in the bitter, corrosive manner perfected in the Pilgrim abode. Deena felt happy at the Bouchers'. Sure, Ken and Eveline mothered her every chance they got—an experience long abandoned by Deena's self-absorbed parents. But even more importantly, Aaron felt comfortable here. This was his safe place. And by extension, so it was for Deena, too.

She stretched against her boyfriend, purring like a cat, cuddling up against his long, lean body. Aaron absently stroked Deena's hair, tapping against the wall with his free hand. She watched him for a moment; watched him lose himself in the music. The last year, while successful, had been rough on Aaron. The aftermath of the gang war, the effects it had brought on his precinct. He'd confided in Deena that the deputy mayor had failed to prepare for not only a transition from federal hands back to local police but for any oversight of those undertaking the process. It had been bloody, corrupt, and divisive. Several cops and Powers had been locked away following vicious hearings. Aaron warned Deena—especially after she'd abandoned a liberal arts scholarship for a criminal justice track—about the graft lacing his precinct. She'd heard him gripe about it before, but now he'd evolved his theories, pointing fingers at everyone from the captain down to Homicide. Aaron had skirted the issue of her father—no doubt hoping to keep his bias from affecting their relationship—but Deena could tell he was hinting in that direction. She still didn't believe it. Sure, the Pilgrims had more cash than a detective's salary should allow, but Waldo—though angry and often broody—was a good man. He protected his city and took care of his family. In the grand scheme of things, where was the harm in that? Deena knew that Aaron wanted to do the same. She didn't understand why the two most important men in her life couldn't get along. They were so similar. But then, Deena knew that if she were forced to interact with someone exactly like herself on a constant basis, she'd probably want to choke the bitch.

She leaned up to kiss him, hoping to draw him into a clinch. He held up his hand, begging her to wait as the rhythm rose and fell across the bedroom. Deena smirked and rested her chin on a hand, propping her elbow atop Aaron's chest. He absentmindedly rubbed her shoulder as he listened to the song, losing himself in the refrain.

"See? Right there," he explained to Deena. "That totally supports my theory."

"Which theory are we talking about? Is it the one where your girlfriend believes you're avoiding sex because you're afraid your mom might hear?"

He laughed. "No, seriously. Listen. Don't you hear?"

Deena rolled her eyes and sat up. "Dude, I hear a lot of guitars and the moment passing you by. That's it."

"The *chords*." His eyes twinkled, reflecting the sunlight streaming through the window. "The same chords again."

Deena flopped back on the bed, arms flailing against the pillow. She groaned. "God. The *chords* again? This may be way on the nose, bro, but you're like a broken record with those things."

This time, Aaron sat up. He ticked songs off on his fingers. "Nine MM's 'Antihero.' Teleportland's 'Red Flannel Cape.' Gorilla Mod's 'Inside Your Mind.' Battleband's 'Give Me Rock or Give Me Death.' And now Little Doomsday's 'Under the Macroverse.'" He spread his hands, wiry arms stretching against his cotton tee. "You gotta hand it to me, lady. There are five songs topping the charts with the same BEEBA chord structure. B-E-E-B-A. Even more when you page through the annals of rock history—"

"Oh, the annals. Yes. I quite like the annals."

This time, he playfully swatted her on the ass. "Seriously, you don't see it? That chord structure, it's like musical magic. It's like an earworm."

"Excuse me? Earworm?"

"Yeah, like that movie where they stick a worm in that dude's—"

Deena scrunched her eyes and stuck both hands against her head. "Agh. No. Stop, stop, stop—la-la-la. I'll be dreaming of worms in orifices all night long."

"I'm just saying. Five songs. Same chords. Tall stacks of American dollars."

They smiled at one another; another sound pervaded the room, a faint hissing from the teakettle in the kitchen.

Deena felt hot. "Stop," she begged him. "You look so serious."

He shrugged. "Happy, I guess."

"Come here." She held out her arms, and after a brief moment, he did. Little Doomsday filled the room, drowning out everything else.

Later, after they'd showered, the couple ventured down to the living room. Eveline was still outside, finishing up in her vegetable patch. The tea had long stopped hissing, and the judge nursed a cup of chamomile in his wide, impeccably upholstered recliner. He frowned at the television, index fingers gently tapping the mug in his hands. He turned as they entered the room and swiftly plastered a smile across his face as he set the cup aside.

He gestured toward the plush sofa, and they arranged themselves across from him where they could both see the TV.

"Your mother's taking in her cucumbers. Then we'll start dinner."

"Pop," Aaron replied, "don't go to any trouble. We'll drop by Tacotown on the way back to Deena's."

"You'll do no such thing. There are several club steaks thawing in the sink. And my Weber could use a test run, make sure it hasn't died during the night."

"Pop . . ."

But the judge wouldn't hear otherwise. "It's done. 'Tacotown'? That's a fine way to get tapeworms, I'm sure. But edible? Hardly."

Deena enjoyed the byplay and lost herself in the cushions. The sun washed the living room with a suffused glow, daubing the furniture and brushing against Judge Boucher's cheek. He winked at Deena, doing his best to elicit a smile. He turned his attention back to the television, where Ted Henry railed against the nation on his popular broadcast, *Powers That Be*.

"Ted Henry rules," she declared, snuggling into Aaron's body.

The judge snorted. "Overpaid, overblown windbag with an agenda. Would sell his own teeth for exclusive dirt."

Deena arched an eyebrow. Ken's reaction surprised her; it had been growled from behind his mug, delivered with animosity she usually recognized in her own father. The judge was generally easygoing—as he'd been during the gang war, presenting opinions and judgments in a calm, even manner. What did he have against Ted Henry? The guy invented Powers news. *Powers That Be* had been the first to report on news of the gang war, the first to break any news regarding the Liberty murders—and there hadn't been much, thanks to police lockdown. Henry, graying and brusque, found angles and exclusives where none could be found. This had many believing he either had powers of his own or an inside track with those that did. Deena didn't care; she idolized the Powers, even if Aaron hated their level of free rein. She'd seen many in action, especially after starting at Emory. Many local Powers were friendly with Waldo and the judge, as evidenced by that horrifically awkward dinner. Maybe that's why the judge had a beef with Henry. *Powers That Be* bulldogged those with powers, playing devil's advocate for those without the courage to ask hard questions. Deena felt, as did Waldo, that someone *needed* to ask those questions; otherwise, who was to stop Powers from abusing their gifts? Who opened debate about the Powers Registry being bandied about in Congress? Who pointed the finger of truth at those purporting to serve it but who actually dragged it through the muck? Ted Henry, advocate for the people. Ted Henry, *that's* who.

"I don't know," she countered, clasping both hands in her lap. "He makes salient points about the Powers Registry."

"*Hmph.* Terrible idea."

Deena frowned. "But *you* said—"

The judge waved a dismissive hand. "Big Brother, that's all it is. Good foundation, born of necessary times. Now used by jackboots and bureaucrats."

Aaron sat up. "Come on, Pop."

Ken pointed a finger at his son. "Tell me I'm wrong. If they truly cared, they'd have done it before the gang war. Long before people died in the streets for no reasons but blood and money."

Aaron grimaced. "You know it can help. It might prevent the next Liberty killer."

Ken snorted again. "As it is, we can't prevent the one we have *now.*"

"That's not fair, Pop."

The judge held his hands out in appeasement. "You're right. I know the police are doing everything they can."

"It's up to ten now."

The judge cleared his throat and drank some tea. Deena took her boyfriend's hand, squeezing it for support. "You'll catch him, Aaron."

"Not me. I'm a junior. They keep me off the big cases."

The judge's mug clanked atop an end table. "How'd he do it the last time?"

"Bludgeoned. Riddled with holes. They're thinking rivets, not bullets. Wounds are machined. Mostly along arms and legs. His head was pulped, like a grapefruit."

Deena's mouth went dry, parched as she listened to the grisly details. Her father barely gave her the goods regarding small-time cases. This, however, was the scandalous stuff—behind-the-scenes details that never made it to the papers. She hung on every word.

The judge went on. "And the tag?"

"Ink this time. With a little paint. Scrawled across the chest."

Deena leaned forward. "What did it say?"

They turned, possibly having forgotten she was there. The Boucher men traded glances, and to her disappointment, the judge slapped his knees. "Let's get those steaks on a fire."

A few hours later, they dug into warm, inviting, home-cooked barbecue. Eveline had laid out corn bread with rich gravy, three kinds of seasoned rice, and a bowl of lumpy hominy. The judge, to his credit, had done the steaks up right: a bit of sea salt sprinkled over grape-seed oil, and then a dusting of peppercorn and a sprig of rosemary. Aaron brought cold beers in from the garage, and Deena had whipped up a fresh summer salad with whatever she'd found in the pantry. The food was delicious, the conversation engaging, and Deena felt more content than she would ever be in her own home. After dinner, there was pie and coffee, and they retired with it to the porch to take in the cool night air. The judge eased into a rocker as Eveline measured out his evening's pills. Deena and Aaron sat double on a wraparound bench, nestled in together under soft exterior lights. Judge Boucher rocked a moment, breathing in the smell of trees and chicory, and then he leaned back and answered Deena's question.

"*'In the Name of Liberty,'*" he said.

"How's that?" She was drifting into a food coma, had barely heard him speak.

"You asked what it said. Liberty's note. That's what it said, what it *always* says."

"Pop."

"Hush now, Aaron. She's got a right to know. Despite ten kills, that little detail's been kept from papers and, god love him, Ted Henry. Or at least someone smart enough paid the man to keep him from screaming it over the airwaves."

Deena's eyes glittered in the moonlight. "What does it mean?"

"S'pose this individual feels his kills are freeing *someone*. All's I know? He's never killed the same way twice. No modus operandi to speak of. Makes him slippery and, frankly, exceptionally clever."

"'Mobile' what now?"

Aaron laughed and kissed Deena on the cheek. "Modus operandi. It means having a method for doing what they do. It's how we catch a serial killer. Most criminals stick to what they know."

The judge reflectively tapped his coffee mug with a spoon. "Not this guy, though. He's smart. Each murder has been performed using the abilities of a certain Power . . ."

Aaron finished his father's thought. "But when the cops close in on the likely suspect? He or she is found killed by Liberty, using another method. The method of the next person on Liberty's list."

Deena thought for a moment. "Who was the first victim?"

"Small-time arsonist. A minnow on the criminal food chain."

Aaron took her hand. "Look, I don't want you thinking police work is all arsons and serial killers, horrible murders and the like. There's a lot of good in being a cop. Protecting the innocent. Making a difference. This stuff? It's few and far between."

She rolled her eyes. "*This* is the exciting stuff. The *glamorous* stuff."

"Not the tenth time, it isn't."

The porch got quiet after that, the only sound the crickets and a light wind whistling through the trees. Aaron tousled Deena's hair, and she closed her eyes, thinking about Liberty's words, wishing tonight would never end. She was so relaxed; so content drifting on the porch, surrounded by love, laughter, and the scent of coffee and cologne. Then a scrape came from the left—someone walking up the graveled drive. Deena opened her eyes, and Aaron got to his feet. The elder Bouchers craned their necks to see who might be calling so late.

"Sure it is," the newcomer scoffed at Aaron's last words, a silhouette framed against the neighboring fence. "It *has* to be exciting, especially when you're kicking butt and taking names. Right, Boucher? You like the *excitement*. The *thrill*. Oh, wait. You only *name* names."

The man stepped into the light, onto the porch. It was Waldo Pilgrim, several cans of Infinity to the wind. Deena set down her mug and joined the detectives at the steps, quickly stepping between them before anything could happen.

"Dad," she said, careful not to push. "Let's get you home."

"I told you not to come here, Deena. I forbade it."

Aaron held out his hand, reaching for her arm. "Hang on a—"

Deena pulled away. "No, Aaron. It's fine." She smiled and addressed his parents. "Thank you for a lovely dinner. I've never had a steak so fine, Judge."

Ken nodded without a smile, steely eyes set on Waldo. "Trick is the grape-seed oil. Controls the char."

Deena kissed Eveline on the cheek and squeezed Aaron's hand. "I'll call you," she whispered. Waldo jerked forward and grabbed her arm, dragging her down the stairs. He unkindly nodded to the judge. "Ken. Eveline."

The judge continued to stare. Then, very imperceptibly, he nodded in return. "See you at the hearing, Wald."

Her father's face flushed a deep, embarrassed red, and he briefly glanced at Aaron Boucher. "Just leave her be. You understand?"

"She's a grown woman, able to make her own decisions."

"Not while I pay her freight. I'm still her father."

"Among other things."

Waldo chuckled, a low and evil laugh. He bit his lip and closed his eyes. "Least I'm honest with who I am. Least I ain't the kind of man who informs on his friends."

"Oh, we're *not* friends, Pilgrim."

"We could've been. I *tried* to be a friend to you, Boucher. But you're too righteous and idealistic to go along. Too proud to understand how it works. So instead, you rat cops out to the press—good men earning honest livings."

"We *both* know there's nothing good or honest—"

"End of the day," Waldo spat, getting right up into Aaron's face. "End of the day, you're worse than Judas, Boucher. You know what I'm talking about. I could name names, too. I could, but I won't. I'm loyal that way."

"Dad, Aaron. Come on." She tried to get between them but couldn't find daylight. Eveline fretted on the porch; the judge's nostrils flared.

"I'd rather be a Judas than a dirty cop," Aaron shot back, looking down at her father, fists clenched.

Waldo cracked a smile. "Now ain't that ironic. Judas died hard, didja know?"

"Yeah? If I gotta go, at least I'll go knowing that you're off the street."

Waldo threw a punch. The younger detective dodged and then drove a fist into the elder Pilgrim's gut. They grabbed one another and wrestled in the dirt, kicking up flowers and trampling Eveline's vegetables. Deena grabbed Aaron's collar and tugged him up, shouting for both men to stop as lights winked on along the street. Neighbors stuck heads out of doors as Eveline shrieked for détente from her chair. Aaron backed off, and Waldo pulled away, rising to his feet and brushing soil from his shirt.

"That's enough, jerks," Deena beseeched the squabbling detectives. Aaron stepped forward, and Waldo stumbled to the edge of the light. "This is ridiculous. I don't know what's the deal, but you have to—"

"Let's go, Deena. Now." Her father grabbed her wrist. She jerked it away.

Judge Boucher rose halfway, hands gripping his chair. A stony expression gave him the appearance of a waxwork, shadows cast across his features by the porch light. Deena swiftly shook her head, indicating that all was okay. She gestured for the judge to sit back down, and after a moment, he did. Aaron stepped forward, gallantly coming to her aid. She kissed him on the cheek. "I'd better go," she said. "Seriously, I'll call."

"You'd better." He halfheartedly smiled, eyes still watching Waldo.

She led her father down the driveway and off the Bouchers' property. He'd driven, of course, and Deena liberated the keys from her old man's pocket. "I'll drive you home."

Waldo grunted and then folded himself into the passenger seat of his old, green Mustang. She got the motor humming, a low rumble filling the air and intermingling with the sounds of crickets and nosy neighbors. Deena looked at the Bouchers' house, a final glimpse before heading home. Aaron and his mother were heading inside; she could see her boyfriend carrying plates in from the porch. The judge sat on his rocker, silently watching the Pilgrims' car. She waved, hoping he could see it through the tinted window, but the old man gave no indication to confirm that he had. Sighing, Deena leaned across and switched on the radio. She landed on a classic rock station playing Battleband, the final chorus of "Give Me Rock or Give Me Death."

Deena took in her stewing, drunken father. His arms were folded, and he seethed in silence. She put the car into gear and pulled away from the curb.

"Hey, Dad?" She waited until he grunted. "Tell you something interesting. Here's the thing." She placed a hand on his knee, and he turned her way.

"What's the thing?" He sat there, arms locked, waiting for judgment or grief.

Deena smiled. He'd get none here. Not like with Mom; not like with anyone who believed that Waldo was a dirty cop.

"You hear this song?" she asked. "Let me tell you something about the chords that you would never believe . . ."

# *10*

-m-

*December. Monday afternoon. 5:23 P.M.*

Malachi Crane looked like an aging pumpkin. Wrinkled and rotten, with a
mouthful of blocky teeth. He stood with his back to the window, hands
clasped and gazing down onto the street. The wide mahogany desk that
dominated his office was sparsely decorated; no photos, merely chrome pa-
perweights and a laptop resting aside three stacks of neatly organized legal
documents. The walls presented a few near-invisible, generic pieces of
hotel room art adjacent to a handful of magazine covers on which Crane and
several dignitaries of questionable moral fiber posed and preened. The office smelled of cigarettes and potpourri. The large picture window offered
an incredible view of the city, the only thing worth noting other than Crane
himself.

He turned to Deena and Kirk—arranged in chairs, waiting in suite 4A
as they'd been for the last twenty minutes in the anteroom below. They'd
arrived unannounced, requesting an immediate audience, explaining no
more than the conversation required. A brief tussle with guards and a rather
insistent secretary ensued; but less than ten minutes later, the two detectives were ushered into Crane's presence and offered coffee, water, nuts, and
fruit. They'd declined them all, focused on the matter at hand.

*And then motherfucking Crane,* Deena thought, *the Great Pumpkin in an*

*Armani suit and loafers, proceeded to waste ten minutes staring out at rush-hour traffic.*

"Mr. Crane," she began again, for what had to be the sixth time. "This really is a pressing matter. If you can offer anything at all—"

A low chuckle was her only answer. Dry and wheezy, the kind an old man gives on his deathbed. Truth be told, at his advanced age, Crane should have been resting comfortably in the dementia unit of a place with the words "Sunrise" or "Pleasant" on the door. Not heading the corporate arm of the world's largest anti-Powers political organization; not sucking in one raspy breath after the other while men of higher ethical caliber had finished drawing their own. This was a man the papers had labeled "the Abbie Hoffman of intolerant humanism." A man who had faced everyone from the Soldier to Olympia to Diamond to Retro Girl . . . and often lost. This was a man who, if he and the backward-evolutionary drones shuffling through the Human Front offices had their way, would not hesitate to euthanize the entire powered population and then order high tea.

In a word, Malachi Crane was *evil.*

But in America, even evil could legitimize with proper legal representation.

Kirk tugged his collar; Deena could see the sweat rolling down the rookie's neck. *Just keep it together. Keep your mouth shut, baby. Okay?* For the thousandth time, she waffled between missing and cursing Aaron Boucher. *Damn his stupid investigation. Walker would be here now, taking point. He knows the history; hell,—he lived it. I know only so much, and Kirk's going to be no help if it comes to dragging this joker downtown past an army of jackbooted thugs.*

*To be honest,* she thought, *even Aaron would be help here. He was there when Crane got rolling. He was on the ground down in Atlanta.*

Twelve years ago, the Human Front had been a collection of intolerant thugs banded together because they were frightened of what the Powers represented. After flashpoints in Detroit, Arizona, Moscow, Berlin, and Seoul, Earth's non-powered citizenry had a legitimate fear of what effect individuals with powers—unchecked, operating on their own terms—would have on the rest of the populace. There had already been post–World War II hot zones that had evolved into full-fledged political conflagrations. Not to mention irresponsible Powers who simply wanted to use their gifts for a life of crime or what they felt to be the greater good: themselves. And so, Powers Divisions sprang up in police stations across the globe. The fledgling United Nations and various unassociated governments around the world put peace-keeping solutions into place. And, of course, Congress began drafting bills that formed the bare bones of an eventual, much-debated Global Powers Registry.

Still, vigilantes gonna vigilante.

And so, a grassroots movement popped up in decaying urban areas throughout the country . . . unofficially labeled "the Human Front." They began with the death of a powered boy in Wichita—strung up, skinned, bloodied, and left for dead. From there, it caught fire, at first only turning gangs of bigots into cells of organized fanatics. As their ranks bolstered, so did their access to resources. Eventually, the Human Front grew from pockets of angry, non-powered zealots into a thriving, dangerous regiment of technologically advanced, well-armed militants. With Crane at their forefront, supported by a legion of radical lieutenants, the Front spread across the globe, attacking powered individuals they felt were undermining humanity; which, they feared, had a good chance of becoming extinct. So they rabbled. They roused. And the Powers fought back, eliciting the help of local, federal, and global authorities.

Eventually, other extremists with a grudge—afraid of what the Powers meant, as well—adopted their mission. The Klan, of course, and what would turn into an underground confederation known as Kaotic Chic. But the remaining arm of the Human Front—nearly eliminated following the violence of the Atlanta gang wars and the original, deadly series of Liberty murders—decided to reinvent itself. As the world marched away from revolution and rage, it donned suit and tie in order to reassert itself in boardrooms across the nation. So, too, did Malachi Crane. He redesigned the Front's sigil—the fist, snake, and bullets—into a slick corporate logo, polishing the edges and retaining the fist. He put his people to work drafting petitions, influencing legislation, and organizing in communities—a quieter form of infiltration, possibly even deadlier than the first. But the Front, now encompassing four of six floors at 500 Fialkov Way, wasn't breaking any laws. Not any laws that Deena could see. No laws at all, save perhaps the law of looking way too much like a rotting, leering root vegetable.

Crane returned to his desk, placing both palms on the blotter as he eased into his chair. "Detective . . . Pilgrim, was it? I assure you, if I had information that might help your investigation, I would provide it. The Human Front is long known for peacefully cooperating with recognized authorities such as the Powers Homicide Bureau." He grinned, his face pulling into a horrible, creased rictus. "A fact your . . . father? Yes. Waldo, no doubt, would be able to corroborate."

*Fuck you, pumpkin.* Deena's face felt hot, and she had to force herself to grip her chair. Kirk gave her a brief, quizzical sidelong glance, which she ignored. Crane had said that to get a rise—his history and knowledge of Deena's own made her vulnerable here, a fact she'd kept from Kirk.

"Even still, Mr. Crane—"

"Please," he responded in an indulgent manner. "Call me Malachi."

"Mr. Crane, your association and enmity with Joseph Monroe is, of course, a matter of public record."

He nodded, eyes watering and cast downward, coupled with a sorrowful frown. "Indeed. I was sorry to hear of his passing."

"Were you?"

"Of course. Despite our . . . cultural differences, the Soldier was a hero. He battled the Nazis, held off the Viet Cong, saved us from the threat of countless alien invaders. How could I not respect the man's accomplishments?"

"Because one of those accomplishments was tossing you in jail."

Crane's lips thinned. "Yes, the Soldier and I oft found ourselves on opposite ends of the battlefield . . . but you must understand, Detective, that we were political warriors. And in any war, though you may fiercely admire your enemy, he is an enemy still."

"Enemy enough to frame and kill him?"

Crane frowned again. "That I did not do. Did I want the Soldier and his kind—enhanced and undisciplined—neutered in some manner? Did I want them restrained from running rampant across the globe?" Crane stood up, voice rising in pitch. He spread both hands out across the desk, looming over Deena and Kirk like a bird of prey.

"Did I wish them," he continued, "to abandon their oppression of we true humans, those armed only with the gifts that God gave us? You're damn right. And as a soldier for true humanity, did I attempt to subdue, maim, kill, and destroy the Citizen Soldier and his friends on the field of battle to ensure that happened? Yes, I did."

He turned to the window again, cracking his knuckles, wiping spittle from his rumpled face with the back of his hand. "But if you're asking whether or not I tied him to a chair and beat the shit out of him? No. That I did not do. What would be the point?"

Deena pushed her cell phone across the desk. The crime scene photos were open as a slideshow. She paged through them, displaying the Soldier's corpse to his greatest enemy, taking care to pause at images that highlighted the Front tattoos.

"And these?" she asked Crane, tapping against Monroe's veiny, bloodied arm. "Who might have something to gain by framing Joseph Monroe? Someone who may have marked him with your logo and colors?"

Crane cast an amused glance at Deena's phone. He chuckled again, an awful sound echoing from the base of his throat. "Why, Detective Pilgrim . . . whatever makes you think that it wasn't Joseph himself?"

"So you're confirming he was a traitor? That Monroe was a member of the Human Front?"

"I never said that."

"You just implied—"

"No, my dear. I played devil's advocate to your inference. I will not comment one way or the other as to Mr. Monroe's involvement with our organization, not yet, but . . ." Crane drifted toward the door. He pointed a finger at Deena, beckoning for her to follow. She got to her feet and gathered her phone and partner and then headed after Crane.

"I will tell you *this*. The past holds more secrets then we dare know. It reveals truths and . . . liberties."

Her eyes widened at the mention of the word, staring into the bigot's own. He smiled, the cracks on his face splintering into a spider's web of creases and divots. She'd reached him now, and Crane held out his hand to shake Deena's. When she ignored it, he used it to open the office door.

"You want the truth regarding Joseph Monroe? I suggest you revisit the sins of the past, Detective Pilgrim. Both his and yours."

She glared at him. "And if I suggest you're facing obstruction charges by not telling me the truth, here and now? The truth regarding Monroe's death and, if I understand your passive-aggressive bullshit, possibly the related Liberty killings?"

Crane smiled and held out his wrists. "Then I would suggest, in return, that you arrest me, charge me, or speak to my attorney when you have some form of legal documentation. Until then, enjoy your day, Detectives."

Deena headed out of the office and stopped, placing a hand on the doorframe and turning back. "One last thing, Mr. Crane. Can you tell me anything about the Rammler Brothers or the whereabouts of Wilhelmina Quince, also known as Willie Wails?"

Crane smiled again, this time with none of the usual charm. "I'm sure I cannot. Any information I have on the Rammlers is classified. Should you desire I share it, I suggest you produce the aforementioned documentation urging me to do so. As to Ms. Quince, I haven't had the pleasure of her company for quite some time. If I had to venture a guess? Wherever the bottom-feeders of this world bide their time until death." He closed the door to suite 4A, shutting them out. "Good day to you both."

Shivering on the street, Deena fumed while Kirk allowed her to calm down. They stood on the top steps of the office building, shuffling in the snow, eyes darting to the scarved, burly security guards flanking the doorway. "Goddammit," Deena seethed. "I let him get my goat. Stupid move."

"Detective," Kirk answered forgivingly, "you're only human."

She pointed five flights up. "That's just it. Not to that guy. I had powers; so did Walker. So did Monroe. That rutabaga up there—"

"Pumpkin, you mean."

She'd made clear her impressions to Kirk on their way down the elevator. She appreciated his playing along and rewarded him with a smile.

"Thanks, *pumpkin* up there sees us as less than human—which, I gotta be honest, is fucking *ironic*. Even still, no way he sticks his wrinkly neck out to sacrifice someone with a snake-and-bullet tattoo. Even if said sacrifice might be the victim himself."

Kirk blew warm air into his hands. "Look, it's no big deal. We just focus on Wails and move to the next name on the list . . . something will turn up."

She closed her eyes and hugged herself. *That's what I'm afraid of. I'm afraid of what* will *turn up, new fish. Fuck Crane. Rubbing my nose in history best left bottled. Why the shit did he bring up my dad, of all people?* Deena's head was all turned around. She hadn't had a minute to think since walking into Monroe's apartment early that morning. And now the only things she *could* think about were Crane's parting words, Aaron Boucher's eyes, the Liberty murders old and new, and of course, her goddamn father.

"I'm gonna be useless for a while," she explained to the baby. "Need a breather, okay? Can you go back and work Wails's whereabouts, as well as the guitar string angle? See if Walker turned up any leads. Avoid the media circus and Captain Cross. I'll owe you a Coke."

"Uh, sure. I can't tell if you're serious. There's a clock on this, remember?"

She clasped his shoulder. "How could I forget? I am serious, and I may have another angle on this, but it's rife with personal attachments. I promise to fill you in over the Coke, maybe a taco or four. Let me work it on my own, okay?"

He eyed the hand on his shoulder, color rising to his cheeks. He agreed, happy to help. "This have anything to do with what Crane said up there?"

Glumly, she nodded in confirmation. "Everything."

An hour and a half later, Deena sat down to dinner in Judge Kenneth Boucher's spacious eat-in kitchen on the corner of Delsante and Lee. A third-floor walkup adjacent to a lovely park, the judge's apartment was filled with mementos that enveloped usually wary Deena in a welcome, nostalgic hug. Near retired, somewhat shrunken with age, Ken had lost none of the twinkle in his eyes . . . though they now peered from behind glasses twice the thickness to which she'd once been accustomed. Aaron, working tieless in shirtsleeves, hovered at the stainless steel range, putting final touches on a dinner consisting of two-alarm chili (laden with short ribs, three kinds of pepper, and two types of bean), honeyed corn bread, sautéed zucchini, and a mango-strawberry salad. The judge was thrilled to see Deena after so long, though his exuberance was somewhat tempered by the news about the resurfaced Liberty killer and annoyance at having been left in the dark as to her presence in the city.

"Mighty sore I'm *just* finding out you're in town." He took her hand in his own, beaming with happiness for having caught up with an old friend.

"I'm in the book."

Aaron grinned over his shoulder, never pausing in his stirring. "Pop can barely *read* the book these days, though he hasn't lost his knack for throwing it at criminals."

The judge raised a hand in dismissal. "Hush, Special Investigator. If that chili's anything less than two-alarm, you're sending out for curry."

Aaron laughed and finished up and then carried the food to the table. They dug in, and Deena felt herself relaxing—not only due to the comfort food but also by easing into the old, familiar intimacy she'd always enjoyed at the Bouchers' table. She rarely felt at ease these days—always looking for the next tragedy, more often than not wallowing in the pain of her past. But spending an hour catching up on small talk, feeling the years fold back, helped strip away the bullshit . . . and despite herself, Deena set the day's horrible events aside. She ignored her pressing case, the four murders, and Walker's sidelining to toast Aaron's mother and then Deena's own. The Bouchers listened to her few humorous case stories and then related their experiences keeping the peace in Texas. Finally, to Aaron's chagrin, the judge reminisced about the various states of undress in which he'd caught them over the years.

"Deena, you recall the time I caught you sneaking out the side door at 3:00 A.M., clutching a shirt and wearing nothing but shorts and a smile?"

She cocked her head and leaned on her elbow. "So retirement, huh?"

"From public service, yes; not from embarrassing my son."

"Okay, Pop." Aaron stood to clear the table. "Time for bed."

"How d'you like that?" the judge said, turning conspiratorially to Deena. "He lives in my spare bedroom, and I'm the one with a bedtime."

Deena quaffed a swallow of beer and then wiped her mouth. "Well, once you venture into nekkid territory, all bets are off."

"Perhaps so," the judge returned, negotiating an escape from the table. He pushed himself to his feet, a bit more shakily than Deena would have liked. "It's been a pleasure. I hope we'll see you soon for more small talk and gleeful humiliation."

She patted his hand. "Get some rest. Still wanna hear more about your travels along the panhandle."

The judge grimaced. "That topic makes me sad, much like our time in Atlanta. Much like these killings. Too much bad road, not enough happy recollections." Aaron stacked the tiny dishwasher, plates and glasses clinking in the background. "Seems to me you've got enough sadness to bear as it is. Best to hold on to the good memories, especially when dealing with trials and tribulation of another's making. You've a challenge on your hands, Detective. A national tragedy. A steadfast fanatic. Murders most foul, rearing their ugly head once more. You need to catch this man—or men—not just for yourself but for every poor soul who lost his or her life back in Georgia."

He stole a glance at his son, busy at the sink, head down and focused on the dishes. Then he leaned down and kissed Deena on the forehead—a soft, moist peck that felt comforting and protective at the same time. "But don't do it alone. You have friends. And possibly more, so be forgiving if you can." Ken's gaze slipped past Deena's eyes, off into some unknown horizon. He might have been thinking of Eveline, because his eyes watered, tears slipping to his cheeks. "Lost loves don't show up out of the blue, Deena. Some are never meant to be. Others take work. But sometimes the work might surprise you. Now good night. I'll leave you youngsters to your sleuthing and such."

"Night," Deena returned in kind.

The judge tottered off and down the hall, shuffling into the farthest bedroom. He closed the door behind him. Aaron finished with the dishes and, absently toweling his hands, turned back to the table. Deena stood up and grabbed the empties, set to carry them to the trash. He stepped between Deena and her destination, placing the towel aside and removing the bottles from her grip. He trashed them and then took her hands in his own.

"Long day," he said, gently massaging her fingers.

Deena rolled her eyes. "Seriously, dude?"

"What?" he asked, taken aback. "It wasn't? Four murders and a standoff. Busy coupla hours for any girl."

"The chili and conversation took my mind off it, so thanks. But I really should go see what kinda trouble the baby got into."

Aaron locked eyes with Deena and toyed with her hair. "You sure you're okay?"

She nodded. "I'm fine."

"I don't believe you."

"I *really* have to go, Aaron."

"I don't believe that, either."

She tried to pull her hand away. He wouldn't let her, and part of Deena was curious to see why. The other part—the part that dealt with countless moments of pain and betrayal over the last five years, the part that sheltered her from letting anyone get close—forced her to back away. He dropped a hand and placed the palm at her back, sliding it ungentlemanly low. Deena blushed, tucking her hair behind an ear. The beer had made her light-headed, and all thoughts of the last several hours seemed fairly unimportant. She reached around and removed his hand. This was unlike her; Deena Pilgrim didn't drop her guard this easily. Not even for the man she once loved. Especially after the way they'd last left it. Deena had never forgotten; the wound still festered.

But still. He smelled really good. They had history.

And she'd been alone for a long time.

"C'mon," she whispered. "What are you doing?"

Aaron grinned and leaned in. "Investigating."

Her mind briefly flashed to Walker, Aaron's raison d'etre for being in town. But invasive thoughts about her partner while so close to Aaron made her feel uncomfortable. She needed to think about something else, anything other than Walker, and feel something other than guilt and horror. Their knees were touching, and Aaron's breath wafted against her nose, sweet and inviting. *This is such a bad idea,* she thought. *Twenty-four hours ago, you hadn't given Aaron Boucher a second thought. You'd gotten over it, numb to the pain. He was a distant memory, one of many bad moments in a lifetime of painful, harrowing recollections. That silly girl you were isn't you anymore, Pilgrim. That isn't your life. Your life is the work now, the badge and ever-present dread.*

*But if so, why am I nearly in his throat and pants, halfway to humping him up against the range?*

*I have a killer on the loose. I have an inexperienced partner who needs me—two, in fact, the second of which I'm remembering what it's like to trust. So why can't I walk away?*

*Aw, hell. This is such a bad idea.*

Aaron pressed against her body. She breathed him in and then cautiously reached up to run her fingers through his hair. They tentatively kissed. Once, twice, and then they dove into it, teeth getting in the way. He slipped a hand down to her ass and drew her near, the other sliding up to caress her cheek. Deena hooked fingers into his belt. They danced around the table, pawing at one another like teenagers, and landed with Aaron's back against the fridge. She broke the kiss, flushed and warm and hoping to grab a breath, get a quick read on a different perspective. This was insane; they'd reconnected hours ago and were now jockeying for position in each other's mouth in his father's kitchen. Aaron had walked out on her years ago, left town without a backward glance. She'd put it in the past, had a new life, a new everything. But everything seemed less important. The Monroe case, spiraling out of control by the nanosecond. Walker's complicated past and uncertain future. The captain and the rookie, eager to solve the case, barely understanding the history shackled to its pedigree. And Deena herself—her father, her hatred of what she'd become, and the life she'd led. The danger of where it might take her from here.

None of that mattered. Only the kiss. His belt. The bedroom. The lights.

Afterward, as they lay tangled in his sheets, it all came rushing back. Dead men in the morning. Deena's near-miss with mortality at midday. The audience with Crane during the late afternoon. Fighting off sleep, she recounted her interview with Crane to Aaron—cryptic remarks included—and wondered whether or not she should call her father in Atlanta.

"Fuck no," he vehemently replied, rubbing Deena's back. "Is that something you really wanna do?"

"Of course not. But Crane mentioned my dad. He urged me to revisit the past."

"Yeah—his *and* yours. With what happened in Atlanta, I wouldn't be surprised if Waldo *did* have something to do with Monroe. But Crane could have been referring to Walker. It's common knowledge you're partners, and he and Crane share history. Maybe he meant Walker's ties to the Soldier. Oh, and let's not forget you're talking about a raging fanatic psycho bigot pumpkin who *may* want nothing more than to discredit the very famous, very dead hero in your cooler. Who just so *happens* to be said psycho bigot pumpkin's sworn enemy."

She looked up. "You don't believe any of that, do you?"

"Would make my job easier were it true. I gotta be honest, Deen, I've never trusted Walker. Or your father. I was right about Waldo. Who knows what Walker might be hiding."

*Not me,* she thought. She'd shared a great deal with Christian Walker over the years, but even still, they had secrets from one another. Her pregnancy, for instance, until he'd found out. And he'd kept his third power set from Deena—cosmic abilities gifted to him by a race of meddling aliens. She'd only discovered later on. She didn't know anything about Walker's family or where he'd come from. She knew he was old from some of his stories and that he dug tacos and bourbon. He favored strong cologne and light jazz. But his mother's name? Number of siblings? Had he ever been married? Deena didn't have a clue. And for a girl whose job it was to uncover clues, that was slightly worrying.

*I haven't seen Aaron in ten years, and I know more about him in a single day than I learned about Walker in a month. Apart from breaking my heart, Aaron has never led me wrong. And I'm sure he had his reasons for leaving. It's only day one now. I bet I get those reasons long before I find out Walker's mother's name.*

*But just like with Aaron, there's history with Walker. And that history is fresh, affecting me on perhaps a deeper level than a college romance ever could. I mean, Walker and I have saved each other so many times. We saved the* world.

But if they'd truly saved the world together, why was Deena here without her dreadnought of a partner, mired in the shit of quadruple homicides with no end in sight? How come Deena didn't know why this case was so damn personal that it fucked with Walker's emotional and professional perspective?

She nestled back against Aaron's chest. She drew his arm over her breasts and gently caressed his palm. "So you think leave Waldo out of this?"

"I think leave Waldo out of everything. Double down on your suspects. Let me help, and maybe we'll have a chance to finally solve this thing."

"The Liberty murders, you mean?"

He nodded. "That, Monroe, everything."

"And Walker?"

Aaron shrugged, rustling against the pillows. "I mean, I hope for the best. I'll try him again in the morning. Meantime, you have Kirk . . . and maybe I can take time off from my job to lend a hand."

Her eyes glittered in the moonlight. "Yeah? Mr. Special Investigator, deigning to slum it with—"

Something vibrated on an adjacent nightstand, positioned between Aaron's bed and an elliptical machine. She craned her neck and, noting the source, reached out to silence her cell phone. Beating her to the punch, Aaron checked the caller ID.

"It's Kirk."

She snatched the cell away and jabbed to accept the call. Deena listened for a moment and then slipped from the sheets and onto the floor, headed for the dresser, upon which her clothes had been strewn. "Great. I'll meet you there."

Deena silenced the phone and danced into her jeans, hopping on one foot and then the other. She tightened her belt and shot Aaron an apologetic look.

"Got a hit on Wails. She's at the Nexus, apparently."

Aaron moved to join, reaching for a shirt that had been tossed onto the floor. "A Powers-hater at a Powers nightclub? That seems unlikely, and could get dicey. You may need backup."

She snorted. "For an aging hippie whistleblower? I can handle it. Besides, I'll have Detective Toddler by my side." She thought for a moment, a pang of guilt stabbing into her side. "Actually, you want to help? Call Walker. Have him meet us at the precinct. We'll bring Wails and grill her quietly. Hopefully, depending on what she knows, we can have Captain Cross's suspect and a signed confession by the morning."

Aaron wheeled around to locate pants, bumping into Deena midway across the room. They stared at each other, faces reddening as they remembered what they'd been doing moments earlier. He stammered, unsure what to say, understanding that time was of the essence.

"Hey, look, Deen . . . I just . . ."

She clutched the front of his shirt, pulled him close, and kissed him hard enough to rattle his back teeth.

"What was that for?" he asked.

"That's for saving my life this afternoon. This one," she stated, moving in to kiss him once again. "This one's hoping it's worth having been saved. Now let's move. I've got a case to solve."

# 11

—*wм*—

Fifteen people writhed along the bar, grinding their bodies to a thrusting, hypnotic beat. They periodically vanished, timing their disappearances to the music. Hundreds of Powers joined them on the dance floor below. Nearby, waitresses dipped into teleportation portals, retrieving arrays of cocktails and exported platters of stalactite sticks and buffaloed space whale. Mistletoe and tinsel hung from skimpy dresses as hostesses led VIPs to sectioned tables in the back. Bouncers, lined along the walls, watched for teleporting undesirables, making sure that any didn't sneak in to Club Nexus through its intimate, darkened corners.

Deena and Kirk didn't worry; their badges were ticket enough. A bouncer waved them past velvet ropes where lines of already inebriated partygoers streamed from six parallel dimensions. He offered to flag down a manager or anyone who would keep the commotion a police presence might elicit to a minimum. Deena assured him it wasn't necessary, but if he felt like pointing out one Wilhelmina Quince, possibly singing that evening, the PHD would be most obliged. The name didn't register, and they didn't have anyone scheduled to perform, so the detectives took their own tour of the popular multidimensional club—brainchild of Christian Walker's ex-girlfriend Zora, the controversial superheroine who'd given her life to save Walker's years before. *Noticing a theme,* Deena mused. *Hadn't Triphammer also died while helping Walker save Chicago? What does that mean for me, I wonder?* Deena was momentarily back in the precinct with her throat in a man's hand, sweating and anxious. Kirk gave her a searching look, and Deena shook him off, throwing herself back into the search.

At midnight she came to the conclusion that Quince was nowhere on premises. Back on the street, bracing against the biting December wind, the detectives weighed their options. Willie Wails may have exited through any of the dimensional portals. She may, as Kirk pointed out, never have been there at all. Perhaps their information had been wrong. That's when Deena noticed the dive bar.

Situated at the mouth of an alley, the bar glared at them from across the street. A handful of filthy signs winked from filthier windows, advertising brews and concoctions by means of vibrating, partially broken, lascivious neon logos. Deena tapped Kirk's arm and gestured. He followed and then furrowed his brow. "You think?"

"One way to find out."

Bits of graffiti had been gouged into the door. *Kaotic Chic,* one read; next to it, a winding, threatening serpent. Between both, a crude fist clutching three bolts. Deena stepped inside, the rookie tagging along in her wake.

The bar's interior offered the reverse of Nexus's ambience and class. Drunks littered the room, grumbling into beers. The drinks looked murky, as did the patrons, and Deena didn't want to be here longer than she had to. *I think I got scurvy by glancing at the menu.*

The bartender was lean and grizzled, with one blind eye. He wore a sleeveless vest and a droopy Santa hat. His arms were riddled with syringe tracks. He looked up as they entered and then hurried away to polish a glass. Three men sat at the window, staring across at Nexus, each burlier and more intimidating than the last. One spat and then swallowed a whiskey. His arms were covered with tattoos—as were half the clientele's. One lady wore a swastika above her left eye; another a trio of thick, interlocked *K*s around her bicep. Two men had draped themselves in motorcycle jackets, each festooned with Kaotic Chic rockers. And, finally, a sullen couple watched the detectives from the bar, forearms covered with Human Front colors. A microphone waited at the far end of the room, placed near an empty stool.

A guitar case rested on the floor, lying open for the audience to toss in cash. Three quarters and a condom were the evening's ultimate take.

Deena leaned over to Kirk. "Head out back," she whispered. "Flank the alley in case someone bolts. Make sure it's covered." The rookie nodded and exited the bar, letting the door slam shut along the way. She stepped up to the couple—a weaselly, red-haired punk and a bottle-blonde cougar in denim. Deena slapped her badge down on the counter, careful to avoid hitting pools of beer and discarded limes.

"Looking for someone," she announced, projecting for all to hear. The men at the window glanced her way; the spitter sneered and then returned to his vigil. *They're watching the club,* she realized. *Keeping an eye on Powers, plotting against them. They're too drunk or fucked up to actually do something. But what happens when Crane discovers this place . . . or places* like *this where one man can buy another's hate for a shot of Drambuie? How will the partygoers across the street react when the patrons of this resentful dive come at them with everything they've got—everything Crane and his people choose to provide?*

She wiped her eyes. *I'm not here to prevent a war between Powers and normals. I'm here to solve a murder.*

Deena pointed at the guitar case. "Willie Wails? You know her?"

The ginger massaged his chin. "Who's asking?"

"Homicide."

The bottle-blonde sneered. "Wrong answer."

"Easy. Everyone chill." The men at the window had started her way. "I'm investigating a murder. Everyone go back to your drinks and . . . window." Slowly, the barflies backed away, returning to drinks and neutral corners. The bottle-blonde tittered, and Deena gave her full attention.

"So. Willie Wails? That's her guitar case up there, isn't it?"

"She kill somebody?"

"Just want to ask her some questions. Malachi Crane sent us. You know him?"

The weasel and blonde exchanged glances, and then the woman pushed out her glass. "Not personally. You a friend? Prove it. Buy me some holiday cheer."

Deena motioned for the barman and slapped some bills down on the bar. "I'll get your next two if you give me something I can use."

The blonde smiled with a predatory leer. She gestured toward a door marked EMPLOYEES. "Willie's through the kitchen, catching a buzz. She likes to get high before her second set."

She thanked the couple and tapped their glasses. The blind bartender hustled over. As he poured, Deena pushed into the kitchen and then out back into a dark alley. The door slammed closed, and she was alone with trash cans, empty kegs, and what appeared to be two people having sex in the snow, based on the moans. After a second, Deena realized the strains of pleasure were actually muffled screams, and she had stumbled onto either a mugging or a murder. Kirk was nowhere to be found. "Hey!" Deena shouted, pulling her sidearm.

The duo quit scuffling, and one of them looked up—he had no face; or rather, his face was hidden beneath a hood. He wore a leather coat and held a knife in one hand. His other arm was busy at the victim's neck, securing her in a choke hold. Deena flashed back to her close call earlier that afternoon and then barked a warning. The hooded man flinched, loosening his arm and giving his captive a moment to breathe. The victim was a woman—Quince, ambushed in the dark.

The hooded man shoved the singer in Deena's direction, putting her between the detective and her target. Deena tried to shoulder Quince aside, but the man tossed his knife away, pulled a gun, and fired twice. Both shots missed Deena, but one of the slugs found purchase in Wails's leg, dropping her to the ground. The hooded man took advantage of the distraction and sprinted, heading for the street. Deena yelled for Kirk, wondering where the hell her partner had gotten himself to, and turned to give chase.

She pounded after the assailant, straining to cover the distance. She could see his coat ahead, flapping as he ran. Deena fired her revolver. All of her shots missed their mark; luckily, the killer stumbled as he hurried to escape. He grunted and then scraped against the wall, faltering and losing ground. Deena tackled him, bringing him down with a meaty, satisfying *thump*. But before she could cuff and unmask the man, he swung out with his good elbow and clocked her in the temple. Deena saw stars and then a dizzying moment of blackness. By then, it was too late; he grabbed her by the throat, lifted her with surprising strength, and slammed her down into the dirt and filth. Then he straddled Deena, placing both knees on her shoulders, a gun at her ear, and a hand at her throat.

*Déjà vu,* she yammered, brain screaming at her to get up. The hooded man's knees locked down atop her shoulders, and Deena's vision swam from the blow to her head. Kirk wasn't here, and Aaron and Walker weren't, either. She needed to break the hold, but he was too strong. She tried to kick, bite, anything—but the second time she snapped, he placed the revolver at her lips. Her nose filled with the scent of metal and oil; she couldn't pull back. Seconds ticked away, and he leaned down, panting into her face, weighing her down.

He squeezed, causing Deena's vision to blacken. Tears betrayed her at the corners of her eyes, and her mind reeled, flashing on faces. First Aaron, and then Walker and the Soldier. Retro Girl. The captain, and then her mother and the judge. Poor, dead Eveline Boucher and the Powers at her parents' table as Aaron berated her father. Kirk's stupid face swam into view and then Walker again, reaching for her hand. She couldn't breathe, but she refused to cry. She closed her eyes, and Zora floated down from the darkness, her hair a corona that lit the world. The hero held out both arms, beckoning for Deena to float, as well.

Something popped in the distance, bringing Deena back to reality. A gunshot or fireworks. She couldn't tell the difference. It may just have been pressure in her head.

"Walk away," the man hissed. She couldn't place his voice—it was deeper than any that she knew. Flat and atonal, electronically altered and with a querulous air. "There's only a few left, and then it will all be over. I can stop. A few more, and I disappear forever. Stay out of my way until then, Detective Pilgrim." He pulled the gun away, resting it against her brow.

Deena hacked and spat. "Over . . . over my dead body."

"If it comes to that. But rather than worry about me, focus on your own. There's a cat in with your canaries, Ms. Pilgrim. You've a traitor in your midst."

"Monroe . . ."

He shook his head, gloved fingers digging into her throat. "No, another. But how is Joe? Not too cold, I hope? I hated to leave him that way."

Deena's eyes widened. She reared to the left and tried to kick the man from behind. He grunted and then smashed the back of her head into the pavement. "Not nice, Pilgrim. Much like your idiot father. Ask Waldo if he remembers me when you wake up, won't you?" He stood up, stepped away, and kicked her in the ribs. Deena moaned and clutched her side. He kicked again; aiming at her head this time.

Then everything went black.

Deena woke in a hospital bed. Her entire body was an inferno of pain. She winced and opened her eyes. Everything was blurry. She wore the same clothes, but her head was bandaged, and tape had been strapped around her torso, probably restraining a broken rib. Machines beeped and dripped, and she could hear the faint sounds of the public address system out in the hallway. Everything smelled sterile. She sat up, but her head spun, and she had to lie back down.

"Good call. Stay there."

Slowly, a shape coalesced into the form of Christian Walker, her worried partner. He sat in a chair, paging through a tabloid magazine with a cup of coffee in his hand, calmly waiting for Deena to find her bearings. He set his periodical aside and edged closer, holding out a hand. She took it, clenching as if afraid to let go.

"What happened?" she asked. "One minute, my head was bouncing on the ground; the next, I'm off-ramping a coma."

"What happened is that I got there too late."

"Say again?"

"Boucher woke me at home. He begged me to come to Nexus, claiming you were taking on a club full of Powers and needed backup. I promised to meet him there."

Deena fumed. "I didn't need that. I asked—"

"Hang on, because if Aaron hadn't arrived when he did, Kirk would be dead, and you . . . well, god knows what would have happened to you."

"What *did* happen?" She rubbed her skull, careful to avoid the tender spots. Her neck stung from where the hooded man's fingers had dug in; several bandages had been placed there, too. "He got the drop but didn't kill me?"

"Did he say anything?"

She thought for a moment. "He knew about my dad." She left out the bit about the traitor. She doubted it was true. The guy was a psychopath. "Aaron was there, you said. Where is he? Is Quince alive?"

"Easy."

"Aaron?"

Walker cleared his throat over the beeping of the machines and the announcements echoing across the hall. "Boucher's upstairs checking on Kirk. He found the baby struggling with Quince behind the bar."

"Struggling? She'd been shot, and he was AWOL. What *happened*?" Deena tried to sit up again, and blood rushed to her head, making her dizzy. Walker gently pushed her back against the pillow.

"Stop. Way it sounds, Kirk found her and tried to stop the bleeding, but Willie Wails was scared. Thought he was trying to hurt, not help. Babbled about Liberty."

Deena sucked in a breath. She waited for Walker to continue.

"Quince got the drop on Kirk and took his gun. Fired one in his leg, the other into his ribs. Pistol-whipped the kid until Boucher arrived and snatched the gun. Kirk will be fine, but he's out of commission. They got Willie at the precinct, booked and in a cell."

She frowned and looked down, biting her lip. "I shouldn't have let him go back there alone."

"It's not your fault, Deena. This is the job."

"I'm his partner. I should have been there."

"You were busy."

She lifted her eyes, searching Walker's for answers. "*Was* it Liberty? Did I let him get away?"

Walker hesitated. "I got there too late. By the time I did, he was gone. But there was a message on the wall . . ."

Deena nodded. " '*In the Name of Liberty.*' Written with what? My blood?" She reflexively touched the bandage at her throat. He must have retrieved his damn knife. She needed a drink. She needed Aaron. She wanted to see Kirk with her own eyes. "Get me out of here."

"Captain wants you tip-top before getting back on the street. He's recommended Boucher take over the case."

"Fuck *that*. I'm not an invalid."

"Agreed. And I don't really trust Boucher, to be honest. But we have to shut this down before the national media picks up the full extent of the damage. It's getting away from us, Deena. And I'm not sure either of us can ignore the personal context."

"No, I meant fuck Aaron taking over. This is still my case, still my neck on the line. What do you mean? You don't trust him?"

Walker put both hands behind his head. "Deena, c'mon. This thing has been against us from the start. It forced me away, then dragged in your past—"

"Which is *exactly* why—"

"And this thing with Boucher has affected your judgment. How convenient is it that he shows up *right* as the killings start again?"

She contorted her face with disdain. "What are you implying? You *know* Aaron was with Kirk while Liberty had a gun to my head."

"Do I? He may have circled back. All I know is—"

"—nothing." She swung her legs off the bed. The beeping intensified as she got to her feet. Walker hurried forward to help Deena, but she slapped his hands away, yanked the IV tubes out of her arm, and stalked toward the door. "Look, don't worry about me. Go back home, and let me handle things. You're fucking crazy if you think Aaron is Liberty or involved with the killings."

"Think about it, Deena—"

She whirled, hand on the doorjamb. "No, *you* think about it. I got jumped twice today, sure. But I'm not distracted by Aaron. I can do my job. Why don't you do yours?"

He folded his arms. "You *know* why."

Deena wiped her brow and sighed. "Know what, dude? I really don't. I can't keep up with the rising tide of your bullshit. At least Aaron doesn't give me passive-aggressive three-word answers. You left, man. You picked your ass up and headed home. And what, that's *okay* now? That's how you deal with horrible shit when the chips are down? Since *when* has that been *us*?"

"Since your boyfriend waltzed in and—"

"No, this is about your moody crap, not Aaron. I have a case to solve. Even if he's taking lead, I'm going to solve it. Are you in? Or would you rather go back to sleep?"

Walker stared at Deena. Finally, she threw up her hands. "Fine. Go home. Mourn your friend. Do whatever you have to do, but back the fuck off. Thanks for saving me—again, but I can take it from here. If you're worried my past is getting in the way of my judgment, then get out of the way of both. You deal with *your* shit. I'll deal with *mine*."

And with that, she headed into the ward, stumbling upstairs to find her wounded partner. Walker remained in the room, watching her go, wondering if he should follow.

Fifteen minutes later, he left the hospital and headed out into the night.

# *12*

~~~

Deena stormed into the interrogation room. She was in a pissy mood, the incident with Walker and her visit with Kirk having set her on edge. She looked right, a flash of green catching her eye. *Well,* she thought with a Grinch-like grumble, *at least I figured out where they stashed the Christmas tree.*

Wilhelmina Quince sat slumped over a wide, rickety table, arms crossed and cuffed to a metal ring. She hung her head, hair falling into her creased, weather-beaten face, hiding her from Deena's hateful gaze. Deena grabbed a handful of locks and yanked hard, pulling Quince back and eliciting a squeal. The woman's leg fell—it had been propped up on another chair, bandaged and splinted—and Quince howled this time, long and loud. Deena clutched the hair and pivoted, swinging it around so that Quince's face descended now toward the table, smashing hard enough that Deena hoped she'd shattered something essential. Blood squirted out along the table, bathing the metal ring in a crimson coat of gore. The drainer was on, covering the room in a sickly glow. Quince had no powers.

*But better safe than sorry,* Deena had decided.

*Though, if I find out this bitch had anything to do with these murders, she's hardly safe from me.*

Deena left Quince to her noisy recuperation. She dragged a chair to the other end of the table and turned it around. Deena sat, crossed her forearms over the back of the chair, and rested her chin against her hands. Quince scrabbled at her nose, doing her best to stanch the flow of blood, crying and cursing so wetly and thickly that Deena couldn't tell where the insults ended and the pity party began.

"You done, cop-killer?" Deena asked the injured, whining singer.

Wails shot her a wounded look. She wiped away tears, smearing blood across her cheeks. She wore spattered orange—prison couture. PROPERTY OF POWERS HOMICIDE DIVISION offered free advertising across Quince's back . . . not that anyone would read it other than the guards and populace of some soon-to-be-decided prison. They had her for assault at least, maybe conspiracy. After visiting Corbin Kirk in his hospital room, Deena was ready to throw the book at Quince—index and all.

Kirk was in a bad way. Quince had pulped his face, shattering a cheekbone and denting his nose. The rookie's skull had more bumps than a maternity ward, and he'd lost two teeth. Doctors had retrieved the bullets from his side and leg, but he'd have trouble walking for a bit, breathing more so. The bullet in his rib had grazed a lung. They'd managed to repair the damage, but one thing remained certain: Kirk was off the case.

The captain had given Deena an earful. Sending Kirk out alone had been a mistake—she knew that—but who knew he'd stop for a piss, as he'd claimed to Aaron? And who knew Deena would have happened upon the killer? Now she was hearing about her fuckup by everyone from the DA on down. IA wanted a word, as did the commissioner. Every news station in town thrust microphones into her business, and a sea of mourners had barely let her pass into the station. The one person Deena *did* want to talk to was pouting at home. Though at the moment, to be honest, she honestly had no idea what she would even say to him were he around.

*Fucking Walker,* she'd thought, seething at Kirk's bedside. The baby's breathing was wet and ragged, and Aaron had rubbed her shoulders as she stared at him in silence. *Walker, what does he know? Look at this kid,* she'd entreated the universe. *Did he deserve this? Why the fuck did I send him out alone? What did I have to prove? Did I think I could solve it single-handedly? In this state of mind? Between Walker and Aaron and the shit I heard from Crane . . . what the hell was I thinking?*

*And now I* have *to solve it single-handedly,* she thought, boring holes into Quince with her eyes. *Kirk's out of commission, Aaron is off reporting to a commission of his own, and Walker's useless. Meanwhile, I get the media extravaganza and am tasked to connect tab A to slot B before the clock runs out.*

*But all I can think about is that hood, my throat, and my fucking father.*

None of which boded well for Deena's only lead, the woman across the table. Cross had balked at the detective's intentions—no way was he letting her in a room with the possible key to solving a rapidly spiraling murder case. But Deena had employed her heretofore-unused feminine wiles, along with a handful of jokes, stories, and outright deals. That had bought Deena twenty minutes in the interrogation room with Quince, and though all she wanted to do was kick the living shit out of the woman across the table, Deena knew she had to make every second count. And she didn't want to be in here any longer than she had to: the smell of pine was driving her fucking nuts. She scooted closer, letting her chair scrape against the floor with an echoing, irritating screech.

"So. Done?"

Quince nodded, a tear clinging to an eyelash and a runner of snot dripping from her mangled nose. She was truly filthy, and she rubbed her wounded leg as best she could, wincing whenever she squeezed too hard. Liberty's slug had struck bone, and though the medics had been able to retrieve the bullet (and were running tests to identify its shooter), it probably still hurt like a motherfucker. *I'll use that, if need be,* Deena realized. *Sweep the leg, Zabka-style. Nothing like a kick to a bullet wound to elicit the goddamn truth.*

"You put a big hurt on my partner, you know. This precinct doesn't take kindly to cop-killers. And I definitely hate having to train fresh partners."

Quince mumbled through her veil of tears.

"What was that?" Deena inquired, cupping a hand against her ear. "Didn't quite catch it."

Quince snuffled and wiped her face. "Said I was sorry. Wasn't trying to kill him."

"Coulda fooled me. And his doctor. But I'll convey the apologies to his mother."

"What do you want me to say?" Quince spread her hands in frustration, rattling her cuffs. "Nearly died. Didn't know who I could trust. Just wanted to get away."

"From the Liberty killer or my poor schmuck of a partner?"

The singer shot Deena a skeptical look. "What? Bitch, I don't know what you're on about. Some asshole jumped me with a knife. Hell, I don't even remember firing a gun, so I want my—"

Deena leaned forward, laying both palms on the table. "So you had no clue your attacker was the Liberty killer. I know that you know who I mean. Don't play cute."

Quince laughed—a short, joyless burst of air. She hung her head and grinned, hair falling into her face. "Dude, Liberty? You're so reaching it isn't funny."

"Am I? Deny you know what I'm talking about. I *dare* you." She pounded the table, and Quince jumped.

"Jeez! Yeah, damn. I know what the Liberty killings are. I never denied that, pigbitch."

Deena bit her lip and tamped down the hate. She felt hot; noise from the precinct filtered through the door, mingling with the static in her head. *Just keep talking. Press her about Atlanta. Don't think about Waldo or Kirk, or you'll gut this slut where she sits.*

"Then how am I 'reaching,' Willie?"

"Because that was, like, twenty years ago. Ancient history."

"Eleven, actually. During the Atlanta gang wars."

Quince sat back and folded her arms. "Whatever, man. I'm not a calendar."

Deena hauled out her phone and maximized some criminal records, crime scene photos, and headlines archived from the *Atlanta Journal-Constitution* and APHD. She placed the device on the table and turned it so that Quince could see. "No, but you are a vindictive, radical, anti-Powers militant. And a whistleblower. Or at least you were, according to records, arrest reports, and court documents. You were Crane's snuggle bunny, weren't you?"

Quince sniffed again, sneering and turning away from Deena's phone. "I ain't seen Mal in years. I don't run with the Front anymore. I'm legit. I sing."

Deena turned the phone back. "And run a little H, maybe deal molly. Part-time hooking when tips run out. That's from this station's records, mind you. And not the ones in Atlanta, dear."

Willie massaged her leg, and Deena inched a heel closer beneath the table. Quince looked at the door. "I want a lawyer."

"For what? I haven't charged you."

"I know my rights."

"Seems like a guilty move, calling a lawyer. Sure you have nothing to hide? I mean, I'm not the one who airholed a cop tonight, sweetie."

Quince exploded, shouting across the table, "Look, I don't fucking know nothing about no goddamn Liberty murders, okay?"

"Well, now. All right. Does Crane?"

"Who—what, *fuck*. I *told* you I ain't seen him."

"You said you knew nothing about Liberty," Deena argued, paging through the files. "But according to these court reports, you testified against several Atlanta detectives who were accused of mishandling the Liberty killings. You said, I quote—"

Quince cut her off. "I fucking know what I said."

Deena put the phone aside. *Dammit, Dad. And fuck you, Crane.*

"So let's try again. Do you know the man who attacked you this evening? Not the man you shot—the first man, in the mask."

Quince shook her head.

Deena continued, "Do you want to venture a guess why he was trying to kill you?"

"I have that kind of face."

"Willie." Deena placed her chair at the left end of the table, sitting with her back to the door and alongside Wails. "Look, the man who attacked you *was* Liberty. Not the moron cops who capitalized on his first killings, pretending to be him in order to clean up the streets."

"I still say you're reaching, bro."

Deena placed a hand on Quince's forearm; the singer flinched. "I know this because he attacked me, too . . . after I chased him down. I woke up in the hospital, after he beat me, and I was told his words had been written above my head. In my own blood."

Wails sneered. "Copycat, like those cops. Liberty disappeared ten years ago . . . and he only ever killed in Atlanta. Besides, why would he want to kill a cop? He went after criminals."

"Because I chased him down. And maybe because though I'm a homicide detective here, I used to live in Atlanta, a lifetime ago. Detective Deena Pilgrim."

Quince's expression went slack after hearing Deena's confession, a spark of understanding flashing behind the eyes. She didn't say a word, but Deena already figured she knew the truth, so she pressed onward. "Okay, so you know my name and what I know about your past. What you *don't* know is that yours wasn't Liberty's only show today. Earlier, we discovered three bodies on a subway car, decapitated several hours ago. The last of the Rampage Brothers."

Quince's mouth formed a letter *O*. "All . . . all three?"

"The hat trick. Somebody's killing Powers-haters." Deena tapped the faded tattoo on Willie Wails's forearm. "Haters with marks like these. I need to catch them as soon as I can. Where were you two nights ago?"

"At . . . at the bar. I had a late set. Billy will back that up."

"Billy's the bartender?"

She nodded, horrified. Deena sat back. "So you didn't kill the Rammlers, let's say. When was the last time you saw Crane?"

"Y-years ago. Before I got involved with Kaotic Chic. It . . . it didn't end well. But I doubt he would have—"

"And the Rammlers?"

"Same time. When I cut ties, I cut ties."

Deena rapped her knuckles on the table. "Okay, let me ask you this. Did you ever meet Joseph Monroe?"

Wails squinted. "Who?"

Deena tried another tack. "Back when you ran with the Front, did you have any interaction with the hero known as the Citizen Soldier? Maybe in battle?"

"Damn," Quince mumbled, "the Soldier? What does he . . . you're all over the place. No, I mean, yeah. I guess. I saw the guy once. But we never fought. I wasn't one of the strong ones. Mal, the Rammlers, Blitzkrieg. Those were the guys that handled the A-listers. I had a fucking guitar. I scared the crowd. Like I said, I haven't been involved. . . . . . I dallied with Kaotic Chic, and I believe in the cause, but stepped away to focus on music."

"And drugs."

"Bitch gotta eat," she replied with a grunt.

"So, you never met him. Crane said nothing about him?"

"Nothing civil."

"But you admit to being involved with the gang war—and I know you testified against those cops. I know you worked for them. Think this might be a revenge thing?"

Wails shrugged. "If so, why wait ten years? I'm nobody now. I sing to drunk assholes in a shitty bar. Why take revenge?"

"Maybe it's a Power out to kill known Powers-haters?"

"Yeah, but why single me out? Plenty of active Front members in the bar last night. Besides, Liberty never discriminated between Power and normal. Killed plenty of Front soldiers, plenty of Powers."

"Could be a Power trying to rub the Front's nose in the mud."

"Could be a lot of things. Could be Olympia back from the dead, wanting my hide because I once gave him crabs."

Deena lifted her phone and scrolled through to the photos of the guitar strings that Kirk had found. She turned it around so Quince could see.

"Recognize these?"

Willie Wails leaned in and squinted. "That a .027?"

"How did you know?"

She sat back, cracking a grin. "Might as well ask how I know one tit's heavier than the other. Strung an old axe with them when I first got to the city. Been out of stock for years. They're tense, see, and—"

"They cause the guitar's neck to bow."

Quince nodded, seemingly impressed. "Yeah, fam."

"We think someone used a set to slice off the Rampage Brothers' heads."

Quince held out her hands. "Fuck, dude. I *told* you, it wasn't me."

Deena stowed her phone in a hip pocket. "And you don't know who else it might be? I can track sales of those strings, Willie. I can find out if you're lying—"

The former radical pounded a fist on the table. "*Hey!* I told you, I'm *out*. I got no beef with anyone no more. I sing my shitty songs and maybe sell an ounce for a hot and a cot, but I don't fucking *know* who Liberty is!"

Deena narrowed her eyes. "Could someone close to you have a set of those strings? Did you ever gift a set to Crane?"

"No. Yes. I don't know. We did a lot of crank back then."

"Tell me about your testimony in Atlanta."

Quince groaned and sank into her chair, looking up at the ceiling in consternation. "Jeez. It's all public fucking record."

"I hate to read. Why don't you paraphrase?"

Quince bent her neck and glared at Deena. "Look. Back on Peachtree . . . you know? It was fuckin' chaos."

Deena edged closer to the singer. "Skip the preamble and tell me."

"Ease off. Okay." She took a breath and sat up. "Look, none of us knew anything about who or what might be killing our crew, right?"

"Sure."

"But thing is, cops weren't eager to figure it out, either. And some of us? It helped us get a little side action with several of Atlanta's finest."

Color rose to Deena's cheeks. She'd heard this all before, of course. Despite her overtures to ignorance, this was, indeed, ancient history. Still, she needed the confession. And perhaps it would lead her closer to wrapping this shit up so that she could maybe go home.

"Coupla us got sprung after Diamond and the Soldier tossed us in the can. Not many—four, maybe six. The Rammlers, Blitz, Hammerhands, me. They ran it past Mal, but he never bit. He wanted nothing doing with APHD."

"Crane had nothing to do with the indicted detectives?"

Quince shook her head. "Mal stayed in jail. Did his time. Rest of us took the deal."

"Which was?"

"You know . . . random acts of violence. Maybe coupla hits against criminal Powers and a few of our own. Look, we wanted *all* Powers to die, so it made no difference which side we hit. Seemed like we were covering up something else, something the cops didn't want us knowing about."

"Like the Liberty murders?"

Quince frowned and shook her head. "Nah. None of the guys or the folks we iced had anything to do with that. But yeah, those cops used his work to cover their tracks. Felt like something else. But . . ."

"But some of your guys *were* killed by Liberty. One of the Rammlers. And Blitzkrieg."

Wails sniffed. "Well, true. But that was separate from our thing with APHD. What I was gonna say . . . some of the guys we iced, the cops told us to tag the scene with his words."

Deena sat up in her seat, heart hammering in her chest. "So to get this straight. The Soldier's crew put you away. Then, some of you were released by cops in order to—what?—kill evil Powers as a distraction from something else. But *not* the Liberty killings, because some of you had been killed by Liberty in turn. And the criminals you *did* kill, some of them you tagged with Liberty's words so that no one knew which were the *actual* Liberty killings?"

"Bingo."

"Could Liberty have simply been that group of cops? Could they have been covering one set of killings up with another? A decoy set of murders, as it were?"

Wails shook her head. "Doubt it. The *real* killer felt like a Power. Like someone with gifts and skills. Atlanta cops weren't the sharpest tools in the shed. They just wanted an excuse to ice bad guys, figured they'd blame it on a serial killer. Hide a coupla murders inside a whole mess of 'em."

*All the cops but one,* Deena thought. "So what I need is to talk to one of the indicted cops and get the truth."

"Sure."

"Which of them hired you?" *Easy, Deena. You're opening a can of grenades.*

"Uh-uh. No way. I want my lawyer."

"After. First give me a name."

"Fuck *that.* How's it gonna look I squawk, draw attention to the cause, Crane, and the cops? How's it gonna be if I give up the guy who hired me to kill a member of the Front and blame the boogeyman? No, I want a deal. I get protection; you get a name."

*I already know his name,* Deena surmised, face and chest growing hotter with every passing moment. "You'll have it. Now give me a cop before I step on your leg."

Quince hesitated, and then she recognized the look of impatience and fury on Deena Pilgrim's face. She slumped down again and mumbled.

Deena craned her neck to hear. "What was that?"

Wails stared Deena in the eye. "It was your father, Detective Pilgrim. Waldo Pilgrim sprung me from jail and hired me to impersonate the Liberty killer."

# *13*

---

*December. Eleven years ago.*
*Friday night. 7:56 P.M.*

"Are you out of your *goddamn* mind?"

The last time Waldo's face had been this red, he'd been through a three-day bender. He stood in the living room, fists clenched tightly, jaw about the same. Deena sensed he might start swinging if she didn't step in, but Judge Boucher, seated on a recliner, held out a hand and waved her away. Her father noticed the gesture and pointed an accusatory finger at his begrudging guest.

"Hey—leave my daughter out of this. Don't look at her! You don't keep *her* confidence!" Waldo advanced on the judge, spittle flying, and the older man rose to meet him. They squared off in front of the love seat, Waldo raging and the judge doing his best to contain the storm. Deena moved into the kitchen, keeping quiet and waiting for an outcome. The rest of the house was empty. Mom had been gone a week now.

"Why don't you drink with me, son?" the judge asked. "Let's discuss this after some liquid balance."

Waldo fumed. "Don't offer me drinks in my own home, Ken. If I want alcohol, I fucking *know* where it is!"

"Is it with your manners? Because I can't seem to locate those anywhere in sight."

The finger went up again, stuck before the old man's eyes. "I only serve goddamn alcohol to people who haven't betrayed me this month!"

"Son," the judge said. "You betrayed yourself."

Deena's father kicked an ottoman and swiped at a lamp, knocking it to the floor. No one scurried to clean it up; the Cubans had all gone, having been let go by her mother before she'd followed them out the door. Waldo stomped across the glass to the liquor cabinet and liberated a bottle of scotch, taking a long, spiteful swallow. He turned back to the judge, lifting his finger once again. "You *screwed* me, Ken. You and your damn kid."

"We did no such thing. You were found guilty by a jury of your peers . . . and half the papers in Atlanta, son."

"Guilty, my ass. You think I'm the only one?"

The judge shook his head and sat back down. "No, I do not. That's why we stripped several of your colleagues of badges, as well. Be thankful that you, at least, I was able to keep out of prison."

Waldo scowled. "That's not what I'm talking about, and you know it. But big deal. Probably safer in jail. I'd have more friends than out here."

This time, the judge raised his voice and stood back up. "That's because you released half the prisoners, you damn fool!"

"Hey, are you kidding me? You don't yell at—"

"Damn right, I'll yell!" It was too late; the judge advanced on Waldo Pilgrim, looming like a grizzly. Deena slunk deeper into the kitchen, wishing Aaron were here, wishing she could hide or turn back the clock. But the damage had been done, and there was nowhere to go but deeper into the abyss. Nothing to do but watch her father figures obliterate the remains of a once-wonderful friendship.

"Thirteen murders," Judge Boucher began, circling Waldo, who had by now dropped into a recliner of his own. "A baker's dozen of corpses unceremoniously dumped throughout the city. Each scene tagged by this Liberty—whoever, whatever that's supposed to be. And have you done *anything* to find the real Liberty killer? Have you turned over rock and root to find this mysterious assassin?"

Now the judge kicked out, striking a soft, leather boot against the Pilgrims' sofa. "No! Instead, you and your crooked group of Keystone Cops stepped aside, took bribes, and released noted criminals—villains, mind you, who have graced *my* bench, subjected themselves to *my* rulings— hoping they'll do what you've failed to accomplish."

Judge Boucher sniffed and then stepped over to the abandoned bottle of scotch and took a swallow. He wiped his mouth and continued with his diatribe. "And what happened, exactly? Half of those villains were *killed,* murdered by this so-called Liberty as cops and Powers alike stood around with thumbs up their asses—that is, when they weren't pretending to be him or raking in kickbacks and partnering with known convicted felons."

Deena's face had bleached of all color by now. She'd heard accusations of the sort from Aaron in the past and picked up whispers from pockets of her mother's conversations with friends. She'd chalked it all up to naïveté, scorn, or do-gooder zeal. But now, faced with reality in the form of printed headlines, television broadcasts covering the APHD trials, and a rattling barnburner of a scolding from her father's oldest, closest friend, Deena finally had to face the truth.

"Ha," Waldo broke in, the crimson in his face whitening to a pale, terrifying pallor. "You got a lot of fucking nerve coming here and saying this to me. *I'm* not the one that hooked up with the Soldier. *I'm* not the one who—"

The judge slapped Deena's father before he could finish. His hand left a mark on Waldo's face. Ken stepped away, chest heaving with fury as her father gingerly touched his raw, red cheek. Waldo sniffed once and held out his hand. "What did you expect me to do, Ken? You took my badge."

"I expected you to do your job."

Waldo shouted back. "Well, now I can't! Now it's gone! Let your arrogant, asshole *son* do it instead! That's what you both wanted all along, *wasn't* it? That was the ultimate plan!"

The judge chuckled. There was no mirth in that laughter, and he started for the door. "No, Waldo. It really wasn't. You essentially killed all those men, even if you didn't pull a trigger or light a fire. Rammler, Blitzkrieg, all the others who died at Liberty's actual hand. Victims who should've been locked away, safe from his wrath. Now all those felons are on the streets—either killin' or dyin'." He turned back to Waldo. "How does that look for you—or for me? What does that say about the weight of my judgments, about the stability of my court?"

They faced one another from across the room. Waldo rubbed his cheek, and the judge donned his coat and hat. A moment went by, long and awkward, and Deena's father spat to one side. "You know that half of what you've said is *bullshit*. You *know* that. But keep up appearances and play the innocent, if you like. Now you got your pound of flesh, Ken. Get the fuck out."

The door slammed, and Deena edged back out into the living room. Waldo ignored her, brushing by as he headed toward the fridge. He rummaged around in the freezer and pulled out an ice pack and then placed it against his cheek. After a moment, he set it aside, opened the refrigerator, and retrieved a beer. He twisted the cap and took a long, determined swallow. He set it on the counter, allowing the condensation to gather, and watched Deena carefully. She held on to the wall for support as she approached. Waldo was simmering with rage, and she trembled with anxiety as he took another drink. Then he put down the ice pack, placed both hands on his hips, and faced his daughter.

"What? Say it."

Her tongue stuck in her throat, but she still managed to stammer out an accusation. "So it's all true. Everything Aaron ever said was true."

"*Fuck* Aaron. You're *done* with that asshole. So am I."

Tears glistened in Deena's eyes. "No. I don't live here anymore, so you can't—"

Waldo jabbed a finger up toward the stuccoed ceiling. "Out in college, you do what you want. But when you're under *my* roof—"

"I'm *not* under your roof. *No one* is under your fucking roof but *you*."

"Fine, then get out."

Deena sneered. "Mom did. Maybe she had the right idea. Maybe she was right this whole time."

Her father splayed both hands against the counter and hung his head. She could see that Waldo was biting back anger, being careful with his next words. "Deena, I love you, but watch it. Things are not what they appear to be, all right? You have no idea what's going on, and I'm not in the goddamn mood."

"What—you're in the mood for stealing and cheating, lying and killing, but not in the mood to deliver the truth to your own daughter? The truth of what they're saying about you on the *news*? Bribery, forgery, racketeering, conspiracy. Everything I'm reading in the papers and hearing from Ted Henry."

"*Henry*. He's another one."

She advanced on her father, blind with anger, shaking with rage. "Everything Aaron said—everything I *never* believed, but the entire time I must have been a complete and utter *moron*. This house, my clothes, the cars—all bought with dirty money."

Waldo smiled at her—an evil, cruel smile. "Don't forget college, darlin'."

She took a swipe, swinging with her left. He caught her wrist, careful not to squeeze and cause a fracture. "Don't do that. I'm still your father."

"Not the one I knew. The father *I* knew was a *good* man, not a dirty cop. I looked up to *that* man—he was the reason I wanted to become a detective. He was my role model."

"I'm still the same man. You don't understand."

"Then come clean, okay? *Make* me understand," she pleaded. "For the first time in your life, tell me the truth."

Waldo bit his lip and shook his head, his hair shaking in his face. "No, I can't. It would hurt you; it would be something you couldn't bear. Like your mom."

Deena laughed. "Dad, I'm nothing like Mom. I can handle this. Please."

"You can't. Look, I'm still your father. I'm a *good* man."

"No, you're not. Not anymore. Not like Aaron."

Waldo released her hand, spinning her away, and spat on the floor. "Then go be with him instead. Get out of here, and don't come back before I *do* tell you the truth. Leave, like your asshole boyfriend. Get out of Atlanta before you get hurt."

She stared, wounded and rubbing her bruised wrist. "What do you mean?"

He grinned as he walked back toward the living room. "Oh, he didn't tell you? Detective Boucher put in for a transfer. Effective immediately."

That didn't make sense. Aaron was the hero. He helped stop the gang war and then effected a series of internal investigations that put five APHD detectives in jail, suspended three of their badges, and removed the Federal

Powers' jurisdiction away from Atlanta. Why would he leave? Who would be left that wasn't tainted by the corruption?

And what would become of their relationship? No, fuck that. He wouldn't leave without talking to her about it. This was just more of Waldo's bullshit.

"You're lying."

He gestured grandly to the door. "Ask him yourself, that son of a bitch." Waldo dumped himself back into his recliner, grabbing the scotch along the way. "But don't come crying to me when your heart gets broken. Don't come crawling back after you finally learn the truth."

She backed out slowly and then spun away, heading out the door. She called Aaron on her cell as she walked to her car, careful not to sprint and twist an ankle. He didn't pick up; she tossed the phone in the back before driving like a madwoman to his apartment.

He was packing when she arrived, placing pans into a box already filled with spice bottles and hand towels. Nine MM played on the radio, streaming soulful mercy throughout the tiny kitchenette. He wore a white T-shirt and jeans; the shirt clung to his skin, and Deena was torn between wanting to hit him and wanting to jump his bones. She glanced around and saw other boxes, labeled and secured, ready to ship. So she landed on the former.

"Hey!" he protested, blocking her attack. "What's gotten into you?"

"You're leaving? Were you planning on telling me?"

He seemed surprised, and his face was pale. "Didn't your dad? I mean, I assumed."

"Yeah, ass. I just found out. But I should have heard it from *you*." Deena closed her eyes and shook her head. "No, we should have *discussed* it before you made a goddamn decision."

Aaron turned back to his boxes. "Really? What would that have accomplished?"

She grabbed his arm and twisted him back. "Why are you being such a dick?"

He pulled away and ran both hands through his hair. "I'm not. It's just . . . look, you know this wasn't just my decision."

She raised an eyebrow. "They're transferring you?"

"No, I mean . . . wait. What did Waldo tell you?"

"He told me you were leaving town—that you put in for a transfer!"

"Oh." He wiped his eyes, and the color seemed to return to his cheeks. "No, it isn't that. It's just . . . my pop is leaving. Moving to Texas. He got an offer, and I'm going to help them get settled."

"I don't understand. They can't go without you? Why can't you go and then come back?" He hesitated, and she knew. "Wait. You don't want to come back, do you? You're using this as an excuse to get away from here."

"No . . ." He shook his head and sat down at the small foldable card table they'd purchased together on a blissful weekend. "I'm using this whole thing—the war, the murders, the trials. That's my excuse."

"Pretty shitty excuse."

He held her hands. "Deena, I can't do this anymore. I can't be the only honest cop in Atlanta. The corruption in this town, it's just toxic."

Deena gripped his fingers. "You fixed that. Waldo, all the shit in the papers. It's done, right? It'll get easier."

Sadly, he shook his head. "I don't know. I doubt it. I plugged a leak, but there'll be others. And the murders. I . . . I failed, Deena. I thought it was someone on the inside, and when we turned the division upside down, all I had was a shitload of rats and traitors. Nothing I did made a difference— nothing I'm doing will change the pit that is the APHD. So I'm done. I can't sit here and wallow in my own failures. I have to start again somewhere else. Somewhere far from the pain affecting my family."

"Okay. I'll come with you."

He hung his head. "No."

She snatched her fingers away. "Why the fuck not?"

"Deena, you have school. You have roots and a family—"

"Not anymore. Not after tonight."

He placed a hand on her shoulder. "Deena . . ."

She moved to the fridge, placing her back against magnets and shopping lists bound for the garbage. "Don't you fucking 'Deena' me. You made this decision by yourself. That makes me feel like shit—like we had nothing together."

"You know that isn't true."

"Then why can't I come? Your parents love me, mine are assholes, and I can transfer to another college or start at an academy nearb—"

Aaron stood up, rubbing his eyes and brow. "Deena, you have to finish college here. You have to live life on your own terms, not latch on to mine. Find a better life—a better man, for that matter. One without attachments and baggage . . . the baggage of my family and yours."

"Are you kidding?" She was pissed now, really fuming. "That's what I get after all this time? 'It's not you, it's goddamn me'?"

"Deen, if you come with me, you're just going to follow my failure. That's all you'll ever see. You need to put this behind you—I know you idolize the cops, the Powers. I know you *glamorize* the Powers. But they'll only hurt you in the end."

"I don't think you're a failure. *You* do, though I don't know why."

"Because I am! I did fail—I failed this city, my father—hell, *your* father. I failed *you*." He moved toward her, taking her shoulders with both hands. His eyes were frightened; she'd never seen him this way before. Never seen the lack of confidence, the anxiety, or pain. Aaron's fingers roamed along her arms, clammy and clutching, and she tried to pull away. He was too strong, though, and leaned forward to lock eyes.

"Don't you get it? Being with you, having you with me in Texas and then wherever . . . I would always be reminded of that failure. I'd never be able to escape it. Seeing you would remind me of your dad and of the mess I'd left behind. I'd resent you for it, just like you might resent me for leaving."

Deena felt numb. She felt dead and betrayed. "I don't resent you, Aaron. I think you're a fucking *coward*."

He let her go and stepped back, wrapping both arms around his body. "Well, at least we agree on something, then."

They stood there for a moment, listening to a clock tick the minutes away somewhere in the apartment. It was his bedroom clock—she knew it well, picturing it on the left nightstand next to where she normally slept. Deena knew every inch of Aaron's apartment. The contents of his drawers, the nuances of every nook and cranny. She'd helped him decorate it when he'd moved in, and she'd always hoped to help him pack after locating a place large enough to call their own.

But he'd found one without her. And now she had to say good-bye. "Fuck *that*," she swore aloud, spitting it with venom across the tiny kitchen. "And fuck *you*, Officer Boucher."

Deena slammed the door as she headed out into the cold Georgian night. The city was quiet now, the wars and battles long having been extinguished. But the city was still broken. A murderer lurked somewhere in the moonlight. The last good cop in Atlanta was pulling up stakes and heading west while his former colleagues—crooks and criminals—scavenged among the ashes. Deena's family was shattered, too, Mom having gone and Waldo a complete disgrace. Deena was fractured, as well, both in her heart and soul. Her two role models, the men who had charted the course of Deena's life, had let her down. They'd perverted and pissed on everything she'd ever believed in. The entirety of her very essence had amounted to nothing in the long run. And so, just as they'd abandoned her, Deena walked out on them both, adrift and alone, without their influence for the first time in her life.

She was broken, sure—wounded and angry, and not for the last time in her life. But despite the pain, she took comfort in one small fact: the steps she took after leaving Aaron's apartment—those first, fateful steps into the cold December night, possibly deeper into sorrow and pain—would at least be Deena's own.

# 14

~~

**December. Tuesday morning. 12:53 A.M.**

Walker flipped the channel.

"—*vigils around the globe, wherein somber orators have draped themselves in blue and crimson and regaled gathered mourners with tales of derring-do and patriotism the like that hasn't been seen for over a decade. Wreaths, tacked to the walls of the police station, painted to match the costumes, are interwoven with handwritten notes—gestures and farewells, perhaps, or simple thank-yous to the man who once epitomized—*"

He flipped again, jabbing the remote with an ink-stained finger. This time, Walker landed on a group debate.

"—*so despite the communal uproar, and ignoring the widespread call for some kind of public service, we enter the second day of what's been referred to as 'CitizenWatch.' I, for one, ask the forum: What is Captain Emile Cross playing at here?*"

"*Oh, agreed, Lynette. And I want to take a moment and point out your choice of words—'playing'—because, as with most matters pertaining to Powers authority via local civic authorities, it truly presents itself as some sick game of cat-and-mouse.*"

"*You mean between Cross and the district attorney, Melvin, or Cross and—*"

"*And the public, Mike. The public. I mean, it possibly goes even deeper, beneath Cross and into something seedier. Are you aware, for instance, that the PHD*" *employs no fewer than six—count that, six—former Powers on staff? And of those formerly gifted . . . and really, Lynette, who's to say they no longer* have *those gifts?"*

"Who, indeed?"

*"But I digress. Of those six, no less than two have direct ties to the Cit—"*

Jab. Flipped a third time. To a commercial, at least. Walker reached for a bottle of Infinity and settled back into his lumpy, poorly stuffed couch. A modestly choreographed seduction played out on his television set—leading, no doubt, to a titillating climax that would be used to hawk perfume, jeans, or perhaps a car. He tuned it out, still listening to the phantom debate trail slanderous accusations in his ear. He swallowed. Walker couldn't sleep. But that was hardly new. He'd been having trouble sleeping, off and on, since Chicago.

The commercial had long moved on (it had tried to sell him on a new kind of sandwich, actually), and now a yammering late-night host in a fashionable suit spewed jokes about local politics, the upcoming holiday, and— of course—the death of the Citizen Soldier. Walker tuned that out, too. He'd mastered that trick over the years, only taking in what he felt important to the matter at hand. It was a valuable skill, one that made him an exceptional detective. Unfortunately, it had made him a lousy superhero.

A good hero, Walker knew, not only focused on the pressing case but also the interconnected multitude of emotional repercussions and possible aftershocks emanating out from whichever decision he or she happened to make. A good hero, he mused while lounging in the common space of his two-bedroom apartment, kept tabs on every facet of every scenario, inspecting all sides before making the right choice. Zora had been excellent at that kind of thing, as had Retro Girl. They both had innate sensitivities for the way their actions—or reactions—would affect people and places that were around them. Triphammer, on the other hand, while having a firm grasp on the inner workings of the most intrinsic and detailed micromachinery, mastering atoms and nanites down to their core molecular structure . . . Harley, Walker had to admit, barely noticed anyone or anything that didn't directly connect to his goal of making the world a better—more powerful— place.

And Walker? He'd landed somewhere in the middle. He always hoped that he was like Zora, empathetic by nature and blessed with the ability to say or do the right thing. But the truth of the matter was that he was more like Harley. Long years spent compartmentalizing his life, gravely understanding that he'd soldier on after everyone else would be dust in the ground, had made Walker cold. He'd worn a mask for that very purpose—not to protect his identity from the public, because when you got down to it, whom was he really protecting? No, Walker had worn a mask because it was easier that way. He didn't have to form personal attachments—Blue Streak, Diamond . . . they'd both been easy deflections from letting anyone get close. No one really knew who he was, no one really cared. And those who did—those who got close—well, that had only proved his point. Anyone who knew that Diamond had been Christian Walker—before Deena had outed him, of course—was now dead. And the joke, the ultimate joke here was that "Christian Walker" himself had been a disguise. Just another name and face he wore to protect his true self from those around him.

Of course, that hadn't worked, either.

Walker finished the beer. He snapped off the TV, plunging the apartment into darkness, and halfheartedly thumbed through the files on his coffee table. But he couldn't focus. He was too busy thinking about Deena, thinking about what she'd said back at the hospital. She was right, of course. She was absolutely right. He'd spent so many days trying to escape the past . . . so much time going *forward,* that he sometimes forgot the need to embrace where he'd been. *That happens when you're immortal, of course. Looking back can be painful. You can't see past the bodies that have dropped in your wake. And there have been plenty of bodies.*

But here was Deena—and come on, that girl had been through hell and gone—attempting to reconnect with the one good thing in her admittedly shitty past. *And what did I do? I pissed all over it. I forget that she isn't always going to be here. I forget that she hasn't always been. I spend so much time fleeing history and forging onward that I forget to face the present.* What he'd said about Boucher . . . Walker didn't know if it was true. He hoped it wasn't. Sure, Boucher was an asshole, but even he deserved a slice of happiness. As did Deena and that poor kid lying in a hospital bed. Hell, if Walker really stopped to think about it, so did he. But that didn't look goddamn likely.

*I'm too busy wallowing in guilt and a sea of terrible memories.*

He abandoned his caseload and wandered the small apartment, trailing a hand over furniture and photographs. He'd hung an abstract near the kitchen a few weeks back, and he absentmindedly wiped the frame for dust. Straightening up, padding around in his bare feet, Walker forced Deena's anger and contempt from his thoughts. He busied himself in the kitchen, washing utensils in the sink as he arranged the day's events, shelving facts in his mind like so many wayward forks and knives. The more Walker concentrated on detective work, the more Deena's flashing eyes swam into view. She'd verbally slapped him, dismissing him as she'd stormed off to Corbin Kirk's bedside.

*You left,* she'd said. *That's how you deal with horrible shit when the chips are down? Since when has that been us?*

Walker set a spoon down on the counter and hung his head. He took a breath and closed his eyes, allowing the torrent of words to wash over him once again.

*If you're worried my past is getting in the way of my judgment, then get out of the way. You deal with your shit. I'll deal with mine.*

*My shit,* he grimaced.

*Since when has that been us?*

Since when. Hell, since longer than Walker could remember. *Walker. It's in my goddamn name, Deena.*

And finally, after decades—no, *centuries* of soldiering on, of plodding forward without a backward glance, it had caught him by the throat. Hell, it had been coming for a while now. Ever since Zora had died, to be fair. Ever since he'd let her die. Since he hadn't been there to save her life.

The bullshit had finally kept pace; the masks were now gone, his past had surpassed his meager stride, and Walker now had to tackle a flood of hard truths and indelicate indiscretions. Worse than all that, though: he finally had to deal with the *guilt.*

Joe was dead, and the world knew the man's secret. Soon, of course, they'd know them all. What that meant for Walker, who could say? The digital age—the information age—had a way of plucking carefully crafted fabrications apart at the seams and then vomiting on the remains with a glut of hateful insinuations, prejudices, and half-truths. Quite possibly, an elite handful of itinerant hackers already knew it all, biding patiently until the time was right to drop it on the public. Walker himself already knew more than he ever had. Joe had been his friend, sure, and they'd worked together on a number of campaigns. But it was clear now that Joe and the APHD had been in secret cahoots—something Walker *hadn't* known. That was a fact that had been kept out of the papers when Waldo Pilgrim and the other cops had gone down years before. Worse, Joe had been covertly involved in mucking up the Liberty investigation by muddying the waters with fabricated murders, murders that had been used for personal, vindictive reasons. Walker knew that Joe had changed at some point—he'd made that point quite clear in Atlanta and had implied it in Detroit years earlier. But Walker hadn't known the Soldier had condoned cold-blooded murder, especially for purposes of revenge. That was something in which Walker would have taken no part. And he never would have suspected the Human Front or Malachi Crane's involvement. That seemed so far out of left field that Walker couldn't as yet process the information. But then, judging by Joe's arms, what Walker knew about the Soldier was so far out of left field that he was possibly stranded somewhere on the first base line.

Walker felt guilty, sure—guilty for not having known, for not having disassociated at the time. But more so angry with Joe for not having painted an entire picture, for having been deceived by one of his oldest, closest colleagues and gotten in bed—even by means of subterfuge—with the same organization that had engendered so many deaths, so much hate. A group that not only stood for everything that was intolerable and repellent to Christian Walker (and Blue Streak and Diamond and Gora) but also inspired those who had misused the mission of the Human Front, repurposing it into a slogan of their own and killing not only a plethora of innocent cops and bystanders but also one of the brightest stars that had ever flown in the sky.

*Retro Girl. That, too, is on me.*

Walker had turned a blind eye, too selfish and caught up in his personal struggles—with Wolfe, with Royale and all the others who'd blocked his interminable, plodding path—and the remorse and sorrow fell squarely on his own broad, slumped shoulders. *I am responsible for what happened to the Citizen Soldier. I am culpable, and what do I do—run? Stick my head in the sand?*

*No, this is on me as much as it is on Joe or Crane or Deena's father or even who-*
*ever is wearing Liberty's mantle. This is my burden—I was there back then, and I*
*did nothing. I am here now and am being forced to do the same. Deena is right.*
*She's right, and maybe so is Boucher. The Powers were as crooked as the villains*
*we fought—and those who weren't should have known better. We should have*
*been the role models we purported to be and not got caught up in the trappings,*
*the perks and packages of being masks and heroes.*

*We are worthy of Boucher's disdain and his commission. We are worthy of*
*Deena's rebuke, her ire and insult. We should have known better. We should have*
*asked.*

Drifting back toward the couch, snapping on the television, Walker continued flipping the channels while wallowing deeper into memories and
remorse. He idly watched the media waffle between equals part tribute and
condemnation of a man the world thought a hero, but the man formerly
known as Diamond and Blue Streak worried might possibly be a traitor.

And as he worried, sitting in the dark with another beer in his hand,
Christian Walker wondered if the same might be said about him.

# 15

—⁓—

*"Too hot for you?" Joe asked Walker, nursing their drinks at the long, mirrored bar. "Maybe you're in the wrong goddamn business." They laughed and turned their attention to the girls, naked bodies writhing across a glistening stage as flashes of hammering gunfire winked outside the only window. The streets burned, riots flared, and people died, but here in the Shaft, the golden gods lived.*

*Detroit had always been billed as a city with more going for it than any other major city in the North. A powder keg of politics and racial divides, stoked by the Vietnam conflict and a growing black voice from the South, Detroit had long been primed to blow. The city's first major league baseball pennant in a while and the burgeoning scene buzzing about Motown's Hitsville, USA, had turned D-troit into the place to be for ambitious folk who hoped for something better. To the north of the city, automobiles thundered off the factory lines, offering work to those willing to put in the elbow grease and security to those looking to settle down. On Twelfth Street, however, in the summer of 1967, the residents of Motown were burning their city to the ground.*

*Walker smiled—he was glad he'd abandoned the full-face mask long ago, adopting a simple domino so that he could drink without interference. He turned to Joe—a vision in primary colors and draped in American finery, every inch the poster boy who'd raced through enemy lines in Seoul and Inchon. Walker raised his drink in salute to his friend. "Plenty hot, sir. But from where I sit, business is good." It was the fourth day of the riots, and both Blue Streak and the Citizen Soldier were supposed to be leading a vanguard against the disobedient mob.*

"Hey, Walker. You still with us?"

Blinking, Christian looked up from his shoes into the dancing, steely-blue eyes of Joseph Monroe. For a second, Walker had to remember where he was—moments ago, he'd been stealing drinks in the safety of the Golden Shaft, a Powers titty bar off Woodward on Detroit's West Side. Joe had been there too. He'd been masked, as had Walker. But it had been a different mask, a different party. He shook the cobwebs from his mind and focused his attention on the circle of laughing, drinking, celebrating friends.

"Yeah. Yeah, I just got lost for a year, is all."

Joe snickered and slapped him on the back. "Well, if it's next year, make sure to tell me who won the Super Bowl. I'd wanna bet it all."

The group broke into sycophantic laughter and drifted back into the dining area—Joe had rented the top floor of Parker/Cooper, one of Atlanta's finest and most expensive Argentinean steakhouses. Beer and booze, cigars and beautiful women filled the room as a handful of the city's top cops and federally affiliated Powers toasted the health of one Joseph Monroe, also known as the Citizen Soldier. Joe was currently attired in a lightweight suit and open-throated white shirt, around which the aging hero wore a ridiculous blue tie riddled with adorable yellow ducks.

The birthday boy grinned and took a puff on his Cohiba. "Seriously, you didn't have to do this, man," he said to Walker. The Soldier slid two fingers down the tie, testing the material, letting it slip through his fingers. "Really. It was unnecessary."

Walker smiled and stuck his own Monte Cristo between his lips. He took a drag, enjoying the corona of ash flaming at the cigar's tip, and then exhaled a cloud of smoke. "I know," he parried back at his friend. "That's why it's such a great gift. You have no use for that tie."

"That I do not."

"Same thing goes for the condoms. I mean, Magnum size? Come on."

"True," the Soldier returned. "Too small."

Walker ashed his cigar. "Ha. Screw you, man. And happy fucking birthday." They shared a brief, brotherly hug, and then the Soldier ventured out into the crowd, welcomed into a grasping, shouting throng of hangers-on and well-wishers. Walker reached for a drink—a gin and tonic from the bar—and then leaned against a lonely wall, idly staring out a window onto the city below. Flashes of light, pulsing beacons littered the skyline. He stared down from thirty stories above the street, noting it less interesting than when he soared even higher and stared down from fifty.

Something exploded. Windows rattled, and the building shook, but the party never stopped. Joe barely noticed, too engrossed in the festivities to care. But then, that was his general attitude these days. As it was for most of the Powers—and, to be honest, the cops—in Atlanta.

*But from where I sit,* Diamond mused, feeling ash and regret at the back of his throat, *business is good.* He set his drink aside. He'd been on assignment in Atlanta for over a month now, asked here by the Soldier and his government handlers. He really hadn't considered making the trip until Zora had encouraged him to go. Triphammer was here, as were Olympia and Z, so at least he didn't feel like an outsider. And this obviously wasn't Walker's first time working with the Soldier, a man he'd known since the Korean War. *A lifetime ago,* he realized. His head began to pound. *Back when we were both very different men.*

He folded his arms and turned to the window, giving his full attention to the firefight taking place between shuddering skyscrapers. A handful of weaponized gangsters had engaged several police copters and an independent team of criminal Powers. Unfortunately, the Powers had underestimated the number of technologically advanced mafioso filling the air and hadn't seen a contracted ion-powered thug floating in their midst until it was too late. The thug charged his fists with electricity, and before Walker could make a move or open the window, a piercing flash of light bathed the city, enveloping it in radioactive sunlight despite the weather and time of night. The partygoers in the steakhouse shaded their eyes and glanced outside, but when darkness returned and only the thug was left standing, they shrugged and went back to their meal. Walker placed his hand against the window, feeling heat, now fading, left behind by the explosive discharge.

He watched as the Power swiveled around, reveling in victory and destruction, and then soared away and into the distance.

*Why didn't I do anything?* Walker wondered. *What is* wrong *with me, with us? They brought us here to rein in the violence, but the cops and feds don't seem too eager to end the gang war. And Joe . . . I get that it's his birthday, but he seems like he just can't be bothered anymore. Which, I suppose, it about par for our last encounter.*

He returned his attention to his party, noting the way Joe circled the room like a shark, drawing minnows into a deadly, charming wake. The Soldier showed not one iota of concern about what had just transpired outside the window. And this was Walker's team leader, the man who gave the orders. If he didn't give a shit, why should any of the rest of them? Why should Walker, for that matter?

*Why do I care? They're criminals. Let them tear each other apart.*

Was that how he felt? Walker hadn't been this way ten years ago, even five. And he definitely hadn't back in '67, the first time he'd truly partnered with Joseph Monroe.

*Joe had been detached back then, as well. That's why we were in the Shaft that night. That's why we'd been drinking our troubles, ignoring the Guard and riot gear and mobs of anti-Powers radicals filling the streets with fire, crowbars, and blood.* Sometime around the second or third day of the Detroit Powers Riots, Joe had shouldered his shield and dragged Walker to a bar. And though he'd racked up an impressive list of victories in his time, something about the Soldier's demeanor forced Walker to defer to the elder statesman. And so, despite the chaos outside, Walker—as Blue Streak, still, before he'd once again swapped identities—straddled the nearest stool alongside the thirsty, grinning legend. Joe had ordered a row of gins and tequilas, encouraging Walker to match him drink for drink as Crane and the Human Front jackbooted their way down Grand Street. Joe showed little interest in returning to contain the civil disobedience—in fact, after their last shared drink in the Shaft, they'd argued long and loud. Walker, as Blue Streak, had wanted to continue assisting the National Guard. Joe, meanwhile, desired another round.

*He'd blamed fatigue,* Walker recalled as he turned down a passing plate of hors d'oeuvres. *I understood. I mean, the guy had been fighting every sort of insurgent since 1951.* Hell, if anyone could understand exhaustion following a long, protracted period of time, brought on by never-ending conflict, it would be Christian Walker. That's why he'd gravitated toward Joe Monroe in the first place. That's what drew Walker to the old soldier, and he imagined Zora, as well.

But when the two heroes stepped out of the Shaft, slightly inebriated and after a fruitless argument about principles and duty . . . when they returned to the smoldering streets of Detroit, Walker hadn't been prepared for Joe's changed attitude toward saving the innocent.

*Joe grabbed Walker's arm and spun him around. Several dancers had followed them out of the Shaft, tits bouncing in the wind, hoping the broad-shouldered man who'd thrown hundreds around like candy might return to the comfort and decadence of the club. But Walker was already fixing his skewed mask, and Joe's face was florid and purple. They faced one another, there on the empty street. A phalanx of cops lined the avenue, backs to the bar, guns raised and pointed toward an oncoming crowd of looting, rioting Detroiters.*

*"Hey!" Joe yelled, drunk and belligerent. "Where do you think you're going?"*

*"To do my job while I still can." Walker tugged Blue Streak's mask into place and then started off across the street to join the cops. Joe followed, too inebriated to remember his mask was down and askew.*

*"Oh no you don't. Your job is finished. So is mine. So is theirs."*

*Walker scowled at his friend. "What are you talking about?"*

*Joe jabbed a finger at the approaching mob. "They won, Walker. Don't you fucking get it? This is what the world wants now. Not us—not someone willing to protect their city in order to make it a better place. Oh, no. They want someone willing to burn it down instead."*

*Walker dismissed the old soldier with a thick, gloved hand. "Come on, you're drunk. This is about something completely different."*

*"Is it, man? Because I've been doing this a long while now—"*

*"As have I."*

*"And far as I can see? No one wants or appreciates my help. They'd rather throw in with guys like Crane or any of the other fanatics with a penchant for tearing down the Establishment. Any why shouldn't they? Look around, Walker."*

*Joe held out his arms, gesturing as if to take in the city, the nation—hell, maybe* even the whole damn world. "It isn't as if the Establishment is willing to negotiate peaceably. It isn't as if they're willing to help. Because if they were, big guy? They'd be walking the streets handing out jobs, not bullets. They'd be turning their Powers into teachers, not weapons. And they sure as shit wouldn't be standing here watching people die. Lord knows I don't want to do that anymore."

Walker held out a hand. "Then why wait? Let's do all of that. Let's start by stopping any more death here today."

Joe closed his eyes and placed both hands on his hips. He took a deep breath, sighed, and faced the sky. "I'm just tired, Walker. It never works. There's always going to be another Crane or Wolfe or god knows. And the powers that be—my bosses, your boss—aren't going to negotiate to stop the bloodshed. I'm just exhausted, man. It didn't happen in Korea. It didn't happen before in Europe and Japan. And it sure as shit isn't going to happen in Detroit—on our home soil, for fuck's sake, where we should be offering flags instead of rifles. Where we should be looking for solutions, not furthering the bloodshed."

Some of the cops were listening to Joe now, ignoring the rioters as they hesitated, rifles unsteady and unsure. The dancers and a handful of barflies hung on every word, ignoring their revels for the moment. Joe had an audience. Everything hinged on what happened next. But before the heroes could make peace between the authorities and the anguished, a shot rang out from Blue Streak's right. Nervous, one of the policemen had accidentally fired into the approaching crowd. A body fell, and the wave of screaming, indignant civilians surged forward, waving bats and weapons. Walker hustled over to help, doing his best to separate combatants without further bodily harm. Joe, meanwhile, just stood there and seethed.

"Come on!" Blue Streak shouted, indicating the violence spreading out in front of the Golden Shaft. "Soldier—help us! Get over here!"

But Joe never looked up. He turned his back on Walker and the rioters, heading east and away from the deadly altercation. One of the militants among the crowd of rabble-rousers—an oafish thug, adorned with the colors of both the Human Front and the Black Panther movement—lunged for several of the Shaft's entertainers. They squealed, and Walker leaped to stop him. The man was inches away from the Soldier's iron grasp, but Joe simply kept walking. Step by step, leaving the fight. He could have stopped the mammoth bigot with a single blow, done something to turn the tide, but instead, he allowed the man to escape when

*Walker couldn't reach him. Joe ignored more than four, if not six members of the Human Front who raced around the tumult, heading deeper into the city and toward the waterfront, running free to spread the violence.*

The pleasant scent of grilled meats brought Diamond back to reality, wafting from the kitchen as the food arrived. Tears stung both eyes, and he rubbed them away. He desperately needed a drink and wondered how he might escape the festivities without offending the guests or, more importantly, his host.

But then, his host hadn't had a problem leaving Walker to his own devices back in Detroit. He'd walked away without a backward glance, doing his country—and its people—a grave disservice by abandoning the field of battle, allowing the riots to continue for two more days without his valuable help. The Citizen Soldier disappeared after that fateful day in 1967, not to be seen again until 1972, during the height of the Vietnam War. Walker himself didn't see his friend until the mid-eighties, around the time he was sleeping with both Zora and Retro Girl, getting ready to set the world on fire by partnering with Triphammer and several others. The feds hushed up Joe's AWOL status—or, at least, it had never become an issue. He was here, wasn't he? And they'd stuck a patsy into his blue-and-red union suit for photo ops, press purposes, and benefits all throughout the rest of the sixties and the start of the war.

But the Soldier who'd returned from 'Nam in 1975 was a much different person from the one who'd inspired a generation in the forties, fifties, and start of the sixties. He'd changed; he'd stopped caring, stopped accepting the weight of his responsibilities. That attitude radiated out to all who allied with the Citizen Soldier throughout the latter half of the century, ever since he caught the last copter back from Laos.

Walker accepted a drink from a passing waiter. He didn't even know what it was—he smelled it, noting the earthiness of bourbon or scotch. He drained it in a swallow, finding himself close to the whirlwind of laughter, Powers, food, and drink. The whiskey was strong, and he reached for another as soon as he could. He hoped to dull his senses, making it easier to ignore the rattle in the windows and sounds of combat filtering in from outside. *I wonder,* he thought, *if this is how Joe does it. If this is how he turns off his*

*sense of duty, his understanding that terrible things are happening around him,*
*but that rushing to the rescue won't matter at all.*

It hadn't mattered in Detroit, where the city burned for five days before
the National Guard had ground the anti-Powers movement to a halt. It hadn't
mattered in Korea before that, and it hadn't in Vietnam a few years later. It
hadn't mattered in the Gulf, or to the victims of the so-called Liberty killer
these past few weeks. Their duty, the responsibility that Walker wanted to
wear like a badge, made little difference to the people who died on the streets
or in the air. The men and women he couldn't save. At the end of the day,
Powers or not, what difference did it make whether Walker was a Power or
cop if neither one nor the other could stop a handful of bigots with ion par-
ticle disruptors from killing each other in the streets? *Better to stay inside and*
*drink. Better to ignore that hollow, horrible, guilty feeling in my gut.*

Walker had reached the tables now, where meats and cheeses were arranged in an enticing buffet. He had a scotch in his hand—his third, perhaps?
He'd grabbed it automatically, by force of habit. Joe sat nearby, entertaining
a circle of admiring Powers with what seemed to be a fascinating, thrilling,
raunchy story. He caught Walker's eye and then beckoned for Diamond to
join the party.

Standing outside the circle, watching his colleagues file in for dinner with
a gaggle of mistresses and cops, Walker wondered what had happened to
the world-famous Citizen Soldier between '67 and '72. He wondered what
had occurred before that day in Detroit, and why Joe had been so emotionally affected, and where his good friend's head was now. For that matter,
Walker wondered—flashing on the riots, thinking about the fires outside and
a state of emergency in Atlanta that reminded him so much of Detroit—
where his own head was, as well.

He finished his drink and discarded the glass. Then he plastered a smile
on his face and headed over to toast his friend.

# *16*

—*uu*—

*December. Tuesday morning. 9:17 A.M.*

They loaded her into a truck. It wasn't much larger than an SUV. He watched them from afar, positioning a telephoto lens through the passenger-side door. His car—nondescript, beige, and badly needing a paint job—lingered on the far end of the avenue, blocked from view by the crowd. The mourners had packed the streets in front of the precinct with camping chairs and pup tents, encircled around podiums and shrines riddled with flowers, photographs, posters, and candles. Blockades of news vans and assorted media helped his car blend in; a phalanx of network reporters kept situating themselves in front of the clunker, obscuring it from any particular line of sight. He didn't worry, though. They wouldn't get in his way; he wasn't watching the precinct.

He observed, instead, the impound lot across the street.

Several cops had escorted the prisoner through an unmarked service entrance—freight or laundry, the man couldn't be sure—and kept her inside a circle of plainclothes detectives as they casually strolled toward the lot. He recognized one or two—from television, perhaps, the news over the past few days. To be honest, he didn't know the cops in this city as well as he'd like. But he hadn't been in town long enough to match faces to names as of yet. Perhaps in due time, should the need arise. He doubted it would.

The work was nearly done, and in a handful of days, he planned to disappear as chaos and scandal swirled around the murders. Just as he had ten years earlier.

He looked back at the lot. They'd secured the doors to the truck and were preparing to leave. He started up his car, twisting the ignition, and both gawkers and mourners glanced his way. He waved them aside, silently asking them to let him through. They shrugged and stepped away, barely giving the man a second glance. Why would they? He wasn't wearing the hood. As far as they knew, Liberty was just another yutz with a POS car.

The truck slid out of the lot and turned left, and Liberty followed, carefully driving through the snow. They wove in and out of traffic. The cops weren't speeding but were clearly determined to finish their trip as quickly as possible. *The Shelf,* he thought, *or another appropriate, nearby prison. No matter; they won't reach it, whatever the destination.*

The truck turned into a warehouse district, and Liberty followed, gunning the engine and making his move. Carefully, trying not to attract their attention, Liberty inched up and drove alongside the truck. He casually surveyed the driver and noted a second policeman in the passenger seat. *I wonder if that's all. I'd been looking away, so I didn't see whether any guards had joined her in the back. I suppose I'll have to be surprised. Won't that be thrilling?*

Liberty accelerated again, easing his car in front of the truck, essentially cutting it off while careful not to skid. He wasn't driving that fast, but the driver of the truck felt the need to pass. The unmarked truck swerved to the left, and the driver pressed the pedal. Liberty smiled and jerked left himself and then back to the right and gave it some gas. He did what he could to make sure the truck couldn't go around. The policeman tapped his horn, offering Liberty a gentle warning. He nodded and waved in response and then sped up, giving the truck a bit of room. The policeman gave up and slid the truck back behind Liberty's sedan, and after several blocks, it seemed the chase had ended. *Pity,* he thought. *I rarely get into car chases, no matter how small. Anyway, time is wasting.* He reached out and stabbed the glove compartment. There, embedded into the metal, sat a trio of custom controls, each with its own purpose. *This is what TV secret agents must feel like,* Liberty thought. *Eeny meeney miney . . .* He slammed down on the first, flat, green button.

A trail of gas seeped out of the car's exhaust, lifted by the wind and fanned toward the front of the police truck. To an outside observer, it might have seemed like another busted piece of an already deteriorating automobile had given way to age and mechanics. But the vapor was no simple emission—it was gaseous acid, toxic and concentrated, and it swiftly ate through the truck's hood, bumper, and windshield. The policemen noticed something was up and slammed on the brakes. Liberty came to a stop, as well, and twisted a second button—a red one, rotating like a radio dial. It opened a hatch in the trunk. The dial adjusted the rate at which the sedan ejected a trunkload of volatile shrapnel.

Fragments of metal, wire, and glass impacted the truck's windshield, shattering it inward and embedding itself into the throats, skulls, and chests of the cops. Liberty's potent extra-strength acid had weakened the custom-fitted titanium-alloy chassis, as well as the fibrous-enhanced friction-resistant windshield with which the truck had been fitted. The policemen slumped against the dashboard, and another two leaped out of the back. Liberty exited his car and lifted a long-range silencer out of his pocket. One shot quickly dispatched the cop on the right; the second dove out of view, behind the truck. He opened fire, and Liberty was forced to hide, sliding back inside his car.

*No doubt at this point the lone gunman has radioed for backup. This is the third time I've had to act fast before the police arrive. I'm getting old, too, like Monroe.*

He reached across and smacked a hand on the final button. This one employed no subtleties; it was clearly made for launching rockets.

A single torpedo emerged from the trunk, blasting the door from his car and setting it ablaze. The rocket hit the truck and lit it up like a candle, sending it off its wheels and forcing it back several feet. The second policeman stopped shooting. Liberty quickly stepped out of the car and strode to the rear of the truck. The remaining cop was dying, gasping on the floor, badly burned and bleeding like a stuck pig. *You should have run,* Liberty regretfully expressed with sorrowful eyes. *I would have let you go.*

Then he shot the cop twice in the chest.

Liberty stepped over the body and swung wide the rear doors. Wilhelmina Quince sat cowering in the corner. She was bleeding—a mess of burns and wounds, groaning with pain. But she was alive. He beckoned for her to exit the truck. "Quickly now," he grunted, "before this thing explodes."

Head bouncing like an agreeable maniac, she scrambled out of the truck. They hurried down the street, away from the burning vehicles. Liberty took Quince by the collar, dragging her forward. He glanced at a street sign. They were on Avenue F and Bernardin. *No, this won't do,* he realized. *We're one block too far.*

"Come on," he whispered to Wilhelmina. "We're going for a walk. It'll do you a world of good."

And off they went down Bernardin, stumbling one block north.

Shortly, drawn by the noise, a lone patrol car rolled up beside the blackened husks of both the beat-up sedan and the once-formidable police truck. Lights bathed the scene, shimmering against pools of blood and reflecting against the snow and the billowing smoke. The front door opened, and a detective emerged. She was tall and lean, dressed in fashionable leather that seemed warm enough despite appearances, a ribbon of faux-fur trim circling her collar. She wore gloves but no hat; short hair severely pulled back, she surveyed the scene with an observant, comfortable gaze. The newcomer sighed, tugging at her jacket, and then she reached into the cruiser to retrieve its radio.

"Dispatch, this is 1-Peter-21 answering a distress call on the old inner harbor. Bernardin and F, north side. Two vehicles, abandoned, officers down and out."

A voice crackled back. "How many officers, Detective Sunrise?"

Enki Sunrise glanced around, creeping unease setting into her bones. She lifted the radio. "Two, Dispatch, maybe three. Front of the truck may hold more answers, but I've yet to approach. Waiting to clear the area."

"Do you require additional backup, 1-Peter-21?"

Enki nodded to herself, wishing she hadn't abandoned her other assignment as quickly as she did. But she'd known this route meant a prisoner transfer related to Deena's case, and she'd been close by. No one else would have gotten there in time to save Quince's life. But as far as Detective Sunrise could tell, looking around, she was too late. Enki was the only person here. The only person alive, anyway.

"Negative, Dispatch," she replied. "No additional backup necessary."

"You sure, Enki? Everything okay?"

She sat back in the cruiser, the wind having been knocked out of her from the sight of the dead men and smoking vehicles. "Not at all, Dispatch. No backup required . . . but I will need a shit ton of body bags."

# *17*

~~~

**December. Tuesday morning. 10:48 A.M.**

Deena mounted the steps, ignoring the smell of day-old marinara and an
assortment of cleaning supplies. Aaron followed, climbing one step at a time
to her two. The staircase was drafty, and she thanked her lucky stars that
Waldo lived on the third floor of a six-floor walkup. Neighbors peered into
the hall—elderly retirees, shut-ins, and grandparents whose family never
came. Deena could understand why; if she didn't have a murder to solve,
and Waldo hadn't been an important piece of the puzzle, the last place she'd
be found was in this building, visiting family.

They'd taken the first flight out, ejecting a couple from Cleveland who'd
been happily diverted to first-class seats on another plane. Aaron had fidgeted the entire way, grumbling beneath his breath and then fitfully snatching
an hour of sleep. Deena, for the most part, had flown in relative peace. A
tall coffee and a cell phone packed with files had kept her company. But his
constant shuffling had eventually gotten to her nerves, and so she'd
swapped seats with a kid she'd convinced that Aaron was a rock star. Deena
had felt bad about that, but truthfully, she needed time to herself. Aaron felt
this was an unnecessary trip, one that could have been solved with a phone
call—and the captain had agreed. But Aaron had insisted on coming when
she'd refused to back down, explaining that she wanted to look her father

in the eyes, force him to finally tell the truth. So here they were: flying south to brace him in person, a man she hadn't spoken to in over ten years. A stranger, though connected by blood, whom Deena was fully prepared to arrest and be done with.

They reached the third-floor landing, and Deena looked over her shoulder at Aaron, who brought up the rear. *He's more nervous than I am. He's afraid that he might punch dear old Dad. Honestly? I might, as well. But I'll at least have the decency to hear him out first. Putting these guys in a room together after all this time? There may be nothing left of my father to hear.*

Not that time and circumstance hadn't already taken their toll. The apartment building . . . *let's call it what it is,* Deena thought. *Six stories of dementia and decay.* She knew that he had fallen on hard times. Waldo still had the old house, the one in Tuxedo Park. But he couldn't afford to live there anymore—not on the money he made working security or guarding banks or whatever it was he was doing now. The old place, her home, was rented. Waldo used the money to subsidize a few places. A modest condo in Miami; a loft in Chicago, which had unfortunately been obliterated; and, apparently, this shit box situated north of Atlanta, miles from what might be considered a decent neighborhood. After all this time, Deena wasn't sure whom she might find behind the door. She didn't really care; all she wanted was answers. All Deena needed was to shine a light onto the past.

She raised a fist, about to knock, but Aaron gingerly took her wrist.

"You sure you want to do this?"

She smiled and sighed. "I'd rather do it alone."

He smirked and caressed her hand. "And deny me the chance to see how far Lucifer has fallen? Come on. I deserve little else, but I deserve that."

He released her, and she knocked. The door across the way cracked open, holiday decorations drooping from where they'd been tacked on. A curious septuagenarian peered out through thick-rimmed bifocals. The man wore flannel pajama tops, fuzzy slippers, a deerstalker cap with earflaps, and nothing more. Thankfully, before he engaged, a shuffle arrived at Waldo's door, the tumbler clicked out of place, and Deena found herself facing the only other man she'd ever truly loved.

"Yeah, what do . . . Deena?" He was shorter than she remembered, which was a neat trick, as Deena Pilgrim wasn't much taller herself. He'd allowed a beard to flourish, cultivating it into a thick, majestic drape of hair. Waldo wore khakis and a tee—the kind they called a wifebeater, a fact in which Deena saw a private irony; he'd never actually struck her mother, but his verbal abuse alone warranted the garment's name. He pulled open the door, giving the detectives a clearer view of the apartment's interior. Small, sure, but well appointed and tastefully decorated, decidedly contrasted with the building in which he lived. A small foyer opened into a common area filled out by a sofa, recliner, modest television, and coffee table—the leather kind, the one that looked like an expensive ottoman but could be purchased in any mall. Just beyond, Deena spied a small kitchen. Steam billowed into the hallway; he'd been cooking, preparing lunch when he should have been at work. Perhaps they'd found Waldo between jobs? She wouldn't be surprised. Staying in Atlanta, even with ten years under his belt, hadn't done much to help his reputation. The past lingers, even when you're trying to move on and forget. Deena knew that. She'd been drowning in the past. And every step forward she'd taken over the last two days had only brought her five steps back.

Waldo stepped out of the apartment. His face had brightened once he'd recognized the visitor in his doorway, and something like hope glimmered in his eyes. He awkwardly lunged, attempting to embrace her, but Deena flinched and stepped away. Waldo backed off, holding up his hands as if he'd been expecting that to happen.

"Hey, I get it," he said as if in response to her thoughts. "No offense taken. But it's like a Christmas miracle. Just happy to see you after all this time."

She folded her arms and sniffed, making a point of looking away. "I suppose one of us should be."

Waldo nodded, as if expecting that, too, and shuffled in his doorway. He rested a hand on the brass doorknob. "Heard from your mom?"

"Not in a few months. I'll probably call her over the holidays. Don't worry. She won't say hello."

Waldo pursed his lips and stared at the floor, embarrassed and uncomfortable. He looked up suddenly, and as if remembering his manners, gestured toward the interior of the apartment. "D'you wanna come in? Have a drink?"

Deena stared for a moment and then silently moved past him as if to enter the apartment. He moved aside to let her pass. Only then did he notice that she had an escort. "Oh, I'm sorry. Nice to meet you, I'm . . . and . . ." He'd begun to lift his hand, an automatic gesture of welcome, but slowly reeled it in after finally recognizing the other visitor.

"I might have known," Waldo said, nodding and smiling as if confirming his worst fears. "So you two are still together."

Aaron chuckled, and Deena's face bleached of color from inside the foyer. A flash of annoyance spasmed across her father's face, but Waldo quickly allowed it to pass. "Something funny? I just imagined you were married at this point, a mess of kids who'll never call me Grandpa."

"No, Dad," Deena replied. "I haven't seen Aaron in ten years. Same as you."

"Then why're you here? Ten-year anniversary of the time he ruined my life? Oh, I know. I know what this is. He finally told you, didn't he?"

"Not exactly. Come inside. You too, Aaron. We'll tell you all about it."

They arranged themselves in the common area. Aaron had needed a moment in the hall—a flood of emotion had overcome the special investigator upon seeing his old friend, his worst enemy. Now they sat on the sofa, side-by-side, and Deena wished again that he'd stayed home to manage the captain and handle the press. Twenty-four hours later and Captain Cross was losing his cool; the DA wanted a name, and media relations was worried that with every passing second, the Soldier's guilty secret had a better-than-average chance of getting out. Deena tended to agree; old, forgotten familial wounds had no place in this investigation. She couldn't allow herself to become further distracted by the history shared between the three individuals sitting in the living room. And, if she was honest with herself, Deena had to let go of the niggling guilt she felt over having left both Walker and Kirk at home, close to the action but momentarily sidelined. No, Deena couldn't afford to be deterred . . . but who knew what unstable emotions this unlikely reunion might unearth? If not for her, then for Aaron. If he needed a moment, a minute to deal and move on, by all means: *take the fucking moment,* she thought. Meanwhile, she looked around. No family photos. No holiday decorations. She felt sad for her father, and then angry. *This was his fucking choice,* Deena reminded herself. *He made this happen.*

Then, after Aaron had handled his shit, they sat across from Waldo and readied to dig him a hole.

Unfortunately, he opened his mouth before they could begin.

"You know," Waldo directed at Aaron, "I never blamed you, even after the money ran out and I had to sell the house."

Aaron raised an eyebrow, curious. "Is that right?"

"It's clear that my anger was misplaced. Look, kid—"

"Don't call me that. I'm not your kid."

Waldo held up a palm as if in supplication. "Fair enough. You did your job. I get that. You did what you had to do, and you played the game. I used to do the same, back when I started out—before I had mouths to feed, you know."

Deena sat forward, clasping both hands between her legs. She felt hot and light, embarrassed but also angry. "So all things being equal, Dad, if I hadn't come along—or my brother—if we hadn't been such a . . . a . . . burden, I suppose." *Now* she was pissed; *now* she knew that there *was* no avoiding the distraction. "If you had been carefree and swinging single, you would've been the Eliot fucking Ness of greater Atlanta?"

Waldo melted back into the plush, upholstered recliner and stroked his beard. "Don't put words in my mouth. Who knows *what* the future would have held? All I'm saying is that what *you* did"—waving in Aaron's general direction—"that was the *right* goddamn thing to do for *you*. Even if the end result fucked me. Even if it did make me lonely, broke, and unemployed."

Now Aaron folded his arms across his chest, resting back against the flowered, slightly stained sofa cushions. "Well, you only have yourself to blame, Waldo."

"Come on. And the judge, in the end."

Aaron sputtered and sat forward again, elbowing Deena slightly aside. "*What?* Hey, *fucker*—"

"Yeah, if the two of you hadn't—"

"Shut your *goddamn* mouth. Where do *you* get the *balls*—"

"Hey!" Deena got to her feet and moved between the two men. "This is pointless. You"—at Waldo, a finger directly in his face—"are the same son of a bitch you were when I left. I'm not here because I thought any different about that. I have no delusions about our relationship, and I'm not here

because I'm looking for reconciliation or any of that horseshit. And you"—
Aaron this time, seething on the couch—"promised to let the past be the past,
shitty as it is. When I allowed you to come on this trip, I had you agree to that.
Yes, he broke my trust, broke yours and my mom's. Yes, he's a terrible father
and an even worse excuse for a human being. . . . I mean, he's sitting here at
noon on a Tuesday and clearly doesn't have a job or a girlfriend to occupy his
time." Her father paled at that; she'd hit too close to his tastefully appointed
yet squalid home. "But I am on the clock, and time is running out. I'd rather
not wallow in the shit anymore. So let's do what we came here to do, and
then I can get the fuck out of his sight and the hell out of this city."

Deena stood between Aaron and Waldo, attempting to catch her breath
and forget the memories that filled the room. Her heart hurt, filled with betrayal and pain, and her vision blurred as she looked from one former role
model to the other. Both of these men had shaped Deena's life. The ideas
and principles, which they had espoused before shattering her once-infallible
vision of father and soul mate, had inspired her to be the detective she eventually became. Now, years later, after what seemed like a lifetime of heartbreak and pain, here she was, forced to make sense of a case that should
have stayed dead. Forced to solve a murder with the help of the only men
she'd loved enough to allow this close, the only men she knew who could
cause this much pain.

Well, there was one more. But the less she thought about Walker, the
better.

She turned to Waldo. "I hate you. I have for a long time. I can't see that
changing just because we sat down after ten years of silence. But I do need
your help. I have questions about a recent murder that connects to a series
of murders that took place in Atlanta, many years ago. I'm pretty sure that
only you can provide the answers I need."

Waldo nodded and tapped his fingers on the armrest. "The Soldier.
That's what you're talking about, right? I caught *Powers That Be* before you
showed up, and they—"

"That's right. The Soldier's dead, but so are a few others. And it all ties
into the Liberty murders."

Waldo opened his mouth, but this time no sound emerged. His jaw
sagged, and he stood up. He headed toward the rear of the apartment,

beckoning for his guests to follow him into the kitchen. "Shit. You don't know yet, do you? We'd better eat, then. Sounds like we all could use it."

Rummaging about half-empty cabinets, they were able to stretch lunch from a small pot of soup into three bowls and some salmon tacos. A handful of beers were passed around, but only Waldo judged it close enough to noon to twist a cap. Hunkered around a varnished wooden table, Deena caught her father up on the intricacies of the case, parceling out just enough information—the Soldier's murder, the Rammlers, Liberty, and both Crane's and Quince's testimonials—to clue him in. Aaron detailed the timeline, as well as the forensic reports from both crime scenes to better paint a fuller picture. They finished talking, and all but the beer and one of the tacos were gone. Deena took a drink of water and then settled back in her chair.

"Where were you this weekend, Dad?"

He cocked an eye and crossed his legs, pulling one heel up with a hand. "Seriously?"

"A name, a place. Anything at all?"

"Come on. Am I a suspect here? I haven't seen the Soldier, the Rammlers . . . anyone you mentioned in over ten fucking years."

"Okay. So the weekend?"

Waldo threw back his head, sending hair and beard fluttering, and blew air between his teeth. "Jeez . . . this is so off the map, but *fuck*. Fine. I was working a private job."

Aaron leaned forward. "Got someone who can verify that?"

"I do, but I don't know if you'll believe him."

"Yeah? Why's that?"

Waldo turned Aaron's way, gave him the sharp stink-eye. "Because he ain't bright and shiny, right and wrong like *you* were, *Detective* Boucher." He said the title with a sarcastic sneer, revealing a bit of dear old Dad.

"Hey," Aaron said, rising up and shoving her father. "I said watch how you talk to me, Pilgrim."

Waldo met his eye, pushing back. "Really? After everything, after all that happened and you *still* want my help . . . you come here and manhandle me? Fuck you!" They started grappling at the table, hands at each other's forearms, until Deena pried their hands apart and forced them to sit down.

"Hey! Idiots! We don't have time for this."

Waldo sneered and wiped his nose as he settled back into his seat. He rubbed his arm; Deena could see the friction marks from where Aaron had grabbed it. Everyone took a moment, and then her father rolled his eyes and held out a hand, as if to offer a deal. "It was a dogfight, all right?"

*Jesus,* she thought. "Of course it was. Here in Atlanta?"

"Over by the train yard. Dogs with Power juice to boost the odds. I do it a coupla times throughout the year; private security puts food on the table. Guy who runs it is named—"

Deena held out her hand and closed her eyes. "Leave it out, okay? Too much on my plate as it is to be running down a Powers dog ring right now."

Waldo leaned back and shrugged. *Mea culpa.* "You asked."

Deena edged her chair toward the table. "Tell me about the Liberty killings."

"It's in the papers, or the library. Or fuck, just ask—" He started to wave a hand, but Aaron cut him off.

"No, *your* involvement. Tell us your part in the Liberty murders, Detective Pilgrim."

He glared at Aaron, and Deena knew that the empty title rankled her father. He was gauging whether or not he might hit the other man, and she half hoped that he'd try. The resentment was still there, bubbling beneath the surface, and though Aaron had been gracious enough to let her lead this thing, she'd be happy to let him finish it. One bad move, one wrong word out of either one of their mouths might send this into fisticuffs and patricide. Then Waldo backed down, cleared his throat, and wiped his eyes. She spied tears glistening on his mustache and knew they'd struck a nerve.

"You really came all this way to do this, Deena? You hate me enough to make me relive my failures face-to-face? This couldn't have been done over the phone?"

She smiled sweetly and then leaned in with a predatory leer. "But then I wouldn't have the satisfaction of arresting you in person."

Waldo nodded and cleared his throat again. "What do you want to know?"

"Wilhelmina Quince."

"Wailin' Willie? Crane's girl. The bitch took the bench, put me away with your boyfriend here's help lo, those many years ago."

Aaron cleared his throat. The steam from the soup had made the kitchen dry. "I'm not her boyfriend."

Deena motioned for Aaron to ignore that. "How'd she put you away?"

Waldo slammed a hand on the table, jarring the empty bowls. "Dammit, Deena. You know."

"Humor me, for old times' sake."

He grimaced. "I put her on the street. Quince and a bunch of ugly fuckers back in the day. Me, Jack Owens, Roman Galenti . . . bunch of guys in the division. We put convicted killers and fanatic bigots back in circulation after the judge or some other schmuck had jailed them. In return, they did some jobs for us."

"Like?"

He shrugged. "Muscle. Arson. Mostly killing. And only killing other criminals who were roaming free . . . those the system had trouble keeping behind bars."

Aaron moved in to cross-examine the defeated former detective. "Like Blitzkrieg?"

"Yeah, and a Simon who operated in Atlanta at the time. Few others, small-timers. And, of course, a few of Crane's nearest and dearest."

"One of the Rammler Brothers."

Waldo absently scratched his throat and then placed both hands on the table, digging into its surface with his fingers. He warily glanced at Aaron. "That wasn't us. That was Liberty."

"But *you* were Liberty. Willie claims you had her tag the murders with his motto."

He smiled. "Yeah, that's right. Just a few. To cover it up. But we were only one of what had to be several killers in Atlanta at the time. No way one guy did all those Powers. No way one guy—or girl, don't shoot me—was that tough." He dug at his neck again, scratching harder now. Waldo seemed flush, crimson creeping up behind his ears and from under the wifebeater. Sweat, possibly an after-effect of the soup and beer.

"You okay, Dad?" She squinted, peering at her father.

"Yeah, yeah . . . just indigestion. A little hot."

"Okay, so you confused the Liberty investigation. That alone was enough to put you away. But they never tossed you in prison. That they reserved for Roman and Owens. Why'd you get off?"

Waldo looked at each detective in turn. "Come on, you both know."

They traded glances. If Aaron knew something that she didn't, he'd been keeping her in the dark. Deena's father chuckled, a throaty laugh that sounded as if it came through a pocket of phlegm. "Let's say some of us cops weren't working alone."

"What does that mean?"

"Put it together, kiddo." Waldo paused for a moment to cough. "Yeah . . . I had help from above. Your murder victim, for one."

Deena rubbed her mouth and processed the information. "Wait . . . are you telling me that the Citizen Soldier, Uncle Sam's poster child, was putting convicted felons back on the street? Which ones, exactly?"

"I dunno. All—*enh* . . . excuse me—throat. All kinds. Mostly Human Front, which I'll admit was crazy. *Nnnngh.* 'Scuse. Again, dammit. Yeah, we made deals, ensured loyalties . . . but I figured out he was working for someone else." Her dad smiled at them both.

Aaron's face clouded over, and he glanced at Deena. "And who would that be?"

Waldo smirked and settled back in the chair. "I'll bet you'd like tha—*koff!koff!*—nnnn . . . 'scuse me." He wiped spittle from his mouth. His eyes were bloodshot now, and the flush had reached his cheeks. "Nnnno . . . no, *Detective* Boucher, I'm gonna—*eeeeennnggh . . . koff!kofffkoff!* Gnnnah . . ."

"Dad?" Concerned, Deena rose from her seat and moved next to Waldo. He waved her away, digging at his collar as he struggled to clear his throat. His whole face had turned crimson, and Aaron seemed uneasy, as well. "Dad, take a drink of water."

Waldo held up a hand, palm out, and shook his head. "I'm fine . . . I'm . . . nnnnngccc . . . chhhh*koffkoff* . . . !" Deena's father stumbled to his feet, kicking back his chair while ravaging his neck with both sets of fingers, clawing and digging with all his might. Deena grabbed Waldo's arm, but he threw her off and pitched forward, face-first onto the table. Cutlery and bowls flew into the air, bottles broke, and the remains of the soup spattered onto the walls. The table splintered, legs heading one way and pieces of tabletop the other. Both Deena and Aaron rushed to Waldo's aid. He couldn't breathe, choking on either the tacos or something else. Deena tried the Heimlich maneuver and then began digging into Waldo's throat when that failed, attempting to dislodge whatever blocked his airway as she would a small child.

"Dad!" she screamed, hoping that she hadn't traveled all this way just to watch her father die. Sure, she hated him, but despite any sarcastic fancies of patricide, she had no desire to see him dead. She worked to save him, trying to free the airway, but his face was growing redder by the second.

"Call an ambulance!" she screamed at Aaron, and he scrambled into the living room to grab his phone. He'd left it on the sofa, and so Deena was left alone to keep her father alive. Every moment stretched into forever, and the longer she watched Waldo clutch and plead, the more she wondered what he might be seeing as the oxygen left his brain. Was it Deena, or maybe her mom? The beautiful life he'd thoroughly destroyed? Or was it, perhaps, the one he'd greedily embraced—the crime, the perks of being a famous detective on the take? What, Deena wondered, did her father wish or regret as his only daughter frantically tried to save him, here on the kitchen floor of a shitty apartment in a town he'd once allowed to burn with abandon?

She grabbed Waldo's shirt and lifted him into her arms. "I'm not going to let that happen!" she shouted. His eyes went wide, searching Deena's. Waldo tapped a finger against his throat, at the bottom of the Adam's apple, reflexively showing his daughter where it hurt oh god where it hurt and please wouldn't she quit fucking around and *save him*? She clawed and compressed and dug, and seconds turned to minutes and then years.

After an eternity ticked by, suddenly, the paramedics arrived and shoved her to one side. Confused, emotionally distraught, Deena briefly wondered how they'd managed to get there so fast but decided in the end that it didn't matter. They were *there,* and they could save her father—a man she once loved, a man who had once loved her. Despite the intervening years, the shit that happened between them and as individuals, they were still father and daughter. And though she might arrest and sentence the man at the end of all this, condemn him to serve his time, she would in no way stand back and watch him die.

Aaron returned, whisking her from the kitchen and out onto the sofa. She broke down in his arms—the first time in a good, long while. It all finally caught up to Deena: the murders, Liberty, Aaron, and Kirk. Her father and her terrible, fucked-up past. A childhood spent under blissful illusion, sheltered from the sinister truth, and a flawed prince in white armor who'd come to save her only to abandon her when the façade came crashing down. Everything plowed into her at once. Malachi Crane's pumpkin-headed prophecy. Walker's selfish, frustrating inner turmoil and retreat. And, of course, Deena's own inability to solve this case. The exhaustion, the constant and overwhelming onslaught of death and destruction, and the horrible realization that even if she felt like saving the day, it might already be too little, too late.

Most of all, though, Deena Pilgrim sat in the living room—not the one in which she'd grown up, not the one in which she'd learned for herself what it meant to be a cop—and mourned the life she'd lost. She felt grief for the loss of how it felt to admire a father and build a future. Or how it felt to yearn for something greater than what she had. How to avoid cynicism and reach for something good, maybe even great. No, instead she sat in the end result of the illusion she'd long embraced. This, *here,* is where everything had led—her mother gone, father disgraced, Deena estranged from them both. Moments ago, she'd almost watched one of them die. And now she sat shaking in the arms of the man to whom she'd given her heart instead—the man she'd left them for, who had offered a separate illusion, only to tear it all away.

She extricated herself from Aaron's arms and wiped her eyes. The paramedics had Waldo on a stretcher, carrying him to the street and toward an ambulance. She gathered a few things—his, hers—and moved to follow. Aaron went after her, heading past and down the stairs with the stretcher as Deena locked up the apartment. But as she did, her heart leaped into her throat. Raw and emotional, wounded and confused, Detective Deena Pilgrim froze before the door to her father's apartment and then leaned against the doorjamb for support. Scratched into the splintered wood, glaring like a sneering threat, someone had gouged five accusing words below the bell and the apartment number.

*In the Name of Liberty,* they read.

# *18*

—◠⌒◠—

Liberty had struck back home, as well.

Numb, Deena cradled the cell phone and listened to Emile Cross's update with half an ear. The captain spoke, relaying Enki's report, but none of it landed. Sitting in Piedmont Hospital's lemon-scented waiting room, crammed amid various midafternoon emergency care victims, Deena slumped into her chair and focused her attention on the cracked television above their heads. Malachi Crane, he of the gourdlike, wrinkled complexion, posed on-screen in a shot taken before the polished steps of 500 Fialkov Way—the Human Front corporate offices. He wore a snap-brim fedora, like a gangster, and a comfortable fleece overcoat. The television's volume had been lowered, so Deena couldn't make out his statement, and the excitable buzz among the patients drowned out whatever she might have heard. Thankfully, Cross managed to break through her emotional daze and explain what was going on: while Deena had been racing to save her father's life, the backstabbing, lying son of a bitch pumpkin held a press conference and tossed a wrench in her ongoing investigation.

"Cap," she apologized to the frantic voice on the phone, "I gotta call you back." She ended the call and launched her browser, swiping to PNN's mobile feed. Tapping the featured video, she flinched as Crane's wrinkled puss sprang to life in full-screen, streaming color. The video was dated several hours earlier—around noon, just as she and Aaron had sat down to tacos. Flanked by cronies, Crane gripped a podium as flashbulbs and ambient light filtered in at the edges of the screen. Deena paused the video. She hesitated, wondering if she should put her phone away.

*What the fuck just happened? My father nearly died. And the man I once loved may have tried to kill him.*

Still processing the events of the last several hours, Deena envisioned the words that had been carved into the door. *There was no other logical explanation. It had to have been Aaron.* Unless she wanted to question Waldo's pantsless neighbor, that is. *No,* she decided, *you'd have to wear at least a modicum of pants when killing a man.*

So, Aaron. It had to be, right? It would make a weird sort of sense. . . . . . and Walker had all but implied something along those lines back home. She would have confirmed his suspicions, but unfortunately, her partner wasn't answering his phone. Probably because he'd been dragged into the media shit storm that had taken place outside 500 Fialkov Way.

*God, it would be so easy to hand off this bag of crap, to give it to those better qualified—anyone, really—to finally solve it.* Another, better detective. The FBI. No one would blame Deena. She wouldn't have to feel the soul-crushing guilt anymore. She could walk away, like Walker. She could recuse herself, because she was just way too close to it now.

*Which, of course, is why I* can't *walk away.* She restarted the stream and kept the volume low.

"—understand this is a time of reflection, mourning, and great personal turmoil," Crane spoke to the cameras. "Every man, woman, and child in America, and perhaps around the world, has been touched by the passing of Joseph Monroe. During this season of goodwill, this time of holiday and celebration, we find ourselves bereft of joy and hope. But we at the Human Front, advocates for those without unusual gifts or talents, see salvation in the passing of a great man. Yes, we may have previously—and publicly— appeared at odds with the Soldier . . . but we equally respected the man. We understood his cause, and though it may have been one in which we did not find common ground, the members of our august body"—at this, Crane gestured to those at his side—"mourn the passing of a hero whose commitment to the common man were nothing short of legendary."

Deena snorted, and a matronly woman gave her the stink-eye. She returned the obnoxious look and shifted left, blocking the video from the lady's view. Crane continued, adjusting a tie beneath his wattled neck.

"I mention the common man not in passing but to create distinction from that of the powered man—or woman, yes; let's not create gender imbalance. You see, Joseph . . . a military hero, a speaker for those with privilege and power . . . he had *two* secrets. The media and the world were stunned to learn that the late Mr. Monroe used to be the celebrated costumed vigilante known as the Citizen Soldier. Tributes have been posted; testimonials and messages of gratitude pass from one hand to another. His death has brought both powered and non-powered people of all nations together in harmonious sorrow."

Crane frowned and scratched his collar. He reasserted his grip on the microphone and gestured to a minion. A folder was passed up, and Crane removed a photograph from within.

"However, the truth, as they say, sets us free. And while the powered community may feel a particular kinship to the masked figurehead Monroe had been, take heart; you may conclude your mourning. You may cease to feel anything but disgust or perhaps heartbreak. For the Citizen Soldier felt no such affinity. In fact, he never felt part of your community at all."

Crane held the photo up to the camera. A black-and-white image of Monroe, dead on a slab, Human Front tattoos plain and center, filled Deena's screen. "Joseph Monroe, a god-fearing man from middle America . . . a dreamer, a patient and forgiving Christian who wanted nothing but to serve his country . . . was enslaved not to the spirit of the nation but to the whims of those who'd broken it to serve their needs. Monroe had been forced— nay, *manipulated* by our government to join the Citizen Soldier program. He'd been muzzled, shackled, and silenced by his superiors. And now I stand here, a private individual, a man with ties to no military entity or self-serving office other than my own, to finally reveal the truth."

Crane set the photo down on the podium. "Joseph Monroe, also known as the Citizen Soldier, was one of *us*—not *you*. He hated his powers; he feared those who controlled him. The man was frightened into submission; fearing for his life, he refused to come forward and tell the truth, after being conscripted into a costume during the heyday of the Cold War. But I am free to confirm that Joseph, the mouthpiece for the Powers movement, was in fact an active and vocal member of my Human Fr—"

Deena turned off the video. She'd heard enough; she knew the rest. And it explained the heightened tension in the waiting room as injured patients debated and gawked while the news played Crane's video on loop. She rested her head against the wall, staring at nothing, wondering what to do next.

*That lying pumpkin. I asked him, point-blank, and he evaded. Well, wait until I get back. Wait until Aaron or Enki drags his ass to the precinct and tosses him into a cell.*

Of course, Enki was dealing with another crisis: Quince was dead. She'd been shot in the throat, killed during a prison transfer on Bernardin and Avenue E. The dead bigot parade continued, and the biggest bigot of all obstructed their investigation live on national television. It wouldn't be long before someone broadcast Liberty's words—painted across a flaming truck, surrounded by dead guards who'd been taking Quince to the Shelf or whichever prison for which she'd been bound. And once that made the news, it wouldn't take long to connect Quince to Crane, and then it was a short line from Liberty to Monroe. Where would her investigation be then? Even now, the division was in media lockdown; no statements, no information until they had something tangible. Everyone had been dragged back in. Enki had been recalled to oversee the investigation surrounding Willie's death, and even Walker had been given a call—though, according to Cross, he'd yet to return. Deena had attempted several calls herself, but no answer. Wherever Walker was, whatever he was doing, he was making it clear that he wanted to be left alone. Meanwhile, as Enki and her team analyzed the gruesome Liberty crime scene, Deena puzzled out the one that had landed in her lap several hours earlier.

*How could Aaron be Liberty?* she wondered. *How could he have killed Willie when I was sitting by his side at my father's table, spooning soup down my gullet? Maybe the rumors* are *true—Liberty is more than one man. Waldo had* all but admitted it, that he and the other cops had co-opted the name to cover their tracks. But that would mean . . . no, if that's true, and . . .

If that were true—if Aaron had tried to kill her father—then not only had they been colluding the entire time, but he was also in bed with Monroe and possibly Crane.

Deena laced her hands behind her head and tried to make sense of it all. He'd denied it. Aaron had looked into her eyes and denied everything, right before he'd left.

*They sat in the ER, huddled against a wall as doctors hurried past. Sodden, ancient Thanksgiving decorations lined the walls and chalkboards, left there by a staff too busy or lazy to swap them out. She stared at a hastily illustrated Tom Turkey and fought back tears. She'd finished crying; Deena had no more use for tears, refusing to be vulnerable in the face of what was to come. Her mind reeled; she'd fought down any raw emotion, the burning questions she needed to ask so that she could be strong for Waldo. But she needed to breathe, and Aaron's arms felt like a prison, so she pushed him away.*

*"What? Deena, talk to me," he said, all eyes and hands and heart. Had it been only hours since they'd been together in his bed, lying in each other's arms? Deena didn't know him at all. How could she have been so stupid? How could she have let down her guard? That was so unlike her. Since when did Deena Pilgrim let a guy lead her around like a lovesick idiot? And why did she allow Aaron to accompany her to Atlanta under the pretense of support when, in fact, what she'd been doing was giving him access to his oldest, greatest rival? Deena had been acting as accessory to the attempted murder of her father.*

*"Deena," Aaron repeated, reaching across the sterile, whitewashed hallway. "Look, Waldo's going to be fine. The doctors will do everything in their power to—"*

*She whirled on him, daggers in her eyes. "Are you Liberty, Aaron?"*

*He was taken aback, shocked and confused. He moved away and stared, stammering for a defense, "What? What are you talking about?"*

*"There were two of us in that apartment. Waldo was fine when he opened the door, and unless one of the geriatrics in his building has been harboring vengeance, or my father invented spontaneous suicide, it was either you or me. Despite vivid fantasies over the last ten years, I know it wasn't me."*

"Come on. The APHD are combing every inch of his apartment. They're testing the food and beer. Maybe someone slipped something into—"

"And the tag? It wasn't there when we arrived. Who carved Liberty's tag into the door, Special Investigator?"

He ran fingers through his hair. "I don't know—maybe someone who saw us go in? Maybe we'd been followed from the airport, or hell, even from the city. Deena, you can't believe that I would do this!"

"Can't I?"

He lowered his voice and took her aside, holding Deena by the arm. She pulled away and gave him a warning look. A passing nurse shot them a quizzical glance, slowing her pace to make sure everything was all right. Deena silently encouraged her to keep walking. She recognized the woman. They might have been in high school together. This whole town was filled with memories and people she'd sooner forget.

"Look," he said, "there's a lyric from the song 'Secret Warmonger' by Rocket to Planet X that goes—"

"No!" she cried. "Shut the fuck up with your music and your lyrics and your fucking universal chords! I don't give a shit about BEEBA or which rock superstar had pearls of wisdom to share. We're talking about my father here, Aaron. Did you or did you not try to kill him?"

"Deena," he whispered, hoping to contain the conversation, "you of all people know how much I fought and scraped to solve the Liberty murders. I staked my career on it—it was the reason, the failure that forced me to leave Atlanta. Why would I have done that to myself?"

"Sounds like a decent cover story to me. A great reason for leaving town."

He smiled. "You always were the better detective . . . but answer me this: there were murders after I left. How could that have been me?"

"Are you kidd—? Waldo just admitted that he and other cops adopted Liberty's MO and name to—"

"Yeah, before I put an end to it. Before we put them on public display and locked half of them away. The Soldier, the Rammlers . . . it wasn't me, Deen. You have to know that. I wasn't there."

She grimaced. "But you were, out of the blue, right as the killer surfaced again. Seems mighty convenient."

"Deena, what do you want to me to say here? If you won't believe me, how can I convince you of the truth? Lie detector test? Cut off my right arm?"

"Just fucking tell me"—she'd gotten loud, and he tried to calm her down—"did you or did you not attempt to kill my father?"

"I swear I didn't."

Her eyes filled with tears. "Then who did, Aaron? He was fine when we got there, and there wasn't a tag on the door. Who put it there, if not you? You left the room—"

"To call 911! Deena, you have to believe me. I'm not Liberty. I've been trying to put him away for twelve fucking years! I love you—"

She folded her arms. "You love me? You don't even know me. You're not in my life, and I sure as hell don't know you."

Aaron grabbed her forearms, and she struggled to free herself. The nurse eyed them again and picked up her phone, weighing whether or not to get involved. Finally, Aaron let Deena go. "Don't you feel anything here?"

"I don't know what to feel. I haven't felt anything but numb in the last five years."

He stopped and cocked his head, concerned. "What do you mean?"

"Forget it. Just let me wait for Waldo in peace."

"No," he pushed. "Tell me what you mean."

Deena whirled around again, eyes blazing. "I mean I'm done. I can't do this anymore; it's too much, okay? Walker, then you and my dad? It's just enough already."

"Deena, this will pass. We'll solve it, and—"

"You're not listening. I don't want to solve it. I want to disappear, Aaron. I don't want to be a cop, not if it leads me here. Not if I have to watch the people I know and love—or once loved—die before my eyes. I just want out, and after I get my father back on his feet, that's what I'm gonna do. You, Walker, Kirk, Cross . . . you can finish this thing, but I'm fucking done."

"Deena . . ." He held out a hand, and she slapped it away. "Deena, you can't quit on this. You've got to finish this case, at least. Get closure. Help me find the same."

"Why? I'm not you, Aaron. Liberty hasn't eaten away at my soul, followed me around for the last twelve years."

"But he will now that your father is involved, now that your name will be dragged into it. Trust me. My father tried the cases . . . his judgments were overturned by your dad and the Soldier. His good name was slandered, his rulings, and it nearly killed him."

*"I don't care."*

*"You will, and then you'll have to finish it. I'll help—we'll put this to rest, and if you still want to quit, I'll throw your goddamn retirement party. But not until we put this to bed. I'll be there—I swear—and I'll help you make that transition . . . but I have a feeling once this is done that you'll want to be a cop more than ever. I know it."*

That was the last thing he'd said—it was hours ago, before they'd stabilized her father. Cross had phoned to tell them about Quince and Crane, the murder and press conference, and Aaron had raced to the airport to lend his support. They'd kissed—briefly, awkwardly—and he promised to call the moment he knew anything. She wasn't looking forward to the conversation. The only man that Deena wanted to speak with wouldn't take her calls. So she sat in the ER waiting room, replaying Crane's statement in her head, fading into the crowd as it buzzed and blabbed about Joseph Monroe, the American traitor. She toyed with her phone, rehashing the day's events and the bitter fight with Aaron, wondering if he was telling the truth and whether or not he might be trusted.

*It had to be him. Who else?*

Crane, perhaps? A slow-acting poison and a silent henchman at the door? Or maybe one of the other detectives, one who hadn't gotten off like Waldo? They might have connections in jail, used an outside party to set it up. Or maybe her father had arranged it himself—an overly dramatic play-act to win back his daughter and put the finger of blame on Aaron Boucher. No, that seemed unreasonable . . . she would have known if he'd been in town, killing Monroe and the Rammlers, and Waldo had seemed genuinely surprised to see her. Her mind reeled, spiraling as she waited for some kind of news, something she could use. Another hour lapsed until, finally, a surgeon called Deena's name, and she followed him back into the ward.

They evaded gurneys, slaloming through the ER until they arrived at a small anteroom in the far-right corner. A jolly-looking two-dimensional cartoon snowman winked down from above the door, giving Deena the thumbs-up. She ignored it, focusing instead on labored breathing from within. She knew that her father lay just beyond the threshold. She turned to the doctor, forcing out all other emotional quagmires, folded her arms, and tried to peek at her father's chart.

"Is he going to die?" she asked. "Am I here to sign a DNR or some kind of living will? Because, I'll be honest, if—"

"Your father will be fine, Detective Pilgrim. He's been cooperating with local police and the APHD. He's responding well to the medication."

"What happened?"

The doctor held up a vial of blood. "We ran several tests, searching for known toxins and possible allergens. The gamut of potential reactants, you know. We checked his food, drink, and the police have swept the entire apartment—they'll grant you access, I imagine. But we found only this."

Deena took the container. "What is it?"

"Hep B."

She raised her eyebrows and nearly dropped the flask. "Excuse me?"

The doctor laughed. "I thought that might be your response. Well, strictly speaking, it isn't hepatitis B, exactly, but a concentrated—and highly mutated—strain. We found traces in his bloodstream, particularly around the arms and a number of minuscule tracks across his right forearm. Someone injected this deadly little cocktail. It was working its way toward your father's liver—it might still, though I believe we've flushed most of it out. In the meantime, it infected his respiratory and circulatory passages, eating at his nerves and deteriorating glands and arteries. We're lucky we caught it when we did; we were honestly concerned it was just a bad allergic reaction at first."

"I thought he was poisoned."

The doctor nodded. "Technically, he was. Did you see anyone puncture his arm, administer something into his bloodstream in any way that might lead you to believe he could have been infected?"

She paused to consider, her mind a whirlwind. *The fight. Aaron and Waldo, arms locked at the table, angry and resentful. Could Aaron have . . . ?*

Deena put it out of her mind, shaking her head. He *couldn't* have. She would have seen. He'd held no injector, no needle. It hadn't been Aaron, despite her various theories otherwise. "No. No, I didn't. What now?"

"Now he recuperates and receives a series of antiviral medications—accelerated interferon and the like. I may zap him with something, depending on what this"—he retrieved the vial and gave it a shake—"turns up.

Meanwhile, APHD will continue their investigation and bring you in whenever you like."

"And can I see him?"

The doctor smiled. "You can. He's resting, but I believe he's ready to receive a visitor who isn't wearing a badge . . . well, wearing a badge and is family. I'll let you know what the lab turns up."

She nodded, and the doctor hurried away, carrying the vial of her father's blood. Deena steeled herself, breathing deeply while processing the new information. Liberty—or someone pretending to be Liberty—had poisoned Waldo, and now once again, she was stuck holding a bag of crap. There were too many connections, too many threads between this case and the ones back home for it to be coincidental. Despite her exhaustion, Deena had to draw them together. Walker, fuck him, wasn't returning calls. Kirk was laid up; Enki had her hands full; and Cross was overwhelmed by a maelstrom of lawyers, government officials, and reporters.

And Aaron . . . she didn't know what to do about Aaron yet. She didn't trust him; still couldn't believe that he was telling her the truth. In her heart, Deena was worried she'd let her father's killer board a plane to kill again—maybe Crane this time, unless they were in cahoots. Maybe Kirk, to wrap up loose ends.

Maybe Walker.

*Walker can take care of himself. He's made that perfectly clear.*

Deena rubbed her eyes, putting it out of her mind. She stepped inside, toward the bed. Waldo, frail and hooked up to wires and blinking machines, slowly opened his eyes. His throat was red. Heavy bags weighed down his eyelids, and an IV tube snaked into his pasty wrist. Deena locked the door, shutting out the world, and double-checked to confirm it was secure. It was the two of them now—the first time they'd been alone in ten years.

Waldo focused his gaze, staring at Deena, and then struggled to sit up. She moved to his bedside, pulling up a chair, gesturing for him to rest. She removed her coat and sat down. He settled back against the pillow, hair splayed out against the crisp, white sheets. Deena shifted in the chair, looking around for a chart. Some data or information she could use or with which she might distract herself. But there was nothing; it was just the two of them.

The two of them alone.

Waldo wet his cracked, bleeding lips, dryness having been induced by an intubation tube that had already been removed. He attempted to build up saliva, and his voice emerged from a crackling, reedy place deep inside his throat.

"Hey, kiddo."

"Hey, Dad."

He reached out, hoping to take her hand. She hesitated and then decided to let him. He'd almost died, and though she hated what he'd done, he was still her father. Waldo seized her hand, clutching it in his clammy fingers, flexing, squirming as if unwilling to let go.

Finally, he gathered enough strength and lifted himself off the pillow. She encouraged him to lie down, not to exert himself, but he waved her off. "No," he wheezed. "No, I'm done taking it easy."

He glared at Deena, staring with fierce, clear-eyed determination.

"There are things you need to hear, and things I need to say. So, Deena . . . Detective Pilgrim . . . I'm done avoiding this conversation. A discussion we should have had long ago. Before I pissed off your mom, before you headed off to college and I lost my little girl."

"Dad . . ."

Waldo gripped her fingers. "No. No more bullshit. No more *lies*. For once in my misbegotten life. . . . . . it's time I told you the truth.

"It's time I told you about the Liberty killer."

# *19*

------

*December. Tuesday night.* *7:48* P.M.

"Joseph Monroe was Liberty."

The words hung between them for a moment. Deena sat back in her chair and assumed a skeptical expression. "Come on. Really?"

Waldo adjusted the IV drip, moving the tubes aside. "Swear to god. The Soldier wasn't the patriotic hero the media made him out to be. In fact, he was secretly aligned with *other* governments. In 1954, for instance, he joined the Communist Party."

Deena rolled her eyes. "Bullshit. This is just sad. You're trying to pin this on a dead man?"

"I'm fucking *serious*. Ask your pal Boucher; he knows."

Deena's heart leaped. "What does *that* mean?"

Waldo peered under the curtain, making sure no one was eavesdropping. "It's like this: Monroe was a Commie; he wasn't spying for the Russians or anything, nothing illegal, but he aligned himself with their beliefs through the remainder of the Cold War. Even after he returned to the home front, the Soldier surreptitiously fraternized with dozens of anti-American and anti-Powers organizations, mostly in defiance of the assholes who filled him full of experimental drugs."

"Wait—he *told* you this?"

Her father nodded. "Had no choice, not if he wanted my help. He revealed his secret to a select few, those of us with no . . . qualms, shall we say, about working with a traitor. He also worked with the Human Front, did you know? Big shock, right, after all the time they were at each other's throats?"

Deena started to respond but realized that Waldo hadn't seen a television in several hours. She feigned surprise. "That's . . . that's amazing."

"You're fucking right it is." He leaned over, speaking conspiratorially. "He basically aided the enemy through Vietnam and then worked against Uncle Sam every chance he got. Now, I met him right when you were finishing high school, around the time the Human Front sank their teeth into Atlanta."

"The gang war, correct?"

His lips thinned, and he shook his head. "Baby, there was no gang war. The Soldier put that together and hired some of us to play along."

"How do you mean?" She folded her arms, raising a foot onto the railing of the bed. "You started the gang war?"

"Atlanta was an up-and-coming criminal destination, see. Close enough to Miami and Mexico, far enough away to steer clear of thriving cartels. Crane, several others wanted to turn Georgia into a launchpad for drugs, chemical weapons, and the like. The feds caught wind and installed Monroe, pairing him up with the APHD and me."

"This was before Aaron was a detective."

Waldo nodded. "Before he was even a cop. Monroe, understanding that graft and corruption had infiltrated the city, chose to create an opportunity in which he would not only set his enemies against one another—some to jail, others to the morgue—but also use the chaos to cover up a series of murders—"

A light turned on in the back of Deena's brain. "The gang war was orchestrated to hide the Liberty killings, in which Monroe bumped off everyone who knew his secrets."

"Exactly. The Rammlers, Blitzkrieg, several others—men and women who knew that Monroe was a secret traitor to his 'people.' He had Owens, me, some others release a number of convicted felons in exchange for them icing those in the know."

"But now *they* knew. Quince, the Rammlers. Why didn't they squeal?"

Waldo settled back, spreading his hands. "He threatened most of them, like Quince. The weak ones, convincing them they'd be excommunicated from Crane's flock. The rest? He killed them, of course."

"That's why there were two Liberty killers. He did his victims differently from Quince, you, and the others. But that doesn't answer who killed Monroe. Who is the *new* Liberty, the one who tried to poison you?"

He cocked his head and softened his expression. "Deena . . . you know."

*No. No, fuck him.* "You think Aaron did it."

"You were always the better detective. You knew how to uncover secrets, like finding hidden Christmas presents."

She rolled her eyes and tapped her heel. "All the secrets but the important ones, apparently."

"Look," he answered quietly. "I don't have proof that Aaron is the new Liberty . . . but he *did* know that Monroe was the original."

She felt light, buzzing and bubbly, as if she'd mainlined ginger ale. Waldo's words rolled around in her skull, and she leaned forward. "What are you saying?"

"Deena . . . you think I cared about what was happening between the two of you? I was high, sleeping with half a dozen of your mom's friends. I couldn't care less what you did. But still, I gave the two of you a hard time. Why?"

"Because I was your daughter. You were protecting me."

He gave her a pointed look. "Does that sound like me?"

"What, then? Why the fuck?"

Waldo stroked his beard. His eyes, half-lidded, were barely focused. But still he went on, opening the floodgates for the first time in her life. "Because Aaron knew. He knew the truth and didn't *do* anything about it. The criminals I put back on the street? Aaron's father—the judge—he'd put them away. His rulings, his judgments, toss 'em in a cell and throw away the key. And here I was, flaunting my authority and recovering that key. I released men and women the judge had jailed in order to catch or kill the ones he hadn't. As an added bonus, I set them after the only people who could finger Monroe, expose his secrets. And all the rest were intimidated, black-mailed, or hobbled."

"And Aaron knew."

"He felt violated at first, sure, threatening to turn me—us—in and put an end to it. But when Monroe spoke to him . . . I don't know, the man had some kind of special connection with the Bouchers . . . and when he convinced Aaron that our actions were in service of cleaning up the judge's spotty conviction rate and putting away those who'd slipped through the cracks, well . . ."

"Wait, wait, *wait*. Hang on. You mean to tell me that Aaron looked the other way in order to tidy up his father's *record*?"

"At first. But then we paid him, like we did the crooks. He worked the Liberty cases to cover his own ass, to make sure nobody knew that he was involved. It removed suspicion. And we kept the judge's record on the bench intact."

"I don't believe you. That . . . no. Just no fucking way." Her heart hurt. If she'd felt betrayed by Aaron before, now she felt devastated. *That prick. That exceptional, lying, scumbag prick. He lied to me—and I slept with him. And the entire time, he was plotting to kill my father. Even back then, he was lying to me as we rolled around and fucked.*

"Believe me, Deen." Waldo sat forward again, and she stood up, pacing the tiny antechamber. "At first, everything was fine. Aaron played the good cop; I played the asshole. But then he started hating himself for sacrificing his principles to protect the judge, and things got ugly. He became . . . distant. You remember that Thanksgiving."

"Yeah." She nodded, stunned and silent, both brain and heart in turmoil.

"That speech he gave—that was *real*. That wasn't an act, and I knew it. Wasn't long after that Aaron learned the Soldier's secret for himself."

Recollections of the last twenty-four hours swam inside Deena's mind, snippets of conversation and what she now knew to be a carefully constructed fabrication. Aaron had known Monroe was a traitor. He knew about the Rammlers and about Quince, their connections to the original murder. *And he'd played stupid, letting me swan about trying to fit slot A into tab X. That motherfucker,* she thought, seething with rage.

"Eventually," Waldo concluded, "he told Ken what was happening. That's why they moved, I'm sorry to say. The judge agreed to keep quiet as long as the killing stopped. As long as we submitted to an internal investigation and Aaron moved away. We agreed, and the judge forked over a handsome sum—which is how I kept the house and stayed out of jail. Course, that didn't stop the Liberty killings—we had to toss out a few more once they were gone, just to throw off any suspicion that might have drifted their way. And also—"

"What about Crane? He must have known . . . I mean, he was in charge of the Human Front the whole time. He must have been involved."

Waldo frowned and shook his head. "I dunno about that. Monroe never discussed Crane . . . who, by the way, was the only member of the Front to *refuse* our offer."

"How do you mean, 'refuse'?" She paced, striding from one end of the curtain to the other, jarring and fluttering it in her wake.

Her father shrugged. "He was the only one who didn't take the deal. Stayed in prison until after the trials, until after the FBI and the Soldier moved out of town."

"Why do you think he did that?"

"Search me. He and Monroe . . . there was something going on there that even Aaron and I didn't understand. You should ask him. He'll corroborate this entire story—that is, if he's willing to admit that Monroe was his pal instead of a lifelong enemy."

She smiled. "You'd be surprised."

"Anyway, that's what I know. I should have told you sooner. I wanted to tell you years ago, but you were so blinded by love that you never would have believed me."

"What makes you think I believe you now? I'm supposed to take *your* word, a man who's lied to me my entire life? I'm supposed to swallow the fact that you were secret besties with the guy I was dating, the guy you hated, the guy you claimed ruined your life?"

"Aaron only ruined my life inasmuch as he blabbed. The perks, the cash, everything else . . . once the judge threatened to expose Monroe and me, the entire house of cards came crashing down. Which was ironic, because—"

Deena stopped pacing. "Because you kicked me out and told me to go to him."

"Well, yeah. I kinda hoped he'd take you away from all this, to be honest. Where you could be safe and sheltered from the things I'd done. From the shameful things I'd done."

"Well, look how that turned out. I'd say *safe* is the only thing I *haven't* been since storming out the front door all those years ago."

He looked up, eyes wide and glazed. "What do you mean?"

Deena glared at the hangdog expression upon Waldo's face. He looked exhausted, spent. She wanted to kill him. *Everything I knew was a lie. Even my half-assed college romance. My hatred for my father, that was a lie too because I should have been angry at him for something* completely *different. For keeping Aaron's secrets from me, as well.*

Her phone rang, breaking the silence. Deena reached over and dug it out to check the caller ID. *Motherfucking Walker. Finally—right at the worst possible time.* Annoyed, she let it go to voice mail and stowed the cell phone deep into her jacket pocket.

"Did you know that I had powers, Dad?"

He laughed in response—a short, brittle bark. "*You* had powers? When? H-how did that happen . . . I mean, your mother and I . . ."

Deena sat back down. "You were terrible together. Because of that, I had to depend on myself for support—you and Mom, you were too busy tearing into each other to care about raising me, so I raised myself. It made me cocky, reckless. Like I knew the only thing that could hurt or help me was *me*."

"Yeah, but *powers*? Where did you—"

"Took a reckless risk on a case. Ended up infected with a virus, gave me powers for a while. Turned me into the infection itself."

Waldo rubbed his mouth. "Jesus."

She laughed. "Yeah. And that was one of the easier cases. That thing in Chicago? Coupla years back? That was me. My partner and me."

"What . . . what the fuck, Deena. Why didn't you tell me?"

Deena smirked and stuck her heel back up on the railing. "Like father, like daughter. You have your secrets, I have mine."

"I have more than you know. I wanted to tell you years ago but didn't think you'd be able to handle it. But tell me more about you first. I want to know about your friends, your job—"

"You don't want to know about my job. You're wasting time."

"I do. . . . That sort of thing. Anything. Everything."

"Tell me first. Tell me what I need to know to put Liberty away."

"I told you: Liberty's dead."

She frowned. "I don't believe that."

"Ask Boucher and Crane. Liberty *was* the Soldier. The killings, the murders—it was him. That's why there wasn't a tag at his apartment, at the crime scene, right?"

"Yet four people died at Liberty's hands *after* Monroe's death. Explain that."

"That isn't my job."

"No, *your* job was to take bribes from crooked Powers and a handful of zealots. To lie to your daughter and cheat on your wife. To kill a bunch of people for terrible reasons and perpetrate massive fraud."

She stood up and loomed over his bed. "*Your* job was to be a shitty role model and even shittier father. Am I right, *Dad*?"

Waldo toyed with his thumbs. "What do you want me to say, Deena? What can I say that I haven't said before? I'm *sorry*. Is that it? Is that what you want me to say? Because I am. Sorrier than you'll ever know."

She gawked at him, looking down on the pathetic figure he'd become. Ruined financially, matrimonially—career in the toilet and facing a minimum of twenty years in prison for his many horrible crimes. She *could* go easy on him. She *could* yell at him a whole lot more. Time was running out, and Deena was forced to choose whom to believe: her former lover, a man who might or might not be a secret killer at worst, a conspiratorial accessory at best; Crane, a militant power-hater who wanted nothing more than to defame America's greatest hero before he made it to the grave; or her father, a scumbag cop on the take who'd been awful to his wife and had lied to his daughter since the day she'd learned to say his name.

Which of them was telling the truth? Which of them had the most to gain or lose? She felt tired, nearly dead on her feet. *This isn't fair. I wanted to recuse myself. I wanted to walk away.*

She flashed back nearly twenty-four hours, to a different hospital bed in another city. Deena had been jumped and beaten, Walker by her side.

*She whirled, hand on the door. "I can do my job. Why don't you do yours?"*

*Walker folded his arms. "You* know *why."*

*She wiped her brow and sighed. "Know what, dude? I really don't. I can't keep up with the rising tide of your bullshit. At least Aaron doesn't give me passive-aggressive three-word answers. You left, man. You picked your ass up and headed home. And what, that's* okay *now? That's how you deal with horrible shit when the chips are down? Since* when *has that been* us*?"*

Deena stared at Waldo, scrabbling for morphine, anxiously waiting for her reaction. She bit her lip and turned to the chair, reaching for her coat. She removed her phone from an inner pocket and swiped until she found a recorder app. Tapping a large, red button, Deena sat back down on the edge of the bed.

"You want to know what to say? Say what you said before. Say it all—everything that you claim is true about Monroe, Aaron, the Human Front, and the judge. Especially everything you claim is true about you. Tell it all. This time, however," Deena Pilgrim said, holding the cell phone out to her recuperating father, "I want you to say it into *this*."

# 20

⌇⌇⌇⌇

*December. Tuesday night. 8:12 P.M.*

Walker held out his badge and gun, testing their weight. The captain's office was mercifully quiet, noise from the bullpen having lessened to a dull roar. Emile Cross sat across from Walker, trying to meet his eyes. But Walker simply stared at the badge, gripped by an uncomfortable sense of déjà vu.

*We've both been here before,* he thought. *This isn't the first time; it won't be the last.* He palmed the badge and placed it on the desk, following suit with his sidearm.

Cross swept them into a drawer, closing it with a bit more force than necessary. The captain sat back, rubbed his eyes, and then steepled his fingers against his chest. "Again, I'm sorry about this," Cross apologized. He anxiously glanced at the third man in the office. After a moment, he turned back to Walker. "You understand why we have to do this, right? This isn't personal, or—"

"I know." Walker avoided looking at either man—neither Cross nor Aaron Boucher, freshly returned from Georgia. Boucher, to his credit, wasn't sporting a triumphant smirk. He didn't seem thrilled about what had just transpired. The special investigator slumped against the wall, ass on a cabinet, hair lightly mussed and sporting bags beneath both eyes. Boucher had already revealed that he'd left Deena in Atlanta the moment Crane's statement had gone national. Walker's partner, handling a shit storm of a case, had been waylaid by a horrible family emergency—her father had been poisoned in his home; another modern Liberty special, but this time in the killer's original stomping grounds. A fresh coat of shame washed across Walker's face. Deena had left—or had tried to leave—several messages on his cell phone since they'd parted the evening before. Blistered by her vicious (though well-deserved) tongue-lashing, Walker hadn't exactly felt like answering. But now he wondered whether she'd been calling for backup or emotional support, reaching out to her partner for a shoulder to cry on or simply because she needed help with the case.

He wanted to dig out his phone and check. He wanted to pack a bag and go. But first, Walker had to finish this ridiculous charade. "Are we done?" he ventured, rising from his seat without waiting for confirmation.

"Walker," Boucher explained in apologetic, placating tones. "You have to know this didn't come from me. I've been so sidetracked on this case, with Deena, and really didn't have sufficient testimony to—"

"I know. I said it's fine."

"I *mean* it, dammit. And this is *strictly* temporary, I swear . . . well, I hope. I'm damn well gonna push for that."

Walker shot Boucher a short, sharp smile. "I get it. There was always a chance it would go down this way. Frankly, I'm hardly surprised." Boucher had been twiddling his thumbs in coach, racing home from Atlanta via US Airways at thirty-five thousand feet, when the order had apparently come in from his mysterious commission. In the face of Crane's exposé, specifically because of allegations against Joseph Monroe and possible un-American activities and associations, Boucher's superiors had decided to pull the trigger. All law enforcement officials with a history of powers—active or dormant—would be immediately stripped of legal authority. Across the nation, good men and women were being forced to submit shields to their superiors much the way Walker had been forced to relinquish his own. Joe had access to the highest echelons of government. Now a different set of men and women—frantic and scrambling to curtail any public relations damage—raced to minimize threats to national security on both domestic and international fronts. Walker didn't give a shit. He couldn't deal with another personal disappointment. His heart had been swept into that drawer along with his badge and gun. Only his heart, of course: Walker believed his soul had been already been swept away the moment he'd first excused the questionable actions of Joseph Monroe.

Crane's revelation—the confirmation that Joe had worked with the THF for all those years—felt like a knife to the balls. He'd trusted Joe, broken bread and hoisted beers with the man. They'd stood toe-to-toe against the forces of evil, and Walker had considered Monroe a friend, despite the apathetic behavior and faulty ethics he'd displayed in Detroit and again in Atlanta. But oh, how it made sense now. How the mighty had fallen . . . and when Goliath fell, a giant of that stature and magnitude, you could be damn sure tremors would follow in his wake.

*That doesn't matter,* Walker reminded himself. *What matters is getting to Deena. Getting to Atlanta.* He clasped the captain on the shoulder and headed for the door. Boucher trailed along, still stammering apologies, but Walker didn't want to hear them. The last thing he needed was to get sidetracked by more bullshit. He headed for his desk to grab his jacket and tried Deena along the way. The cell phone put him into voice mail. *I deserve that, too,* he thought while jamming his phone into a back pocket. He would listen to her messages on the way to the airport, right after he booked a flight. Boucher was still attached to Walker's hip, offering inane platitudes. The former Power rolled his eyes and snaked his jacket from a desk he wasn't sure he'd ever see again.

"Christian?" He turned to find Enki Sunrise striding across the aisle, carrying a tablet and a steaming cup of coffee. She wore little more than a T-shirt and jeans, despite the frigid weather, and raised her eyebrows with concern. "Happy holidays, dude. You okay? Tried to raise you coupla hours ago, bring you back in on that exploding truck."

"Thanks for handling that, Enki. I appreciate it."

She glanced at his jacket. "Going somewhere?"

Boucher piped up. "He's going to Atlanta."

"What the hell is in Atlanta?" She checked out the special investigator, a virtual stranger to someone who'd been away from the precinct for twenty-four hours. "And who the fuck is this? I go on one little drug stakeout and someone switches all the cops."

Walker shouldered into his jacket and moved for the door. "Detective Enki Sunrise, Special Investigator Aaron Boucher. Boucher, Enki. She's one of the best, and he's Deena's ex. Oh! And also the guy that took my badge. He's like the Grinch who stole law and order."

"Wait. Took your what, now?"

"Hey," Boucher interrupted, "that's not fair. Look, Walker, going to Atlanta is a terrible idea. Right now, Deena—"

That was too much. He'd tolerated the yammering and frigid détente he and Boucher had mutually obeyed . . . but now he'd reached the limit. Walker rounded on the smaller detective, fists clenched around his keys. The hubbub of the precinct faded away as the tension of the last twenty-four hours—discovering Joe's body, getting sidelined by bureaucrats, fighting with Deena, and getting shit on by Crane—all came roaring at Walker like a freight train. Thousands of years, a lifetime of patience and passages, and even still a pissant like Aaron Boucher could manage to get on his nerves. Everything—the anger, the guilt, the overwhelming shame and humiliation—came burning through Walker's chest and into a single finger: just one, an index finger that he used to poke Boucher in the chest.

"Deena *what*? You tell me, Boucher. *Tell me* she doesn't need me. Because, look!" Christian fairly shouted, holding out his phone. "See, she's been calling. So I *know* she wants to talk, despite everything that went down between us. Now, I don't know what happened between *you* in Atlanta, but don't fucking stand there and tell me it's a terrible idea. When it comes to saving my partner, *no* idea is terrible. No fight or distance is too impossible to overcome. So *tell me again*," he repeated, jabbing his finger into Boucher's shoulder. "Deena fucking *what*?"

Boucher batted Walker's finger aside. "I'm just saying, leave her alone for a minute. Waldo almost died, and yeah, things didn't end well between us. We come down on her with caseloads and evidence and our own insecurities and feelings—even if it means solving other people's murders, murders possibly connected to the attack on her father—it's just gonna break her."

Walker smirked. "Boy, you don't know her at all. This could never break her."

"Oh, yeah," Boucher posed, ignoring the circle of gawkers that had drifted over to bear witness to the confrontation. "Do *you* know her? Dude, you don't know anything about her—or about me. The things Deena told me—about the job, the way she's been feeling. . . . . . did *you* know she was ready to quit? That she wants out?"

Walker bit his lip and glared at the special investigator. Enki took the brief silence as a moment of opportunity to step between them. "Fellas, I don't know what's going on, but—"

Boucher barely cast his eyes her way. "Stay out of this, Detective. Look, Walker. I know you carry a grudge against me, but I'll be blunt: I don't know why. I'm not your enemy—*you* are. All I did was come to do a job."

"I don't care about that."

"What *do* you care about?"

Walker leaned forward. "I care about Deena, which is more than I can say about you. Otherwise, you would have stayed in Atlanta. You wouldn't have raced back, even at the beck and call of your master's voice. That's what a partner does—or a friend. He stays, even when the going gets tough—I know that now. That's what you do."

"And I didn't? She basically forced me to leave."

Walker laughed. "This time, maybe."

"What the fuck does *that* mean?" It was getting heated now, and Enki glanced in the direction of Cross's office, searching for backup. A crowd had formed, encircling the desk. Even the perps waiting to be booked had stopped to listen, waiting for Walker's reply. Boucher stepped closer, nose to chin with the larger detective.

"It means I know more than you think. For instance, I know that Waldo Pilgrim brought you into the APHD."

"So? He was friends with my father. A family favor for a promising young cop."

"He was friends with Monroe, too. See, I knew that even *without* having to dig through files. Remember: I was *there*. Sure, I had little to do with Waldo, but the Soldier and I were 'thick as thieves,' remember? In fact, I was at his goddamn *birthday party*. But you wouldn't know that."

"Why not?"

"Because you were at a different party that night, out in Tuxedo Park."

Boucher thought back for a moment, the audience of cops and criminals hanging on every word. "You're talking about Thanksgiving. That one at the Pilgrims'."

Walker nodded. "The very one . . . when you scolded the cops and Powers, claiming you were the only honest law dog in town. Here's the thing, Aaron: You were there *why*? To berate a bunch of crooked cops and terrible heroes? While criminals were burning down the city? No, you were there to pick up your father."

"What? Yeah, I took my parents home. So wha—"

"You knew the judge was in danger that night. Why? Sure, there was a war, and he'd put some of the combatants away . . . but that wasn't it. What else happened that night? You remember."

Boucher set his mouth into a determined line. His hands were at his side now, balled into fists. "A Liberty killing."

"That's right. And everyone in Atlanta knows now, thanks to the press, that most of the Liberty killings were undertaken on behalf of Waldo Pilgrim. But what they don't know—what isn't exactly public knowledge—is that many of Pilgrim's contract killers were Powers and bigots that the judge himself had put away. Yet here they were—back on the street."

The crowd murmured now. Enki had abandoned them, having gone to retrieve Cross. Walker didn't care; he'd be done by the time they returned. "More importantly . . . the victim that night was one of the criminals the judge had *not* put away—one who had gone free, evading your father's justice. I can show you, if you like. I did my due diligence; that's why no one could reach me these last few hours. I've been in the files, at the library. I've been *working the case*."

He moved in for the kill now. "So you knew the judge was in danger because a Power or Front associate he'd convicted was out killing rivals, criminals the judge had let go. And you knew that the judge might be next— one can never anticipate the whims of a jealous felon. You knew Waldo and the others were releasing killers onto the street. This was before the hearing, before it all came out. Before Pilgrim and his pals were drummed out of the APHD."

Walker edged closer, sneering at Boucher. "But *that's* not why I have beef—though, to be honest, it's enough to make your life extremely difficult should I inform the right people. Your commission, perhaps. Taking my badge, coming after me with everything you've got—that's fine, too. Here's the reason I really hate you, Boucher. Why I said the other day it would never work between us, because there was too much history."

Boucher met Walker's eyes. The big detective could see the other man's pain, disdain flashing beneath a hooded brow. "What's the reason, former detective Walker?"

Walker whispered, keeping it low and between the two of them. "It's because even before I partnered with her, I knew what you did to Deena Pilgrim. I'd never met her—*hell*, I barely knew Waldo. What I *did* know was that they'd both embraced the Powers community while you'd showed us nothing but resentment. And I knew that the two of you had dated; that much had circulated around Atlanta for me to get a read on Deena and who she was."

He smoothed his shirt and stepped back to leave, elbowing his way through the gathered mob. The captain had arrived, curious and worried, but Walker held out a hand to demonstrate that he was finished. "I don't think you used her, per se—I actually think you *did* love her. I'm not disputing that. But you treated her like shit, man. You offered her your heart—your values—and after she dived in with both feet forward, you let her fall."

*That* got Boucher angry. He stalked after Walker, shoving cops aside. "Shut your fucking mouth. You have no *idea* what I felt for Deena. What I *still* feel."

Walker swiveled, walking backward toward the door with his palms raised in supplication. "You're right. I don't. Honestly? I don't much care. What I do care about, however, is that you left her again—you think she really wanted you to leave? I made that mistake, friend-o, and it was the stupidest mistake I've made in the last few hours."

He stopped at the door and looked away, settling his gaze on Enki and Cross. He smiled, hand resting on the handle. "But, hey, the last time you left Deena, she ended up becoming the world's greatest detective. So, again, I'm good with all this. Look, I just care about my partner, and I feel like an ass for not having stayed. Even with all the shit going down, with all your rules and threats, Captain . . . I never should have walked. That's not what a partner does. He stays, even when the going gets tough. Even when he might end up as part of the story. He stays to support his partner. And now," he announced, bringing the diatribe to a close, "I'm going to pack a bag and do exactly that."

"Walker." Cross stepped forward, features stoic and severe. Enki touched the captain's arm, and her grizzled, beleaguered superior shook it off. The room was silent, the entire bullpen having been drawn in to the tense and heated drama. Walker eyed Cross, waiting for the hammer to fall. But the captain placed both hands on his hips and motioned toward the door. "Call us when you know our girl's okay."

Walker raised his hand in a stiff salute. He nodded at Enki, raising an eyebrow, and then was out the door.

Standing alone at Walker's desk, seething with anger, Aaron barely gave the dispersing crowd a second glance. Awash in humiliation, regret, and justifiable anger, he reached for the phone and, getting an outside line, dialed a number. Aaron Boucher stood there alone, toes tapping against the floor, anxiously waiting for the party on the other end to answer his call.

# 21

—mm—

He'd managed to book a red-eye flight, arriving in Atlanta around six in the morning. Walker lurched about his spartanly decorated apartment, tossing clothing and assorted toiletries into a makeshift go-bag. He'd tried Deena twice since leaving, both calls heading to voice mail with all the others. He'd debated leaving a message but decided to let it alone. Some things had to be said in person, as he'd managed with Boucher to exceptional satisfaction. Walker couldn't spend too much time basking in the glow of verbal triumph. Not when he had to get to Georgia—not when his only job was being there for Deena.

*I don't have a job. I'm unemployed during the holidays.* It felt weird to say, even in his head. Walker had been unemployed before. In fact, this wasn't even the first time he'd been without work since becoming a cop. The roller coaster of the last few years had torn his badge away more times than he could count—some by choice, more often by decree. This time, however, he was glad to be operating on his own. He didn't have to deal with the whirlwind of crazy that had descended on PHD. The Human Front allegations and mounting body count were no longer his headache. Even the specter of Joseph Monroe—what his death represented, the damage its truth would effect—that, too, was no longer his concern. He didn't have to save the day or solve the murders. That was someone else's problem now—Enki, perhaps, or Corbin Kirk, when he was back on his feet.

But still . . . the guilt remained.

The adrenaline high had worn away, and Walker slowed down, folding a T-shirt, pacing the bedroom as he considered next steps. Despite claims otherwise back in the bullpen, he *was* running away. Not from Deena but from her case. From facing past mistakes. He did know more about the Liberty killings, about what had happened in Atlanta than he'd let on, as he'd revealed to Boucher before thirty cops and a handful of hookers. Christian Walker—Diamond then and Blue Streak years before—hadn't been blinded by glamour and idealism. He was aware of the corruption that had permeated Atlanta. Like Z, a former colleague who'd used his powers to criminal advantage, Diamond knew something was shady about the Citizen Soldier. But he'd left it alone, even after what happened in Detroit, no doubt due to the respect he still afforded the elder statesman.

But perhaps he'd also left it alone because of his distaste for the opposition—men and women clamoring for the death of the powered individual. *The Human Front.* Malachi Crane and his pack of wolves. And sure, if a Power capped a few . . . even if that Power lived on the wrong side of the law . . . then what was the *big deal*? Sure, guys like Boucher—with anti-Powers vitriol and cries of corruption—yeah, they could be a hassle. But at least Boucher was a cop; Diamond had known, if push came to shove, that Boucher would do the right thing. The same couldn't be said for THF goons. And so, Diamond—like Triphammer, Zora, and all the others—had looked the other way. He never questioned the Soldier's directives (or, mostly, lack of directives) and did the job to the best of his understanding.

Thus, the guilt. The realization that he'd actually been wrong. As was Triphammer, as was Zora. They'd all fucked up, and now it was coming back to bite them on the ass, because the goddamn Citizen Soldier was a traitor. And truthfully, Walker *did* care. He couldn't walk away, not until he assumed responsibility for his actions . . . or as the case might be, his inaction.

He tried Deena again, and when the machine picked up, he tried Enki instead. Another drive to voice mail. Walker abandoned his bag and the half-folded, discarded clothes. He walked into the kitchen and opened the refrigerator door, bathing in the bright light as he searched for a drink.

Then the doorbell rang.

At ten-thirty on a Tuesday night.

*Could be Enki,* Walker thought. *She may have followed me home, wondering if I'm okay, maybe offering to come along to see Deena. Another great partner—that's probably why I couldn't get her phone. Terrible Wi-Fi in these old lead-and-asbestos prewar buildings.* He marched to the door, catching the knob on the second ring, and twisted it open.

"Enki?" But it wasn't Enki. It was a man in a hood. Shorter than Walker, which wasn't unusual, but dressed in a coat, jeans, and a pair of bloodstained sneakers. The man clutched a crowbar, a fact that entered Walker's mind at the moment he dimly remembered to slam the door. Unfortunately, it was a moment too late.

The hooded man swung the crowbar, catching Walker on the side of his face. Christian stumbled back into the apartment, blood gushing from a tear at his cheek, jaw damaged as he fell onto the floor. The hooded man advanced, entering the apartment and closing the door behind. He lifted the crowbar, raising it above his head, but Walker regained his senses and kicked him in the gut. The invader doubled over and dropped the crowbar; Walker scrambled toward his bedroom, racing for the revolver he kept beneath his bed.

He didn't get halfway across the apartment.

The hooded man grabbed Walker by the ankle, clamping down with a viselike grip. He grunted, never uttering a word, and tossed Walker into the television. Christian soared—having been lifted off his feet—and his back smashed into the flat-screen, shattering it into millions of pieces. He was in pain. Whoever his attacker was, whatever his agenda, it was clear that he possessed powers of some kind. Despite his short stature, the invader was strong and *fast*. He was on Walker before he hit the ground, reaching down to snake the large detective's collar and towing him toward the kitchen. Walker grabbed for the masked man's hands, hoping to break his grip, but his assailant wouldn't be deterred. The hooded man used his free hand to pummel Walker's face, tearing a gash in his cheek. Blood dripped onto the small knockoff Persian rug that Walker kept beneath a coffee table. The hooded man paid no mind; he continued their brief trek to the kitchen, dragging Walker along the way.

Walker extended his arms and flattened both palms against the wall to either side of the kitchen. The hooded man bent down to pry one hand away and then the other, but not before Walker raised his chin and butted the invader in the face. The intruder grabbed his own nose and stumbled backward onto his ass, giving Walker the opportunity he needed to get to his feet and tackle the trespasser. They grappled in the galley, and Walker understood that without powers, he was completely outclassed. He loomed above the masked man, sure, but couldn't match his strength and speed—not to mention his vicious ferocity. Walker disengaged and scrabbled around the counter, grasping for knives or utensils. The hooded man had beaten him to the punch; he swung a meat tenderizer (a gift from Deena, who enjoyed a fine club steak tartare), bashing it into the side of Walker's head, sending him sprawling back into the common area.

Walker clawed his way onto his stomach and crawled for the bedroom, shoving aside the coffee table along the way. The hooded man followed, and so Walker tossed furniture and knickknacks in the shorter man's direction, doing his best to slow him down. Finally, he clambered over the remains of the television—Walker's palms dug into glass, jagged pieces tearing into knees and hands. He lifted a larger piece and, rearing up like a Neanderthal warrior (*Not too far a stretch,* Walker gibbered in his head; *I* was *Gora*), the battered detective launched himself at the hooded man and jabbed the glass into his shoulder.

Walker's assailant grunted and then blindly lashed out with his right arm. He connected with Walker's chest, smacking the injured cop and sending him crashing through the bedroom wall. He landed on the bed and then bounced off, landing next to the far-left nightstand. *Excellent,* Walker thought, struggling to catch his breath. *Just where I needed to be.* Something hurt inside; a broken rib, maybe several. He hoped he hadn't punctured a lung. He really couldn't breathe . . . and he worried that the wheezing might give him away as he scrabbled beneath the mattress. His fingers connected with a small briefcase, and Walker dragged it out, undoing the latches to reveal a handheld machine pistol—semiautomatic, loaded, and ready for emergencies like this. The last few years, Walker had been ambushed in his apartment—as he was now—by an assortment of Powers, crazies, girlfriends, and would-be gods, both cosmic and mythological. In fact, Satan himself had targeted Walker . . . or so the whack job had him believe. Not that a gun would do anything against the Prince of Hell, but it might put a small hole in a short, little Power with a shard of glass through his left shoulder.

Walker pulled himself to his feet. He raised the pistol and turned to face the demolished bedroom wall. With any luck, half the building had heard the commotion and called a cop or three. Enki wasn't coming, and Deena wasn't, either. Walker was alone until this was over . . . or until some well-meaning, concerned citizen managed to convince 911 that the building was falling apart around them.

*Not on my watch. Not if I have to feed this guy the bullets myself.* Determined to make that happen, Walker advanced on the wall—

—only to have someone other than the hooded man tear the pistol from his hand.

Surprised, Walker glanced right. A second, taller masked man cocked his head and examined the weapon. Exerting little effort, the second intruder twisted the gun into an unrecognizable lump of metal. Walker lunged, but like his shorter associate, the man in the hood was faster. He slapped the broken detective into his equally broken wall. Walker landed on his back halfway between both rooms. He looked into the common area and spied the first man, massaging his shoulder.

The second man stepped through the bedroom door—it was still intact, swinging on loosened hinges. He stared at Walker and then up to his colleague.

"Couldn't have left some fight in him?" Walker didn't recognize the man's voice; muffled by the mask, the hooded man had erred on the side of caution and spoke through a vocal synthesizer. The words were electronically amplified, reverberating throughout the apartment. "I know I'm late, but that's just rude."

The original assailant stood up, brushing away dust from his battered coat. "This is taking longer than you suggested," he replied, voice digitally altered, as well. "Let's finish it already."

The second man returned his attention to the gasping detective. "Hear that, Walker? My colleague wants you to go out with a whisper, not a bang. Now, me? I disagree."

The man hunkered down into a crouch, hands hanging between his knees. He reached out to tap the broken plaster. "See, I think you deserve to go out the way you do everything. The way you screw up your relationships. The way you solve cases. The way you flew above the city, inspiring others down below."

He gloated into Walker's ear, laughing with a shrill, sibilant whisper. "Magnificently. Good night, Christian. I'm sure you didn't think we'd forgotten you."

With that, the hooded man grasped a portion of the wall and tore it apart, throwing chunks of plaster against a beam that ran perpendicular to the building. A load-bearing beam, Walker recognized.

*Shit,* he complained to the universe, frantically pleading for a bit more time, *I wasn't fucking serious about the whole building-falling-apart thing.*

After that, all that Walker heard was the screech of shifting iron and the crumbling roar of thousands of falling, broken bricks. That, and triumphant laughter.

Then, mercifully, the enveloping rush of silence.

# 22

—⁓—

**December. Wednesday morning. 7:10 A.M.**

Deena sulked and waited in the austere, glass-enclosed suite that served as the central boardroom for the Human Front. Snow dripped from her hair and her coat, pooling on the floor and the wide, oval table that dominated the space. She glanced out across the hallway—most of the offices were still dark; business wouldn't commence for another two hours. Or maybe everyone was just away visiting family for the holidays. Still, she'd assumed the organization would be in lockdown following Malachi Crane's blatant—and, to be fair, ballsy—shot across the prow of the government and authorities he'd rebelled against for most of his life. *That's what you get when you assume,* she thought, sanity and good sense pinwheeling away with every passing moment she spent soaking in this tastefully decorated fishbowl. *You make an ass out of every shit heel you meet. Even yourself.*

*That isn't how it goes, is it?*

Before she could elaborate to herself, Crane appeared as if from nowhere, his pumpkin head beaming with a cutaway, raggedy smile. Two bodyguards flanked the door, waiting just outside to prevent any trouble. *Smart,* she acknowledged. *Trouble's my middle name. Well, that isn't true. My middle name is Olivia, but let's just keep that to ourselves, boys.*

"So," Crane began, voice thick with oil. "Detective Pilgrim. You're back from Atlanta. Did you bring me a souvenir?"

She wasn't surprised. Deena had tried to keep her trip under the radar, but the Human Front had their claws in every city, informants in every cop house and hospital from Carlsbad to Key Biscayne. Hell, Waldo's doctor or one of the nurses—that *bitch,* the one who'd nearly gotten between her and Aaron—probably owned the private line to Crane's little kingdom. Fuck, as far as she knew, Aaron could have made the call himself. Deena didn't know who to trust anymore. But that's why she was here, dripping on the carpet of Satan's war room.

She'd boarded a plane late last night, hitting the snow-dappled tarmac again around 5:45. Deena hadn't traveled alone; she carried documents and records from Waldo's private files, carefully hidden away in a storage locker on the Atlanta piers. She also carried hours upon hours of testimony—her father's words, implicating Monroe as Liberty, suggesting that Aaron Boucher couldn't be trusted, either. First, she'd stopped at home and up-loaded her recordings to the cloud. Then she'd showered and changed, her mind still a whirlwind of betrayal and insecurity, after which she'd taken a circuitous path to 500 Fialkov Way. There had been reporters still camped out front—the Media Watch never stopped—and that was the last thing Deena had wanted. She'd been keeping this under wraps, playing the cards close to her chest. Launching herself up the stairs, elbowing past PNN, Channel 7, and all the rest would only serve to catapult this very personal evidence onto the world stage. And though it would probably come to that, Deena wasn't yet ready for that yet. First, she needed confirmation. She needed Crane to corroborate Waldo's accusations and admit—on paper, on digital device, whatever—that Joseph Monroe was Liberty. That members of the Human Front were, indeed, paid off by the nation's Top Cop to sub-due and murder individuals who had legally been granted their freedom in a court of law . . . or who hadn't been given the chance to be convicted in the first place. She needed Crane to exonerate Aaron Boucher of any in-volvement with the Liberty killings. She needed to know, to believe in the man she once loved. She needed to confirm that the man who had been the catalyst for her life behind a badge was truly clear of all wrongdoing . . . and that everything she'd heard in Atlanta was just a series of far-fetched allegations.

And so Deena had shivered on the outskirts of the media encampment, waffling between paying off a cleaning lady for entrance and simply storming up the stairs, hurrying through the crowd and into the building. Thankfully, the decision was taken out of her hands: moments after arriving on scene, Deena was approached by two of Crane's sinister aides and escorted into the offices via a side entrance.

Now here she sat, face-to-face with the embodiment of intolerance, hoping to confirm the words of a crooked cop. *What the fuck am I doing? Why not take this to Cross—or to Walker, if I even knew where the hell he is? Why am I here, talking to this demented pumpkin, depending on this hateful scarecrow to be the arbiter of truth?*

"Tell me," he began, settling in at the head of the table, "how is your father? Road to recovery and all that?"

She flinched and then decided to fuck it all. She slapped her phone down on the table and set it to Play. Waldo's voice, wheezing and addled by pain medication, drawled throughout the boardroom. The file played, and twenty minutes later, Crane reached out to shut it off. He sniffed once and then clasped his hands on the surface of the table. Crane stared at her, curious yet dismissive, waiting for Deena's opening salvo and truly looking as if he didn't give a shit if it ever came.

"Why not cooperate?" she began. "Your pals did. Quince, the Rammlers. They all took the Soldier's deal. Why not you?"

Crane's face widened to a smile, and he leaned back in the chair, holding out his hands. "My dear detective, even if this were true, I can't be held responsible for all the decisions made by poorly informed, weak-willed underlings, can I?"

"So you deny that it's true? That Monroe and my father *didn't* pay members of the Human Front to kill Powers and cover it up? Because I can show you stacks of depositions and courtroom testim—"

"Of course it's true. But a few bad apples don't represent the orchard."

"Goddamn—look, speak like a human being, okay?" Deena leaned forward and tapped her phone. "Did you or did you not refuse an offer by Joseph Monroe to kill specific individuals in exchange for financial gain?"

"I did."

"You . . . you did?" Stunned, she sat back. The room spun, and she had to grip the table to keep from falling. "Why refuse?"

"Simple," he replied with a wave of his hand. "At the time, Joseph Monroe was my enemy. We'd clashed in Vietnam, Detroit, and several other battlefronts along the way. I'm not in the habit of abandoning my principles and getting in bed with enemies, especially for something so crass as *money*."

"But he *wasn't* your enemy. You said it yourself: Monroe belonged to the THF. I've seen the tattoos in person."

Crane nodded, the wattle in his neck quivering in an obscene manner. "Yes, but that was much later. After we'd incorporated."

"Why? What changed your mind—or changed his heart?"

Crane grinned again, wrinkles cracking across aged, withered skin. "That's not for me to explain—or your shell of a father, my dear. That's someone else's story entirely."

"And if I told you again that by withholding that name, you could be charged with obstruction of justice?"

Crane stood up, still smiling, palms down on the table. "Then I'd tell you again that with the proper documentation, you'd be well within your rights to drag me downtown and hold me in one of your depressing little interrogation rooms for twenty-four hours. To save you some time, however, let me say this: in the end, we would arrive at the same conclusion. Me, a full day short. You, lacking the evidence and name your heart desires."

He circled the table and stared out the window, hands clasped at his back as he'd been the first time Deena had visited his office. *This guy sure likes to look out windows,* she thought, frustrated and grasping at nonexistent straws. "So you'll at least admit to the fact that Monroe, through Waldo, was releasing criminals and paying them to kill other criminals?"

He looked over his shoulder, nodding in confirmation. "I will."

"And that he did it using Liberty's name, creating a second persona under which he and several others stalked and murdered over fifteen powered and non-powered individuals?"

"I can corroborate that Mr. Monroe was involved, yes."

Deena raised an eyebrow, along with her voice. " 'Involved'? What kind of evasive fucking statement is *that*?"

The guards, alerted by Deena's sudden increase of antagonistic volume, turned and entered the boardroom. Crane waved them away; everything was fine. "If I'm evasive, Detective Pilgrim, it is only due to my continued reticence in telling another man's story. Joseph was involved with the Liberty killings, yes."

"Was he or was he not Liberty?"

Crane smirked and turned away, heading for the door. "Exactly that."

*What the fuck?* Deena stood up, melted snow sliding from her lap and onto the floor. "Hey, I'm not finished."

"But I am," he announced with an air of finality. "My offices are shortly about to open, and a phalanx of devoted staffers should be streaming from the elevators at any moment. I have answered every question I'm likely to answer, Detective, and should you require I do anything more, I suggest, for the third time, that you produce a document urging me to do so. Now, if you don't mind, please clear my boardroom and exit the premises. One of the men will show you out."

"Yeah? And what will you do?" She snatched up the phone, stamping toward the hallway. "Stir the pot some more? Announce the exact opposite of what you've told me? You've done it before."

Crane leered at her, flashing that blocky, pumpkin-headed smile once more. "If that's the way you choose to see it. As I said, I've explained everything I'm likely to explain. You asked what I planned to do now. I believe I'll put the coffee on before the receptionist arrives."

Five minutes later, Deena was back on the steps, shivering in the wind. Reporters surged forward, recognizing her and peppering her with questions both piercing and inane. She ignored them, shoving her way through their ranks with a few well-placed elbows. The parking lot had filled up since she'd gone inside; the denizens of 500 Fialkov Way were arriving for the day. She wanted to question them all, but she knew if she tried, Crane would release his goon squad. Anyway, she had plenty to figure out based on their meeting. A great deal to decide before she made her next move.

Deena headed north, leaving footprints in the snow as she left her car and pointed herself in the direction of the precinct. She didn't know if that was her final destination, but she knew she didn't want anyone trailing her steps. Losing a man on foot was easier than in a car; you could go down a subway, in a doorway, onto a roof. The city was Deena's fortress, and she knew ways to assure her solitude. She glanced back. She'd picked up two tails—one across the street, another on top of the adjacent building. Deena grinned, waved, and smiled. They both disappeared, respectively hiding in a doorway and ducking out of sight. She rolled her eyes and shook her head and then jammed both hands into her pockets. She looked back again and gestured for her tails to follow. "Come on! Let's go for a five-mile walk!"

She lost them in Tyler Square amid hordes of commuters. Deena turned left down Connor Street and doubled back on Hudson. She located a small bistro—the Armenian kind, one you could only access by walking downstairs—and settled into a corner booth with a piping cup of tea and a plate of *gatah*. She watched the door, waiting for men with snake-and-bullet tattoos to come wading into the café. But no one did; she owned the place, and the proprietor, delighted to have an early morning customer with a taste for his native delicacies, offered Deena a hearty bowl of *kalagyosh* with a stack of spiced croutons. She thanked him and ate slowly, placing her jacket on the back of a chair and consuming the first true meal she'd had in nearly a day. The *kalagyosh*—a vegetable stew—warmed her belly, and the tea soothed her throat, sore from having yelled at so many people in so short a period of time.

As Deena ate her breakfast, she considered the testimony that had been presented to her since she'd left for Atlanta. *On one hand, can I believe the word of a crooked cop?—Even if he is my father, Waldo was dirty and corrupt. That's not up for debate. Everyone has read the papers and knows what happened after the gang wars came to a close.*

*And can I believe the corroboration by a noted, manipulative, anti-Powers fascist who may simply be trying to further smear the once-sterling reputation of a living legend . . . and by doing so, clear a path to do the same for anyone connected with that Power?*

*Or do I believe the man who once owned my heart? A man who betrayed me before, who isn't the man he was back when I fell in love. A man who inspired me to be a good cop, even if he eventually turned out to be a rat bastard.*

"There's no way," she said out loud. "No way Aaron could have done the things my father said he did. Not for those reasons."

"Hm? Yes, yes. Coming right up," the bistro owner responded from the kitchen, having thought that Deena was asking for more croutons.

Aaron Boucher had left Atlanta because of men like Waldo, despite his obviously skewed confession. Aaron had been exhausted, tired of being forced to work with men who profited from the innocent and dealt dirty with the law. He left because Atlanta was dangerous—for the entire Boucher family—and he needed to get them away from the graft, corruption, and lies. No, Aaron might be a grade-one dick bag, but the only thing he was truly guilty of was betraying Deena Pilgrim and breaking her goddamn heart. She knew it.

*But still . . .*

Something didn't sit well with Deena, and it wasn't the *kalagyosh*. For one, who had infected her father? Nobody else had been there, and Waldo had been fine when he came to the door. A slow-acting virus? Timed to release and then spread quickly through his bloodstream? It made little sense to Deena. But then, none of Liberty's crimes really connected in any way. The MO shifted from place to place, and the victims—until now, until this new batch where various threads of the past found themselves centering on Joseph Monroe—had previously been random kills. So . . . maybe. Maybe it *was* Liberty.

*But again, there were three of us in the apartment: Waldo, Aaron, me. I know I didn't do it. Aaron claims he didn't, as well. Would my father have infected himself, knowing that Aaron and I would find a way to save his life? Would he put his life in that kind of danger, hoping for an honest moment—or perhaps to throw off the scent—in order to place the finger of blame on someone else? Someone he hated, like Aaron Boucher? Okay, let's say that's true. Then how the hell did the Liberty tag get on the door? We were with him the entire time. Did he pay someone else to do it, maybe the pantsless basket case across the hall? Or was Waldo working with someone else—Crane, perhaps, lying again to me?*

"No. I'd know," she muttered to herself, polishing off her *gatah*. *It made more sense that Aaron had placed it there, probably when he left to call 911 after surreptitiously injecting Waldo . . . or maybe when he'd first lingered in the hall.*

"Fuck!" she cried, banging a hand on the table. "I don't know *what* to believe."

The proprietor shuffled out. "More tea?"

"Keep it coming. Gonna be a long morning." The man smiled and hurried off, darting into the pantry for a fresh mug.

*I can't do this myself. I've tried; I'm too close to it. I have the word of three very different men, and I can't believe a single one. The only man I* can *believe, that I* can *trust, won't pick up his goddamn phone.* Deena glanced down, staring at the dark, dormant cell phone next to her plate. She willed it to ring, wishing that Walker would get over his bruised ego and call her the fuck back.

*Screw this. I'm going over there. He'll help me figure this out, right?*

She lifted the phone and willed it to ring one more time. *Walker!*

The device shuddered in her hand and started to vibrate. Deena jumped, taken aback, and nearly dropped it on the floor. She checked the number. It wasn't Walker, but she tapped to receive, anyway. An awkwardly posed image of Detective Enki Sunrise filled her mobile screen, saved to Deena's caller ID.

"Enki," she inquired, happy to hear a familiar and welcome voice, "where have you been?"

"Deena. I'm at Ellis General. You have to get down here right away, okay? Where are you? I'll pick you up."

She sat up in her chair, quickly tossing a handful of cash onto the table as she prepared to make her escape. "The hospital? Is it Kirk? Man, I feel like I've been in more hospitals—"

"Not Kirk," came Enki's response, somber and succinct. "It's Walker."

Deena's stomach leaped into her throat, and she knew with certainty that it wasn't the food. She grabbed her jacket from the back of her chair.

"I'm on my way."

# 23

⁓⁓

*December. Wednesday morning. 9:59 A.M.*

"—viewers tuning in, this is Collette McDaniels at Ellis General. Late last evening, yet another devastating, Powers-related catastrophe struck our city . . . circling at the edge of an ongoing national tragedy. According to eyewitnesses, two men entered a fifth-floor apartment at 44122 Andreyko Place—one in early evening, the other just after ten, moments before the building was destroyed. Over thirty-five injuries, fifteen near-fatalities, and at least six deaths were the result of an unknown altercation involving the owner of the apartment, Detective Christian Walker of the Powers Homicide Division. Walker, as regular viewers may recall, formerly operated as the masked vigilante known as Diamond. These days, he finds himself powerless, an unfortunate set of circumstances that landed Walker—no doubt at the epicenter of the wreckage—in Ellis's intensive care unit. More recently, Walker had been a key contributor to the terrible series of . . . wait . . . wait, hang on. Someone's coming through the door. Yes . . . yes . . . *Manny, bring the camera!* Walker's partner has arrived at Ellis, currently lead detective in the . . . *here,* I . . . Detective Pilgrim! *Deena!* This way. A moment for *Powers That Be*?"

"Are you fucking kidding me?"

"*We can edit that in post* . . . Detective, care to comment on—"

"Seriously, stick that camera in my face again, and you'll be picking glass out of your teeth."

"Really, Detective, our viewers just want to understand—"

"And *you*. Come near me—or Walker, for that matter—with a recorder, phone, chalkboard, or quill and I swear to fuck I'll boot you right in the dick."

"Well, that's just the kind of ill-mannered—hey . . . *hey,* where are you going?"

Deena hurried away from the salivating vultures skulking by the door. She flashed her badge and sidestepped the triage area of Ellis's emergency ward, casting about for a doctor, nurse, or familiar face to point her where she needed to go. The ward was loud and hot, littered with gurneys and wailing family members. She tried to flag down one of the orderlies, but every able-bodied professional had his or her hand in a wound or body. It felt like the last days of war, the screaming for help, and Deena whirled around at the nurses' desk, unsure where to go. She was especially disoriented after elbowing through not only a horde of journalistic bloodhounds but also an army of hysterical loved ones, not to mention angry protestors picketing on the street. Deena had already seen video of crowds like it around the city, either riled up by Crane's intolerant rhetoric or indignantly fighting against Human Front wackos who aimed to marginalize their right to powers. Three days after Monroe's death and the city was ready to blow. She hoped it wouldn't happen until after she solved his murder or at least got a chance to see her partner one last time. Deena spotted a tiny phalanx of cops and plainclothes detectives at the far end of the ward. Steeling her resolve, she headed in that direction.

"Deena!" She turned left and was elated to see Enki Sunrise hurrying down the hall with an armful of snacks. Enki handed Deena a pack of M&M's she'd retrieved from a vending machine. They hustled away, avoiding stares and possible distractions.

"What happened?" she asked Enki as they ducked into an empty room.

"Still piecing it together. Could be Liberty; could simply be an enemy with a grudge. Could also be an exploded gas leak. We'll know more soon, for sure."

"Was there a tag? Why do we think it could have been Liberty?"

Enki shrugged and poured candy down her throat. "We're not sure," she mumbled through a mouthful of chocolate. "Building's rubble; won't know if it's been tagged 'til we sift through the wreckage . . . or Walker comes to."

Deena touched Enki's forearm. "He's alive, though. Is he okay?"

Enki frowned. "He's stable, at least for now. Walker's a bruiser—and he used to have powers. That's why the doctors think he's not a puddle. But he is in pretty bad shape. Broken bones, contusions, heavy blood loss."

"But he'll live?"

Enki nodded in reply. "More than we can say for some of these poor bastards." She gestured to the sea of gurneys. "You think it was Liberty?"

Deena stepped aside to avoid a passing wheelchair. "I thought Liberty was with me, down in Atlanta . . . but so was Aaron, and then Aaron came back . . ."

"Right before Walker got hit."

Deena peered around the ward. "Where's Aaron now?"

"Last I saw him—and really, I only met the guy last night—he was stewing in the bullpen. He and Walker have history?"

"Not Walker. Me."

Enki raised an eyebrow and opened her mouth, and then she thought better of it and let it go. "Want him found? I can make some calls."

Deena vigorously shook her head. "Not yet. I need to work shit out, confirm a few things before we do. Can I see Walker? They admitting visitors yet?"

"Captain's been in, a coupla lawyers. No family as of yet."

Deena grimly stuck out a thumb and pointed it back and forth, between the two of them. "Family's here. Let's go."

Moments later, Enki closed the door, shutting out the madness, as Deena pulled a chair to Walker's bedside. Her friend, her partner, was stretched out amid a tangle of tubes, wires, charts, and sheets. A single window let in the light, casting it across his bed in a bright-yellow rectangle. Deena reached out to take Walker's hand, and her heart thudded against her chest. *I should have been here. I should have done something,* she thought, *instead of being so focused on the shit pile I left behind. You were right,* she admitted. *I was distracted—by Aaron, by Waldo, all that bullshit. I should have listened to you this one time . . . because face it, Walker, I'm usually the one that's right . . . but this time . . . this time it was* you.

She wiped a tear away. Enki, arms crossed, leaned against the wall and seemed amused. "What is it?" Deena retorted. "Didn't think I could cry?"

"It's like watching bears masturbate. Something you never see, something you aren't sure you ever wanna see again."

"Funny girl. Sit down; think on this with me a bit."

Enki pulled up a second chair. The room shut out all the noise, all the insanity waiting in the ward. Their world narrowed down to two detectives, an injured partner, and the incessant beeping of many, necessary machines.

"Fucking hospitals," Deena opined. "I really should see how the newborn is doing upstairs. Fuck, I was *just* here for him. First Kirk, then my dad. Now Walker. One more ER visit and I get free ice cream."

"Share it with Liberty. He's the one who got you here."

Deena pursed her lips. "It wasn't Liberty."

"How's that now?"

Leaning forward, she clasped both hands between her knees. "It wasn't Liberty. Monroe was Liberty."

Enki sat back and rubbed her jaw. "Busy man. First a hero, then a bigot, *then* a corpse . . . now a serial killer from beyond the grave. Great work ethic."

"No . . . he *was* Liberty the first time around. These new killings? That's somebody different. Listen . . ." Deena launched into her story, explaining to Enki what she'd learned from Waldo and Crane, leaving out only her father's last, secret bit of information—a tidbit she had yet to corroborate. She related what Quince had revealed in the investigation room and then tacked on her own suspicions about Aaron—as well as Walker's. *I should have listened,* she reminded herself. *He was right. He's generally right. Guess that's what happens when you're a goddamn superhero.*

"Wait," Enki responded. "So the Citizen Soldier was not only an antipowers militant but *also* a noted—and as of yet unconvicted—serial killer?"

"Yes'm." Deena polished off the M&Ms, tossing them down her gullet one by one. The sounds and heavy breathing coming from the bed faded into the background. Everything came down to the data—the facts—evidence that she, Kirk, and Walker had gathered over the last few days. *I wish I had a blackboard or some way to spread it out. But all I have is a cop on a chair and a pig in a blanket. And, of course, a heart full of regret. I wish the son of a bitch would just wake up so I can alleviate that . . . apologize and explain how much I need his help.*

*Then again, if I'm wishing for shit, how about strippers and a pony, God?*

Enki continued her summarization. "Monroe, working with your dad, released convicted criminals—Powers and anti-Powers both—in order to kill other *unconvicted* criminals and, what, clean up the streets?"

"I guess."

"Meanwhile, the cops and Powers look the other way and your dad has the released criminals tag their murders with Liberty's catchphrase. Because the Liberty killings were already a thing—the Soldier, operating on his own. Yes? But then what was the Soldier's original agenda?"

"Search me. Secretly killing Powers, I guess. The guy's a proven bigot."

Enki shook her head. "No, no. Some of his victims weren't Powers, re-member? The Rammlers—or at least the one who died years ago—he didn't have powers. So, again, *why?* And why didn't Crane take Monroe's deal? Sentimentality? He didn't wanna kill his own people? No, it's all kinds of interesting."

"Not to mention," Deena added, "my asshole former boyfriend *knew* about it, even though he claimed to be the last good cop in Atlanta, and he allowed it to happen until his pop was in danger."

Enki furrowed her brow. "You think the Bouchers were in on it? You said the victims were all men and women the judge couldn't convict."

"No," Deena assured the other detective. "You don't know the judge. I . . . I . . . just, the guy's the epitome of what it *means* to be a good man."

"You thought the same about Aaron, not to mention your father."

Deena frowned and sat back, folding her arms. *I don't buy it. There's no way the judge is involved . . . but Aaron? Do I believe for a second he might be lying, might have helped Dad in order to straighten up the judge's spotty record? I didn't two days ago, but now . . . now, I can't be certain.* She looked over at Walker, eyes closed and breathing through a tube. *You would know. You were certain. Wake up, dumb-ass. Wake up and help us.* But Walker continued to sleep, his ragged breath vibrating the IV drip. Deena motioned for Enki to drag her chair to the window, away from the bed, and she followed suit. They hunkered, dropping voices to a whisper, passing facts back and forth like a football.

"Okay," Deena started, "so we know the killer can't be Monroe. Because, I mean, weird shit happens in this town, but I know for a fact that dude's cooling in the morgue."

"Right." Enki nodded, counting on her fingers. "So that leaves Crane, Aaron, your father . . . ?"

Deena shrugged. "Crossed my mind. Waldo could have poisoned himself."

"Yeah, but he was in a hospital bed while Walker's house fell down. Not to mention while Quince was shot on Bernardin and E. Plus, you know, it coulda been a host of other folks connected to the original killings, the gang war, and the Front."

"See . . ." Deena rubbed her brow with both sets of fingers. "That's what's getting me. Who says it's *one* guy? Who knows if we have one or two killers on our hands—one here, one in Atlanta—and it's some kind of fucked-up revenge scheme?"

"You think there's a dark horse?"

"Hoping." She didn't want it to be the most obvious choice. But Deena knew in her heart of hearts that Occam's razor would prove out: the simplest solution usually turned out to be correct. "Hoping, but I doubt it. The main issue we've always had with Liberty is that there's no pattern—no two killings happen the same way or at the same location. There's nothing that connects one killing to the other."

Enki thought for a moment and then stood up. She breathed onto the frigid window, cooled by the December chill. "Okay, let's go with location. Murder one?"

"Here in the city, 851 Taylor."

Enki used her finger to write it onto the window. "Then the Rammlers at Ellis Station." The second location quickly joined the first. "Okay, that's two," she said. "Next was Quince. The Nexus Club, or nearby."

"Yeah . . . no, no, wait. That's where Liberty *attacked* Quince, but she didn't die until—"

"—she got to Bernardin and E, where I found the poor girl." Enki nodded and, misting the lower half of the window, added it to the list.

"Okay, so my father was in Atlanta."

"Right, and Walker was here. Andreyko Place. But we don't know that was a Liberty killing yet. Plus, don't forget, Monroe's crime scene also had no tag."

Deena rubbed her temple. "Fuck. This is giving me a headache. What the hell do all those locations have to do with one another?"

Enki studied the list. "Not much. It's letters on a window. No connection."

Deena glanced up. *Hang on.* "What did you say?"

"Letters on a window. What?"

Deena stood up. A light came on inside her mind, illuminating a wonderful—possibly horrible—truth. She'd felt it before, on earlier cases. The moment where the tumblers unlocked and everything clicked into place. Enki had been on the right track—the locations being the tenuous connection—but the addresses or general locations . . .

. . . *the specifics. The devil in the details.* She stepped over to the window, elbowing her friend aside. Out in the hallway, she could hear cops and doctors arguing outside the door. Deena didn't care—no one was getting inside, not until she pieced this together. *And I think . . . I think I'm close. This is important. The details. Both of the case and maybe my past. Shit, I hope I'm right.*

*Shit, I hope I'm not.*

Deena marked a letter next to the first location, 851 Taylor. It was the letter *B.*

Enki looked confused. "I don't get it."

"Not yet you don't." She continued to write, inscribing a letter *E* adjacent to Ellis Station, and then circled the *E* next to Bernardin.

"'*Bee*'? We looking for an apiarist with a grudge?"

Deena sighed. "Seriously, shut up. Look: Monroe was killed in apartment 3*B.* The Rammlers? We found them on the *E* line."

Enki nodded and then pointed to the circle. "Oh. Okay, I get it. I get it. They all have a letter in them. Bernardin and *E.* What's Walker's apartment number?"

Deena shook her head. "See, I don't think Walker was part of this. I think that was . . . that was removing a potential obstacle. He just got in the way."

Enki seemed skeptical. "I dunno. Seems convenient to leave it out."

"Trust me. I don't think Walker's building was supposed to go. He was just collateral damage; if Christian had walked away, if he'd just kept his mouth shut, he would have been allowed to live. That's why the commission, all of a sudden—assuming there ever *was* a commission—broke protocol to move him aside. Maybe. That seems too much like a conspiracy rabbit hole I don't want to go down, though."

"Wait, wait, *wait*. You think . . . you think *Aaron* is the killer. Right?"

Deena teared up as she traced a line to the letters. "I know he is, and this is the genius in his plan: he left a riddle that no one could solve but me. . . . . . or maybe his father, depending on his history with the judge. That's why he sidelined me in Atlanta. That's why he left me behind."

"Deena . . ."

"Look. Look at this." Her finger strafed the surface of the window. "*B . . . E . . . E . . .*" She brought the line up, back toward Waldo's location. "And *B*."

"There a *B* in your dad's address?"

"No. But Liberty used hepatitis B as the murder weapon."

"Again," Enki reiterated, "I dunno. Seems like an awfully convenient acrostic. And what the hell does 'beeb' mean? Like 'the Bieb,' that singer? Is it a music thing?"

Deena pointed at Enki in triumph. "Exactly. But not exactly."

"*The* chords." *Aaron's eyes twinkled, reflecting the sunlight streaming through the window.* "*The same chords again.*"

*Deena flopped onto the bed. She groaned.* "*God. The chords again? This may be way on the nose, bro, but you're like a broken record with those things.*"

*Aaron sat up and spread his hands, wiry arms stretching against his cotton tee.* "*You gotta hand it to me, lady. There are five songs topping the charts with the same BEEBA chord structure. B-E-E-B-A. Even more when you page through the annals of rock history—*"

Deena smiled. Her heart hurt, and she was sad, but she'd managed to pull her shit out of the wreckage yet again, and so there was triumphant satisfaction, as well. "I quite like the annals," she echoed herself, and then she explained Aaron Boucher's chord theory to Detective Enki Sunrise.

"Okay," Enki acknowledged, "I mean, I guess it fits. But you're missing a letter, right? Where's the *A*?"

"Not sure. Could be a location, a method, a secret codename, anything." Deena wracked her brain, racing to think. If it were a location, where would that location be? She ruled out the precinct, Ellis General, and her own apartment, not to mention Enki's and the captain's. Anxious, desperate to put it together, she ran through the names of all individuals she could possibly connect to both the Monroe and Liberty cases. And then it hit her. If everything that her father had told her was true—if Monroe and Aaron had quietly been working together in Atlanta, and Aaron was using the new murders to tie up loose ends . . . to finish off those in the know . . . then there were only two possible victims. Aaron would never kill the judge, so that left only one possible location . . .

"500 Fialkov Way, suite 4*A*." Horrified, she turned to Enki Sunrise. "My crazy ex-boyfriend is gonna kill Malachi Crane."

Enki nodded and hustled to the door. She wrenched it open and stuck her head into the hallway, snapping to the cops for help. "Hey—I need a current location on Aaron Boucher. He's that special investigator over from Washington, dragged in to help on the Liberty murders. APB, wide, focused on the area around Fialkov Way, the Human Front building. Find him; get him locked down and in cuffs."

Enki came back inside. "You think we missed him? Should we call Crane?"

"No, I'm going over there. This ends before noon."

Enki placed a hand on Deena's. "I'm with you."

"So am I," Walker suddenly chimed in.

Surprised, they turned back to the bed. Walker was sitting with his feet on the ground, naked from the waist up. He was busying himself at his wrists, trying to remove the IV since he'd already pulled the tube out of his throat. His voice was dry and raspy, and he looked as if he'd been on the losing end of a fight with a Mack truck. But his eyes were clear and determined, despite the medicine pumping through his veins.

"Fuck that," Deena replied, moving toward the bed. She grabbed one arm, Enki the other, and they wrestled the injured, protesting detective back onto the sheets. "You're staying here and getting better. Remember? You're off the goddamn case."

A beat cop ducked into the room, addressing Enki and then smiling when he saw that Walker was awake. "Detectives? We have a location on Special Investigator Boucher. Hacked into his rental's LoJack system; tagged him on Paige, coming up on Fialkov Way."

The ladies traded knowing glances, and then Deena barked at the cop, "Get a team out there, nice and discreet. Cut him off before he gets to 500 Fialkov; keep him quiet until I arrive. Don't alert anyone in the building—if he makes it that far, and he should *not* make it that far. I'll join them presently. And someone call Judge Kenneth Boucher—his number should be on file. Get him down to the station—keep him situated until we get back there with his son."

The cop nodded. "I'll keep it on the local dispatch, contained frequency. They'll send a few cruisers down." He left the room, leaving the three detectives alone.

Walker tried to sit up again. He grabbed Deena's forearm, and she looked down and then lost herself in her partner's steely, watery eyes. "Deena . . ." he began, wheezy voice wavering on the edge of forever. They hadn't seen each other in a day, but the previous twenty-four hours had put each of them through the wringer. They had everything to say, yet nothing was required; as partners, they were allowed that shorthand. Anyway, it would have been awkward. She'd basically reamed him out in a room very much like this one, back when she'd been on the other end of the pain stick . . . and to be honest, her neck and head still throbbed. She was dealing with her baggage, Walker his own. And Deena also knew there was something else going on— something about Monroe, about the last few days, that she would never truly understand. She could let that go. Not knowing all of Walker's secrets didn't mean she couldn't trust him as a partner. She had secrets of her own— as had her father, Aaron, and all the rest. But partners had to put that shit aside.

Walker would open up when he felt it necessary. He'd unload his doubt, guilt, and the history that weighed him down—whether related to this case or something completely new. One day—probably not today or tomorrow.

And that was fine. Deena, meanwhile, would endeavor to do the same. She'd hopefully explain her recent emotional roller coaster . . . the lies and truths she'd discovered over the last three days. That was coming—but for now, they needed to trust one another, work together to solve the maelstrom on their doorstep, and put an end to the rich history of death and lies.

Walker opened his mouth again, trying to explain or apologize, but Deena cut off the big man before he could continue.

"No, jerk. You're staying here. Enki and I got this one. And keep your mouth shut; I know what you're trying to say."

Walker shot her a quizzical glance and then lifted himself off the pillow.

"No," she answered his unspoken question, coupling it with a smile. "There isn't any fuckin' coffee."

# 24

-ıllı-

**December. Wednesday morning. 11:42 A.M.**

Enki's Range Rover swerved around the corner of Parker and Haspiel and then shot across an alley to connect with Fialkov Way. They were five minutes out, and Enki did her best to ensure the SUV didn't skid in the freshly falling snow. Wipers squeaked against the windshield. Deena covered her ear with one hand, ignoring the complaining wipers as she earnestly spoke into her cell phone.

"Yes," she confirmed for the cop on the other end of the line, "I know he's no longer on the force, but his life is in danger. Move him off the ward and into protective custody *now*. That's right. Waldo Pilgr—what? Hey, look; no one's asking you to . . . no . . . no, hey, are you a *cop*? Oh, an *agent*. My apologies." Deena rolled her eyes as Enki grinned in the driver's seat, gripping the wheel and slaloming past Fialkov's 800 block. "Look, Waldo Pilgrim. He's involved in the Liberty murders—remember those? *Yeaaaah*. There you go. Just get him into custody. Lock him up for all I care. But you have to *protect* him until he can testify. Okay? Okay . . . great. Thank you again. And for the other thing, right. I appreciate it all. You, too."

Deena sighed with frustration. She took a breath and held on to her seat belt as Enki steered toward their destination. They'd had no report regarding Aaron's arrest, and Deena wondered if he'd gotten to the building before anyone could pick him up. They had to try and stop him before he killed again. Before Liberty took revenge one last time.

*I still can't believe it. How many times did he bitch and moan about putting Liberty away? How many times did I lie in his arms, sit on the porch, and listen as he went on about doing it* by the book? *Due process, a trial of one's peers, all that happy horseshit. And all that time, this douche bag was lying straight to my face. I wonder what the hell* else *he was lying about.*

The events of the last three days caught up to her like a freight train. A whirlwind of victories and betrayals flashed before her eyes. Aaron had known about the Rampage Brothers; he'd known about the guitar strings that Kirk found in Ellis Station. Not because he was a musical enthusiast, but because they were the strings he'd purchased and used to snick the Rammlers' heads from their beefy German shoulders.

*And he'd known about Monroe's ties to Liberty and maybe even the Human Front. He had to have known,* right? *He probably knows why Crane refused Monroe's deal. Why else come here other than to get closure, to finish the job? Crane had stayed in prison; he didn't mar the judge's track record. No, it had to do with Monroe . . . with his tattoos and hatred of powered individuals. That made sense, right? And Dad . . .*

. . . Deena's father—what had *that* been about? Shutting Waldo up or getting revenge? Did Aaron try to kill him because he was gonna squeal? That was ridiculous. Waldo had stayed inside his little hole for the last decade, barely coming out to even call his daughter. What did he care about Aaron or Kenneth Boucher after all these years? He didn't, nor did Aaron care about him . . . but Aaron had been afraid of what Waldo might say when faced with a daughter seeking the truth. *Maybe the mutated hep B was meant for someone else—Crane, Walker, or another target we don't yet know about?* Was Aaron that desperate and clever, and was his plan unraveling so badly that he'd take a shot at her father and seamlessly fold it into his insane, horrible plan?

*For that matter,* Deena wondered as Enki rocketed up the street, *what about the fact that he fucking strangled me the other night? Liberty said that I'd been betrayed. I thought he meant Walker—because, well, Aaron had been there for me and Walker was disengaging. But now I know, don't I? Sure, he probably hoped I'd immediately focus on Walker, too. Aaron hates Walker—afraid, no doubt, that he knows something and might expose his string of murders. Walker had been local during the gang war—we'd never met, but I think he knew Waldo. I know he knew Monroe. Maybe Aaron had opened his investigation as a way of getting Walker out of the way without having to kill the guy? Or maybe . . . once Walker wasn't a cop anymore, Aaron felt he could ice him without being a cop-killer? I don't know. He's been three steps ahead, betraying us all.*

*God, I want to kill him. No . . . I just want this to be over. And then . . . and then I'm out.*

"Let's go."

Deena looked up, jarred from her reverie. They'd arrived at 500 Fialkov. Enki had pulled her SUV around the edge of the crowd, skirting the sea of fanatics and rabid reporters, aiming for the parking garage in the back of the building. There was a gatehouse, and Enki flashed her badge at the guard. He waved them forward and then reached for his phone. Deena pulled her gun and aimed it at his face.

"Open up," she barked, gesturing toward the gate. "Seen a guy come this way, thin and dark? Maybe looks like a cop?"

The guard frowned. "Seen a lot of guys today maybe look like a cop."

Deena motioned forward. "Open the fucking gate, will ya? No one likes a gut shot wiseass." The guard nodded and raised the barrier. Deena waved him out of the gatehouse with her gun. "Around the building, toward the front. Don't call anyone; don't warn security. Give me your phone."

"What?"

"Your phone," she said, gesturing with her hand. "Let's go. And your cell."

Curious, the guard slowly handed over the wireless handset to the gatehouse phone and a tablet. Deena snatched them from his grasp. She smashed the handset and snapped the cell in two, tossing the pieces out the window.

"Hey!" the guard objected. "What the fuck do you think you're doing?"

Deena stopped him with a finger and a scowl. "You know who I am? I'll find you. You know who I fucking am?"

The guard, taken aback by her tone, stopped and shook his head, sweat flying from the brim of his cap. "No. No, I don't."

Deena smiled. "Great. Have a nice day."

Enki drove into the garage and turned the corner. Before them, parked on an angle, were two police cruisers. Their lights were flashing, red and blue painted against the garage's peeling walls. Enki stopped short, put it in park and then leaped from her seat and drew her sidearm. Deena followed suit, edging out the passenger door and quietly creeping up on the leftmost cruiser. Just beyond, splayed out on the floor, she could see unconscious cops. Looming over them was Aaron Boucher, dressed in shirtsleeves, jacket and coat draped across his parked sedan. His hair was atrocious—corkscrews spiraling out from both temples, mussed by what had to have been a brief but invigorating round of fisticuffs. He was breathing hard, glancing at the detectives as they approached from opposite ends of the cars, guns and faces drawn.

"Hey, Deen." He waved, somewhat cavalier, as if Deena were meeting him for lunch instead of coming to arrest him. She squinted, lining her sight along the center of his chest. "Don't 'Deen' me. You know you're fucking under arrest, right?"

Aaron stared and then laughed. He wiped a hand against his shirt, knocking his tie askew, and then ran it through his unkempt hair. "See, I told you that you were one hell of a detective. Figured it out, huh? Sure took you long enough."

"Well, my partner's been out of commission, and my father nearly died, so as you can imagine, I've been a bit distracted."

Aaron held out his hands in supplication. "I'll admit to the latter, but as far as Walker, Deena, you know I—"

Her sidearm vibrated as she spat in his direction. "No, I don't fucking *know anything*. I *used* to know I loved you. I *used* to know I respected you, despite the fact that you dumped me without an explanation. But at least I know why now. At least now I know that you broke it off because you were afraid I'd find out you were worse than my father."

Deena advanced, and Enki followed. Human Front security, alerted no doubt by the untrustworthy guard, would be on them at any minute. But Deena had to get this out while she had the chance, to distract him until they could get him into cuffs. Her heart was brimming with hate and pain; this had to come out now before he took another step. "You inspired me to be a cop. Did you know that, Aaron? You and Waldo, the two assholes in my life. Because of you, I *made* something of myself. And you know what? I fucking hate you for making me realize that it was for *bullshit*. There are no good cops—not anymore. Maybe there never were."

She gestured toward Enki. "Well, maybe one or two."

Enki nodded, faced forward, arms extended and aiming at Aaron's face. "Thanks for that."

Deena heard footsteps in the distance, slapping against pavement and snow. She didn't know how close they were, so she rushed to finish. "You . . . you were *never* a good cop, Aaron. All this time, you were in on it. With Monroe, my dad. And you just . . . you wore a *mask,* like all the other Powers. You wore a mask and pretended to be somebody else. Someone I never should have trusted."

Aaron stuck his hands in his pockets. "I'm sorry you see it that way. But there's more to it, Deena. There's more you aren't aware of."

She laughed. "There *always* is. That's what we do—you, me, Walker. We hoard secrets. We can never trust anybody but ourselves, and so we hide the truth from those closest to us. You know the funny thing about Walker and the Powers? At least they're honest. They wear . . . wore masks in the open, so we *knew* they were hiding something. You and I? We don't even have the balls to be as honest as *that*."

She stopped talking, listening again for approaching footsteps. But the garage was silent as a tomb now; Deena stood there, pointing a gun at Aaron's chest, glancing down at the comatose policemen and fervently hoping they were still alive. Aaron fidgeted, shifting on the pavement, and she snapped back into position, aiming at his heart.

"Now what?" he asked. He held up his palms, waiting for a response.

Enki reached for a pair of handcuffs. "Now you have the right to remain silent."

He moved back, close to the wall, angling for the door that led out of the garage and into the building. "Come on. She just said there's no such thing as a good cop, and now you're playing one to her bad? Fuck . . . I mean, come *on*. Don't be absurd."

"Shut up, Aaron," Deena warned him, continuing to advance.

He turned toward her, ignoring the other detective. "Where was law and order back when Monroe killed random criminals because he hated what they stood for? Where was justice when Waldo gathered bribes and colluded with the enemy? No, don't make me laugh, Detective Sunrise." He held a finger out to Enki, pointing at her chest. Aaron's voice was loud and abrasive now, echoing throughout the garage. "You're arresting *me*? Your partner, Walker, *he* was the real bad guy. Him and Monroe. Walker was Blue Streak—did you know? He killed thousands of mafiosi . . . never brought them in by the book, he and his crew. And Diamond? That guy palled around with a traitor to his own people—don't tell me he *didn't fucking know*! They were longtime pals.

"No. . . ." He ran fingers through his hair again. "Walker's the criminal. Crane, Deena's father. The Soldier. Me? I just did what I've always done. I protected my family and the ones I loved. And I brought criminals to justice my *own* way. The *right* way. The way Monroe did poorly and for selfish reasons all those years ago."

Deena bit her lip. The gun wavered in her hand, waggling at Aaron. *Fuck him,* she thought. *Nothing but excuses and crazy manifestos. But there are no excuses for what he's done. He's no different from any other whack-job banger or half-pint kingpin we take down on a daily basis. He believes in rhetoric; he believes in his truth. But the only truth here is that there is* right *and there is* wrong. *And as a wise man once wrote, that distinction isn't difficult to make.*

*But still, I can't just shoot. I mean, there's history. And just like Walker had to step away from the Monroe case to get perspective . . . maybe I'm too close to all this. I don't love the guy anymore—like I did; I'm not that much of an idiot. But I'll admit I felt* something *for him these last three days. Yeah, there's heartbreak and betrayal, but also longing . . . and there were good times, too, no? I mean, he's a killer, don't get me wrong. But so am I. And Walker. We've killed in the line of duty, seeking justice. We killed men and mobsters, gods and glamazons. And who did Aaron kill? Intolerant hate-speeching, militant bigots? Superpowered thugs and hooligans? He tried to kill Waldo, but let's be honest, Deena . . . your father is as guilty of betraying the law as Blitzkrieg or the Rammlers or half a dozen criminals on Liberty's hit list. So who's to say that Aaron is wrong?*

Deena swallowed, desperate for a drink. And the answer came. Walker. *He tried to kill Walker. Even me, even Dad—those weren't as bad as trying to kill my partner, you righteous asshole. I loved you once, long ago. I was* inspired *by you. But you tried to kill my goddamn partner, and that cannot stand.*

She motioned for Enki to cuff him, covering from her side. But she'd waited too long, and before either detective could make a move, Aaron sprang and swept the gun from Enki's hand.

*So fast*, Deena gibbered inside her rapidly processing mind. *How'd he get so fast?* She steadied her pistol, preparing to fire . . . but she hesitated again, and he was on her like a cat, slashing at her wrist with iron fingers. She dropped the gun and kicked out, but Aaron spun Deena off her feet, sending her ass over teakettle onto the ground.

Enki scrambled for either gun, but Aaron danced her way and stepped on her leg, breaking an ankle. Enki muffled a scream and tried to grab his foot, but Aaron swiftly lifted up and kicked her in the head. Enki fell to the floor, skull colliding with one of the unconscious cops. She lay silent in a discarded heap.

Deena struggled to get up, but Aaron was already halfway toward the door. She shouted, and he turned back, staring over his shoulder.

"Give up, Deena. You can't stop me. You must know that by now."

She tumbled into a somersault, expertly snatching her gun as she came back onto her feet. But Aaron merely smirked.

"Don't take another step," she warned him. "So much as move toward the door and you're my personal Christmas turkey shoot."

Aaron glanced back at the gatehouse. Footsteps and commotion had returned, getting closer, angry and concerned strangers scurrying into the garage. Deena remained vigilant, keeping her gun trained on her former flame, edging closer to Enki to make sure her partner wasn't dead. She carefully bent down and checked for a pulse and confirmed that her battered friend was merely knocked out.

"No door," Aaron replied, chuckling to himself. "You got it." He bent slightly at the knees, gathering momentum. The concrete vibrated and then splintered around his shoes, a spiderweb of broken pavement radiating out across the garage floor. Deena watched, eyes wide and jaw slack. She barely had a moment to react when Aaron Boucher, the boy next door, leaped into the air and smashed through the ceiling. He was a blur of motion, hammering with his knuckles one floor above Deena's head, leaping and burrowing through to the second floor. Plaster and metal broke apart in his wake, showering down to the garage below.

Deena stood there dumbfounded, lowering her sidearm, just as Crane's goons arrived with weapons of their own.

*What the fuck just happened?* she wondered. *What the fuck did Aaron just do?*

# 25

⸺〰⸺

**December. Wednesday afternoon. 12:03 P.M.**

*I have powers. That's my secret. But I have another.*

*Nothing extravagant—exceptional enhanced strength, extra stores of speed, but most importantly, a severely accelerated supply of white blood cells protecting me from harm. It's like superimmunity—not only do they keep me safe from disease but the little buggers also make me resistant to foreign contaminants such as poison, powers, and the like. That's a little tidbit of information that few know. I can absorb most anything that comes my way: radiation, energy weapons, you name it. Anything that isn't a projectile. I can absorb, adapt, and make myself immune to it. But Malachi Crane will know all too soon—right before I snap his weaselly little neck.*

Aaron burst through to the third floor, punching his way through carpet and steel, scattering furniture and a handful of receptionists. He leaped up into a cubicle farm and started for an elevator on the far end of the floor. Office drones scrambled the other way, desperate to avoid the new arrival. Aaron didn't mind. He calmly walked to the elevator bank and jabbed the button with his index finger. He listened to shrieks as the third-floor residents continued their impromptu evacuation. *Calmly. Quietly. That's the way I had wanted to do this. Get in, get out.* He checked his watch: just after twelve.

*I figure fifteen minutes until the guards make their way to my location. Plenty of time.*

The elevator arrived, and he stepped inside. Aaron reached out again, stabbing the fourth-floor button, and then he settled back against the wall. He remained calm, as he'd been for the other murders. That bit with the ceiling, breaking through from the garage—that had been out of character. He'd prepared for this, understood it was a necessary end. Not just for Crane—who, let's be honest, deserved to die—but for Aaron, as well. And for Liberty and everything that name represented. Even still, there was a way to do these things. And Deena and Sunrise had fucked that up.

*One more floor. One last act and everything is over. My life, career, and any chance I ever had for love. Ironic, really. All this time sporting a name that I could never embrace. I never had freedom, the liberty to live the way I wanted. Love the woman I wanted. No—another person made my choices for me, set me on this path. There was a deal that had to be made, and I accepted it with eyes wide open. I became Liberty to save someone else's life, but not my own. This? This is me bringing the contract to a close.*

*Now I'm going to kill a man and by doing so, kill three: Crane, Liberty, and myself.*

"I'm coming," he spoke aloud, hoping the elevator had been fitted with bugs and cameras that might pick up the threat. "I'm coming for you, Crane. I'm coming in the name of *Liberty*."

The doors slid open. Aaron looked around the lobby of the Human Front's executive floor. The circular room, warm and inviting, was done up in neutral colors, inlaid with mahogany and bands of polished chrome. A large reception desk dominated the space, staffed by an attainably attractive brunette and littered with telephones and bowls of sugary treats. Two leather couches lined the walls, set adjacent to matching chairs. Racks of magazines—quite diverse, dated no earlier than the previous week—had been affixed to the wall along with tasteful, generic pieces of art. By looking around the lobby, one would never know that he or she was standing in the foyer of the most aggressively intolerant incorporation of bigots in the nation—that is, if their eyes hadn't been drawn to the carefully inscribed logo looming above the desk: a bronze depiction of the fist-and-lightning symbol the Human Front had adopted as their corporate mark.

Aaron's eyes *had* been drawn to it; he approached the desk, ignoring the screams filtering in from the floor below and the blaring alarm that now shrieked throughout the building. The receptionist stood up, greeting him with a smile and then with an illegal Glock, lifted into view from where it had lain hidden beneath the desk. "Can I help you?" she sweetly inquired. "Do you have an appointment?"

Aaron broke into a grin and beckoned for the woman to shoot.

# 26

‑‑‑‑

Deena continued staring at the ceiling, watching frantic staffers rush to the nearest exit. She was astounded. *Aaron Boucher has powers. I mean, what the holy* fuck?

All her life, the single constant remained that Deena felt she'd understood the man who'd inspired her to be a cop. Despite Aaron's treating her poorly and cutting off the relationship for what she'd felt to be an insufficient reason, Deena at least had taken comfort in the fact that she'd loved a good man. The last good man she truly ever knew.

But these past few days . . . getting to know Aaron, immersing herself in his life once again, the layers of his carefully constructed façade had been peeled away—like a rotten onion—and now she knew him for what he really was.

*Also? Aaron Boucher has powers. Are you goddamn* kidding *me?*

He'd been the poster boy for hating the powered community, just shy of tattooing a fist-and-lightning onto his bicep. Not that he ever showed disdain for what a powered hero could be . . . there were many that he *did* commend and use as example. Aaron only hated the Powers he *knew.* The ones in Atlanta, the ones who'd let the city down.

Now she discovered that he was one of them. He could have saved so many lives, could have ended the gang wars by *being* the poster boy for his own kind, rather than deceitful, deceptive Monroe. But instead, he chose to wear his mask—yet another in a succession of equally disappointing masks. Now, she learned Aaron was using his talents not to uphold law and order, no, but instead to undertake acts of vigilantism. *He used his powers to kill criminals. What a fucking hypocrite.*

Sudden noise dragged Deena back to reality. Wet boots clomped on the cracked pavement, indicating the arrival of Malachi Crane's goon squad. She dragged herself away from the hole above her head. Four well-armed bigots arranged themselves in a circle around the two detectives—and the comatose policemen—decked out in head-to-toe lightweight armor emblazoned with the colors and logo of the Human Front. Their faces were hidden beneath what appeared to be a set of motorcycle helmets; the visors were drawn, and she could see herself reflected in the glass. Each thug carried a two-handed, technologically advanced machine pistol, tricked out with laser sighting, flamethrowers, and computer-enhanced smart-tracking capabilities. Measuring one of the weapons, Deena could see the way it corrected its aim every time she swayed to the left or right. Thin beams of crimson light bounced across the cruisers, bodies, walls, and cars, and three of them sighted her chest, zeroing in on Deena's heart.

She held up her piece and widened her eyes, showing them that all was cool. "Hey," she carefully stated, "I'm not here to cause trouble. I'm here to stop it, okay? Malachi Crane? Your boss? He knows who I am."

One of the goons raised his chin, indicating for the thug to his left to take her into custody. The second goon stepped forward, right hand leaving the machine pistol, reaching out to grab Deena by the arm.

"I wouldn't do that if I were you," she warned him. "I'm just here to save your boss's life. And I want to make sure my friend," Deena continued, pointing to Enki on the floor, "is A-okay. Okay?"

The building shuddered, and Deena heard a fresh set of squeals emanating from the floors above. Everyone in the garage looked up as dust and plaster rained down from the ceiling. "See?" she explained. "It isn't me. It isn't Enki here or any of the cops. Us cops? We're here to help. But you have a killer on your ha—"

The first helmeted goon gestured in her direction again, and the second guy advanced once more, placing a gloved hand on Deena's forearm. Scowling, she grabbed the hand and twisted left, dragging him over her body and onto the hood of a car. Deena flipped her sidearm, butt-first, and slammed it against the helmet, shattering the pane of glass. The goon blinked rapidly as the visor shattered inward, doing his best to avoid shards in his eyes. Deena held a hand to the thug's throat and snapped up the other, aiming her gun at the other three.

"I told you assholes, we don't have time for this. There's an unregistered Power running amok in your corporate office, hell-bent on icing your esteemed CEO. I suggest you either call for backup and get on up there to get your jollies . . . as you anti-Powers nut bags love to do . . . or else drag these cops," she indicated, gesturing to her colleagues on the floor, "and my friend back up the ramp and head for safety. Either way, your beef isn't with me."

The guard on the car struggled against her grip, both hands wrapped around Deena's wrist, trying to break her choke hold. He attempted to kick, but she adjusted her stance, twisting away so that his feet struck air. The other three shifted and stared at one another. A private, silent conversation took place before Deena's eyes, and a moment later, the Human Front goons reached down and started dragging cops up by their armpits. Deena nodded once and then released the fourth guard. He coughed for a bit, massaging his throat, and faced off with the surly little detective. She sneered in his face, and he backed off and then gingerly stepped around her, headed to help Enki to her feet. Deena gave him a hand, wincing slightly as the garage shook violently. The goons traded frightened glances and hurried to drag the beaten policemen out past the gatehouse. Deena ducked her head and faced Enki one more time. She was moaning, low but audible. Deena smiled and then patted her friend on the arm. She picked up Enki's discarded gun, stood up, and barked instructions at the remaining guard.

"Get her out of here, back beyond the media, and find someone to set her leg. Have your men establish a barricade or police line until my backup arrives. If you don't hear police sirens in the next ten minutes, call it in. Got that?"

The guard nodded to confirm, eyes still blinking rapidly beneath the broken helmet. He gently took Enki in his arms and started up the ramp. Halfway, he turned back and shouted, "How do I call it in?"

"What's the matter?" Deena jibed, sprinting for the building entrance. "Can't spell the word '911'?"

# 27

~~~

A bell rang behind Aaron, and he turned aside, swiveling in time to see Deena barrel out of the elevator, a pistol in both hands. The office receptionist opened fire and Deena flattened herself on the ground, scrambling for cover behind one of the wide leather couches. Aaron pivoted and then pushed away from the ground with a heel, vaulting across the lobby to land on the mahogany desk. Astonished, the receptionist lifted her gun, but Aaron kicked out and broke her wrist, sending the Glock clattering to the floor. The poor woman's jaw dropped as Aaron kicked again, shattering several teeth and sending her to join the fallen weapon. Leaping, he landed on his feet and transitioned into a sprint, avoiding two bullets that Deena had fired from behind the couch.

He shouldered through a set of double doors, splintering them in his wake, and stumbled into the wide, marbled hallway of the Human Front's executive wing. He grabbed a random desk and dragged it to block the doors, ensuring himself a bit of time as Deena worked to get past it. Aaron walked into the hall. Glass doors and windows stretched as far as he could see, sectioned into offices and a partitioned conference room in the middle of the floor. A lone office dominated the far-left wall—this one wasn't transparent but rather done up with artfully crafted opaque doors, shutting out visitors and staffers alike. Another receptionist sat in front of the office, and when she spied Aaron standing in the hallway, she lifted her telephone and whispered into the handset. Then she dropped it and ran. *Smart girl,* Aaron thought. *She'll go far.*

Not as far as the rest of the executives, though. Despite their corporate, buttoned-up appearance, many of them put up a decent fight. Aaron waded through a gauntlet of handsome, expertly trained vice presidents armed with bats, crowbars, knives, and guns. Bullets flew, and blades flashed; Aaron ducked and weaved, feeling for the first time like he could flex his muscles. He lashed out and clotheslined three assistants, each armed with deadly-looking swords. He sank his nails into an aluminum file cabinet, crumpling the metal like papier-mâché and then tossed the cabinet at a handful of brass-knuckled interns, sending them through a window to the street below.

Inwardly, Aaron cursed Deena's timing. If her plane had been late . . . if she hadn't figured it out for another hour, he could have been in and out with minimal damage. But Deena Pilgrim was a damn good detective; that was something he'd always known—what he'd bet on, leaving her the chords as clues. And now he was exposed—not only his face and mission but also his ties to the other murders. He'd left the hood behind, wanting his victim—Crane—to know his murderer, know that he'd been beaten by a Power before dying a failure. And even if Aaron had succeeded, he never would have gotten away. She would have found him, tracked him down, and slapped a drainer around his balls. If not for what he'd done to Waldo, then for what he'd done to Walker and to her heart. Aaron knew there was a possible chance, should he survive, that he was heading to prison. If he knew Crane, however, if he hadn't underestimated the man, there was a better chance that he wouldn't make it out the door. No matter what, though, Aaron was finished lying. Finished hiding behind a mask, behind another man's name. But if she'd been an hour late, if Deena hadn't put the pieces together so quickly . . . maybe Aaron Boucher could have done this quietly and disappeared. *Just me and my pop, easing into retirement.*

*But what kind of life would that be? Hounded by heartbreak, weighed down by the price of betrayal. No, this is better. No masks, no secrets. Open and honest, as every good relationship should be.* He headed toward the opaque doors.

Moments from now, Crane's elite guards would breach the fourth floor. Then Aaron would have a fight on his hands, not this ridiculous farce, these fat former militants who did their fighting in the boardroom now instead of on the battlefield.

He checked a nearby clock. Twelve-ten. Five minutes before the cops or cavalry arrived. Plenty of time to finish it. Plenty of time to kill three men and call it quits.

Aaron kept walking, stepping over unconscious bodies, heading for suite 4A.

# 28

～～～

*December. Wednesday afternoon. 12:11 P.M.*

Deena crouched low and held out both revolvers. She was glad that she'd lifted Enki's. Glad that she'd brought along the extra firepower. She would need it. *Sucks, though, that I didn't take one of the goons' super-rifles. Or that they didn't offer to hand me one before choosing the better part of valor and running away. Cowards,* she thought. *You just can't buy good fanatical help these days.*

After checking Enki's vitals, Deena had sprinted into the elevator, heading to the fourth floor where she'd met with Crane twice before. She'd hoped the other guards—the ones on the street, or Crane's personal thugs—and cops on the square below had heard the commotion and were on their way. Just in case, she'd asked the goons to call for backup. Hopefully, they'd listened. For now, unfortunately, Deena was on her own.

She wormed her way around Aaron's barricade and carefully leaned out into the executive hallway. The gunfire and fighting had stopped. The hall was empty now apart from shattered glass and broken bodies. Everyone else had fled. She hurried past the fishbowl conference room toward Crane's private suite. The doors were open, and a faint glow spilled into the corridor. Deena recognized that glow for what it was and realized that if Crane was truly crafty, this fight might already be over.

She crossed the threshold of the office. The walls were illuminated, thrumming with circuitry and tinged viridian green. It was like standing in a giant, toxic box. Thankfully, Deena knew the only one in any real danger was Aaron Boucher. He leaned heavily against the hardwood desk, gasping for breath, sapped of power. Crane had cunningly fitted his office with hundreds of tiny power drainers, disguised and obscured from sight. They'd been affixed to photo frames and lined the baseboard molding. Minuscule dots, stuck to the floor, now lay revealed and glowed green. But that wasn't the most unusual sight in the office, not by far.

Standing behind his desk, safely beneath a sheath of metal and plastic, Malachi Crane preened and grinned like an armored death's-head pumpkin. A steel-and-plastic helmet cushioned his head, wrapping around his ears, seamlessly fitting into a sheet of bulletproof glass that protected his face. His arms were encased in sturdy alloy gauntlets, both of which ended in a pair of deadly gloves that looked strong enough to crush an elephant's skull. The rest of the exoskeleton—from pneumatically enhanced greaves to a set of compartments used to house power cells, tools, and supplies— had been designed to inspire awe and fear, finished with a glossy sheen of red and black. The Human Front logo was engraved into the left breast over a solidly built piece of enamel. Deena recognized the suit from photos she'd seen during the gang war. *This was his supersuit,* she thought. *The one he wore to fight the Soldier, Olympia, Zora, and Walker.*

Crane smiled through the helmet, blocky teeth parting to reveal a laughing, dancing tongue. The glass muffled his voice, so he triggered a dial at the base of his neck, turning on a sound system so he could be heard.

"Welcome, Detective," Crane gloated. "Didn't we *just* have a meeting? I'm afraid that my calendar has been busy as of late. I tend to forget."

Deena lifted her revolvers, pointing them at the cyborg-militant's neck. "Stand down. Give me room to cuff Boucher, and we'll be out of what's left of your hair."

Crane indulgently waved his hand. "By all means. Oh, and feel free to thank me for the drainers whenever the mood should strike."

She moved toward the desk, one gun trained on Crane's suit, the other on her now-powerless ex-boyfriend. "Don't expect a card. Come on, Aaron. You're under arrest."

Aaron looked sick; the drainers had clearly gotten to him. His face was pale and waxy, slick with sweat. He struggled to catch his breath, hand clutching the front of his shirt, the other roaming the surface of the desk. Aaron looked up at Deena, eyes bright, teeth bared in a horrible rictus. "Honey . . ." he stammered, "honey, I . . . I don't think this is working out anymore."

Deena set her jaw and aimed both guns at Aaron's head. Her hands shook, but she was ready to shoot. Ready to do what needed to be done. *I'm ready,* she told herself, turning it into a mantra. *I will shoot you.*

"You have the right to remain silent. Anything you say can and will be used against you in a court of law, where they'll throw the book at you for poisoning my father, shooting the newborn, and nearly killing my partner."

Aaron laughed, and Crane stepped away from the desk, back toward the green-tinged picture window. Deena heard shouts and commotion on the plaza below—Crane's evacuating staff, no doubt, alerting the media and the authorities. She also heard movement in the hallway—shuffling feet, somebody drawing close. Either one of Crane's goons or, hopefully, a magically splinted and recovered Enki Sunrise.

Aaron wiped perspiration from his face with the hand that had been clutching his shirt. "When you put it like that . . . it's pretty clear, no? It's . . . it's not you, D-Deen . . . it's me." His free hand, roaming, shot out and clutched something hidden from her view. Crane balked and rushed forward, but before either of them had time to react, Aaron pitched a paperweight across the room and glanced it off Deena's brow. Her head snapped back as she fired, but the shot went wild, burying itself into the wall.

Growling, Aaron launched himself over the desk and grabbed for Crane's throat. He looked fine now—completely normal again, barely affected by the power drainers. A thin seam existed between Crane's helmet and torso; Aaron snatched a letter opener and jabbed it into the bigot's neck. The suit's servos whined as the exoskeleton's gauntlets reached up to pluck Aaron by the collar as one might a cat or child, lifting him out of the way. Crane used the other gauntlet to rip the opener from his throat, spewing a ragged fount of blood onto the desk and carpet. Aaron freed himself from Crane's iron grip, and Deena—recovered by now—ordered him to stand down. Still recovering from the drainers, Aaron steadied himself against the desk. Deena started over, ready to slap on the cuffs, but Aaron jabbed a finger in her direction.

"Stay there, Deena. I don't want to hurt you."

"Neat trick, if you can manage it," she retorted. "Not looking too good. Those drainers pack a wallop, I hear."

"What, these?" he asked, gesturing around the room. "No . . . I'm good. It's like . . . I feel drunk? Maybe buzzed, because there's so many of them. But otherwise, I'm golden." To prove his point, Aaron stood up and sank his fingers into Crane's desk, splintering the wood and jarring the knick-knacks and papers so that they fell onto the floor. With a grunt and heave, he tore the desk in half and lifted both pieces—one in each hand. He smiled, a spasm of exertion or pain flitting across his face, and he smiled at Deena.

"See? Good as new. Here's my other secret, Deen. The drainers . . . energy blasts . . . anything you throw my way. I just absorb it into my system. I'm superimmune. You can't stop me."

"Is that how you poisoned Waldo? The hep B was on you when you fought, but there was no chance the injector could accidentally hurt you in the scuffle?"

Aaron's smile nearly reached his ears. "Not exactly. Actually, I just stuck it in his beer while the two of you were fighting. Then I carved the tag on the door when I went to call the paramedics."

Deena raised her gun and fumed. "I fucking knew it." She fired a shot; Aaron deflected it with half the shattered desk, forcing the bullet to ricochet away and into the bookcase. He turned to Crane and apologetically ducked his head. "Sorry to you both. Not the way I'd hoped this would go down." He hefted the other piece and flung it at Crane's exosuit. The cybernetic bigot leaped aside, lashing out with a robotic arm, and the desk glanced against the metal and flipped up and over, smashing through the window and falling to the street below. Crane was shaken, and Aaron took advantage of the moment by gently sliding the other half of the desk at Deena. She stumbled back, bracing for impact; a moment flashed before her eyes, and it was the last moment she'd expected to see.

*Two cops met in an office. Deena, younger, slouched against the wall in a T-shirt cut short to expose her stomach. Walker leaned halfway through the door, bantering with the captain. He'd been saddled with a leftover from a case—a little girl, abandoned and alone.*

*"I have cases," he explained, attempting to pawn the girl off.*

*Cross wasn't deterred. "And that's why we have day care. Drop her with Babs for the shift, and we'll see what we can do."*

*Deena looked up, giving the handsome, square-jawed detective a sidelong glance. "How old is she?"*

*"What?" Walker finally noticed her but barely looked her way, focus still on the captain. "I don't . . . I don't know. Six or—how can you tell?"*

*"You could ask."*

*Now his eyes slid in her direction. "I'm sorry," he asked, irritated that she had interrupted the back-and-forth. "Who are—"*

*"Oh, I'm Deena Pilgrim. I've just been reassigned."*

*"Oh, uh—congrats, I guess." He seemed confused, slightly distracted. "Pull the short end of the . . ."*

*"Nope," she said, interrupting him once again. "Requested."*

*"Seriously?"*

*"Totally."*

*That seemed to land an impression. His hand still rested on the doorknob, as if unwilling to commit an entrance into the office. "Huh," he breathed, genuinely surprised.*

*Deena wasn't sure why he would be. "So did you, right?"*

*He just stared at her as a beat passed. Then he glanced at the captain. "So what floor is day care?"*

*Cross leaned back into his chair, hand lazily gesturing in Deena's direction. "Third," he replied. "Take your new partner with you."*

*Walker's eyes darted right again, taking in said partner. "Huh," he repeated, and this time, he said it with a lift in his voice.*

*"Huh yourself," she answered.*

*"No," Walker stammered, "I . . ."*

*Deena smiled. "Let's go." And go they did.*

That moment, the day she'd been partnered with Walker, it seemed like a lifetime ago. And it meant more to her than anything else she cared to remember—more than her childhood, more than her *Hindenburg* of a relationship with Aaron Boucher. Only one other moment could possibly compare, and that was her last day at the academy. The day she'd finally been able to call herself a cop.

But that was over now. She was about to be flattened by a solidly built, unjustly shattered piece of overpriced furniture. Deena closed her eyes and said a prayer.

Footsteps stumbled against a marbled floor, and hands reached out from the hallway. Powerful fingers grabbed Deena's arm, pulling her out of harm's way. The desk smashed against the doorframe and wedged itself between Deena and the office. She looked up, pushing matted hair from her eyes and quickly raising a gun toward her attacker.

Broad shoulders, kind steel eyes, and a square jaw filled her vision. Walker reached down and offered a hand, involuntarily smiling despite himself. He wore a novelty T-shirt and a pair of faded jeans—where he'd found them, Deena had no idea. His left arm was dotted with blood and bruises—probably from the IV tubing he'd torn away. He looked like an exhausted, battered mess. He'd deliberately ignored her instructions to stay behind. But Deena had never been so happy to see his stupid face in all her miserable life.

"Remember that first day?" she asked. "I had to give you babysitting lessons."

"All I remember is that belly shirt you were wearing."

"Gross. Help me up."

Walker did, and the partners faced one another in the hall. Grunts and crashes filtered out from Crane's office. "You okay?" she asked her partner, genuinely concerned.

"Yeah. You?"

"I will be. Enki's downstairs."

"Yeah," he said, nodding. "I saw her on my way in. I followed you from the hospital. Took my time. Hung back until you needed me. Backup should be here any minute."

"Great . . ." She couldn't stop smiling. Deena jerked a finger toward the office. "We should probably do this now."

"Yup." Walker grinned in return. "Hey, that was a great first day, you know."

"Retro Girl died that day."

"Yeah," he said, pointing between them. "But this . . . *this* was born."

"Ugh, shut up." Deena really couldn't stop smiling. She heard shouts and movement from the far end of the floor, along with the sound of metal clacking on metal. Crane's guards, no doubt, unlocking safeties on their superweapons. "Do you hear yourself when you talk? I think I like you better when you're an asshole."

He smiled back, placing a hand on her arm. "I missed you, too."

They turned back to the office as the Human Front elite appeared around a corner. Walker grunted and slowly moved aside the fractured desk, wincing from the pain, and the partners stepped inside.

# 29

⁓⁓⁓

*December. Wednesday afternoon. 12:32 P.M.*

Metal squealed as Aaron wrapped his fingers around Crane's arms. He tore away the gauntlets, dusting the floor with a shower of sparks. Crane kicked out, connecting with Aaron's knee, and the powered vigilante crumpled into a crouch. Deena started forward, but Walker blocked her from advancing.

"Cut off those guards—get them to make sure the building is evacuated!"

Deena shook her head. "I'm not leaving you. We can take this douche bag!"

Walker locked eyes with his partner. "Trust me. I've survived one collapse today; I don't want to do it again. But the way these guys are goi—" A shorn sliver of metal flew by, embedding itself into the wall. Walker tossed Deena back, out toward the hallway, and dove into the action.

Three Human Front goons—clad in heavy body armor, each engraved with the THF logo—jockeyed their way down the hall. They all held expensive, advanced machine rifles, and they raised them to target the intruders in Crane's office. Deena grabbed the first goon's weapon and pushed, just before he unleashed a torrent of bullets. She took advantage of the confusion and jabbed an elbow into his neck, choking and forcing him to drop the rifle.

The other two came at her. She snapped up the fallen gun, holding the guards at bay while Walker put an end to the fracas at the window.

Malachi Crane hadn't been in a fight in a while, and it showed. He recklessly attacked, and Aaron took advantage of his looping punches to duck in and disassemble the suit, piece by piece. He dug into seams, ripped away joints and connections, removing the shell and gaining access to the flesh beneath.

A dull whine echoed throughout the office, and Aaron's eyes widened. He backed away just as a porthole on Crane's chest fired a beam of viridian light. It burned into the adjacent chair, setting it on fire, and Walker ducked around the combatants to smother it with his shirt. Naked from the waist up, Deena's partner waded into the fray, grabbing her ex-boyfriend by the arm. Walker spun Aaron around and clocked him on the nose. Aaron stumbled and smiled through a trickle of blood.

"Walker . . . you little secret-keeper. Do you have your powers back?"

The bigger cop sneered. "I don't need powers to deal with you, Boucher. Remember when I said I'd break your face? Well, here it comes."

"Not so fast. It's my turn. I've wanted to do this for a long time."

Aaron returned Walker's blow, and the former Power's head snapped back. He lurched, nearly falling off his feet, but managed to right himself against a wall. Crane, meanwhile, came up from behind and put Aaron in a metallic bear hug. His captive smiled and flexed both arms, shattering the remains of the metallic torso. A violent flash of energy flared against the tattered remains of Aaron's shirt—where he'd backed against the porthole on the exosuit's chest—and a contained explosion shoved both militant and vigilante apart. The rest of Aaron's shirt was burned away, and Crane resembled a wrinkled turtle, unable to rise due to the weight of his suit. Laughing, Aaron stumbled over, ready to dispatch Crane into the next life. Before he could get closer, Walker tackled him to the ground. They wrestled for a while without either gaining an inch until Aaron lashed out with a burst of adrenaline. He kicked Walker away and scrambled to his feet.

"This was fun," he breathed. "But my immune system is through the roof, Walker. I'm just going to heal, and you're going to get buried again."

Aaron stuck his fingers into the wall, parting the wood paneling like butter, continuing through drywall, metal, and glass until he came to the structure beneath. "I've done this trick already. I generally don't like to repeat myself, but this one time, I'll make an exception. *In the name of Liberty!*" Aaron flexed and pulled forward, tearing the structural beams away from the building. Half the ceiling shifted and fell, burying Aaron beneath a pile of rubble, obscuring him from view. The office shuddered, and the guards' eyes widened. They stepped back into the hallway and darted for the exit. Deena fired twice, missed, and then turned back to see what was happening inside the room.

Crane had unburdened himself of the suit and was hustling toward the door. Walker, negotiating falling plaster and sliding furniture, hurried toward the intolerant lobbyist and caught him by the throat. He lifted Crane, holding him high as the building fell around them.

"Now what, Diamond?" Crane sneered, baiting the former hero. "We have moments before this place crumbles at our feet. Will you save us both? Or like all Powers-loving swine, will you look out for yourself and leave the Powers-hater to the mercies of shifting bedrock?"

Walker scowled and slowly lowered Crane to his feet. "Fuck you. I'm not that man; I never was. I'm bringing you in by the book."

Crane dusted off his shirt, blackened and tattered by the ruptured armor. His flesh had melted, as well, stuck to frayed fabric. It didn't bother the man—or if it did, he had a surprisingly good sense of self-control. "I doubt that. You, Joseph, Olympia, Boucher . . . all you Powers are the same. Above the law, unwilling to—"

Walker slapped a hand over Crane's mouth. "Hey, I'd love to debate this to death, but if we don't move, that's exactly what's going to happen. Until it does, you have the right to remain silent. Got that?" Crane nodded and pushed Walker's hand away. They angled toward the door, heading for safety. The office had returned to its usual tint—the power drainers having been deactivated as the building tore itself apart.

Before they could escape the wave of drywall and steel, Aaron Boucher burrowed up from beneath the floor and wrestled Crane back into the wreckage. He kicked Walker aside, and both bigot and vigilante were lost amid the thunderous fall of debris. Deena briefly caught a flash of glass and light, and she saw something—someone—fall through the fragmented picture window.

Walker snatched Deena by the waist, lifting her over his shoulder despite her unladylike protestations. He pounded down the hallway, outracing a maelstrom of metal and concrete. Coming to an access stairway, Walker wrenched the door open, launched himself inside, and leaped down flights as fast as his legs could carry him. He came to ground level just as the staircase started to topple, and he put Deena down, shouldering his way into the lobby. Glass shattered around the partners as the infrastructure collapsed in on itself, crumpling like a cake as one level fell on top of the next. They sprinted across the lobby, dodging to avoid pieces of ceiling and imploding glass. A large section of recessed lighting glanced against Deena's shoulder, and she nearly fell to the ground from the weight. Walker grabbed her by the crook of her elbow and lifted her up, propelling her toward the exit. The ceiling gave way, and the first floor descended into the lobby. Broken furniture, reams of paper, mounds of plaster, and computers all slid toward the detectives in a vicious, powerful stampede.

They reached the door—the frame only, bent and twisted, the glass having exploded into the street. They sprinted down the steps toward a hastily erected barricade on the far end of the square. The evacuated inhabitants of 500 Fialkov Way watched with bated breath as the detectives outdistanced the debris wave, holding hands up to protect their eyes as a rolling cloud of smoke washed over, heralding the demise of the falling building. Walker ducked beneath the barrier, joined by Deena a moment later. The larger detective struggled to catch his breath—his wounds from the night before had opened, rivulets of blood coursing down his chest, arms, and brow. He slid behind a news van, and Deena motioned for several THF guards to attend her ailing partner. She stared as the last of the building thundered to the ground, and a fleeting moment of panic set in—had Enki gotten help? Walker said he'd seen her, but . . . ? She glanced wildly around, eyes darting between hordes of wailing ambulances and arriving police cruisers. Finally, at the far end of the square, Deena spied Enki Sunrise, hunkered down amid the cowardly goons, icing her bruises and receiving medical attention. Three cops hustled over and promptly arrested said goons; they put up a struggle, but after a moment, they realized that they were overpowered and gave up.

*Enki's fine. Walker's going to be fine. Me, I'll be fine.*

Deena took in the demolished building.

*Aaron . . . what the hell happened? Did you get out?*

Deciding it was worth the risk, she ducked back beneath the barricade, despite warnings and protestations. Deena lunged into the roiling, sulfurous wall of smoke. The remains of the building's framework were still on fire, and she carefully navigated through the haze. The fallen structure shifted around her, creaking and settling somewhere in the expansive wall of white. She unholstered her gun and warily walked to the spot where Crane's office had once overlooked.

She heard groans, muffled through the crackling flames and falling rubble. Deena climbed a mound of damaged computers, scrabbling for purchase as she made her way to the epicenter. Her foot slipped, and something dug into her heel. Cursing, she picked up the offending aggressor. It was part of a helmet—plastic and steel—and the top had been severed, leaving an exposed, dangerous edge. She recognized it as the top of Crane's armor. She noted dismantled portions of the exosuit, stained with blood and gobbets of human remains. Gingerly moving forward, careful not to step in detritus, she scanned the area for signs of additional bodies.

More groans, this time from her left. Deena raised her gun and started in that direction. She didn't have to go far. Over a wide outcropping of wood and steel, trapped beneath a steel beam, Aaron Boucher worked to free himself from under the fallen superstructure. His face was black—singed and burned, skin having melted from bone near his temple. A chunk of shoulder had been shorn away. His fingers were broken, and though he fought for purchase on the equally blackened beam, Aaron couldn't move the object from atop his sunken chest. And he couldn't remove the jagged piece of crimson-and-black steel that had pierced his abdomen. Blood poured from his belly in a sluggish stream, and he was valiantly—though unsuccessfully—attempting to stanch the flow. He struggled for breath and blindly looked around, trying to see through the wall of fog.

Deena stepped closer and tripped on a leg—Crane's, severed from the rest of his body. Aaron heard her falter and started to shout, his voice thin and desperate, begging for someone to take away the pain. Tears sprang to the corners of Deena's eyes, and she lowered the gun, holstering it. She stepped around the beam and came to Aaron's side.

Deena Pilgrim sat next to the man she once loved. The man who'd killed a legend, attacked her father, and nearly destroyed her life for the second time in ten years. She reached out and took his hand, caressing his maimed fingers in her own. He started and then wildly looked around, eyes glassy and insane. Once he saw who it was, Aaron's face relaxed into an easy smile. He took a breath, and she heard it gurgle inside his chest. He tried to grip her hand, but his fingers wouldn't cooperate. Instead, he stared into her eyes and settled back against the debris.

"Hi, Deena," he said, voice thick with blood and emotion.

"Aaron," she answered, head shaking with dismay. "What . . . what did you do?"

She shuffled closer and lifted his head into her arms. Aaron was dying; they both knew it. He wasn't healing—something had broken inside, and superimmunity wouldn't save him from fatal wounds and perforations. This wasn't a toxic dose of drainers or an energy beam. This was a piece of metal to his gut and a building on his chest. This time, there was no shrugging off the inevitable.

Aaron gathered strength and lifted his head off her arm. She encouraged him not to exert himself, but he waved her back. "No," he wheezed. "No, I'm done." He glared at Deena, staring with clear-eyed determination. "I'm dying."

"Hell you are. You think I'll let you off that easy, Aaron Boucher? You're gonna live, for nothing more than the fact that I want to see you rot in prison."

He laughed, and the effort pained him. Blood dribbled from his lips, staining her sleeve. "There are things you need to hear," he whispered, "and things . . . things I need to say. I'm done avoiding this. A . . . a discussion we should have had long ago."

"Aaron . . ." Déjà vu washed over Deena. She'd heard a confession like this before, from her father.

Aaron flinched and grimaced. "No more *lies*. It's . . . it's time I told the truth. It's time I told you the truth about the Liberty killer."

# 30

⁓

"Joseph Monroe wasn't Liberty."

The words hung between them for a moment, swirling away with clouds of smoke. Deena's heart felt heavy, as did her arms, and she gently laid him back onto the rubble. He coughed and then continued.

"I loved you, Deena . . . I . . . I still do—*koff!*—b . . . but I was *this* . . . what I am . . . first, and longest. You have to understand that."

She felt numb and wiped her eyes. "So it was always you. Even then?"

He stifled a cough, and a bubble of blood appeared on his lips. "I wasn't the first. I won't be the last. But Monroe . . . he was . . . was Human Front, sure . . . but never . . . *koff! KOFF!* . . . n . . . never this."

"And Waldo? My father? Did he tell me the truth about anything?"

He weakly nodded. "Cops . . . Liberty, too. *All* in the name of Liberty."

"So you lied about everything. The Powers and hunting down Liberty to put him away. Everything about you was a lie."

Aaron shook his head again. "Not everything. Not the way I felt about you."

"Bullshit. How can I believe that? And why did you even come back? If you got away with it, all the murder in Atlanta, why start again?"

He closed his eyes and pursed his lips, holding back gasps and coughs. Then he turned to her, eyes overbright, and quietly launched into his story.

"I . . . I never 'got away' with the murders. They haunted me, following me from place to place along with what I did to you. I had to leave; don't you understand that now? If I stayed . . . you might have found out . . . and . . . and—*koff!*—and you might have hated me for it."

"Damn right," she hissed.

He nodded. "But I had to come out of exile . . . out of 'retirement,' if you will. Had . . . had to assume the name one last time to protect my father."

"Why is that?" she asked with a quizzical look, "What does the judge need protection from? All his enemies are dead or retired."

"Exactly . . . and Pop wanted to do the same—retire, not die. But with Crane out there, your dad . . . he kept looking back. He . . . he was too afraid, with all our secrets hanging over his shoulder."

"So you took it on yourself to tie up loose ends, is that it?"

He dipped his head and took a minute, hands roaming against his wound, as if trying to locate the source of his troubles. "I did it . . . I did it in the name of Liberty. In *his* name. The villains, your father . . . everything in Liberty's name. N . . . never meant to hurt you . . . but I hurt you most . . . most of all."

She stared at him, head throbbing and heart blazing. *Don't you fucking put this on me!* she shouted at Aaron inside her mind. *Don't blame your sins and troubles on your relationships with other people. You did this—not the judge, not me—and you won't win sympathy or absolution by asking for forgiveness on this makeshift deathbed. You* did *hurt me. You hurt a lot of people with your secrets and lies. I once thought you were a good cop, Aaron Boucher, and the man of my dreams . . . but I know now that you weren't even a decent human being.* She said all these things to herself and more, raging into the whirlwind behind her eyes. But in the end, she took his fingers and simply held them, realizing that telling him those things would solve nothing. Monroe would still be dead, as would Quince and the Rammlers, Crane and all the rest. He still would have attacked her father, as well as her partner. Nothing could change the past, despite their existence in a world with those who might.

She felt betrayed, her sense of self had taken a hit over the last three days. Deena had originally patterned her life and career on the choices and decisions that Aaron Boucher had made. He'd been an early hero, and to a lesser extent, the man she'd thought her father had been. Aaron was a role model when Waldo had failed to live up to the task. Now she knew that the two were more alike than she'd ever before realized.

*Now what?* How could she go back to being a cop, justifying her actions when the examples she'd followed turned out to be the wrong ones? When Aaron had turned out to be no better than the crooked cops and criminal Powers he'd railed against so many years before? He'd lied to her at every step. He'd lied, and now he expected Deena to forgive him in death. To be the better person. Be the *good* person.

*Well, fuck that. I'm also not the person I once was. I've killed men, as well—and I've done things I'm not proud of. These last few years, working with Walker, surviving the beat and the bureau . . . it changed me. The virus, the pregnancy, Chicago—I'm not a good cop, either. I don't know that I ever was.*

*The difference is this: I was always trying to be. I never lied, and the masks I wore were for me alone. Not for my friends, partners, or family. I'm not a good cop. But I wanted to be. And my life, my* history, *never really gave me that chance.*

So she sat by his side, letting him ramble on about devotion and love. He confessed to killing the Rammlers and Quince. He admitted to poisoning Waldo and attacking Deena in the alley across from Nexus, having digitally altered his voice to avoid being recognized as he had been by the Rammlers. He felt bad about having deceived and beaten Deena, but he'd had to commit to the role in order to throw her off his tracks, and buy himself time to get away without being forced to shake her on foot. Aaron had also shot Kirk and butchered Crane, of course. And he'd always known about Monroe's ties to the Front . . . what he did back in Atlanta and how the hero had lived his life.

"Is that why you killed the Soldier?" she asked, dimly realizing that she should have been recording his confession this entire time.

Aaron smiled, blood leaking out the sides of his mouth and coursing down his chin. He coughed, spewing spittle and gore. "H . . . H . . . his name," he repeated, the words fading. "All of it . . . in *his* name."

"Whose name?" she shouted, voice carrying across the square. "Whose name do you mean? Liberty? If he wasn't Monroe, then who? Crane, Waldo . . . come on! Say it so I know it's true!" Deena grabbed the sides of Aaron's head and shook it, begging for answers. He just kept smiling, eyes rolling back to reveal the whites. Her face was hot, and she started to weep, shaking with rage. *You don't get to die!* she demanded. *You don't get to die while I'm still here, miserable and alone with failed purpose and a shattered heart. You don't get to die until I know why.*

"You don't get to die!" she screamed aloud, but he wouldn't respond. His mouth opened, and his body went limp. "Not while I'm alive."

"I can't tell you how many times I've thought that very same thing."

A calming presence appeared at Deena's side—a broad hand on her shoulder, offering consolation and support. She looked up, and of course it was Walker. Deena took his hand and squeezed. He helped her stand, and she brushed dust from her tattered clothes. They looked down at the body beneath the beam, pinned by the remains of the man he'd come to kill.

"Backup arrived," Walker announced. "Enki's fine. Pounding headache and a broken leg, though."

Deena nodded and looked around. The smoke was starting to dissipate, and the blur of the barricade could be seen from where they stood. "We'll get a team in here to clean this up," Walker said. "Gather Crane's remains; get him and Boucher to the morgue. The rest of the guys are corralling the last of the Human Front security team, confiscating illegal weapons and charging them with a loose variety of creative violations. That should be good to start. Then we'll have to deal with reports, media blowback, parsing the truth about what really happened."

"I know what really happened. He pretty much confirmed it."

Walker looked down on Boucher's body. "Did you record it?"

She glared at him, eyes hooded and embarrassed.

He understood and nodded. "Then we still don't know, do we?"

Grateful, she took his hand as he led her from the wreckage. She glanced back, taking in her former boyfriend one last time. Aaron looked so small from far away, receding into the distance as she walked. Receding from her life as she moved on, left with the same mysteries and questions as before, but this time having added several murky, distressing answers. Alone and adrift, Deena Pilgrim walked away from Aaron Boucher—the man she'd thought she loved, the man she'd thought had inspired her life—left with nothing now but pain, heartbreak, and heroes with feet of clay.

# *31*

—⁄⁄⁄⁄—

*December. Wednesday afternoon. 5:35 P.M.*

"Joseph Monroe wasn't Liberty."

Deena nodded, bent over on a chair in the captain's office. She'd been sitting in silence for half an hour, sipping lukewarm coffee, cleared by the medics to attend this debriefing. Walker and Enki flanked her seat, arms folded and nursing wounds of their own. The doctors had balked when the trio of detectives refused to stay for further testing—Walker especially, having survived two falling buildings in a matter of days. But Deena's larger, male partner—*did she have two now or three, assuming one added absent, recuperating Corbin Kirk into the mix?*—Walker, in any event, seemed to be healing just fine. He leaned against the window, as per usual, and glowered as Emile Cross clued them in on the current state of affairs. Enki, meanwhile, sat beside Deena. Her leg had been fitted for a cast, and a pair of crutches rested against the captain's desk. The blinds were closed, and Deena spied frantic activity just between the moving slats. She could see a handful of curious coworkers lingering by the window, hoping to glean a bit of confidential information.

Deena didn't care. She sipped the coffee, which was terrible, and stared at nothing in particular. Until this moment, the captain's words had filtered in through one ear and out the other. She didn't want to hear it; she just wanted to go home and fall into bed. But then Cross had mentioned Liberty, and his phrasing so closely mimicked a portion of Aaron Boucher's final worlds that she had no choice but to perk up and pay attention.

"Whassat, Cap?" she inquired.

Cross turned her way, paging through a catalog of digital reports on his tablet. "I said Monroe's clean of the murders, as far as the public knows."

"Even if Boucher's testimony—unrecorded hearsay—is found admissible," Walker argued, "it conflicts with Waldo Pilgrim's, which is captured and on the record."

"And Waldo's aligns with the public hearings they held in Atlanta ten years ago," Enki pushed, "which only continues to prove that Monroe was Liberty."

"Yeah," the captain replied, settling into his chair, "but we're taking the testimony of a known liar, a crooked cop, and putting it up against that of a detective known for impeccable service—"

Deena rose up, flushed. "'Impeccable'? He brought down a building! He killed nearly thirty people in the last week alone. We have eyewitness testimony from—"

"From who?" Cross asked, innocently swiveling in his chair, lacing his fingers. "Human Front guards? A handful of gun-toting receptionists? Hardly individuals with strong moral character . . . plus, they could be continuing the smear campaign begun by their late, martyred leader."

Deena sat down, astounded. "Are you fucking kidding me?"

"Relax, Pilgrim." The captain leaned over the desk, splaying both hands on its surface. "Nobody is glossing over what Boucher did, nor are we going to ostrich it under the table. Aaron Boucher killed Malachi Crane and destroyed 500 Fialkov Way. He murdered Wilhelmina Quince and three of the Rammler Brothers, and he attacked Detectives Christian Walker, Deena Pilgrim, and Enki Sunrise . . . not to mention Waldo Pilgrim, formerly of the Atlanta Powers Homicide Division. Aaron Boucher was Liberty. We're only saying that Joseph Monroe was not."

Deena was confused. "But he was—my father's testimony—"

"—can never leave this room."

That statement, delivered with forceful finality, stuck a pinprick in the room and let the air out of the conversation. The four cops sat there, processing Cross's declaration, until Deena stood up and slammed her cup on the desk.

"This is *bullshit*."

"Deena, this is what the country needs right now."

"'*Needs*'? America *needs* to be lied to about—"

Cross pointed to the chair. "Goddammit, Pilgrim, sit down!"

She fumed, but complied after a moment of indecision. Cross continued, "Look, this didn't come from me, okay? I get it—Monroe was involved, even if it didn't come out until ten years later. But you have to understand the larger picture, and what this does is condemn the actual Liberty killer, while still providing a hero to our nation."

Deena scowled and started to speak, but Walker interrupted her unspoken diatribe. "What do you mean, 'hero'? Joe was still a traitor. The tattoos, Crane's press conference. The guy was a discredit to other Powers, no?"

Cross's face flushed a dull red, and he wiped a hand across his gleaming skull. "Not anymore. Official reports will declare his tattoos part of a recent undercover sting. The Soldier's plan to infiltrate the Front, befriending Crane in their old age, in order to destroy it from the inside. Crane, angered, had the Rammlers kill Monroe when he discovered the truth and hired Boucher—as Liberty—to clean up the loose ends. He used Joe's tattoos against the man in order to destroy the legacy of the Citizen Soldier."

"Why would Boucher go along? He was a Power. He hated the THF."

"Officially? To avenge the Soldier's death, but also to finish Monroe's final mission. That's why he killed Crane, attacked the Human Front, and decimated 500 Fialkov Way. Illegally, mind you—as a vigilante and not working on behalf of the PHD or any known federal agency."

Deena's head was throbbing. This was so much contrived bullshit. "And unofficially? What about my father? Not to mention Walker and me?"

Cross gazed into her eyes. "The two of you got in his way. And Liberty was a vigilante. He killed a bunch of people for reasons of his own, a fact that had been covered up—and taken advantage of—by your father, Pilgrim. Could it have been secondary revenge? Beats me. Point is, Boucher takes the fall. Malachi Crane is worm meat and the Human Front disbanded. Joseph Monroe is a national hero again. The guy's dead already; arresting him will do no good. Why prosecute his legacy? It will only do more harm than good. This way, Boucher and Crane are the bad guys, the Liberty cases are finally closed, and everybody wins."

Deena traded glances with Walker and then stood up once more. "Everybody but those who care about the truth. No, screw that. I still have one last ace to play, and I'm going to get the *real* truth right fucking now."

Cross rose to meet her, lifting a finger and jabbing it at her face. "I'm warning you on this. I can't help you here, Deena, if you choose to make it a thing. This comes from Washington—even the commissioner's hands are tied. You open your mouth, you leak *anything* . . . your ass lands out of this precinct and maybe in federal jail."

Walker pushed away from the window. "Least she'll have company."

Enki looked up. "You going rogue on this, too?"

"Already did," he retorted. "Remember? No badge or gun, no license to cop. And yet everyone on that square saw me race out of that building. No way the commission doesn't toss me into some kind of superprison."

"Oh, that," Cross said, distractedly reaching into his drawer. He retrieved Walker's gun and badge and placed it on the desk. "Congratulations. You're hired. Again."

"Cap?"

"In light of your actions during the recent investigation, and due to the incriminating evidence piled against the late Aaron Boucher, the commission has decided, well . . ."

"To give back a job they never should have taken in the first place?"

"You solved a long-standing and embarrassing open case. You saved the lives of countless people in the line of duty. Everyone is satisfied in allowing you to continue performing the duties of a homicide detective. Mazel tov. You still get paid shit."

Walker gave the captain a nasty look. He started to speak, thought better of it, and reached down to take his personal effects. Enki patted him on the arm and smiled, but he didn't return it in kind.

"What?" Enki asked. "Isn't this what you wanted?"

Walker shook his head. "I'm not sure that *I'm* satisfied in allowing myself to continue performing the duties of a homicide detective."

Cross slapped both palms against his face and wiped his eyes. "For

Christ's sake, what the fuck now? Would you just take the win, enjoy being right for once in your miserable goddamn life?"

Walker pursed his lips. "But I'm not right, Cap. None of this is. Joe was Liberty—he was guilty, same as me."

"You?"

"Guilty due to inaction. Guilt by association. Sure, Boucher may have been the killer, but you can't say that either one of us is completely innocent."

Cross slammed a palm down on the desk, rattling his tablet and several sheaves of paper. "Dammit, Walker—leave it alone. That's a goddamn *order*. Welcome back. You've got open cases, same as the two of you. Get out of my office, and don't speak a word of this to fucking *anyone*. You understand me? You don't have to like it, but if I read about this in the papers or hear word one from PNN, you'll be walking a beat in Des Moines."

The detectives nodded, biting their tongues. Walker handed Enki her crutches and helped her hobble out the door. Deena followed, closing the door, glaring at Cross one final time. She found the captain's head lowered into his hands, elbows resting against the desk. His fingers were hooked into claws, and she realized that the dejected cops weren't the only ones being forced to swallow a line with a smile. She gently shut the door and turned to follow her partners.

Enki limped to her desk, and Deena helped situate the injured cop. Walker seethed and fidgeted nearby, glancing at the captain's office, shaking his head in disbelief. The din of the bullpen rose and fell about them, a handful of lawyers packing up cases and infinite perps protesting their innocence to a mob of unfazed policemen. Names and crimes were bandied about like trading cards, particular interest being paid to notable masks and abilities. Detectives filed reports as clerks gathered research, and despite her having helped bring a high-profile case to its close, no one paid much attention to the foul mood that had settled about Enki Sunrise's desk.

"Complete and total bullshit," Deena said, resting her ass on a vacant chair. She toyed with her cell phone, staring at the files containing Waldo's testimony.

"Look," Enki suggested, "at least Boucher gets blamed for his crimes, right? We got Liberty in the end."

"No, we didn't. Not yet, anyway."

Enki rested her leg on the desk. "Whaddya gonna do? They're all dead. You're going to defame an icon just so you'll sleep better at night?"

"The world needs to know!"

"Does it?" Enki looked skeptical. "I mean, yeah, people were sad when they learned Monroe died. But when they found out he was a *traitor*? I mean, I've never seen some dude burned in effigy before this week, is what I'm saying."

"Wait," Deena posed, "so, you're saying we should spare everyone's feelings?"

"Let it alone, Deena."

She looked up. Walker was staring off into space, scratching the back of his head with one hand. "You're good with this?" she asked her partner. "You're fine with lying *again* . . . with keeping *more* secrets for douche bags that ruined your life?"

"I'm not 'good' with it, no. But I can't fight it, either. It's like all the rest—Chicago, the bureau, Wolfe. It eats away at me, but what can I do about it?"

"You can—"

He turned to her now, earnest and red. "No, I can't. I feel totally hollow inside, Deena. Guilty for what I let Monroe get away with, angry with myself for not doing more. Like I didn't do with Z or Triphammer or any other Power I let use his abilities for personal gain . . . or avoid using them because he or she simply didn't give a shit."

Walker leaned down, whispering to his partners. "I should have given a shit. I should have done something back when I could. But now . . . now what can I do? If I speak, if I tell people the truth, I'll just end up hurting them. And I've hurt too many people already, including the people I love."

He'd glanced at Deena for that last bit, and she snorted in reply. "Me? You feel bad for me?"

"Yeah; I hurt you. Aaron hurt you. Your dad hurt you. I don't want to add to anyone else's pain, okay? My job is to keep that from happening. I'll call this the win they want me to believe it is."

Deena stood up and got right into her partner's face. "You think I'm in pain? Dude . . ." She waved her arms around, taking in the bullpen. "I'm numb to all this already. I'm beyond fucking pain."

She stepped away and walked to the middle of the aisle, narrowly avoiding impact with a passing clerk. "This 'win'? I'm hollow inside, too. I have new contempt for the man I called my father. Now I can add to it the man I'd idolized—a guy I'd have been happy to avoid seeing for another ten years. The man I looked up to, who was, in actuality, a vigilante-murdering-Powers psycho with stained, conflicted principles. Oh! And one of his victims? Yeah, *that* guy *also* helped kill a mess of people . . . and *I can't bring him to justice.* So tell me again: *How* is this a win?"

Enki watched the byplay, concern spreading across her face. She reached out to Deena but was too far away to take her hand or touch her arm. "Hey," she said, attempting to verbally step between the partners. "Come on . . . it may not be a win, and I know it's close to the heart, but we finally closed the Liberty case. That has to mean something, right?"

Deena screwed up her face and shook her head. "No, not to me. Not anymore."

Walker raised an eyebrow. "What does that mean?"

"Means I'm done. Been saying all week that I need to talk to Cross about it. But I . . . this was it, Walker. I'm finished with this shit."

"Yeah, you keep saying that. But you always come back. After the virus, and after Chicago. You always end up back behind the badge."

She grabbed his shirt, crumpling it in her fist. "Don't you see, though? I used to have a reason. Something . . . someone was always out there, pushing me. Inspiring me. First Waldo, and then when he let me down, Aaron. Even though Aaron had been a grade-A asshole and walked away, I still believed him to be a *good cop*. That's what brought me back . . . that and the drive to keep the peace, do the right thing. And now?"

"Now?"

"Now I'm finished. Someone else can keep the peace. You do what you want, but once I go deal with the last piece of this, I'm *done*."

Enki opened her mouth, about to pose arguments, but Walker sighed before she could get started. He hung his head and rubbed his eyes with two fingers. Walker was battered and tired—they all were, the last three days having taken an exhaustive toll. The drone of the bullpen washed over the trio, and Enki waited for Walker's measured response. Finally, the former hero lifted his eyes and stared at his smaller, younger partner.

"You do what you want," he told Deena. "I won't stop you. In fact, if this is what you need, I'll support it. I'm your partner, but I'm also your friend." He reached out and placed a hand on her shoulder. "If you're done, I'll stand by that."

Surprised, Deena dumbly nodded her head and then clasped Walker's hand with her own. They stood there, and Enki watched them closely, unsure what to say.

"Before you do that," Walker continued, "before you walk into the captain's office and lay your badge on the table . . . first you have to walk an old man to see the body of his poor, dead son."

Deena looked up, tears streaming from her eyes. Walker placed the other hand on her opposite shoulder.

"First you have to show Aaron's body to the judge so he can confirm it, and by doing so, condemn it."

# 32

—⁓—

**December. Wednesday night. 7:55 P.M.**

A father sat by the corpse of his son, head lowered, hands clasped in his lap. Eyes closed, lips pursed, he breathed deeply and evenly as two detectives kept a respectful distance. The body was covered up to the chest, naked and cold, lips tinged blue from having been stored in a locker for the better part of two hours. It lay in a bag, zipped down and strategically positioned so that the father couldn't see the damage inflicted on his poor son's torso.

Judge Kenneth Boucher sighed once and then lifted his eyes to meet those of Deena Pilgrim. He looked away, the pain too great to maintain eye contact. Before he did, she noticed that tears clung to his glasses, twin trails coursing down his weathered cheeks. She started to speak, keeping her voice measured and soft, using discretion and restraint in retelling the events of the past three days. The judge listened patiently, taking in the details, nodding every now and then as if unsurprised to be hearing the story of his son's final days on Earth. Walker glanced from Deena to Boucher, back and forth like a tennis match, gauging the old man's reaction as the case unfolded. Deena confirmed that Aaron had been Liberty, eliciting yet another knowing nod, and revealed that the partners—and the federal investigators—knew about the secret conspiracy between Aaron, Waldo, and the Citizen Soldier. The judge's son had killed Joseph Monroe, Malachi

Crane, and the remaining members of the original Human Front. He'd poisoned Waldo Pilgrim and attacked both Walker and Deena during the course of his carefully executed swath of betrayal. Deena explained that Aaron had undertaken the recent actions in service of one thing, in her opinion: eliminating any connection to the original Liberty killings through the use of secret powers.

"See," she continued in the silence of the station morgue, "all Aaron had wanted to do in the first place was clean up *your* record. That's why he'd worked with Waldo and Monroe . . . he didn't care about the money. He cared about *you*. But . . . I think he also felt disgusted by it, which is why he hated my father—not to mention the Powers—and was eventually forced to leave Atlanta."

The judge kept his own counsel. He stared at Aaron's body, sorrowful and humble, barely glancing in either detective's direction.

"Or so he wanted us to believe. Isn't that right, Ken?"

The judge looked up again as if being dragged from a harrowing daydream. Rheumy eyes bored into Deena's own. "What do you mean?"

"You know what I mean."

Ken seemed confused and disoriented—which was fair, having just been presented with his son's corpse. But Deena's tone, her determined gaze, set him on edge, and he straightened his back. Walker was confused, too. He glanced in Deena's direction, but his partner held out a hand, gesturing for the larger detective to wait.

"Waldo," she continued, "laid out how he and Monroe used the gang war as a cover to not only remove certain . . . threats but also managed to clean up *your* spotty record. They freed criminals you convicted in order to kill those you hadn't. They did that before Aaron ever even got *involved*. Before he began tying up the loose ends as Liberty, killing those they'd released. Was it coincidence, Ken, that Waldo's and Monroe's enemies . . . the people they freed, the people they killed . . . were also your own?"

The judge finally spoke. His tinny voice, choked with emotion, echoed against the freezer compartments and reverberated throughout the room. "I'm not sure I like your tone, Deena."

She headed toward the compartment on which lay Aaron Boucher. "I know. I don't like it, either, but that's my problem. Once I open my mouth, it's hard to stop. Someone closed my mouth a few hours ago, keeping me from singing this song, but see? I have it on the cloud." She retrieved her phone from a pocket, holding it out so Ken could see. "Every detail, explained by your former friend—my father—and confirmed by APHD in a sworn affidavit by my request. But I'm sure you know the details, Ken. I'm sure you know what I'm driving at."

Ken's chest hitched, and he let out a sigh. The judge wrung his hands and looked down again, hiding his eyes. Walker, curious now, joined Deena by the corpse, coming around to flank the judge.

After a moment, the old man looked up again. "You always were the smart one, Deena. That's why I was thrilled when you and Aaron ended up together."

"Don't cruise down memory lane, Ken. Start talking, and I'll start taping, and we can get out of here before the dinner rush."

"Deena . . ." Walker warned her, holding out his hand. She slapped it away. The judge flicked his eyes in Walker's direction and then nodded his head.

"You were a clever one, too, Diamond. That's why Joe kept you close. Clever and dangerous—too many years in the eyes."

The judge dusted off his clothes. He sniffed, rubbing fingers over his nose and settling back into the chair once more. "I knew that Aaron had powers. Is that what you're asking? Of course I knew. And no, he didn't act alone."

Walker raised an eyebrow. "So Joe *was* Liberty, too."

"Not exactly. But, yes. Liberty was more than one man." The judge turned to Deena, eyes clear now, somewhat bemused. "Who told you?"

Deena held out the phone. "Live and clear, fifty-five minutes in. Waldo revealed all and confirmed it to the APHD when I called to acquire federal protection for my dad. I know, Ken. I know it all."

Walker snorted. "I don't. Someone had better tell me what's going on."

Deena tapped Record on her phone and set it on the tray next to Aaron. She pulled up a chair and sat down and then held out an indulgent hand to Judge Boucher. "Be my guest," she said, giving him the floor.

Boucher cleared his throat and rested a hand on his dead son's chest.

"Very well," he agreed. "This has gone on long enough. Here, to clear up all confusion, is the absolute truth about the Liberty killer."

# 33

~~~

*July. Twelve and a half years ago.*
*Saturday night. 9:57 P.M.*

*They sat on the porch, rocking in faded recliners that wouldn't last the summer. Each of them sipped a tall, cool glass of iced tea. Only two smoked fine cigars. Joe was the exception; he seemed ill-at-ease, constantly checking the street as if he might be recognized by a reporter or ambushed from the darkness. Waldo, of course, was most relaxed. He puffed the last quarter of a Macanudo Maduro and stole swallows from a flask he kept sneaking from his pocket. Joe and the judge pretended not to notice. It was understandable; this kind of conversation allowed for that sort of indulgence. Eveline busied herself in the kitchen, out of sight, and Aaron wasn't home—either on patrol or at the Virgin Megastore on Peachtree, sifting through the racks.*

*Ken rocked forward, ashing his own cigar, and gazed out into the night. The block was silent, the evening serene. He hated to ruin it by continuing their conversation.*

*"Who's first, then?"*

*Joe traded looks with Waldo and shrugged. "Start with someone . . . someone invisible, maybe? Save the heavy hitters for last."*

*Waldo agreed. "Whassat girl's name? Crane's girl, you know the one."*

*Joe reached for his drink. "Quince. Willie Quince."*

*"Yeah, that one. We'll send her after . . . I dunno, give her a challenge."*

*Ken smiled and leaned back into the chair. "Ernst Rammler."*

*Joe scoffed and shook his head. "She couldn't handle a Rammler. No, I want that to be special. Let's save him for later—we'll set Blitzkrieg on his trail. Send a German to fry a German."*

*Waldo didn't care. "I'm agnostic. You gents pick the targets. As long as the checks clear, Owens and I will release any con you want."*

*Ken placed a hand on his friend's arm. "I appreciate that, son, but despite the appearance of random violence, there's method to my particular madness."*

*"I know . . . I know. We'll only pick targets based on the list you compiled."*

*Ken's mouth tightened as if he'd been eating lemons. "Thank you, yes. That list contains all the cases . . . the defendants who slipp—"*

*Waldo Pilgrim stood up and held out a hand, flicking the remains of his cigar onto the pebbled drive. "Save it. Honestly, Ken? Point, shoot, and pay me. Your reasons are your own."*

*"My son," the judge cautiously inquired, "has he said anything? Since the last time, I mean."*

*Pilgrim sighed and breathed in the secondhand smoke. "Yeeeah . . . he's been sniffing around. Interested in why I'm partnering with the Soldier, other Powers. I set him straight. I mean, APHD can always use extra hands, ain't that right?" He grinned in Monroe's direction, but Joe looked away into the trees.*

*"Once you get a few on the street, and the fighting begins . . ."*

*"The kid'll change his tune. Hopefully, Officer Boucher will be an asset to us in the coming gang war."*

*Ken frowned. "I don't want him to know about this. Him, Eveline, no one else."*

*Pilgrim belched and started down the steps. "Mum's the word, Your Honor. Now, if you don't mind, I have a date with a faulty prison cell. Then home to check on m'girls."*

*"Give Deena my love."*

*Waldo returned the nod, lifting his thumb and cocking an index finger, firing an imaginary bullet in assent. He moseyed down the driveway and into his car. Moments later, a pair of headlights stretched away from the Boucher home.*

*They sat there, just the two of them. The smoke drifted away, and an evening breeze ruffled their hair. Ken settled back again, whistling softly. Joe sipped his drink and listened to Eveline putter around in the kitchen. Finally, Ken had endured the silence for too long.*

*"You think he knows?" the judge asked the incognito legend.*

*Joe held out his hands, unsure. "Could be. He's paid well enough to keep it to himself. Who wants to ruin a good thing, right?"*

*Ken smiled and placed a soft palm on the back of Monroe's broad, veiny hand. "Exactly."*

*Joe snatched the hand away, glanced back through the window. "Are you an asshole? She's right there."*

*Ken smirked. "Live a little."*

*"I thought the whole point of this war was to keep our secret, well, secret."*

*Ken chuckled and lifted his sweating glass of tea. "Relax, hero. Your masculine, American façade is safe with me. Remember? I'm the guy who jailed all your fascist playmates. I'm also the guy paying to have them killed."*

*"Seriously, keep it down. The wind carries here."*

*Ken scoffed and looked around, gesturing to the silent, darkened homes. "To who? Retirees and eccentric millionaires? There's nobody listening. No one who cares that the Citizen Soldier and his lawyer are fucking like bunnies. I'd be more worried about keeping your other secret." He pointed to the Soldier's open-throated shirt, revealing vivid, lurid tattoos. Monroe started and looked down, reflexively palming the symbol on his arm. He rolled down a sleeve, hiding the Human Front colors from sight.*

*"I mean it, Ken. I love you and all, but I have a lot more to lose than you do."*

*Boucher drained his glass and set it down on the floor. "Not according to the drunk that just left. He thinks we're doing this to settle up my 'spotty' record. Never thinkin' for a minute that even judges might throw a case for the right man."*

*Joe smiled. "That's sweet. I'm the right man?"*

*Ken leaned over, surreptitiously checking the window before pecking the Soldier on the cheek. "The right one for me."*

# 34

---

"Wait, wait, wait . . . hang on." Deena massaged her throbbing brow, struggling to keep up with the latest bombshell. "You and the Soldier were lovers?"

The judge nodded in reply. "Joe's tie to the Human Front wasn't his only secret. Yes, he'd allied himself with that gargoyle Crane's campaign of intolerance. In fact, Joe had originally been recruited to the Communist cause during Korea. They were quite convincing, and he saw an argument against the global policing that America—and the fledgling United Nations—was doing in other parts of the world. He resented the government for turning him into a figurehead, and so . . . he sought ways to rebel. It was Crane who convinced Joe that it would be more effective to fight from the inside."

"That makes sense," Walker interjected, the curtain drawn away from so many shady memories. "That's why Joe was odd in Detroit. He was already working with Crane and the Communists."

"Not to mention any and all anti-Powers, antigovernment movements he could find, short of the Nazi Party. He worked with the Black Panthers and then Vietnam protestors. He helped them flourish—in secrecy, of course—but most of the key fomenters faded away, keeping their heads down and simmering in silence as they started families or a new beachhead from which they could strike via the middle class."

"But the Soldier kept fighting?"

"Well," Boucher explained, "he still had Crane. The Human Front wasn't going away—they hadn't yet begun to evolve into the corporation they are today, but Crane was starting to organize. His troops were maturing from being uneducated, grassroots thugs into well-trained, well-armed, sophisticated killers. And the more Crane preached hatred regarding all things 'non-human,' fighting new Powers and operating in public . . . the more Joseph fought to publicly distance himself from the organization."

Deena understood. "Yeah, makes a ton of sense. That's why the Soldier was the Human Front's biggest enemy. That's why he put them away."

"Well," Boucher tentatively corrected, "that was mostly to keep them locked away. He wanted to maintain his cover and live in peace, and who would the public believe? The word of jailed, bigoted, rhetoric-spewing militants . . . or one of the nation's greatest heroes?"

Deena snorted and folded her arms. "Fucking ironic."

The judge agreed. "Truth be told, I was surprised it took Crane this long to play his cards. See, Malachi quickly discovered Joseph's other little secret. Yes, he was a traitor to his own kind, but he was also . . . he was also, well . . . you get it."

Dawning realization smacked Deena in the face. She was transported back in time, years ago, to a brisk Thanksgiving evening on her parents' porch.

*The judge grinned. His cigar blazed, enveloping his face in a cloud of smoke. "Love—or hell, even lust—is nothing to hide. Don't be embarrassed or keep it secret. Never be afraid to seize love. You'll regret it when it's gone and mourn after it's far too late."*

*Deena's face felt hot, and she nervously played with her hair. "I'm not in love."*

*"I'm just happy for the company, dear."*

*"I mean . . ." She searched for the words, feeling them slip away. "I don't know that it's love. But I will say . . . I'm excited about his passions—the music and being a cop."*

*The judge playfully poked her arm. "And what do you like? Don't get lost in another person's passions, Deena. Have your own beliefs and principles—desires and dreams independent of the man you love."*

Back in the morgue, Deena goggled at Judge Boucher, one of her father's oldest friends. "You didn't become Liberty to clean up your record. You became Liberty to cover up your *affair*."

The judge smiled tightly and stared at his feet. He nodded slowly. "You always were the smart one, dear."

Walker was still putting it together. "So, wait. Who else knew? Joe was handsy with the ladies, and I never heard word one about Crane opening his mouth or any form of blackmail."

"No," Boucher confirmed. "Malachi found out somehow. He knew that Joe had begun an affair with the man helping put his colleagues away, and while he never openly revealed our secret, Crane felt deceived. He could abide Joseph's betrayal of the Human Front but not the thought of a notable Power in an—at *that time,* you understand—'perverse' relationship with a Power-lovin' liberal."

"But he never said anything," Walker reiterated. "Not even while he was in jail. I was there; I would have heard."

"No, Crane never did squeal. But he *did* put a price on our heads. That's why we started the gang war—to fight money with money."

Deena cut in, already picking up on the thread of the judge's narrative. "Liberty . . . the killings were put into effect so you and Monroe could have an excuse to kill Crane's associates. That way, once-convicted Powers—happy to get paid in order to kill Powers-hating bigots—took out the Human Front one by one."

Boucher dipped his head again. "That was the plan, yes. And we asked your father to mix the pot, to free some Front soldiers to go after the Powers, as well. This would give Atlanta the illusion of—"

"—an out-of-control gang war. During which you could pick your enemies off with ease, keeping the secret safe by killing the folks Crane may have blabbed to."

"More importantly," the judge clarified, patting Aaron's corpse on the cold, pasty arm, "it kept our secret safe from family and superiors who wouldn't understand. Eveline, especially; I *never* wanted to break her heart."

Walker cocked his head. "But Crane knew. And he never took Waldo's deal."

Boucher nodded, wringing his hands in dismay. "No, he never did. And he hung it over our heads, threatening to expose us when we least suspected it. He was safe in prison—protected from Liberty and our plan. We had no way of getting to him, nor could we try without revealing ourselves. And he used it to leverage special privileges from Joseph, as well as an early release."

Deena stood up and paced the width of the morgue. "Okay, so we've established that you and Monroe were Liberty, along with my father, who adopted the name to do some of your dirty work for money. And since we're all history students, we know you got away with it and left my dad holding the bag. So why come back? Why resurface? And how did Aaron get dragged into it? He told me to my face that he was Liberty, but Waldo told me it was you and Monroe."

Boucher's face flushed a bright red; he was obviously embarrassed about what came next in the story. "Well, after we left Atlanta, my plan had been to disappear. Aaron knew about the gang war at that point—I'd told him, brought him in on the plan. He thought, like Waldo, that we were killing people to protect my reputation. And he knew that Crane was gunning for me for killing Human Front soldiers, which is why he was all fired up to protect me that Thanksgiving night. You remember, Deena?"

The vision on the porch came roaring back, as did the uneasy feelings Deena associated with her family and heartbreak. She nodded, and the judge went on.

"After Eveline died, rest her soul, Aaron and I bounced from town to town, constantly checking our shoulders. The Liberty murders had never been solved, and we left a lot of baggage in our wake."

Walker interrupted. "Joe couldn't protect you?"

"After the events in Atlanta, we felt it best to table our relationship for the sake of putting distance to the past. Joseph and I still had feelings, but he was already on a slow, downward spiral, and I had a family. We saw each other a few times after that, but it was never the same. Then, of course, I didn't see him for years. Not until last week."

"When you killed him."

Boucher turned to Deena, noting her expression, measuring every inch of angered disappointment. "Yes, child. When I killed him."

# 35

*~~~~~*

*December. Saturday morning. 3:00 A.M.*

*Joseph thrashed against his bonds, too weak to snap the ropes. Ken, hooded and silent, knelt by his side. A handheld drainer rested on the toolbox, emitting a faint, green glow. Ken didn't believe it was really necessary—Joseph's powers had long since faded, as had his will. It had been that way for years now. Maybe even since Atlanta.*

*He secured the ropes, pulling them tight. Joe grunted and moaned, possibly trying to beg for mercy. Maybe doing his best to pledge a love they'd both long forgotten. Ken didn't know; he'd decided to remove Joe's tongue, along with most of his teeth. This way, Ken wouldn't be swayed by his former lover's pleas of mercy.*

*This way, it would be easier. His heart and the memories wouldn't get in the way. He would do what needed to be done. He didn't want to listen to Joe—seeing him this way brought back painful memories. A life they could have had instead of this one. A world that could have been different if Joseph hadn't been too chicken-shit. And if Ken, scared and taking Joe's lead, hadn't been the same.*

*He leaned forward and whispered to his prisoner. Ken reminded Joe about the past—why this had to happen. He spoke about Aaron and Malachi Crane, and all the loose ends they'd left behind in Atlanta. Joseph didn't respond to any of it. All he cared about was pain and mercy. Ken understood that. The events leading to the night's proceedings were not as important as Joseph's pain, betrayal, and shame.*

I loved you, *Ken thought, spitting venom at the former hero inside his mind.* But you abandoned me. You abandoned yourself. And you chose the coward's route. Now you've decided to change that? Fuck you, Joe. If you ever truly loved me, you'd know that your sudden reversal would only engender the end of everything I hold dear.

*But he said none of that to the bound, captured hero.* "That's it," *Ken said instead.* "Not so bad. We're nearly done. Just two things left, and it will all be over."

*He tore open the front of Joe's shirt and leaned over to roll back his shirtsleeves. He arranged Joe's arms so that both hands rested palm-up. Then he stepped away.* "There," *he announced.* "That's one."

*He took a moment to look around. He'd been too focused to appreciate the ambience of the apartment, such as it was.* Look at this dump, *he thought to himself.* How the mighty have fallen. *Served Joseph right. He'd allowed this to happen—just as Ken had allowed himself to go from a beautiful home in suburban Atlanta to grubbing for condos in Texas, Illinois, and now here. Nothing suggested the beauty and gravitas of the man Ken once knew. Nothing at all, except his ornate shield.*

*He picked the shield up, remembering how he had once used it as a coaster to Joseph's chagrin. This wasn't Ken's first time holding it, but it would be his last. The thought made him sad for a moment, and then it was time to move forward.* "Now," *he began, speaking from beneath Liberty's hood.* "Just one more thing."

*He had to do this. For Aaron and for himself. It had to be done.*

"You know I have to do this. Right?" *Ken said it out loud, to himself as much as to Joseph. He started to cry, as did Joe, and Ken realized that they had nothing left to say. It was one or the other. Joseph had been unreasonable. Crane was out there. It had to fucking be done and over with.*

*Ken swallowed beneath the hood and reached down for the shield.*

# 36

*December. Wednesday night. 8:49* P.M.

"I wanted to retire," the judge revealed. They'd been talking for nearly an hour, and everyone needed a drink. Walker didn't want to go, and Deena didn't, either. So they sat and listened, waiting for Boucher to explain how his son had been involved.

"Aaron was concerned, you see. We'd built a career out of watching each other's backs. Eveline had never known the truth—oh, she knew that Aaron had clashed with Waldo and that a fresh start was necessary. But she went to her grave believing her son was a hero and her husband a good man."

He cleared his throat. "Following her death, I decided to retire. That's when Crane reappeared in the form of a nasty e-mail—he'd caught wind via the politician's grapevine. He knew, and he threatened to reveal my secrets. Crane wouldn't let me retire—no peace for the men who'd killed his friends. So, I came to the city and met with Joseph."

"Wait," Walker said, attempting to clarify, "you met with Joe before showing up on his doorstep Sunday night?"

"Briefly. We had coffee, and I asked for his help. But Joseph was no longer connected to anyone or anything and felt he could weather the blow. Who would care that we'd been lovers? He was a nobody at this point, and my wife was dead. Our relationship would be celebrated now, no longer taboo. But I choked. I was too burdened with my past. I was afraid my secret relationship and the ensuing media spectacle would ruin my good name, overturn my decisions, and destroy what was left of my family."

"So instead," Deena snarked, "you beat Joe to jelly with his own shield."

Boucher ran a hand across his face, cheeks flushed. "I reassumed the mantle of Liberty to engender confusion . . . and, as I had in Atlanta, to cover my tracks. I planned to tie up all loose ends, eliminating the remainder of the Human Front members that had been involved in our Georgian deception. And I would finish with Crane, killing him before the man could make good on his threat."

Walker frowned. "You hoped that Joe's secret would be more important than your own. If you worked fast, you could tie up every loose end before disappearing again. This time for good."

The judge smiled weakly. "Gold star, Diamond."

Deena's face was as red as the judge's now, but for different reasons. "That still doesn't explain Aaron's involvement, Ken. You admit to killing Monroe, but Aaron did the same as he lay dying. Which of you was *actually* Liberty?"

Boucher sat back and steepled his fingers by his lips. "Both of us."

"Not Monroe?"

He shook his head. "Eleven years ago, my son discovered my secret. Waldo Pilgrim, being an untrustworthy drunk—no offense, dear."

"None taken."

"Anyway, Pilgrim's loose lips sank Aaron's opinion of his father. He knew that I was working with Liberty, but only to clean up my inconsistent record. He knew nothing about my relationship with Joseph or the Soldier's ties to the Human Front. He pleaded with us to end the gang war, to put a stop to the corruption and murder. You would have liked him that night, Deena. It was a great speech."

Deena remained stoic, unwilling to give the judge an inch. She twirled her finger, urging him to get on with it. Boucher continued, "Aaron suggested we leave Atlanta, despite your relationship, dear. He wanted to start over far from where I could tarnish the family name and the good work that he'd been doing. So I agreed. As we put it together, Aaron looked the other way, continued the charade we worked up with Waldo and Monroe until I went into seclusion. Both Aaron and I abandoned our lovers and our city, hoping that the burgeoning Human Front would forget that either of us existed."

"Hang on," Deena asked. "Aaron didn't kill anyone in Atlanta? He wasn't involved, didn't take bribes from Waldo? All he did was keep quiet?"

Walker cleared his throat. "Which is bad enough, in and of itself."

"Dear," Boucher interjected, "I don't know what your father told you or what Aaron told you. But what *I'm* telling you? This is the truth. Why hide it now?"

*Dammit,* she thought. *They lied to me again. And none of Waldo's testimony will ever see the light of day or be useful to anyone. Thanks for nothing, Dad.* Boucher continued, speaking to Walker while Deena covertly reached over to her phone and deleted Waldo's recording. The testimony he'd lied about in order to get in good with his daughter.

*Fat lot of good it did him,* she seethed, setting the phone back on the cooling slab.

"Joseph threatened to expose our relationship," Ken was saying, "and I killed him to hush it up. And I told Aaron the truth because, well, I'm his father, and I needed his help. I'm sure you can understand that, Deena."

"So Aaron wasn't Liberty when he arrived in the city. He was legitimately here to investigate and prosecute Walker?" The big detective stared bullets at the old man, waiting for an answer.

"Yes, oh yes. Aaron donned the hood only recently. He may have already felt like part of the legacy, due to his knowledge of our decades-old conspiracy, but now he officially accepted the mantle. He was younger, more agile, and willing to internalize my secrets—as he had his own secret powers and personal turmoil."

Walker pressed the judge for an admission of guilt on behalf of the deceased. "So Aaron killed the Rampage Brothers. Then Willie Wails. He poisoned Deena's dad—"

Boucher cut him off. "No, I killed Ms. Quince. That night in the alley; that was Aaron. But the one who pulled the trigger? That was *me,* Deena."

She bristled. "I still can't believe Aaron put me in the hospital."

"You nearly put him in the morgue. And he tried throwing you off track, pointing the finger of doubt in another direction. Hoping it would save your life. We never meant to hurt you, dear . . . but then, I suppose he had to in order to escape."

"You both had me believing it was Walker."

The judge spread his hands. "You believed what you wanted to believe."

Undeterred, Walker continued to press. "So Aaron attacked Waldo, even though the man didn't know the full extent of the lies."

"That may have been personal—as were you, Walker, when we tag-teamed you the other night. Aaron . . . his powers . . . he got carried away. But I killed Quince, after which I planned to eliminate Crane, once and for all. Unfortunately, Aaron beat me to it before I could reveal myself. He was one step ahead of everyone—even me. He wanted to end things on *his* terms, planning to do exactly what he accomplished. He killed Crane and Liberty at the same time, ensuring that I remained a mystery . . . as did my relationship with Joseph Monroe."

"Not anymore. We have the truth—*your* truth—saved to the cloud now."

Boucher grunted with exertion as he got to his feet. He leaned over and kissed Aaron's brow, a tear splashing against the side of the corpse's cheek. "You do. Aaron took my secrets to the grave, but thankfully I've been able to reveal the truth about the men I loved—Joseph and my son—to the detectives who knew them best. What you do with that truth is not for me to decide. I'm finished holding lives in my hands."

He patted Aaron's cheek and stepped away, turning to Deena and holding out his wrists. "Now . . . my son is dead, and I'm an old man who has lived too many years and lied for most of them. Please," he asked the partners, his soft pleading echoing around the empty room, "finally, do your job.

"Arrest me," Kenneth Boucher begged, "in the name of Liberty."

# 37

~~~

**December. Wednesday night. 10:48 P.M.**

"So, then what happened?"

Corbin Kirk shifted toward the window, careful not to interfere with his dangling IV tubes. The rookie's face, bloated and unshaven, had come alive with interest and concern as Deena related the tragic events of the last two days. The door was closed, and the room's television tuned to a muted newscast—Collette McDaniels, live from the PHD station.

*One day,* Deena warned the bitch on the television. *One day, you and me.*

Kirk stole a quick sip from a crumpled juice container on his dinner tray and then waggled his fingers for more of the story. "Come on, I'm dying here."

"That's not funny."

"Seriously," he cajoled his superior office, "what happened next?"

What had happened was simple: Judge Kenneth Boucher, a.k.a. Liberty, had been incarcerated until such time as he could be arraigned and sentenced. Joseph Monroe, a.k.a. the Citizen Soldier, meanwhile, was posthumously cleared of all wrongdoing—his calamitous death and subsequent framing having been labeled a sadistic, tasteless ruse perpetrated by Malachi Crane, a notably vehement Powers-hater. The late Mr. Crane had been a founding member of the notorious group of militant activists known as the Human Front. Despite THF's recent politicization and incorporation, the Unites States government had seen fit to seize their surviving assets and place all remaining members in prison without bail. The Citizen Soldier, poster boy for the Powers community, was a hero once more. And only a handful of detectives and several federal agencies knew the actual, sordid truth.

Deena glanced at the television. PNN was broadcasting clips of vigils from around the city. *A return to mourning and eulogies . . . which, I guess, is better than vitriol and lynch mobs,* she decided. Hand-drawn banners and touching photographs graced miniature shrines. The camera panned across a sea of candles and flowers strewn throughout public parks, local landmarks, and the entrance to the apartment on Taylor in which Monroe's body had been found. Deena shook her head. Not seventy-two hours ago, she'd entered that apartment, a rollicking pop song fading from her lips. That moment seemed like a lifetime ago. The moment she'd stepped over the threshold—a lifetime that had been led by a completely different person.

But Kirk was waiting, recuperating, and hungry for information.

So she continued, "Walker and I reached out to the Atlanta Powers Homicide Division again. They had Waldo formally arrested—no protective custody this time. He's cooling in lockup until he can be formally charged and thrown into some minimum-security prison, no doubt. But that's okay. He's finally where he should have been ten years ago. In a cell with Owens and all the rest."

Kirk raised an eyebrow. "You're okay with that? He *is* your father."

She sighed and smiled. "He is, and I am. I'll visit at some point. Another ten years should be long enough."

"What happens to his stuff? All your family mementos and such?"

She shrugged and reached for the juice container. "Dunno. Trash? To be honest, rook, there isn't much left from that life I truly care to remember."

"That's ice cold." She ignored him and he finished his drink, then settled back against the pillows. She felt gloomy and hoped Kirk wouldn't pick up on it. *I came here to cheer him up, hoping it might cheer me up, too. But rehashing this shit isn't helping. I'm wallowing; I coulda done that back at the station. Or in a bottle.*

Deena had left the precinct thirty minutes after the judge was arrested.

She'd wanted to walk, to clear her head. Loitering around the cop house, finishing the required paperwork . . . it made her sad. Made her angry. And she was worried that another case might come along. Deena nursed deep wounds and even deeper betrayal, still committed to turning in the badge. She'd considered marching into Cross's office the moment Boucher had gone but had hesitated. Then other detectives had wandered over to congratulate the partners—Deena, Walker, and Enki—and that had been too much. She didn't want to be praised. Didn't anyone get that? She wanted to *quit*. She couldn't be a cop anymore—much less a *good* cop. Not after the lies. Not after another blatant cover-up positioned as a win for the city, its populace, and the well-meaning, hardworking detectives of the Powers Homicide Division. Not after the destruction of what had been the inspiration . . . the very bedrock of Deena Pilgrim's law enforcement career.

So she'd pushed through the doors and lurched into the snow, walking aimlessly in no direction at all. She was searching for definitive answers or maybe some kind of sign. Eventually, she'd found one: It read ELLIS GENERAL. And so Deena had entered a hospital for the fourth time in three days and ridden the elevator to visit her recovering junior partner.

Kirk reached for a pudding cup he'd missed. A wailing mother clutched a Citizen Soldier doll on the TV. Her little son, awake far past what should have been his bedtime, picked his nose as his mom poured out her heart to PNN. Deena reached out, stole the remote, and clicked it off. Kirk didn't mind. He was too busy gossiping. "How did Walker take it all? He must've been happy, getting his badge back."

Deena leaned back and scratched her head. "You'd think . . . but you know Walker. Well, maybe you don't. The guy's a dictionary model for Jewish guilt, despite his atheist leanings."

The newborn smacked his lips on the spoon and then slid the cup aside. "Okay, so he feels guilty. Because of the death? The murders?"

"He feels a sense of responsibility for the Liberty cases . . . or a lack thereof, as it were. Me too. But he's getting over it. Typical male, distracting himself with a project."

"Yeah? What's that?"

She smiled. "He's aiming to close all the open murder cases from during the period in which he was stationed in Atlanta. Most of them tie to

Waldo and the Bouchers, to their fake gang war. But, as with all riots, there are your unsolved strays. Walker figures that this is his way of making up for dereliction of duty. I think he's an idiot, personally. Best to leave the past in the past. I learned that the hard way . . . again."

Kirk stared at her, face drawn and solemn. "But you're going to help him, anyway."

She stood up. "Not me. I'm done."

The rookie's eyes narrowed. "What do you mean, 'done'?"

Deena fidgeted and stared at the frost-covered window. She could see bulbous Christmas lights across the way, winking at the other end of the hospital. The streets were clearing as midnight approached, apart from bands of pious stragglers heading to mass. Snow fell on the city, blanketing the streets in layers of pure, welcome white.

"Detective Pilgrim," Kirk repeated, craning his neck to get her attention. "Deena . . . you're going to help Walker, right? On to the next fucked-up case and so on?"

She faced him again and stuck both hands in her jacket pockets. Her right knuckles scraped against the badge, and she could feel its weight. It was heavy—like her heart—and she toyed with the idea of throwing it out a window or into a garbage chute. She really wanted to fling it at the captain or Walker or maybe use it to smash Collette McDaniels's dumb face and say good-bye to everything. To dead Powers and lost friends. To innocence, family, and ill-fated romance. To her hope, to faded ideals. To everything and anything. Deena had nothing left that mattered—even her job. Two cops had let her down—both of them, father and former lover, had been the standards of excellence to which she had ascribed. They had inspired her to pick up the badge. And now, years later and after hundreds of lies, she wanted to throw it in their stupid faces.

*And you know what?* she realized. *I'm not even properly angry. I'm just fucking exhausted. After all the death and loss, all I want to do is crawl into a corner of my bed and shut out the world. I want to hide from this harrowing, horrible planet on which would-be gods can decimate cities and jealous assholes can kill a heroine trying to make a difference.* That's *why I want to quit. Not because of stained principles or a broken heart. I'm just tired of the endless flood of bullshit. I'm tired of thinking that one good cop can make a difference. Because from what*

*I've seen, there are no good cops anymore. Only secrets, lies, and bullshit. Why the fuck would I want to be inspired by that? Why would any cop?*

*So I'm done. I'm quitting today.* She gripped the badge in her sweaty, clammy hand. *Kirk can have this piece of empty metal for all I care. He can give it to the captain or Walker. I just want to say good-bye and walk away. Maybe that's why my feet led me here: because I felt guilty that the newborn got in the path of my drama. That he got himself slugged on my behalf.*

"Hey, rookie," Deena said, removing the badge from her jacket. "Look, I just wanted to say that—"

"Uh-uh," Kirk cut in, interrupting the half-assed speech in which she'd planned to wrap her badge. "Don't even say it. You were done before; you'll be done again. That's how this thing works."

Deena laughed at Kirk's sudden onset of balls. "Seriously? How do you kn . . . no, listen, you don't understand."

"I think I *do* fucking understand." That was the first time she'd heard the baby curse. She wasn't sure she liked it; it felt like watching grandmas screw. But Kirk kept rolling. "Yeah, it sucks. You got lied to, and lots of people died. The shit with your father, the stuff with Walker and Boucher . . . sounds like a hectic, painful three days."

She nodded and held her tongue, curious to see where he was going with this.

"But, Detect . . . Deena—you *have* to look at the big picture. You closed the Retro Girl murder. You helped save thousands of lives in this city, then again in Chicago and Los Angeles. You faced down mobsters, Internal Affairs, a Federal Powers conspiracy, the Powers virus, a brush with super-powered Ragnarok . . . and you're *still fucking standing.* Sure, this last week was dogshit. Yes, people got hurt and killed. Damn straight, you had personal challenges that tested both your limits and friendships. But that's the job, isn't it? That's what we signed up for. And you've been doing it full-tilt since day one after Retro Girl fell into your lap. Hell, you were doing it before. You've been at this for so long that they're studying your cases at the academy."

Her brow furrowed. "What's that now?"

"Oh, you don't know?" His hands shook with excitement now. This was the most confident she'd seen Corbin Kirk since the day they'd met—and this with bullet wounds in his gut and legs. "Oh, man. Yeah, that interrogation shit you pulled with Jon Jackson Stevens, the Retro Girl case, and that was case *one*. You and Walker, you're kinda like . . . legends to new cadets."

Deena blushed and carefully eased the badge back into her pocket. "You're joking, right? I used my tits to elicit a confession."

"Come on, Detective. I've watched you work up close. Don't be modest—it wasn't only Retro Girl . . . every situation that followed, every case. The research and legwork you did on the Rammlers? You could have easily leaned on Walker's reputation. His history and . . . his abilities, y'know? But you never did. You never took the easy way out. You honed your skills, worked crime scenes, and hunted down leads. A lotta the other detectives on the job . . . well, I mean . . . they're fine and all. But what *you* bring to the table is something innate. Something that can't be taught. That's why I asked Cross to partner on this. That's why I wanted to work with you."

She was confused. "Why? I'm jaded and bitter, dude. I'm two seconds from tossing my badge in the river. Once I leave here, I'm hanging it up to write shitty, self-published fan-fiction. Why the *fuck* would you want to work with a cop like that?"

Kirk stared her down and placed his hands in his lap. "Because you're *honest*. You're a cop with integrity and determination, and so is Walker. You've seen and done it all, and you *Keep. On. Going.* Despite all the horrible shit you've experienced on the job, you're still here. And so are your principles. At least, as far as I'm aware."

They sat in awkward silence for a minute, listening to the muted beeps of Kirk's monitor and a muffled announcement over the public address system. Snow fell harder outside the window.

"What are you saying? No, you're way off base. I'm a fuckup pariah, newbie. That horrible shit I've 'experienced'? You think I did it out of a sense of adventure or responsibility. But it just fucking *happened*. It's bad goddamn luck, and thankfully, I've managed to survive it by the skin of my teeth. But hey," she offered, "if you want to partner with Walker and 'experience' all that horrible shit? Be my guest." She dug out her badge and held it to her face. "I was two seconds from chucking this at you and walking away."

"But you won't."

"Why the fuck not?"

He smiled. "Because of Walker. You don't want me to be his partner. He already has a partner. A good, honest partner. One who inspired a kid named Kirk to pick up the badge himself. You were *my* example, Detective. You're one of the reasons I became a cop and then joined up with the PHD. And it would truly suck if this newborn returned to work without having someone around to belittle him and show him the ropes."

Deena's jaw sagged. She was speechless, apart for a short surprised grunt. She quietly returned the badge to her pocket, patting it once to keep it secure. She looked at Kirk, shook her head, and offered a confused, embarrassed smile. "You're crazy. I'm no one's role model. This is a huge fucking mistake."

He held out his arms, taking in the room, the hospital, the falling snow. "So was heading out behind Club Nexus by my lonesome. But I'm chalking it up to 'experience.' And I was glad to have lived up to your reckless ideal . . . or at least . . ." Kirk rubbed the back of his head and offered a sheepish smile of his own. "At least to have tried."

Deena folded her arms. She tapped a foot and then headed for the door.

"Hey," Kirk asked, "where are you going? What are you going to do?"

She rested her hand on the doorjamb, taking one last look before walking away. "Thanks, Kirk. You did good." She slapped the wall and slipped into the hallway.

"Detective!" he called after her, voice carrying into the hall. "Will I see you back at the station?"

But Deena Pilgrim was down the hallway and out the door, barreling into the purifying fall of snow. Kirk's words echoed in her head, cleansing her, she felt for a moment, of pain and anger.

*That's not true. I still feel shitty. And I'd like to jam this badge up the ass of the next beat cop I see. But still . . .*

His confession, Kirk's sentiment, had struck a nerve in Deena. Sure, she would always be pissed at her father and at Aaron. She would probably never feel the same way about being a cop. Not like she did back when she'd finished at the academy. Not like she did in Atlanta, before everything went to hell. But what Kirk had said made her realize just how much time she'd spent inside a bubble of cynicism, so much so that she often couldn't see outside. The newborn had penetrated her little cloud of pain and betrayal. Just because she'd lost her inspiration and the roots of her desires to be a detective had been poisoned with wormwood, that didn't take away from her accomplishments. *Deena* had put away Jon Jackson Stevens, not Aaron. *She* had helped shut down the bureau, not Waldo. And *she* had inspired Corbin Kirk to join the force, not the men from whom she'd taken her earlier cues.

*I inspired someone. Me. The snarky little midget with an attitude. The jaded cop who accidentally killed a mobster the first time she got herself some powers. Just because my dad and Aaron were awful cops, it doesn't mean that I can't change the cycle. It doesn't mean I can't be the role model that one of them should have been.*

Deena hunkered down against a flurry and beelined for her car. She wrapped the jacket around her torso and pushed through the snow, suddenly having places to be.

*Besides,* she concluded, *I actually do have a good role model. A good cop, if there ever was one, even if he may not believe it right now. And he's sitting in a records room, no doubt, digging through cold cases and trying to make amends.*

Deena grimaced. That seemed to be going around. Making amends, that is. She arrived at her car and opened the door. Easing herself into the driver's seat, she pulled her hands from her jacket to take the wheel. Deena's right fist palmed her badge, tingling from the cold. She looked at it, noting the serial number. The little golden shield had lost its pallor over the years, its edges having rusted and dulled. She smiled, set it on the dash, and started the car. As she steered through the garage, she clicked on the radio and flipped around for an upbeat song. Anything she could find with more than five chords.

Deena Pilgrim drummed against the steering wheel of her late-model sedan, carefully navigating out of the hospital parking lot. She passed the attendant and flashed him the sign of the horns. *Rock and roll.* She head-bopped to the beat as he opened the gate.

The attendant stared at Deena for a moment and then looked back at his cell phone as she sped away. She laughed. He didn't understand. *This right here,* Deena Pilgrim said to herself.

*This right here is the high point of my day.*

# *38*

---

*December. Wednesday night. 11:53 P.M.*

Walker sat alone in the interrogation room, boxes spread out across the table. He picked at the remains of a half-eaten value meal, mostly cadging french fries as he pored over documents. He preferred to dig through printed files. Something about the digital archive seemed too easy—like less work. The purpose of this exercise was to avoid cutting corners. This was his penance for Atlanta, and before that, Detroit. This was Walker's way to make up for not getting involved. For literally being an absent badge in a city that sorely needed one.

*Maybe it's something more. I'm beating myself up for throwing irresponsible pebbles onto an eight-lane superhighway. Sure, I've had moments of apathy. After that disaster with the bureau, I basically walked away from everything. I didn't give a shit—like I didn't in Atlanta and other times in my life. But let's be fair: I've lived a long fucking life. And yeah, I'm not going to be conscientious the entire time. There* will *be moments of detachment over the years. So why am I beating myself up over looking the other way twelve years ago? It's not like I was alone, right? Why am I the only one dredging up the past, forcing myself to make amends?*

That's when he realized the obvious answers: the rest of them were dead or imprisoned. And though there would, indeed, be indiscretion during his never-ending lifetime . . . guilt would undoubtedly follow.

*It's my secret,* he recalled. *My weakness. That, and my friends.*

Deena. Enki. Kirk. Joe. Each had suffered; one of them had died. And though Walker wasn't the reason for any of that, a possibility existed that he could have changed events by simply giving a shit. *Too late now,* he mused. *But that's why* I'm *here. To quell the guilt and do right by my friends, even if they're dead and gone.*

Walker had seen too many friendships wither and die over the years, whether due to the passage of time or some dumb-ass thing he'd said or done. Joe was gone. Harley was gone. Zora, Calista, Janis, Z. He'd lost them all, and time marched on. Soon he would lose the rest. Cross. Enki. Even Deena. One day, he would turn around and the world will have changed. But the guilt would remain, the overwhelming feeling of loss . . . and there was nothing he could do about it.

So he pored. He filed. He checked and cross-checked as some small measure of looking back. He could try to solve the past—do right by those who'd fallen along the way—even if he had to do it alone.

He looked out the open door. The bullpen was dim, few lights other than those strung around the rafters. A gaggle of detectives lingered by the duty desk, sipping coffee and exchanging gifts. Walker smiled. He swallowed a fry and spread his hands across the table, shifting stacks of folders. He lifted a paper cup from his side, sloshing with coffee, and downed it with a swallow. He crumpled it and tossed it at a nearby trash can. The ball missed, hitting instead a foot wedged into the doorway. Deena Pilgrim lingered in the hall. She glanced at the throng of detectives and then to Walker, curiosity radiating across her face. Her hands were in her pockets; a coat of muddy snow caked her feet.

Deena thumbed in the direction of the bullpen. "What's going on? Not-So-Secret Santa?"

Walker pointed at the neglected, forgotten tree, quietly sitting in the corner. "That's right. And I'm in charge of decorating. This year, I thought we'd use cups of swill and stockings full of case files."

"Ho fucking ho."

"I believe 'ho fucking ho' is in section 653 to 653.28 of the penal code." Walker cast about, dragging his hand through a random box. "It's in here somewhere. I'll find it, I swear. Maybe by Easter."

Deena smiled. "Good luck."

"Wanna help?" Walker held out his hand, sweeping over the contents of the table. "Cold hamburgers and colder cases. It's like the cop equivalent of Chinese food on Jewish Christmas Eve. Best part? You won't want to dig in an hour later."

"Tempting," she replied, reaching out of sight. "But I have a little Christmas gift for you that could make it that much sweeter."

Walker rose from the chair. "Oh, hey . . . I was kidding, Deena. You didn't hav—"

Deena returned with two steaming cups, purchased from the diner across the street. She handed one over and popped the tab on her own, bending her mouth to lap sweet, sticky foam. Walker sipped his own and then looked up.

"Wait. Where's the fuckin' coffee?"

"Hot chocolate. Yum."

He had to agree. They sat across the table from one another, quietly sipping their drinks. Deena idly paged through a file, barely committing to one before checking out another. She leaned back, tilting her chair onto its rear legs.

"So . . ."

"So, indeed."

She set the cup aside. "Seriously, asshole. Do you want my help or not?"

Walker placed his beverage on the floor, careful to move his foot in order to avoid a spill. He laced his fingers and rested his mouth on the back of his hands, elbows placed on the table. A telephone rang. One of the detectives detached from the desk and drifted off to answer.

"That depends."

"Depends on what?"

"You staying?"

She nodded, sipping her drink. "For now," she replied, wiping her mouth with the back of a hand. "Probably not long enough to get through this library."

"But you're staying."

"Seriously, we should get men in here to sift through it all. Top. Men."

"Deena . . ."

She returned his gaze and set the drink aside. She was tired, but Walker noted that she seemed lighter. She seemed at peace. Six years working with the same partner, you got to pick up on things like that. Changes in mood. Adjusting attitudes. Living a mortal life in an immortal body had helped, as well. Taking in his exhausted partner, Christian Walker realized that Deena Pilgrim was going to be just fine. They'd been through the wringer before; they'd experience it again. As long as they trusted one another, all the bullshit, guilt, heartbreak, and pain would be just another set of cases they needed to solve. Just another hardship they'd be able to overcome.

Walker reached for a handful of folders marked DETROIT—1968. His partner snatched files of her own. They sat in silence, reading and sipping, enjoying each other's company and the inaudible shorthand they'd developed over the years.

"Walker?"

They looked up. The detective who'd answered the phone was standing in the doorway, anxious and armed with information. Walker closed his folder. "Yeah?"

"Got a live one. Call about a giant bookie, tossed off some kind of flying vehicle. Splashed into the fountain in New Vokes Square."

"This giant bookie's a heavy hitter? Lots of clients?"

"Uh . . . no. The dude's an *actual* giant. Like, eight feet. The fountain's shattered to shit. So's the body. Thought you might wanna take a look."

Walker finished his drink. He looked up and Deena was following suit. "You can sit this one out," he offered. "Go home. Catch some shut-eye. We'll pick it up on Friday."

Deena balked at the notion. "What—and miss some horrible new shit? Not a chance. What about this?" She waved at the table, indicating the boxes.

Walker grinned and grabbed his jacket from an adjacent chair. "Top. Men."

"Oh, nice. Excellent call back."

He stopped her at the door, pausing the banter with an open hand. "Hey, Deena," he said. "I wanted to say one more thing before we go."

She stared at her partner, waiting for the other shoe to drop. "What's that?"

He smiled. "Merry Christmas, partner."

Deena rolled her eyes and shouldered past, exiting the room with a wiseass smirk. Walker laughed and closed the door behind them, heading into the bullpen, off and running once again. "Bah, humbug," she replied, slapping Walker on the back.

"And Merry Christmas to you, too."

# *Epilogue*

―∿―

**June. Ten and a half years ago.**
**Sunday afternoon. 1:07 P.M.**

Birds wheeled above the academy grounds, flying in formation beneath a brilliant azure sky. The sun was shining on the bleachers as row after row of prospective policemen and policewomen filed into seats. Family members milled about on the grass, beaming with pride as they aimed cameras and phones. Bunting and congratulatory banners hung across the aging tree line; the groundskeepers had gone overboard, but that was most often the case when it came to graduation.

A dais ran against the main building, looking out and onto the grass. Several dignitaries and special guests climbed a staircase, dressed in tailored uniforms and carrying speeches and documents of distinction. One of them approached center stage and tapped on the microphone. The family members ceased their milling and drifted toward waiting white seats. After they'd settled, the president took his place at the podium and began the official ceremonies. The graduating cadets fidgeted in their seats, ready to join the ranks of those who chose to uphold the law. They searched for their families, spying parents in the crowd, husbands and wives happily cheering from the seats positioned on the lawn.

Deena searched the sky instead. She watched the birds, dress hat nearly falling from the back of her head. She caught it, setting it right. The starched, ironed uniform felt perfect against her skin. She clasped both hands in her lap, anxiously tapping one thumb against the other, ready for the formalities to be complete and the work to begin. The afternoon's festivities were the culmination of five long, hard months. A little over nineteen weeks learning the ropes, immersing herself in a world of which she'd always longed to be part. Waldo had refused to include Deena in his work life. He'd refused to help her see this through, and Aaron had disappeared; she had no idea where the Bouchers had gone. Last she'd heard, the judge graced a bench in Dallas, and Austin before that. Aaron was undoubtedly at his side. He definitely wasn't in the crowd, waving and cheering in Deena's direction as he snapped pictures.

*That's fine,* she had decided, putting on a confident face. *I did this on my own. And no one can take credit for that. No one else can take this from me.*

She stared at the birds and clouds one last time. A contrail streaked across the sky—a jet, perhaps, or a commercial airliner. She squinted into the sun; it wasn't either. It was a man in scarlet armor. He carried a large, metallic hammer, and his face—though it would have been a blur at this distance—was hidden beneath a bullet-shaped helmet. Several other cadets raised their heads to watch him go by, as did a handful of spectators. The Power must have sensed their attention; he glanced down and saluted them with his hammer. Moments later, the unknown Power rocketed into the distance, tattered clouds and a tinny burst of sound left in his wake.

Deena lowered her head, adjusting her cap once more. A memory stirred, and she closed her eyes, drifting back to November two years before

*when a noise captured her attention, the sound of war coming from the city. Cops and Powers joined her on the porch, investigating the commotion without leaving the house.*

Fuck, *she'd thought.* I'd be off like a rocket. If the APHD allowed, I'd be out there myself, fighting the good fight. *But that would be a long time coming. Deena had to start college, hadn't even lived on her own. She had to abide her father's rules, follow his word.* Not for long, *she'd promised herself.* Before you know it, I'll be out of college and deciding shit for myself. What to think. What to eat. Where to live. And no one will tell me what to *be.* I can be anything I want. Even a cop. *Especially* a cop.

Deena opened her eyes. She found herself in the moment, within a *sea* of cops sitting at attention, clad in their dress blues. She watched the reactions of her fellow graduates. Many were smirking, grab-assing with their friends. Several were quietly conversing with family in the audience. Only a select few were listening to the speeches, faces drawn and solemn, rapt with attention.

Even fewer had their eyes closed, as Deena had, lost in private thought, overwhelmed by the moment, the pomp, the ceremony. This was her family now. These were her people, the men and women with whom she couldn't wait to serve. With whom she couldn't wait to partner.

It had been a long, painful road from Atlanta. But here Deena stood, beneath a hopeful sky, less than an hour from succeeding. She had done it herself but was far from alone. She felt her colleagues in the crowd: the solemn cops, those with something to prove. And the honest ones, dedicated to being just and true. They were everything that Deena hoped to be. Everything that she'd longed to be.

She had done it by herself, arriving beneath the clear, blue sky. She'd endured five months of heartache and hardship and planned to savor the moment forever: the exact moment that Deena Pilgrim could refer to herself as a good cop. Maybe the last good cop she knew.

First, though, she would have to endure the rest of the speeches.

But that was fine. Deena was on point. And she had survived worse in order to become a good cop, to accomplish her mission.

And everything she'd survived, she'd survived in its name.